The War Between Us

Sarah Creviston Lee

For Lynée –

Congratulations! I hope you enjoy
your time in River Bluff and
fall in love with the characters
as much as I have.

Sarah Creviston Lee

이서라

The War Between Us
Copyright © 2015 Sarah Creviston Lee

ISBN-13: 978-1516988679
ISBN-10: 1516988671

Cover design by Cindy Canizales
Author photograph by Keslie Houser

Cover photo from shutterstock.com

For Katherine, my fellow 7th grade
writer in crime
For Mairi, who was there from start to finish

And for my Great Aunt Elaine,
who had the courage to be different

Chapter One

STARES AND WHISPERS accompanied Alex Moon his entire trip. Without even touching him, the other passengers poked and prodded, assailed his privacy, wearing on his already fragile patience. At each stop, the experience was renewed as old passengers disembarked and new ones took their place. Alex's confidence shrank away as quickly as his beloved California faded behind him. If being sent from home to live with his uncle in Washington DC wasn't bad enough, his father's disapproval still stung, trailing after him like the cloud of steam from his eastbound train.

He turned away from the racing view of darkened farmland to make eye contact in the crowded car with a plump woman wearing a funny hat. She glowered, *harrumphed*, and turned away. "Brazen Jap!" Her words cut through the air like a whip, drawing more stares. He turned back to his little window patch of isolation, trying to look past the hostile reflections, but with night obscuring the landscape, it was hard to see anything else.

He sprang to his feet as the train wheels squealed to a stop. The conductor had mentioned River Bluff, though this meant nothing to Alex. Restlessness ate at him. It didn't matter where they were, as long as he could get off the train and away from these people.

The August breeze lazily stroked his already damp skin. His neatly parted, pomaded black hair remained unruffled. He strode across the platform to the train office, enjoying the fresh air outside the stuffy train car. A dozen other passengers followed suit.

On a whim, Alex sent a telegram to his mother. She was worried. He didn't need to see her to know. Especially after the way he left with shouts of defiance at his father.

Telegram sent, Alex emerged from the office, tucking the change into his old black wallet. It was worn out, its stitches coming undone. He'd put off getting a new one, funneling all he could toward his secret stash of savings. Besides, it had been a gift from his friend, Danny, and he hated to part with it. Perhaps when he got to his uncle's in Washington he'd get it repaired.

Placing the wallet into his pants pocket, he patted his jacket's breast pocket. His savings. Still safe and sound. The fat envelope reassured him. The end of this train ride didn't have to be a dead end to his life.

He walked the length of the platform to stretch his legs. The train was delayed for twenty minutes. Earlier that day, at another long wait in Indianapolis, he'd watched train cars bursting with smiling, energetic, young American soldiers setting off to unknown fates in Europe or the Pacific. He didn't envy them, and more than anything he was happy he wasn't on that kind of train.

He turned the corner and walked to the end of the station. He rubbed his neck, trying to work out a knot of tension. It had materialized as soon as the train had removed him from the comforting sight of desert and mountains, launching him into an endless expanse of grassy plains. The flat scenery left him feeling exposed, on edge.

River Bluff, Indiana was no different from any other small mid-western town. Various businesses extended out from the train station, but trees and night obscured the rest. He longed for his familiar sprawling town and sunny beaches. When would he see them again? When would he see his family again? See his mother's smiling face, hear his little sister June's laughter? He even missed the bickering with his older sister, Esther. One thing he wouldn't miss would be his father's constant lectures, the unrelenting disapproval. Always being at the mercy of trying to live up to his older brother Henry's shining example.

Rowdy, shouting curses and loud laughter drew his attention. Two middle-aged men stumbled from around the corner and up the station steps. It was obvious they were drunk. About ten feet away from Alex, they faltered to a stop.

"Hey, Homer. Izzat what I think it is?" One of them slurred loudly. His stubby finger pointed crookedly in Alex's direction. Alex's shoulders tensed, waiting for the inevitable to arrive with grating familiarity.

"What?" Homer grunted.

"That's a Jap, ain't it?"

Alex dug his nails into his palms, teeth clenched until they ached.

Homer leaned forward, his large frame tall and domineering. He squinted. "Yeah, Jake, I'd say that was a Jap. What I wanna know is what the hell's he doing *here*?"

Heat rose in Alex's face. There was no point in arguing the difference of Korean versus Japanese. Instead, he turned on his heel and quickly walked back toward the train and the safety of his seat on board.

"Hey, he's gettin' away," Homer roared. "Grab him, Jake."

The two men moved faster than Alex believed them capable, and a few feet short of his train car, Alex was wrestled to the ground, arms pinned, cheek flat against hard pavement. Foul, alcohol-laden breath fogged the side of his face.

"You kill our boys down at Pearl Harbor, and you try to run?" Jake growled. "Uh-uh. No Jap runs away from me and lives to tell about it."

"Teach him a lesson," Homer urged.

The man was heavy, and Alex struggled fruitlessly. Jake shifted his bulk to lift Alex to his feet. Alex pushed his weight back, throwing the man off balance. Jake tumbled onto his side. Alex leapt up and spun to face his attackers. Homer grabbed his arm, but Alex launched a blow at his stomach. Jake came at him, and Alex fought hard to protect himself without much success. Each punch to his gut or side was like fire, but he continued to fight, throwing in as many strikes as he could.

His heart leapt in relief at the faint shrill of police whistles. He turned to see the approaching policemen, but his world burst into a blaze of light as a fist connected with the side of his head. He stumbled and fell to his knees, vision reeling.

Piercing whistles cut through his pain. Running feet pounded the platform, and he was roughly dragged to his feet. The cold bite of steel stung as handcuffs were locked onto his wrists. He desperately tried to make sense of what was going on amidst the commotion. Struggling against the police officer holding him, he was dealt a second blow to the head. The two men loudly claimed a tumble of lies. Alex had provoked them, threatened to kill them, and insulted the United States Army. Regardless of these accusations, the police put the drunken men in handcuffs as well.

When questioned, Alex protested and insisted there were a dozen witnesses who could verify he was a passenger and had only stepped outside briefly to stretch his legs. However, to his horror, no one would vouch for him. Faces turned away in embarrassment, and a few shot him dirty looks that plainly said, "*You don't belong here.*"

***

"Reverend Hicks, thank you for coming," Sheriff Wilcox boomed, getting to his feet to shake hands. He was a tall, broad-shouldered man with a graying mustache and a personality that filled the room. "Miss Lonnie, how are you this evening? Did you come with your uncle to visit the poor sap we picked up last night?"

Lonnie bobbed her head, awkward with the unfamiliar surroundings. She'd never had cause to step foot in the police station before now. Dressed in a rust-colored, shirred dirndl dress, brown hat and gloves, she stuck out amongst all the dark uniforms and brass buttons.

The sheriff motioned Lonnie and her uncle, Reverend Phillip Hicks, to follow him down a dimly lit staircase and through a hallway to the jail cells. "I don't know what this world is coming to," he said, shaking his head. "I can't get anyone to speak up for him. He got into a bad fight, but from what I can tell he dished it out pretty well all on his own, so don't be startled by his appearance. It's not as if we have any hard evidence, just accusations, so we can't hold him for much longer. We mostly kept him in for his own protection being that he looks for all the world like a Jap, though he claims adamantly he isn't. I dare say he'd much rather see your pretty face than ours, anyway." He laughed, nodding in Lonnie's direction. She blushed.

"Now, Sheriff," Uncle Phillip spoke up with a frown. "She's not here to be a pretty face, but to assist me in my ecclesiastical duties."

"Of course, of course." Sheriff Wilcox unlocked the door and led them through.

They entered a cramped square room with a desk manned by a police officer, the far wall lined with four barred cells. Tiny windows set high in the bricks let in the late afternoon light giving the room a cheery feel despite the dingy surroundings. The officer scrambled to his feet as they approached. The sheriff nodded at the man. All the cells were empty but the one at the end of the row. "Just down here, Reverend. Mr. Moon, you've got company." He wrapped on the metal bars with his knuckles, making a dull, metallic thunk.

Only the iron bars of the jail cell separated Lonnie from the man on the other side. He sat calmly on the narrow bed, legs folded, reading a book. His scuffed shoes faced outward by the cell door as if waiting to go out for a stroll.

The young man flicked his gaze up toward them, and Lonnie unconsciously sidestepped to hide behind her uncle. Her eyes widened and tiny fingers of fear paralyzed her sensibilities. His golden face was a mass of bruises, bloody cuts, and a blackened eye. Even his hair, sticking up every-which-way, still appeared to be in shock from his violent scuffle.

An image of a comic in yesterday's newspaper popped into her head. It showed a Japanese man with squinted eyes, a pig nose, and buckteeth. This man didn't resemble the comic at all, but she couldn't help but wonder—was he Japanese? And if he was, how in the world had he landed in their small town?

Lonnie lost her shelter as Uncle Phillip stepped forward.

"Mr. Moon? I'm Reverend Hicks from one of the local churches. This is my niece, Lonnie Hamilton. Sheriff Wilcox has apprised me of your situation, and I've come to offer any advice or counsel you might require during your stay here."

The young man set aside his book, studying them. His eyes locked onto hers, and Lonnie steered her gaze away, flushing.

"It's Alex, if you don't mind, sir." His voice was a smooth tenor, his accent decidedly American. Lonnie started in surprise. She'd expected some clipped Chinese-type speech.

"Of course. Alex." Uncle Phillip took position in the chair the officer had left for him outside the cell. Lonnie shifted her weight between feet, tightly clutching her bible. Her hands were sweaty inside her gloves. How long were they going to stay?

"Are you far from home, Alex?" Uncle Phillip asked.

"Yes. I'm from Los Angeles."

"Goodness that is a long way. I've heard the California beaches are beautiful."

"They are." He looked Uncle Phillip square in the eyes with a confidence that unnerved Lonnie. His back was straight, his face passive. He was amazingly certain of himself for a criminal.

"We haven't any beaches, I'm afraid," her uncle continued, "but we have a particularly inspiring view from the bluffs overlooking the Ohio River." He paused for a moment. "I'm sorry your first experience in our town has been such a negative one. I was disturbed to hear about the violence toward you at the train station. Is there any way I can help you? Anything you need? Do you have family back home waiting to hear from you?"

Alex shrugged. "My family won't be expecting to hear from me any time soon, but I'm worried about my suitcase. It was still on the train."

"I'll stop by the station and speak with Mr. Carter, the stationmaster."

"Thank you."

"Please forgive me for asking, but are you by any chance a Christian?"

Before he could answer, a police officer appeared at the door that led upstairs to the police station. "Reverend Hicks? Sherriff Wilcox wants a few words, if you don't mind."

Uncle Phillip smiled an apology to Alex. "Pardon me, please." He turned to Lonnie, his expression meaningful. "Perhaps you can share that passage of scripture we discussed?"

Lonnie hesitated, then nodded. The next moment her uncle was gone, the officer went back to his duties, and she was left to face Alex Moon alone. She had no idea what to say. Weren't the Japanese supposed to be heathen? Would he welcome what scripture she had to share?

She studied him discreetly. His face was soft, his eyes intelligent. Maybe he wasn't Japanese. Maybe he was a Christian. She didn't know anything about him except he'd gone back to reading his book. It was like he was trying to ignore her. Maybe he didn't know what to say either.

Lonnie sank into the chair and stared into her lap, studying the worn, black leather cover of her Bible, its gold leaf script on the front worn off long ago. She ventured a glance at him. He was her age—nineteen, maybe twenty? Surely, there was something they could talk about, even if it wasn't the strengthening power of God's word. Maybe films, school, or books? Lonnie tilted her head to the side to read the spine of the book in his hands, but he moved before she could.

"You want to ask me something?" Without warning, his eyes bore straight into her, pinning Lonnie to her chair.

"What?" Panic surfaced, and she blurted out the first thing that came to her. "Are you—are you Japanese?"

"No." His answer was quick and hard.

"Then what—"

"What am I?" He leaned forward. "A human."

Lonnie's mouth dropped open a little. "Well, I didn't doubt that."

"You're just like the rest of them, aren't you?" He scowled.

"Wh-what do you mean?"

"Ignorant and judgmental."

Lonnie gasped at his rush to verbally attack her. "You don't know anything about me."

A bitter smile tipped the corner of his mouth. "I know enough to see you're just a hypocrite with a Bible; professing to be a Christian while practicing nothing of the sort."

She leapt to her feet in indignation. "How d-dare you," The words jammed up in her throat. "I haven't even said anything to you."

"You didn't need to."

Lonnie was mystified at the wounded look in his eyes. What had she done to hurt his feelings?

She took a few deep breaths. Taking in Mr. Moon's present position—injured, friendless, and no doubt suspicious—her heart slowly softened. Now that she was closer, the blood crusted on his cuts and the swelling on his face were more pronounced. This young man needed help, and right now she was the only one here to give it.

She turned to the officer on duty. "May I have a glass of water please?" He nodded and returned shortly with her request. Pulling a handkerchief out of her pocket, she soaked it in the water and strode to the jail cell where she draped it over a crossbar. "You should clean your cuts before they get infected."

The astonishment that flickered in his dark, almond-shaped eyes was the last thing she saw before walking out.

Lonnie waited for Uncle Phillip on the front steps of the police station, glad of the deep, cooling shade the brick building behind her provided. It took a few minutes before the racing in her chest finally calmed.

Usually helping Uncle Phillip in his ecclesiastical duties meant visiting the widowed, the sick, and the poor. It was something she enjoyed, but after this encounter, an irrational outrage burned in her. The scripture of "I was in prison, and ye visited me" jabbed at her mind, but she crossed her arms stubbornly, readily recalling Alex's smirk and insults.

The last of the pedestrians enjoyed the night air—an older couple out walking their dog, a small knot of laughing kids from the high school, business owners closing their shops. Only the young men were missing, leaving a glaring vacancy in the familiar landscape of the town. Even her own cousin, David, was stationed somewhere in England fighting Hitler.

It wasn't long before her uncle appeared at the top of the stairs, a worried frown wrinkling his brow.

"Is everything all right?" she asked, standing.

"I didn't expect you to be out here. Was the young man disagreeable? He was sorry you left."

Lonnie shrugged. *He* felt sorry? "I just needed some air, that's all. I should be getting home. Mother will be expecting me."

"It's getting late, isn't it? Thank you for accompanying me. I know it was a little unusual, but I think we brought him a bit of comfort, don't you? Gratefully, he'll be released tomorrow morning. I'm not sure what he'll do after that, but I've told him where to find me."

Lonnie squeezed her bible tightly, eyes widening. Did that mean Alex Moon wasn't leaving? The possibility of him staying was unsettling.

"Well, I would walk you home, but . . ." Uncle Phillip shifted uncomfortably as he always did when the topic of his younger sister was brought up. Lonnie regarded her uncle with sympathy. The itch to know what had happened between him and her mother all those years ago was strong, but the bravery to pry always escaped her.

"I'll be all right." She waved farewell.

Her walk home was uneventful. The streets were considerably quieter as dusk claimed the nooks and crannies of the town. Street lamps left little pools of sanctuary light. Lonnie stepped in and out of them on her way—light, dark, light, dark. Insects fluttered at the lamps, and she batted a few of them away from her face.

Ten minutes later, she reached home—a cozy, squat craftsman tucked onto a tranquil back street. She quietly let herself in and tiptoed toward the stairs to her bedroom.

"Lonnie, is that you?" Her mother's sharp voice pierced the air.

She took a deep, steadying breath. "Yes, Mother."

"Where were you?" Her mother appeared out of the living room. Harriet Hamilton was tall and thin, her pale hair swept back into a simple wave and bun that was ragged after a long day working at the local glass factory. She wore a plain housedress and had one of her perpetual cigarettes dangling from her fingers, its white smoke wisping up in fading curls. Her face was severe and unforgiving.

Lonnie debated about whether she should tell the truth or not. "I was out with Uncle Phillip on his rounds."

Her mother's lips tightened in anger. "Is he that incapable that he needs *your* help? Stop wasting time with that good-for-nothing brother of mine and keep your worries closer to home."

She took a long draw on her cigarette and blew out a fierce, stream of smoke. "I noticed you left a number of chores undone before you went out. From what I can see, you don't have time to spare traipsing around town when you have household responsibilities. I can't do it all myself, Lonnie. Marty and Tunie have enough to worry about with their studies. You need to take your duties more seriously if you expect to continue living under this roof. Either that or find a man and move out. I'm sick of lecturing you."

Lonnie hung her head, fighting back the stinging tears. How many times had she been given this same rebuke? She'd lost count. "I'm doing my best, Mother. With my job, and cooking all our meals, and taking care of Marty—"

"I don't need to hear your excuses," Harriet shouted. "If you don't want to be treated as a child, then stop acting like one." She stomped back into the living room and switched on the radio. Laughter from the evening program assailed Lonnie as if the radio audience mocked her in her moment of chiding.

Defeated, Lonnie headed into the kitchen to finish the dishes and empty the garbage pail. By the time she trudged into her darkened bedroom, her younger sister, Tunie, was already asleep. Lonnie quickly prepared for bed, then slipped between the covers.

As she lay there, she allowed the quiet of the dark to relax her anxiety from the encounter with her mother. Tears slipped down her cheeks into her hair. It wasn't the first time she'd had to let the dark cover her tears. Ever since her father had left home seven years ago, her mother's temper and gloominess had steadily grown worse. As the oldest, Lonnie usually took the brunt of it. Her mother's lengthened hours at the factory for wartime work didn't help.

Lonnie's heart ached, longing for her father. He would've known what to say, how to soften her mother's temper. She could barely remember the last time his arms had gone around her in his warm embrace smelling of spicy, sweet cigars. It was like chasing slowly fading smoke. The more she tried to grasp at the memories, the harder they were to recall. Every photograph of their father had disappeared after he'd gone. Had her mother merely hidden them or had she burned them to irretrievable ashes? The question plagued her.

Luckily, Lonnie kept a box of her father's letters hidden at the back of her closet—secret communication they'd kept up through the years, even now with him in the army in Europe somewhere. When would she hear from him again? Once more, her heart squeezed painfully.

She whispered a prayer, hoping for comfort. Instead, all that came to her mind was that strange Oriental prisoner. The image flashed in her memory of his youthful face creased in anger, his eyes full of some nameless injury. Meeting Alex Moon had triggered something inside her. Beyond the sting of his words, there was something raw, undiscovered. Her curiosity burned, as if he was a mystery to unravel. Of all the places around the world she'd studied in books, she had yet to discover the Orient. Where exactly did his family come from? What was his culture like? Why did he come here? And if he wasn't Japanese, what was he?

Lonnie desperately wanted to know the answers to these questions. Figuring out Alex Moon could potentially add another piece to the puzzle of the extraordinary world that lay shrouded beyond the borders of her town; a place that was exciting and different. Everything River Bluff wasn't.

She sat up and wrapped her arms around her knees. Something else struck her now that she'd had time to cool down. The vulnerability in his eyes—they'd reached out to her as if begging for acceptance, for help. What had happened to him that he'd look so lost? Compassion crept into her heart. Maybe if she got to know him, became a friend . . .

The thought made her squirm in protest. What utter nonsense. He was a perfect stranger, *and* he was Oriental. He could be an enemy, even if he did deny being Japanese. His words didn't prove anything.

Lonnie frowned and lay back down, pulling the covers to her chin. There was no point in getting upset about Alex Moon. He'd be released from jail and disappear, leaving nothing behind but an uncomfortable memory.

***

The cracked, dimly white ceiling of the jail cell was hardly inspiring to the imagination, but it did serve as a blank canvas for Alex's memories of the past twenty-four hours. He turned over bitterly, the pitiful bed squealing in protest. His humiliation snapped at him like an angry dog. To his frustration, those offensive men had been released that morning while he still lay here in jail, falsely accused and friendless.

Everywhere he'd been since leaving home a week ago, he'd received the same treatment—suspicion, fear, hatred. Some people had openly insulted him as they walked past his seat on the train. Alex conceded that he understood their feelings. The hostile Japanese had attacked their country. Pearl Harbor burned with hateful memory for every American.

Of course, it was obvious what else everyone was thinking— he was one of *them*, the Japanese. If only they knew. If only they'd listen or take the time to see past their own noses. They were all just like that young woman, Lonnie. She'd regarded him with fear and fascination. It disgusted him that no one could see him as a person, someone with feelings and fears of his own. And wasn't he as American as they? He was born in California, went to an American school, spoke like an American, thought like an American. For heaven's sake, he *was* an American.

His eyes found the handkerchief still hanging from the jail bars. Pride prevented him from touching it while anyone was around, but now . . . Alex rolled painfully to his feet and retrieved the smooth, delicate fabric. It was mostly dry now, retaining a bit of moisture in the sticky humidity. It was useless to him, and he crushed it in his fist. She'd left it out of charity. Not because she really cared. She pitied him, and that was almost as bad as cursing at him because he looked like a Jap when he wasn't one.

Chapter Two

LONNIE SLIPPED OUT to the back yard in the weak morning light. A crust of yesterday's bread in hand, she passed the dew-glazed rows of tomatoes, corn, beans, and cucumbers in their Victory garden. Fruit bushes huddled in shady corners by the fence, and the lone apple tree swished its upper branches in a lazy breeze.

She came to the chicken run, smiling at the four hens trilling and pressing against the wire at her approach.

"Good morning, girls." She crouched and broke off a piece of the bread. Four beaks thrust through and grabbed at the crumb. "Mrs. Cooper's dog didn't bother you last night, did he? He sure kept me awake."

She glowered in frustration. In truth, Alex Moon had kept her awake. The hurt in his eyes from their argument still haunted her.

"What am I going to do about him?" Lonnie asked the scrabbling hens. "How do you get to know a man like that, anyway?" She tossed them the rest of the bread. "He's being released today. Where's he going to go? Do you think he'll just get right back on the train and leave?"

She inhaled sharply, disturbed by the slight sink of disappointment from her words. Lonnie brushed the crumbs off her skirt, whisking away any further thoughts with them.

She went back to the kitchen to meet Marty shuffling his way to the table. Her eight-year-old brother's wheat-colored hair stuck straight up on top while it was mashed up on the sides. His striped pajamas were wrinkled, and his shirt was one button off, leaving a funny bulge in the middle.

She laughed and tousled his hair. "Morning, sleepyhead."

"You're up early," he said, rubbing his eyes. "Avoiding Mom again?"

She grunted at his intuitiveness. "Yeah. She's not too happy with me right now. I hope she doesn't take it out on you."

He shrugged. "Don't worry. She thinks I'm an angel compared to you."

Lonnie playfully shoved his shoulder. "Aren't you a little too smug for so early in the morning?"

Marty smirked and poured himself a bowl of Cheerioats while Lonnie popped some bread into their finicky, heavy chrome toaster. She fried an egg and hurried to pack lunches of egg and ham salad sandwiches, leftover cookies, and some carrot sticks for herself, Marty, Tunie, and her mother.

All of a sudden, Marty shouted. "Lonnie, it's smoking!"

With a cry of dismay, she rushed over to the toaster and pulled out the two planks of charred bread. She sighed. "This blasted toaster."

"Why don't we just get a new one?" Marty wrinkled his nose at the burnt smell wafting through the room.

"We can't get any new appliances because of the war. We'll just have to make it work. Maybe I can take it over to the repair shop one of these days." She set the toast on the table. "In the meantime, this is all we've got until I can make some more bread."

"Well, I'm not eating that," Marty stated.

Lonnie ate her egg and resigned herself to the burnt toast, regretting feeding what she had to the chickens. She scraped away the black as best she could and hid the rest with a generous portion of butter.

Fifteen minutes later, she was on her way to work. She was an hour early, not an uncommon occurrence for her mornings. With an issue of *Reader's Digest* tucked under her arm, she wasn't afraid of the long wait. Avoiding her mother was worth it.

She slowly strolled down the sidewalk, relishing the cool morning before the heat of the day. It was the best time of the day. Only the milkmen in their familiar white trucks were out on their rounds, and the early paperboys slung papers onto front stoops from their bicycles. The tranquil morning belied the true reality of war raging in far off lands Lonnie had only read about in the newspaper or heard on the radio.

The sun skimmed the rooftops in a golden glow as she passed the police station. She stopped. When was Alex going to be released? No doubt, she'd miss him while she was at work. With a sigh, she fully acknowledged her disappointment. The idea of getting to know someone so culturally different was intriguing, even if he was completely rude. She probably wouldn't get that chance at all now.

As if to prove her wrong, the door to the police station opened and Alex Moon stepped out, a suit jacket draped over one arm. She gasped and ducked beside the wall of the staircase out of sight.

His footsteps descended and paused at the bottom. Lonnie peered around the corner as Alex felt in the pockets of the jacket, his face growing increasingly worried. He pulled out a wallet, but quickly snapped it shut and cursed. Then he stalked off in the opposite direction of her hiding place.

After he was safely out of sight, Lonnie reemerged, curious about his actions. What had he meant by that outburst? And where was he going? The train station was in the opposite direction.

Lonnie moved to follow him, but decided against it despite the curiosity that pulled at her. There was no use getting worked up about a perfect stranger. She continued on her detour to the train station, mounted the steps to the platform and found her customary seat under the shelter of the station office overhang. She flipped open her magazine and began reading the article that piqued her interest—"The Westerner's Crowning Glory." It was a history about Stetson hats in Texas.

"Another early morning, Miss Hamilton?"

She smiled into the kind eyes and wrinkled face of the stationmaster. "I'm afraid so, Mr. Carter."

"Well, you're welcome to stay as long as you like, as always. The eight-ten will be right on time today, I think." He consulted his large, gold pocket watch, nodded, and walked away whistling.

She leaned forward, peering down the track, a familiar wistfulness filling her with an ache like an old wound. How many times had she watched the trains come and go? And not once had she ever been aboard. At least not further than the county seat. What was it like out there? The things she could discover were innumerable. She'd long since exhausted their library's limited resources about cultures near and far. She wanted to know more. Everywhere was more interesting than River Bluff, especially while she remained under her mother's thumb. Why couldn't she just step on a train and leave everything behind, allowing the tracks to steal her away?

She imagined herself, for the thousandth time, boarding the train, choosing a seat, the anticipation for her journey filling every cavity of her lungs. Where would she go? East to New York? West to California? Would she board a boat and sail across the ocean to some foreign shore?

Before she could picture herself in some far off exotic place, the train came and went, blowing a great gust of hot air and ashes. Lonnie was left on the bench as usual. She stared with longing after the receding caboose, her magazine lying neglected in her lap.

***

Lonnie arrived at the office of Pickering Insurance Company in town just as her boss, John Pickering, got there. He was a large, meticulous man with a propensity for being opinionated and nosy, but he was a decent employer. They greeted each other, and Lonnie followed him into the building. She took her place at the small desk behind her worn Remington typewriter from a previous decade. Mr. Pickering disappeared into his office and shut his door with a loud click, leaving her in the yawning expanse of solitude that was the front office. Lonnie stretched, beginning another long day of typing letters and reports and answering the occasional phone call.

By the end of the day, she was irritable and tired. She blamed it on the boredom, but mostly on Alex. Her mind inevitably wandered, and he was the one who filled it. Memories of their brief discussion at the jail irritated her. What had made him dislike her so quickly? Had he even been grateful for her handkerchief? Would things have gone better if she'd just kept her questions to herself and done what Uncle Phillip had asked by sharing the scripture passage with him? Her head ached from these incessant thoughts, and she couldn't wait to curl up in her window seat with the distraction of a book.

However, halfway home, she remembered she was supposed to meet up with her friends later. Before she left, there was laundry to be done at home, dinner to be made, and homework to oversee as well. Lonnie bit her lip, frustration building behind her eyelids in the form of hot tears. She blinked to clear them.

The moment she walked in the door at home, she spotted Tunie at the kitchen table, books spread out in front of her. Honey brown hair curled around her shoulders, held back with a blue ribbon bow. Her youthful face of fifteen frowned in concentration.

"Where's Mother?" Lonnie asked.

Tunie jotted something on her notebook paper. "She said she was taking on another shift. They're really behind on some of the glass orders. And before you ask, Marty is playing in the garden. As for me, I'm dying here. This essay is going to take forever.

History is such a bore." She finally turned despondent gray eyes toward Lonnie, sagged in her chair, and pouted.

"What's your paper about?"

"Some dusty old British kings and their tiresome battles."

Lonnie laughed. "Sorry, I can't help you there. I could never keep those kings straight."

Tunie gave Lonnie a hopeful smile. "Anything good for dinner?"

"I was about to figure that out." Lonnie surveyed the options in their refrigerator: milk, butter, a few glass-lidded containers of leftovers, and some celery. She knew there were onions in the onion box and a couple cans of Heinz Vegetable Beef Soup in the pantry. The green peppers were ripe in the garden as well. She called out to Marty to pick some. He brought them in and was gone again.

Lonnie set about making a batch of biscuits. She poured the cans of soup into a baking pan, stirred in the chopped vegetables, and laid cut biscuit rounds on top. Thirty minutes later, the three of them sat to eat at the table in the kitchen.

After saying a prayer, Lonnie asked about their day at school.

Marty and Tunie exploded in a torrent of chatter, each talking over the other until Lonnie had to hold up her hands. "One at a time, please."

"The whole school is buzzing about that Jap that got captured," Tunie said.

"Someone said he's a pilot that crash landed somewhere on the other side of the river, and he's a spy." With large eyes, Marty leaned toward her with the importance of this bit of information.

Lonnie's face clouded. "Who came up with that idea?"

"I don't know, but don't you think it might be true?" He looked so hopeful.

"We would've heard the plane, silly."

"That idea is nuts," Tunie agreed. "I heard he was in this huge brawl at the train station and now he's rotting in jail. In fact, Phyllis and I went there after school today. The stationmaster wouldn't say much, but he pretty much confirmed it."

"Well, never mind." Lonnie scooped a bite of the casserole onto her spoon. "I'm sorry I asked. Let's just finish eating and clean up. I've got somewhere to go later." They obeyed with muffled grumbles.

After dinner, Lonnie hurriedly folded the pile of laundry that waited for her and put it away. Once Marty was finished with the dishes, she set him to the task of his homework. At last, she hurried upstairs to get ready to go out. She changed into a fresh dress, lamented her tattered pair of silk stockings, and hoped her hemline would hide the worst of them.

She was touching up her hair and makeup when Tunie came in.

"Where were you last night, by the way?" Tunie asked. She perched on the edge of her bed. "Mother was livid, going on and on about how she was going to teach you a lesson for staying out when you were expected home by six."

"She must not have remembered I said I was going out with Uncle Phillip."

Tunie scoffed. "I'll bet she didn't. Why do you go around with Uncle Phillip, anyway? How boring. Don't tell me you want to be a nun."

Lonnie ran a tube of Tangee over her lips and pressed them together. She examined the gentle rosy blush it added to her lips. "We'd have to be Catholic, dear. I just like helping, that's all. And Uncle Phillip is all on his own, at least until I finally succeed in setting him up with Mrs. Godfrey."

Tunie laughed loudly. "Oh, that would be perfect. She's so bossy, and he's such a push-over."

Lonnie frowned. "Don't be mean, Tunie."

Her sister sniffed. "Well, it's true. Anyway, where did you go? Anywhere interesting or was it the same old widows and orphans?"

Lonnie shook her head. "Why do you have to be so callous about it? They can't help themselves. But if you must know, we went to the police station, and yes, I met someone interesting, but extremely rude."

Tunie bounced on her bed excitedly. "Oh, do tell. Was it a prisoner?"

"Yes."

Tunie rolled her eyes. "Well? Spill it."

"I have to leave, Tunie."

"How typical. You never tell me anything." Tunie crossed her arms in a huff.

Lonnie gazed at the square of shifting green light from the tulip tree fluttering outside their window, recalling the visit. "He was about my age. And . . . he was *Oriental.*"

Tunie gasped. "The Jap? So it's true. And you spoke to him? What could you possibly say to a creep like that? Did he even understand you?"

"He speaks perfectly good English. And I didn't say he was Japanese. I said he was Oriental."

"Isn't that the same thing? He's the enemy. What are they going to do with him? Shoot him?"

Lonnie eyed her sister in disgust. "Good heavens, of course not. Besides, Oriental and Japanese aren't the same thing. Don't you learn anything at school? Anyway, he's not Japanese at all. He told me he wasn't."

"Of course he'd say that. They lie and cheat and—"

Lonnie scowled. "This is why I don't tell you anything, Tunie. You just overreact. I have to go." She pinned on her hat, grabbed her purse, and went to the door.

Her sister was quiet for a second. "How do you expect me to sleep tonight? The enemy is in our town. He could bomb us like at Pearl Harbor."

"That's just stupid. Do you think he's carrying the bomb in his back pocket? Criminey, Tunie, you've got nothing to worry about."

Tunie's hushed voice trailed after Lonnie. "Wait until I tell the girls at school."

***

Halfway to her friend Rose's house, Lonnie met up with Gladys, a pretty brunette with well-developed curves and a forward personality. Tonight she had on a new blue dress with a red piped keyhole neckline and matching red pumps with pompom bows, making Lonnie queasy with envy.

"Lonnie." Gladys waved from across the street. She crossed over and linked arms with her. "How was work?"

"Long and tiresome. How about for you?"

"Oh, it was as thrilling as ever. You wouldn't believe the juicy things going on in this town."

Lonnie shook her head with a smile. Gladys worked as one of three telephone operators in River Bluff and made it a hobby of eavesdropping on conversations. "Thanks for the reminder to never use the telephone when you're on duty."

Gladys smirked. "By the way, did you know there's a Jap being held at the jail? They caught him back on Tuesday."

"He's not Japanese," Lonnie said.

Her friend glanced at her sharply. "How do you know?"

Lonnie squeezed her eyes shut in annoyance. She shouldn't have said anything. "I went to see him with my uncle yesterday."

Gladys stopped in her tracks, dragging Lonnie to a stop as well. "What? How did I not hear about this yet?"

Lonnie laughed. "Gossip is not the surest way of finding out quality information."

Gladys sniffed, and they continued walking. "Well, it's the fastest way to find things out anyway. Besides, how do you know he's not a Jap?"

"He told me."

"Well, what is he then?"

"He told me he was a human."

Gladys snorted. "At least that rules out Martians. So what does he look like? Is he like those nasty little comics? You know the ones—squinty eyes, piggy nose, and big lips." She screwed up her nose and squinted her eyes to mimic what she meant.

Lonnie raised an eyebrow.

Gladys smoothed out her face and batted her eyelashes. "What?"

"He wasn't like that at all, actually. He was about our age. Dark hair, interesting eyes, though he was terribly beat up. . . and I don't know. Why? Does it matter what he looks like?"

Gladys pursed her lips. "Oh, I thought I might keep an eye out for him, that's all." She gave her a bright smile. Lonnie was suspicious of her intent, because it was hard to tell what was on Gladys's mind all the time.

They finally reached Rose's house, a pretty, red brick two-story with a white front porch and giant hydrangea bushes. When Lonnie knocked, Rose herself came to the door.

Rose Everett was appropriately named. She had gleaming dark auburn hair, soft brown eyes, dimples in her pink cheeks, and a peaches and cream complexion. She and Lonnie had been fast friends since they were little girls.

"Come on in. Walter and Teddy are already here."

A tall, sandy-brown haired young man with light blue eyes and dark-rimmed glasses fiddled with the knobs on the radio in the front room. He beamed and greeted the girls as they entered, though his eyes stayed with Lonnie.

Lonnie smiled. "Hello, Teddy."

Teddy strode over to her, concern etching his face. "Are you all right? You seem like you're tired."

"I'm fine. I just went to bed late and got up too early."

"You need to take better care of yourself, Lonnie. We can't have you falling sick."

"I know." Lonnie placed a hand on his arm. "Thanks for looking out for me. I'm okay though. Really."

"She looks fine to me," Walter mumbled from his place on the couch.

Rose emerged bearing a plate of bread and a toaster. Gladys followed on her heels with a tray of different spreads.

"I thought we could have a toast party," Rose said. "What game do you all want to play?"

"How about Monopoly?" Walter suggested. "I still have to redeem myself from last time."

Lonnie moaned. "I was hoping for something less committal, like Chinese Checkers."

Teddy positioned himself close to Lonnie. "Chinese Checkers sounds good."

"Yes," Gladys agreed. "I'm afraid of your aggressive tendencies, Walter. Monopoly just brings them out in you."

"I don't know what you mean." Walter scowled causing Gladys to laugh. Broad shouldered, outspoken, and athletic, Walter could've been the ideal soldier. An unfortunate motorcycle accident the previous summer had left him with a terrible limp— and unfit for service. His bitterness hung around him like a cloud, leaving him more belligerent than ever these days.

"I was hoping for Monopoly too," Rose said, "but it seems we've been out-voted, Walter."

Soon, bread was toasting, and they were well into their game.

"How's David doing, Lonnie?" Gladys asked.

"I think he's all right. Aunt Millie says he's having a grand ol' time."

Gladys batted her eyes. "He sure makes one dreamy soldier. I still remember the day he shipped out in his uniform . . ."

"Hey," Walter protested.

"I'll make sure to tell him you said so in my next letter," Lonnie replied. "Better yet, why don't you write him yourself?"

"You better not," Walter threatened.

Gladys's plump lips curved up innocently, and she blew him a kiss.

Teddy spoke up in annoyance as he moved a marble. "My mother cries at least once a week over my little brother Eugene. He's a terrible writer, so she imagines the worst—he's in some Nazi prison camp or dead on some mysterious battlefield."

Walter balled his hands into fists. "What I wouldn't give to get my hands on some Nazis or Japs. It doesn't matter which."

Lonnie moved one of her marbles. "Part of me wishes I could join up myself, to see new places and new cultures. But I can't seem to work up the courage. I'd like to be able to do more than type insurance forms all day long. It's not even something for the war effort."

"Uh oh. Are you going to start waxing poetical about your grand adventures, Lonnie?" Gladys poked her arm.

"No." She swatted away her friend's hand.

"You do far more than that, Lonnie," Rose said. "You help care for your family while your mother works at the factory. You're a whiz at figuring out what to cook and bake, especially with the sugar rationing. My sisters and I barely have enough imagination to figure out what to put between two slices of bread."

Gladys laughed. "Rose is right. You're practically a saint with all the charity work you do with your uncle. We all have to find our niche in doing our bit. Teddy helps his father manage the glass factory, Walter helps his mother keep up the farm, and Rose teaches at the school. Even I do my part." She grinned broadly and Walter scoffed.

"Yeah, you have your own version of war work, and it involves way too many soldiers for my liking." He frowned gloomily, and Gladys flashed sparkling teeth.

"Keeping up the moral of our fighting men is a serious job."

"You better take me with you to the next dance, Gladys Marshall," Walter insisted. "I wanna make sure none of those boys gets the wrong idea about you."

Gladys touched his arm. "If you weren't such a bad dancer, I'd take you in a heartbeat, Walter, dear."

"Gladys," Lonnie cried and Rose gasped. Only Teddy laughed.

Walter shrugged it off. "I'd go as your bodyguard, of course. I don't mind being muscle. Besides, I hate dancing anyway."

"Speaking of *men*," Gladys cooed, glancing slyly at Lonnie. "You all heard of that Jap they caught and put in jail? He's quite the interesting character, isn't he, Lonnie?"

All heads swiveled toward her, making Lonnie blush. "He's not a Jap," she said, voice soft. "And besides he's not in jail anymore." She broke off a tiny piece of her half-eaten piece of toast, avoiding locking glances with anyone.

Gladys squeaked in surprise. "You never mentioned that."

"I only saw him this morning. Now, can we talk about something else, please?"

Teddy frowned. "Where do you think he went? Is he just wandering around town unsupervised?"

"I hope they've got someone tailing that guy. Just because they didn't have any evidence, doesn't mean he wasn't guilty." Walter pounded the table with his fist, causing the marbles to jump and everyone cried out in dismay as they skittered to different holes.

"Don't you think they let him go because he was innocent?" Lonnie kept her eyes on the marbles as she replaced them.

"I think they should've held him longer," Walter said. "What do they know about the guy anyway? Why was he in town to begin with?"

"You know, Lonnie," Gladys said, a mischievous twinkle in her eye. "He may be wandering around trying to find a familiar face."

"What's that supposed to mean?" Teddy asked, turning his head back and forth between the girls.

"Maybe he fancies our sweet little Lonnie here. She did get to have a nice chat with him. Maybe he wants to steal her away. I'm sure they got real chummy in his jail cell."

Lonnie grew red-faced, embarrassed at her friend's implications.

"Shut up, Gladys," Teddy snapped. "That isn't funny."

"Yes. What a horrible thing to say." Rose turned to Lonnie. "Just ignore her. She's only sore because you knew something she didn't."

Gladys's breath rushed out in irritation. "Don't snap your cap. I was just joking."

Lonnie kept her eyes on her hands clenched in her lap.

"I think I'll head home." She slid out of her chair, and Rose grabbed her arm.

"Don't go, Lonnie. Gladys was being a beast like always."

"I was *joking*," Gladys said. "Sorry, Lonnie."

Lonnie smiled and shook her head. "It's all right. It's been a long day, and I'm more tired than I realized. I'll finish the game next time." She gave her friends an encouraging smile and left the house.

Once she was outside, she fumed. That Gladys, always opening her mouth and saying whatever idiotic thing came to her mind. Lonnie shut her eyes briefly and took a moment to steady her temper.

She started for home, but turned back at hearing running footsteps. Teddy caught up to her, his breathing a little wheezy. "Don't mind, Gladys. You know she always wants to be the center of attention."

"I know. You didn't have to come after me, Teddy. I really am tired."

"Don't be ridiculous. That dirty Jap is out wandering the town somewhere. You didn't think I'd let you walk home alone did you?"

"You shouldn't have run, though. Won't it make your lungs worse?"

Teddy swatted the air. "Nah." To his betrayal, he started coughing and had to stop walking until it was under control. Lonnie smiled in sympathy. He'd been plagued with weak lungs since he was a child and had frequently missed school as a result. Many times, she'd gone over to bring him his homework and to keep him company.

"So how is it working for your father at the glass factory? I've heard it's gotten busy. My mother took on a second shift today."

Teddy moaned. "Brutal. The factory is going 'round the clock. It was pretty enjoyable when we were just making plate glass windows and lamppost covers and the like. Ever since we got converted to making things for the war it's been non-stop madness. I've been busy training and doing all the lousy paperwork." He moaned again. "The paperwork."

"It sounds exciting to me. Much better than being stuck in a boring old office typing forms and letters by myself all day long."

"I'd love some isolation like that."

Lonnie shrugged. "I long for seeing what's out there, you know? You've seen that new poster for the WAVES at the post office, haven't you? I've considered joining—"

"For heaven's sake, don't do that." Teddy's eyes were wide in shock.

"Why not?"

"You can't leave."

"Why?"

"Well, who else would I have to walk home?"

Lonnie laughed. "You have a never ending supply of deserving young ladies in town."

"They're not like you, though," Teddy mumbled.

They arrived at her house. "See, you needn't have worried. We arrived without any criminal sighting."

Teddy glanced around. "He could've been following us. Now he knows where you live."

Lonnie shook her head. "Goodnight, Teddy."

"Goodnight." His voice was doubtful.

They waved at each other, and he turned back toward Rose's house.

When he'd gone, Lonnie surveyed her street. Children were still out playing on the sidewalks in the last of the day's light. A few older boys and girls were riding their bikes in the quiet side street. Everything was as it should be, though her thoughts still turned to Alex. Where was he? What was he doing? She doubted he'd be wasting his time following her around. She wouldn't be surprised if he was long gone already. A haze of regret trailed after her as she went into the house.

***

After everyone had gone to bed, Lonnie still lay wide-awake. The conversation at Rose's house annoyed her and it still stung like a rug burn. She got up, threw on a robe and snuck barefoot down the stairs and out to the front porch.

She sat in the creaking porch swing. Her feet pushed the old worn bench, then dangled as they rose in the air. Back and forth. The air was cooling and sweet with late summer flowers. It was quiet as the street sank deeper into dusk's embrace. Lightening bugs flickered above the lawn like drifting embers from the dying sun.

Usually seeing the lightening bugs triggered her smile, but tonight they filled her with melancholy. She remembered sitting on the porch as a girl with her father right before he sent her off to bed, his arm close about her shoulders. He blew smoke rings from his spicy-sweet cigar to make her laugh. She would rattle off funny little poems she'd read or made up, and he'd chuckle heartily for each one, then tweak her nose, saying she was his clever bug.

Tears welled up, and Lonnie let them fall, her heart aching for her father. Where was he? Was he safe? Would he see the sunrise tomorrow? If only the war would end. But even that thought was bittersweet. Even if the war did end, he wouldn't come home like all the other fathers. He wouldn't be welcome here. He hadn't been for a long time.

Chapter Three

ALEX WAS DISCOURAGED after one of the restaurants in town turned him away with a scowl and insults. He didn't bother checking out the other two. He had two dollars to his name, but what good did that do him when no one would serve him?

Once he'd been released, the officer on duty had given him his belongings back. His jacket was a mess of rips and stains. He still had his wallet with ID, draft card, and a couple bills, but the envelope with his money, along with his uncle's address, was missing. All his hard-earned savings—just gone. The full realization made him weak with helplessness.

His stomach grumbled unhappily. Before being released from jail, Sheriff Wilcox had seen to it Alex had a cup of coffee and a donut. The meager meal was hardly enough to sustain him for the whole day.

He wandered, unsure of what to do or where to go. He walked the length of the town, avoiding people as best he could. His favorite place was the park at the peak of the bluff, which wasn't high at all—maybe a hundred feet above the wide, brown river. The view, however, was just as inspiring as Reverend Hicks had promised. Flat prairie rose up to rolling farmland, hairy with stands of trees breaking up the smooth fields. They stretched out from the river in the opposite direction as if he stood on the edge of a different map. Roads spidered across the scenery between farms, and Alex could even see the railroad track gleaming tauntingly as if it had somewhere to go, but he didn't. And he couldn't.

Four hours later, the sun blazed high in the sky as Alex rested beneath a sheltering oak halfway down a block of houses. Not a soul was in sight. He wasn't surprised. Cicadas buzzed like rattling phantoms in the treetops, heat wavered drunkenly from exposed pavement, and the air was thick with humidity. It was as if he was cushioned in a sticky cloud of moisture that refused to be free of him. He leaned against the trunk, faint with his misery.

The roasting weather wasn't the worst problem by any stretch. His situation was serious. It was doubtful he'd ever see his savings again. A hundred dollars was a lot of cash. No one in their right mind would turn it in. He couldn't even contact his uncle to tell him what had happened. Alex's chest rose sharply in a half-hearted chuckle. There was no use denying he was glad the address was gone. It made his journey momentarily impossible.

On top of that, the ticket to Washington was missing too, and there was no way to get back to California. He was well and truly stuck in the middle of nowhere, confronted by suspicious, wary glares from strangers on every side. They were like ghosts of his memories, bringing to life his father's scornful disapproval. Their argument that launched him on this trip in the first place still battered at his mind.

"I want you to follow Henry's example," his father had said. "Tomorrow morning you will enlist in the Navy." The hardness in his father's voice signaled there would be no argument, no possible way to plead his case.

Alex balled his fists, clamping down on his desire to outright rebel. Instead, he resorted to pleading anyway. "*Abeonim*, please. I just want to go back to school. Can't I finish my degree and then enlist? At least let me finish out the term. It's humiliating to leave early, as if I couldn't cut it. You must see that."

His father's face was stone. "I don't need to see anything, Yeong Su, except your obedience. The freedom of Korea is far more important than your American education. Why is that so difficult?"

A dozen reasons flew through Alex's head. The words rushed out before he could stop them. "I can't enlist, *Abeonim*. Not after seeing what happened to Danny. They made his family line up on the street. He barely had time to pack or for his family to sell their things. He didn't even have time to say goodbye. He's as good as in prison, and only for being Japanese. It isn't right." There. He'd said it. If the government could do it so easily to the Japanese, what was preventing them from moving on to the Koreans? To many they were one and the same, which of course wasn't true. His father felt the distinction was important to fight for. Americans needed to understand Koreans were different. Their loyalties lay completely with the United States, and the Japanese were truly the ones to be suspected and feared.

His father's nostrils flared. "I never approved of your friendship with him. The Japanese deserve to be in camps after what they've done to our people. Every single one."

"You're wrong!" Alex shouted.

Without warning, his father backhanded his face. Alex cried out at the sharp sting.

"You never should have placed your trust in him. Danny Tamura and his family are where they belong." His father's chest rose and fell with deep breaths of agitation. "I'm finished with your defiance. From now on, you're going to be in my brother's care. I hope he'll be able to talk some sense into you. When you've truly learned what it means to be Korean, and you've rooted out these preposterous ideas, then you may come home. I expect you to be packed by the end of the day."

Now, a sneaking fear coiled itself into his heart like a black weed. Those same feelings, like an echo from the past, pounded louder and louder in his head until they began taking over his rational thinking. What was he going to do? Where was he going to go? The last thing he wanted to do was to spend the night on the street. But what other choice did he have? What if someone found him and beat him up again? Or worse—killed him?

As if to calm his fears in a single stroke, a bell rang out, calling out the time of three o'clock.

A church.

Two other bells sounded from different parts of town like giant iron birds calling to one another across the swaths of winding streets and sun-drenched trees.

Alex scrambled to his feet and followed the last ringing tones hovering in the haze. His mother had faithfully taken her children to church their entire lives, having had Christian-converted parents since she was a girl. His father grew up in a Christian home himself, but didn't observe regularly. Alex had always found comfort and peace when walking through the front door and hearing the organ played. The bells awoke in him a freshened sense of hope. There was always hope found at church.

He turned down another quiet street and came upon a pretty, white plaster church with a steeple and simple stained glass windows. A familiar form was outside sweeping the walkway.

"Reverend Hicks?" Alex asked. Relief flooded him at this sudden change of luck as the man caught sight of him.

"Alex, how good to see you." With a broad smile, he reached out a hand and they shook. "Please, come in."

Reverend Hicks led him into the dim, cool foyer and on into the main chapel filled with wooden benches facing a plain pulpit.

The stained glass windows glowed spectacularly in the late afternoon light, giving the room a comforting feel.

"Lovely, aren't they?" Reverend Hicks said proudly. "The local glass factory donated the windows back when the church was first built thirty years ago."

"They're beautiful."

"Why don't you come through to my office?"

Alex followed him into a small room lined with brimming bookshelves. A large, single window highlighted the wealth of dust and an untidy desk in the middle of the room. "Please, have a seat," Reverend Hicks encouraged.

Alex sat in the worn, green leather chair across from the reverend.

"How can I help you?" Reverend Hicks leaned forward, an expectant smile lighting his face.

Alex opened his mouth, but he had no idea what to say and shut it again. His pride choked out anything that had to do with asking for assistance. But he knew he needed help. How should he ask?

Reverend Hicks seemed to sense his discomfort. "You know, I was just thinking I could use some extra help around here. I have my regular duties of writing sermons, paperwork, visiting the members of my congregation, and such. I have a small budget to hire a woman to come and clean the inside of the chapel, but any other things like repairs and outdoor work are stretching me a bit thin. You wouldn't by chance be in need of some work would you?" He gazed at Alex expectantly.

The tremendous sense of relief at this man's kindness and understanding was overwhelming. "It seems as if I'll be in town for a while, so I'd be grateful for the work." For a while was an understatement. Who knew how long he'd be stuck here?

"Wonderful. It's settled, then. You can get started right away. I'll show you where the shed is. It's not a full-time job, and you're welcome to go find more substantial work. I'll put you up for tonight in exchange for mowing the lawn. How does that sound?"

Alex barely kept the grin from his face. "It sounds good. Thank you."

Reverend Hicks showed him the tool shed and where the push mower was located. "The blades have been sharpened recently, so it shouldn't be too hard a job. Do you have anything else to wear?"

Alex shook his head and surveyed the damage. It was no wonder they'd refused to serve him at the restaurant. His trousers were torn and filthy. The rest of his clothes weren't any better. He practically looked homeless. All of his spare clothing and things were in his luggage. As far as he knew, it had been abandoned in Washington DC.

"I'll loan you a shirt and old trousers," Reverend Hicks said. "I still have some of my clothes from my pre-minister days, though they'll be terribly outdated."

"That's fine. I don't mind."

***

Alex enjoyed the constructive manual labor after hours of reading and inactivity in the jail cell, and before that, the long, uncomfortable travel on the train. He pushed the mower methodically, carefully overlapping his rows. The freshly cut grass and rich, earthy smell grounded him. There was something soothing about the whir of the spinning blades, a satisfaction of seeing the green grass flying away from the mower to leave a neat trail in the lawn.

He finished the job and pulled the mower back to the shed, wiping it down with a grease-stained rag he found before putting it away. Reverend Hicks emerged from the side door of the church, beaming as Alex closed the shed.

"Look at this lawn. I'm being honest when I say I couldn't have done a better job."

"Thank you."

"I'll give you time to wash up inside, and we'll have a spot of supper. My house is just next door there."

Alex emerged refreshed and dressed in a set of Reverend Hicks' old trousers, shirt, and vest. They sat to a humble supper of bread, canned soup, and cheese. Reverend Hicks bowed his head, said grace, and they ate in companionable silence.

After a while, Alex spoke up. "I know some of this may have to do with your job as a minister, but why are you being so kind? People around here are pretty suspicious of me. Why aren't you?"

Reverend Hicks swallowed his mouthful of soup. "Well, you're right. It is part of my job as a spiritual leader in this town, and indeed, I see everyone as God's children." He paused for a moment and continued, "The other part is your eyes."

"My eyes?"

"I can usually tell by looking someone in the eyes what sort of person they are. You've heard the phrase 'the eyes are the window to the soul'?"

Alex nodded.

"When I look in your eyes I see an honest young man who's had the misfortune of being subjected to a sad misunderstanding."

"How can you know for sure?"

"I can't. But I'm offering you the gift of trust, and I'm hoping I won't be disappointed."

Alex nodded. "I won't disappoint you. Thank you again for giving me some work and a place to stay."

They cleared up the table and moved into the living room.

Alex took a seat on the couch and Reverend Hicks settled into his well-worn armchair. He leaned over to a small, boxy Philco radio sitting on a side table nearby and turned the knob with a click. Crackling and whistling filled the air as he fiddled with the knobs until the strains of classical music came through relatively clear. He leaned back with content, closing his eyes. They listened for a while, the swell of music washing over them.

For the first time in a long time, Alex relaxed. He was safe, warm, and fed. He was extremely grateful to have met the kind-hearted reverend. He honestly didn't know what he would've done without the man's generosity. No doubt, he'd be sleeping in some dark alley, cold and hungry. Homesickness stole over him with a sharp stab to his chest. Shutting his eyes, Alex saw his mother before him, eyes crinkling in a smile, her arms outstretched to give him a warm hug. His breath caught in his throat, and he opened his eyes again. He needed to distract himself.

"Are you all alone then?" Alex asked and then mentally kicked himself. "I'm sorry. It's really none of my business."

Reverend Hicks smiled. "It's all right. I never got around to getting married." He chuckled. "I've been chided by a number of people in my congregation saying I should be setting a good example, but I suppose I've always been too consumed with my ecclesiastical work." He paused. "Frankly, I'm just too shy."

Alex laughed a little. "Really? I don't see you that way, sir."

"Well, that's what my sister Mildred tells me anyway, and usually she's right; though if you meet her, don't tell her I said so." They laughed together.

"Do you have just the one sister?" Alex asked.

"No, I have two. There's Mildred, myself, and then Harriet, Lonnie's mother. She's the youngest. And you? Do you have any siblings?"

"Yes. I have three. My older siblings, Henry and Esther, and then my younger sister, June."

"I'm sure they miss you a great deal."

Alex nodded and stared at the floor. The homesickness returned, but this time the image of June flooded him, her sleek black braids bumping wildly on her back as she ran after his Washington-destined train on the platform, tears streaming down her face. His heart mourned from remembering, and he was unprepared for how forceful the memory was. He took a deep, shuddering breath to clear his mind.

After a moment the reverend said, "Have you given any thought to what your plans are? I've contacted the stationmaster and he's working on getting your suitcase."

Alex slowly rubbed his hands together, working any agitation he felt into the mindless action. "I lost all my money somewhere between the train station and the police station. I'll have to find a job and earn it back. So I think I'm here for the time being. I'll find another place to stay as soon as I secure a job, if that's all right."

Reverend Hicks nodded. "I'll keep an ear to the ground for any jobs. There's always the glass factory. They've recently been hiring a lot of people. Mr. Stanton tells me they're having trouble keeping up with the orders. Do you have any specific skills?"

"My father runs a mechanic's shop back home. I'm pretty good with a wrench," Alex said. "And I was studying engineering before I came out here. I'll take whatever job I can find, though."

"I think we'll be able to find you something." Reverend Hicks switched off the radio. "I think it's time for both of us to get some rest. I'll fetch you some linens." He left and quickly returned with a soft blanket and fluffy pillow. "Make yourself comfortable." He picked up Alex's folded pile of spoiled clothing from the sofa. "I'll see to having these cleaned and repaired."

"Thank you," Alex said, taken aback at this further kindness.

Reverend Hicks smiled. "I'll see you in the morning. Oh, and before I forget, if you need to write a letter to contact your family, you're free to make use of the materials at my desk. Goodnight."

Alex got ready for bed. Ten minutes later he lay on the couch, his head propped up by one arm as he stared up at the dark ceiling.

Twenty-four hours ago, he'd stared at an entirely different ceiling. It was as if he'd traveled a thousand miles but hadn't really gone anywhere. He tried not to think of what he was going to do next. If he thought too far ahead, the feelings of responsibility and duty he'd been trying to ignore would come crushing down on top of him again.

He turned over on his side and tried to get comfortable on the stiff couch, appreciating how much better it was than the jail cot. Crickets chirped loudly outside the living room window, bright moonlight streamed in through cracks in the dark curtains. He studied the patterns of light.

After fifteen minutes of sleeplessness, he snapped on the lamp. Duty had won out. He rummaged for a piece of writing paper and a pencil and easily found both at the reverend's writing desk. He perched in the chair, his hand hovering above the paper. What should he write? Enough sparing information to make his parents not worry? Or should he just lay everything out? If his mother knew what he'd been through the past few days, no doubt she'd take the next train out here to rescue him herself.

No, he wasn't going to tell them everything. He needed a carefully worded letter to assuage their concern and to delay any action on his uncle's part. While he was reluctantly resigned to being sent to live with his uncle, this one day of freedom, however horrible it had been, was his first. As for tomorrow, he looked forward to it with a tentative optimism. He had to take full advantage of his unexpected independence before it was taken away again.

Soon, Alex finished his letter, scanned the *hangul* for any mistakes or untidiness, and then readied it for posting. His uncle deserved a letter as well, but his address had been wadded up with the lost money. He'd have to wait to send him something until after he heard back from his parents.

Alex lay back down and tucked his hands behind his head, the image of his mother filling his mind like a burst of sunshine on a dreary day. To feel her comforting arms around him, to drink in her warm, contagious smile . . . He'd give anything for that now. He closed his eyes, picturing her. Slowly he slipped into sleep with the sound of her laughter in his ears.

***

Sunday beamed bright and glittering after an early morning storm that swept through. Green leaves and small branches littered the street and lawns. Alex, taking a glance out the window, saw he'd have some work cut out for him the next day caring for the church grounds. As it was, he dressed quickly and got to work sweeping the sidewalk leading up to the church doors and making the front at least look tidy.

He got ready for church, and after a refreshing shower, he stopped to examine his cuts. His lip was healing quickly, and the bruises were yellowing and fading, but the cut by his eyebrow had been deep. He'd have a scar, no doubt, and a permanent reminder of his attack.

Once he was presentable, he walked next door to the church. An older woman was at the organ warming up. Reverend Hicks was nowhere to be seen. Alex took a seat near the front of the empty chapel. Soon other people started arriving, their footsteps on the stone floor echoing in the chapel. Their whispered conversations added a soft background cadence to the organ.

One set of sharply tapping shoes grew louder until they stopped abruptly beside the end of Alex's pew. He glanced up, prepared for an unfriendly scowl. His nerves settled into amusement to find the reverend's niece, Lonnie, staring down at him in surprise. Her mouth hung open.

"Am I in your seat?" he asked. The question filled him with an unexpected wicked glee.

"W-what are you . . . why are you . . ." Her mouth snapped shut, and she marched to the pew in front of him, followed by a girl with light brown hair who appeared to be a younger sister. Also filing into the pew was a bright-eyed boy of about eight or nine. His shirttail hung out of his pants and as soon as they were seated, Lonnie leaned over and hissed for him to tuck it in. Peeking over her shoulder at Alex, the younger sister's eyes widened. She nudged Lonnie.

"It's that Jap guy," she whispered loudly.

Alex winced, but didn't bother to comment.

"I told you, Tunie, he's not Japanese . . ."

This he couldn't let pass. He leaned forward. "How charitable of you to notice, Miss Hamilton."

She craned her neck to regard him icily. He winked at her, and she whipped her head around. He wanted to laugh out loud at her embarrassment, but Reverend Hicks emerged from a side door, walked up to the pulpit, and began delivering an inspiring and energetic sermon. Alex relaxed, happy to finally be getting to see this side of his new friend.

The last hymn was one that he knew, and he sung out with the rest of the congregation. He grinned at hearing Lonnie's pleasant voice grow louder to match his own. After the last notes of the organ faded, Alex stayed in his seat, his eyes following Lonnie as she filed out of the pew with her siblings, completely ignoring him. As the boy passed him, his face lit up with interest. Alex gave him a little smile. At least someone wasn't appalled at the sight of him.

He was grateful he'd sat up front. He didn't have to live through anyone's reactions as they walked past him to exit. He suspected the day's sermon on "judge not lest ye be judged" hadn't sunk in deeply with most of the congregation.

Alex waited patiently until the church quieted before he left his seat and walked back toward the main door. As Reverend Hicks shook hands in farewell with one of his remaining church members, a middle-aged woman with short, graying curly hair and a bustling demeanor approached him.

"I thoroughly enjoyed your sermon, Reverend. Quite inspired. But then, your sermons are always so wise and insightful."

Reverend Hicks caught sight of Alex. "Why, thank you. Mrs. Godfrey, I'd like to introduce you to a friend of mine. This is Mr. Alex Moon. He's visiting our town for a while. Alex, Jane Godfrey is a neighbor to Mike Hardy, one of two mechanics in town and a good friend of mine. She also has a delightful rose garden."

Mrs. Godfrey's eyes widened in horror as she turned to Alex. Nevertheless, he extended his hand. He even threw in a warm smile.

"It's a pleasure to meet you, Mrs. Godfrey."

She glanced nervously between Alex and Reverend Hicks, who was trying to hide his humor. No doubt, his sermon she'd just complimented was on her mind. Mrs. Godfrey collected herself and weakly shook his hand. "M-Mr. Moon. A pleasure." She withdrew her hand quickly. "I do apologize, but I need to hurry home. Goodbye, Reverend." She sped away.

"I'd say you put her on the spot," Alex remarked good-naturedly, tucking his hands in his pockets.

Reverend Hicks chuckled. "I suppose it was rather wicked of me, but it couldn't be helped."

Alex raised his eyebrows.

"Mrs. Godfrey has her sights set on me. My niece, Lonnie, has been doing her part to throw us together. She doesn't like to see me all alone, I suppose. I'm not too fond of the idea myself. So I sabotage when I can." He coughed a little to clear his throat and looked away. Alex laughed.

"You're a surprising man, Reverend Hicks."

"Oh? Am I?"

They walked back inside the church. "You know," Reverend Hicks said, "why don't you join me at my sister Millie's house this evening for dinner? Lonnie will be there, and I think she'll enjoy having another young person to talk to."

At hearing Lonnie's name, Alex found a smile tilting his lips. "I'd love to."

Chapter Four

LONNIE ARRIVED AT her Aunt Millie's just as the clock on the mantle chimed six. Her aunt greeted her at the door.

"Appalone, my dear, come in. It's been too long since you've come to visit me. I was tickled pink when Phillip suggested we get together. Of course, I tried inviting your mother; I even called her up on the telephone, but naturally she hung up. It's too bad your brother and sister couldn't come too."

"I know, but they have school tomorrow. Mother wanted them to stay home and study."

"Keep them under her thumb more like," Aunt Millie grumbled. "Phillip, Appalone is here. Oh, and by the way, your uncle brought that young man who's staying with him for a few days. Alexander, was it?"

She led Lonnie into the spacious living room and both men stood as they entered. Lonnie's heart dropped to her stomach. How could *he* be here? Alex was smartly dressed and impeccably groomed, his cuts cleaned and bruises healing. It was a huge transformation from when she'd seen him in jail. It was bad enough he'd been sitting in her pew at church, making her flustered and jittery. Now she had to face him for the entire evening. How could Uncle Phillip not even mention he'd invited Alex?

"I didn't know Alex was staying with you, Uncle Phillip," she said.

"It's only for a few days."

Alex didn't say anything, but his gaze followed her and she fidgeted, removing her gloves and clutching her purse tightly.

"Shall we go into dinner?" Aunt Millie asked. "I don't know about you, but I'm famished."

They pulled up their chairs around the beautifully laid table, the men at each end and Lonnie facing her aunt. Aunt Millie had a flair for hosting parties and this small, intimate gathering was no exception. Her best silver was laid out along with china place settings and crystal goblets. The elegant blue willow dish at the center of the table glamorized the tiny pork roast, carrots, and potatoes into a feast.

After Uncle Phillip said grace, Aunt Millie dished up the food, chattering away. "You have no idea how thrilled I was to have a dinner party. It's been ages since I've gotten the good dishes out. Not since George rejoined the army and went off to Britain. I can hardly believe it's been almost a year."

"Time is strange. It feels like they were here yesterday," Uncle Phillip mused.

Lonnie ate quietly, letting the talk surround her. She tried not to let her eyes wander in Alex's direction.

"I'll just be glad when they can come home," Aunt Millie said. "I don't mind doing my bit for the war effort and all, but I was born to be a housewife, not a factory girl. The sooner I can get back to throwing dinner parties, cleaning my house, and switching on the six o'clock news and not hearing any news reports on the war, the better."

"I think we all look forward to that day." Uncle Phillip nodded.

Lonnie laughed a little. "I definitely don't see you as a factory girl, Aunt Millie, but I think your work with the local OPA board, the AWVS, and the Red Cross is extremely admirable."

Her aunt beamed. "Well, you're right of course. My talents do lie outside a factory, thank goodness. Speaking of which, Lonnie, there are a few volunteer opportunities I was hoping to talk you into doing for me. We can speak about it later so as not to bore the men." She smiled round at them, and Lonnie bit her cheek to hide her amusement. Her aunt could be so grandiose.

Uncle Phillip cleared his throat. "This pork roast is delicious by the way, Millie."

"Why, thank you, Phillip. It's much more cheerful to be able to share it with you all." She raised her glass. "To George, David, and the end of war."

Lonnie raised her glass. "Here, here." They clinked glasses. Lonnie's eyes slid over and met gazes with Alex, then flicked away.

"Aunt Millie, have you heard from David? How's he doing? The last time I heard he was stationed in England."

Her aunt sighed. "Yes, that's about as much as I know. I wrote him not too long ago using that new V-mail service. It's wonderful, do you know? The reply to one of my letters from George came two and a half weeks later. I don't like that I'm not getting his actual letter, only a picture of it, but it's better than waiting for ages."

"I need to write Uncle George a letter. And David too. It's been a while since I've done that."

"Oh, I know David would love to get a letter. He's been asking after you."

Lonnie felt Alex's eyes on her, but she continued to ignore him.

Aunt Millie turned her attention to Alex. "So, Alexander, my brother tells me you come from Korea."

Lonnie straightened in attention at her aunt's question. He was Korean?

Alex's jaw tensed. "I was born in Los Angeles, and my parents and siblings still live there. My grandparents live in Hawaii. They immigrated from Korea a long time ago."

"Oh, Hawaii. I've always wanted to go there, though not now perhaps. Things are a little different . . ."

"Millie." Uncle Phillip chastised gently, glancing over at Alex. There was an awkward silence.

"Have you ever been to visit them, Alex?" Aunt Millie continued primly, trying to recover the conversation.

He nodded. "Once when I was young. I don't remember much, but I do remember the large waves coming onto the beach." He turned to Lonnie. "Have you ever been to the ocean, Miss Hamilton?"

She tried to avoid his eyes. "Um . . . no. I haven't."

"Never? Not even to the Atlantic?"

Her face grew warm. Of course, he was more traveled than she was. He'd just come from California.

"No." She hadn't meant to let on she was so testy about it, but what else could she say when she hadn't been anywhere outside Indiana? Her jealousy must've been apparent because she caught him muffling a laugh with a burst of coughing. She glowered and went back to ignoring him.

After a satisfying dinner, they congregated in the living room, and Aunt Millie put on a record. The smooth croon of Buddy Clark's voice filled the air. She and Uncle Phillip settled in to play a game of dominos. Lonnie found an interesting book on the shelf and settled at the end of the couch. Alex cornered her, taking a seat right next to her.

He didn't say anything at first, but only watched as she read. Lonnie felt his eyes boring into her, and the temperature in the room steadily rose until she was uncomfortable. After reading the same paragraph three times, she dropped the book to her lap.

"Is there something you want?" She finally looked him full in the face, showing a confidence she certainly didn't feel.

"I suppose you know how it feels now, don't you?" His eyebrow was cocked in a challenge.

"What are you talking about?"

"To be stared at. To be studied like a bug under a magnifying glass."

He must be referring to when she'd visited him at the jail. She opened her mouth to speak, but nothing came out. Her mind was a complete blank.

He leaned in close, locking eyes with hers. "It's very disconcerting, isn't it?"

Lonnie swallowed, her heart pounding hard. She nodded silently. His dark amber eyes were impossible to avoid; his breath was warm on her face.

Alex moved back and laughed. She started, astonished at how much his face was transformed—it just lit up, his eyes curving into little half-moons. Her pulse raced miles faster than before, and she tore her eyes away.

Her mind was all jumbled. First, he was angry. Then, he wanted to teach her a lesson. And now he was laughing at her. How could one person be so confusing? Something about Alex pulled her in, but at the same time, he terrified her. He was *Korean*. What did that even mean? How was that different from being Japanese? And where was Korea anyway?

Her eyes met his, and her heart jolted. There was that vulnerability again. Her whole being filled with pity for him.

Alex regarded her. "I don't know what to make of you, Miss Hamilton. You seem completely unfazed by me."

Lonnie blushed. "Not completely." She stared down at her fingers woven tightly in her lap. "There's a lot I don't understand about you, Mr. Moon. I'd like to, but . . ." She met his gaze. "Instead of laughing at me, why don't you teach me?"

Alex frowned. "Teach you?"

"Yes." She turned her body to face him straight on. "Teach me about the culture you come from. Then I'd be able to understand."

Suspicion etched his face, and strangely, disappointment too. "What's there to understand? I'm an American, same as you."

She opened her mouth in momentary speechlessness. "Well—well, isn't it obvious?"

"No." His expression was steely. He was shutting himself away from her.

"You're Korean, aren't you?"

To her surprise, his eyes narrowed. A seed of fear began to grow in her chest at the sudden anger she saw flame up.

"It seems we're right back to where we started," he murmured, his voice wary and low.

"What do you mean?" She wanted to shrink away, but her back was jammed against the arm of the couch, and he was still very close.

"You only see me as an *immigrant*. I'm better off going back to where I came from. Is that it?"

Lonnie gaped, his words assaulting her again. "No. You're just different, that's all. I only want to learn more about you."

He crossed his arms and scoffed. "I find that hard to believe. Everyone else sees me as some piece of Jap trash they wish would drop off the face of the planet, and they're too scared to consider anything else. Why should you care? Why should I say anything just to satisfy *your* curiosity?"

Lonnie was in over her head. What was the point in even trying with this man? She'd wanted to be friends, but her efforts were going nowhere. It was obvious he wasn't interested in being friendly.

She dug her nails into the edge of the couch cushion, leaned forward and glared, their faces inches apart. "Well, I'm not everyone, Alexander Moon. You should take a good look in a mirror to see who's really scared. If you had any sense, you'd try making friends while you're here. It's a shame you're off to such a terrible start."

"Are you saying *you're* trying to be my friend? What a joke."

She stood abruptly, stiff with anger. "You couldn't spot an honest intention if it bit you on the nose."

"Lonnie, what's going on?" Uncle Phillip's attention diverted from the domino game. Aunt Millie stared, open-mouthed.

Lonnie's face flushed. How much had they heard? She cleared her throat. "I should be getting home, Aunt Millie. Mother likes to have me home before eight."

"Oh. Well, all right, dear."

"I'll give you a ride home," Uncle Phillip said. "Alex and I came in the car."

Lonnie gaped in mortification. She'd have to ride home with Alex? After the heated words they just exchanged? "Oh, you don't have to do that. It's out of your way. I can walk."

"Out of the question, Appalone," her aunt scolded. "Be a good girl and let Phillip drive you home."

"I brought the car with that in mind, my dear." Her uncle smiled over his spectacles. "It's hardly out of my way."

Lonnie reluctantly gave in. After an effusive farewell from Aunt Millie, they climbed into the old, but well maintained black Ford. Lonnie occupied the front with her uncle while Alex climbed into the back.

As they set off, Alex bent forward to lean on the back of their seat. "Did I hear Mrs. Smithfield say your name was Appalone?" His voice betrayed his delight in finding something to tease her about.

Lonnie pursed her lips.

Uncle Phillip answered for her. "Yes, she did. An interesting name, isn't it?"

"I've never heard it before. Where does it come from?"

"I believe it was Lonnie's three times great-grandmother's name. Other than that, we don't know much about it."

"No one calls me that," Lonnie finally butted in. "It's just Lonnie."

"*Sagwa*," Alex said.

"What?"

"*Sagwa*. It's Korean for apple." He grinned wickedly.

Lonnie gritted her teeth in annoyance. He'd made such a fuss over her saying he was Korean, and now here he was speaking the language? "My name isn't Apple. It's *Lonnie*."

"Her sister's name is Petunia," Uncle Phillip volunteered.

"We call her Tunie," Lonnie retorted. "Really, Uncle Phillip, do you have to go about revealing all of our embarrassing names?"

"I think Petunia's nice," Alex remarked. "It's a sweet smelling flower."

"It doesn't match her personality, I'm afraid," Uncle Phillip added.

Alex laughed. It was hopeless.

They finally reached her house, and she turned to her uncle. "Goodnight, Uncle Phillip. Thank you for the ride."

"Goodnight, dear. I'll see you on Sunday."

She reached for the door handle, but Alex was already there. In one smooth movement, he'd opened the door and taken her outstretched hand to help. Her breath sucked in with a hiss at the touch of his warm, strong hand. It gripped hers for a mere moment.

"Goodnight, *Sagwa*." His tone was gentle, but it was laced with the smugness that was half-concealed in his smile.

Flustered, Lonnie yanked her hand away and hurried into her house without looking back. She shut the door and leaned against it, hearing the car rumble off down the block. She took a few measured breaths, filled with relief from the solidity of the door behind her. Why had she ever showed an interest in him? Now what was she going to do when she saw him again? It seemed he was sticking around for a while, and it was hard to avoid anyone for very long in River Bluff.

✳✳✳

Alex leaned back in his seat. "Your niece is an interesting person, Reverend Hicks."

The reverend glanced at him through the rear view mirror. "I don't know of any young lady who is as sweet and thoughtful as she is. She's a big help to me and does a great deal to help her family at home."

Thoughtful maybe, but Alex wondered about the sweet part.

They pulled into the church drive and parked around back. Just outside the front door of his house, Reverend Hicks placed a hand on Alex's arm. "Please be cautious, Alex." It was hard to read his expression in the darkness.

"What do you mean?"

"I hope you don't misunderstand me, but a friendship between you two might be out of the question. Lonnie is under a great deal of stress at home. She bears up fairly well, but I worry about her. Her father isn't around, so she's my responsibility. I know you've just met, and I may be rambling on like an old fool, but please tread carefully. Don't cross over any lines that might be deemed inappropriate."

Alex was a little stung by his words. "I'm sorry, sir. A friendship with Lonnie?" He laughed lightly. "Honestly, I doubt she'd be interested. Both times we've met, we've argued. It's not like I meant to, she just—"

Reverend Hicks nodded in understanding. "Just be careful. Goodnight."

The reverend disappeared into his room, and Alex plopped down on the couch, absorbing everything the man had said. He'd barely met this girl. Why would he be warning him off a friendship?

Lonnie's image hung before his mind's eye—her delicately curling golden hair, her blue eyes, and her shy smile. He wouldn't go so far as to say she was stunning, but she had a beauty about her, a gracefulness that complimented her.

But if anything, Lonnie Hamilton was confusing. What had she meant by learning about his culture? What was there to learn? He was American, but it was obvious she didn't see it that way. Why should he even bother?

Though, like an itch he couldn't scratch, a tiny corner of him wanted to know more about her. Why did she want to get to know him? Why wasn't she afraid? Being seen with a man like him would be death to her reputation. Why would she risk something like that?

Alex shook his head roughly to clear his mind and got changed for bed. He yanked the blanket over himself and frowned. He was better off making a plan. First, he'd get a job, scrape together enough money, and then either head back to California where he came from or resign himself to his duty and continue to Washington DC. He hadn't made up his mind yet. Either way, there'd be no attachments, no ties left behind. And no Lonnie Hamilton.

Chapter Five

THE NEXT DAY, Alex's luggage arrived back at the River Bluff train station. The stationmaster sent them to the reverend's house via a delivery boy. Opening the case on the couch, Alex searched the contents. Nothing was missing. He breathed a sigh of relief. If it hadn't been for Reverend Hicks's quick action in contacting the stationmaster, his luggage very well might have ended up abandoned in Washington. His money, however, had not appeared even after a search and inquiry at the train and police stations. Not that he expected to find the money at all.

After stowing his suitcase away, he walked to one of the mechanics who was seeking extra help. Alex stood at the open garage door watching an older gentleman with his head deep underneath a car's hood.

"Hello? Mr. Hardy?"

Mike Hardy, a man of about sixty with a full head of flyaway white hair, turned around, his hands covered in grease, and a cigarette dangling from his lips. A thin cloud of smoke drifted near his head. "Can I help you?"

Alex stepped forward with a smile. "My name is Alex Moon. Reverend Hicks sent me over. He said you might be in need of another pair of hands. I'm looking for some work."

The man wiped his hands on a grease-stained rag, giving Alex a once-over. "You're not from around these parts are you?" he drawled.

"No, sir." Alex waited uncomfortably for the barrage of questions that were sure to come. *Who are you? Where did you come from? Are you a Jap? Why aren't you enlisted?* But the questions never came.

The man grunted, seemingly satisfied. "It's not like I couldn't use the help." He nodded in the direction of the car. "What do you know about cars?"

"I've worked repairing machinery and cars in my dad's shop since I was ten. I suppose I've got a knack for it. May I?" Alex approached the car and the man stepped aside. He poked around for a minute under the hood and gave his diagnosis.

The man nodded again. "I was thinking the same thing. I'll tell you what, go change your clothes, and you can start today. Business has been busy, and I can't keep up with the demand. Where are you living?"

"I've been staying with the reverend, but that's only temporary," Alex said.

Mike scratched his head in thought. "I've got a spare room above the garage. One of my boys used to stay up there. It may need some fixing up, but the bed's still good. Might be better than Reverend Hicks's couch. What do you say?"

Alex was elated. "That would be perfect. Thank you, sir."

Mike grunted. "I'll have to take food out of your wages."

"That sounds fine, Mr. Hardy."

The man reached out and offered his weathered hand. "It's Mike."

"Alex. Thank you for taking me on, sir."

The man guffawed. "Just Mike is fine. I'll see you in a bit then."

Alex agreed and thanked the man again before hurrying back to the reverend's house. He packed his things into his suitcase with a grin on his face. For the first time he was getting somewhere in this town.

After packing and changing, Alex notified Reverend Hicks of his job success. He bade his friend farewell and promised to continue helping with the yard work at the church. Alex was back at Hardy's Garage within the hour.

Mike allowed him to tidy up the room above the garage before starting work. Alex swept and moved boxes of junk to one corner, made the bed, and wiped down the windows to let the sunlight in. He smiled, surveying where he'd be living. It was the first time he'd had a place to call his own, even though it wasn't really his own. It wasn't attached to his parents' home though, and that was all that mattered.

Soon after, Alex got to work with some direction from Mike. He was happy to get his hands into a car again. There was something soothing about being able to fix problems he understood and analyzing mysteries that always had a solution. He worked in perfect contentment until lunch when Mike called him over.

"Soup's on. Wash up and come on inside." The man disappeared through the door into his house.

Alex washed up in the garage sink, scrubbing his hands and arms well until most of the grease was gone. Then he followed Mike inside.

Mike Hardy lived in a modest single-story bungalow on the edge of town. The inside was neat and tidy. Photographs lined the hallway to the kitchen—gray-tone images of a younger Mike, his arm around a wavy-haired woman with a beautiful smile, rough and tumble boys all arms and legs laughing and pointing at the camera, a jubilant Mike in a stiff tuxedo, the same pretty woman beside him in a bridal gown. There was even one of Mike posing proudly in an old Army uniform from The Great War. Alex stopped to study the photographs with a smile.

He wandered out into the living room, and his jaw dropped. An enormous world map occupied the main wall. Pins with mini flags attached were stuck all over the map; most were clustered in areas of Europe and the Pacific. Three black flags jumped out at him—one in Hawaii and two over the Pacific Ocean.

His eyes traveled to some framed photographs next to the map of three young men, all smiling, all in uniform. Each had a black ribbon decorating a corner of their frame. His eyes continued on their path left to the front window. There hung the white, red-bordered flag signifying Mike's sons in service with three stars—all gold. Immediately his heart jolted. This man's sons were all dead? And they were killed by the Japanese no less. A deep sadness filled Alex; to have lost all three sons in such a short time. What must Mike have gone through?

Alex's stomach churned. What must Mike think of him? Here he had, bold as brass, come and asked for a job; he who looked to everyone like the enemy. Why hadn't Reverend Hicks warned him?

"Food's in here," Mike said from the doorway into the living room, making Alex jump. "Come on."

Alex followed him into the kitchen where they sat at a small round table set with two mismatched chairs. "My wife passed a few years ago, and I don't have company much," Mike said as explanation. The table was set with two bowls and spoons, glasses of water, and a small pot of soup, a packet of saltine crackers and a dish of margarine.

Alex was nervous as Mike dished up his own bowl of soup, wondering if Mike was going to say anything about his impolite snooping. But the man only started slurping his soup noisily, so Alex served himself and began eating.

"Campbell's is my best friend these days. Hope you don't mind." Mike laughed gruffly at his little joke, slathering a generous portion of margarine on a saltine.

It took a second for Alex to realize he was referring to the brand of soup. The empty tin sat on the counter. Alex smiled. This was his second meal of canned soup served by a man living alone. He imagined himself having a long-time relationship with canned soups now that he was on his own without the comforting umbrella of his mother's home cooking. He tried not to think about it.

"I don't mind," he said.

The rest of their meal was filled with the sound of slurping and the crunch of crackers, but the knot in his stomach about his predicament never went away. When was Mike going to ask the fateful questions or make the pending accusations blaming him for the death of his sons? Alex felt it looming on the horizon, and yet Mike still said nothing, seemingly content with his warm and simple meal. Alex certainly wasn't going to bring it up. And so his wait began.

***

Lonnie paced back and forth in an aisle at the library. Should she ask? She already carried a small stack of books on the topic, but they weren't really what she was searching for. Sometimes this library could be so frustratingly insufficient. Their world history section was all right, but it was heavily biased toward European history.

She thought about going to the librarian to request the books she wanted. Would the woman ask questions? Would she wonder why Lonnie wanted books on the Orient and Korea? What if the librarian got the wrong impression and thought she was friendly toward the Japanese? Would the woman say something to someone?

She bit her lip, pausing in her fretful pacing. Why did she have to be afraid? She was in a library—a place for pursuing knowledge. She should be able to ask for whatever books she wanted as long as they weren't banned.

She filled her lungs to steady herself, squared her shoulders, and marched toward the librarian's desk. It was a busy day at the library. Saturdays usually were. Lonnie tried to avoid the busy times, but the past week had been impossible. To be more accurate, her mother had been impossible. She barely had time to leave the house with all the work her mother loaded onto her.

Lonnie was impatient as she waited in line. Everywhere people sat at tables, chatting in hushed conversations, perusing the shelves, or hurrying with their selection of books to check out. The Roman-columned library wasn't tiny, but it wasn't substantial either. Many times, she had to request books to be sent from other libraries.

Lonnie finally stepped up to the desk to face the trim little woman who was stationed there, waiting expectantly.

"I was wondering—"

"Speak up, please," the woman urged.

Lonnie glanced around. "I'd like to request some books about the Orient."

The woman nodded. "Have you gone through our card catalog?" She indicated the wooden cases of multitudes of tiny drawers to her right. "I know we have a number of books on the Orient."

Lonnie nodded. "Yes. I found a few things, but not really what I'm searching for."

"What specifically about the Orient were you wanting to learn?"

Lonnie swallowed and lowered her voice. "I'd like books about Korea."

"Korea?" The librarian said the word more loudly than was necessary in Lonnie's opinion. The woman frowned and moved over to the card catalog case. Lonnie gritted her teeth with impatience. Didn't the woman realize she would've already checked there? Lonnie smiled in apology to those waiting behind her. They didn't seem particularly interested, but it didn't quell her queasy stomach.

The woman came back from her search. "Yes, you're right. We don't seem to have any books on that topic. If you could fill out this request card, I'll submit it, and we'll see what turns up, shall we?" She slid a piece of paper across the desk.

Lonnie quickly filled in the short form and handed it back to the woman.

"Not many people are interested in the Orient in this town. I'm curious as to why you so specifically would like to learn about Korea."

Her mind scrambled for an answer. "It's for research," Lonnie mumbled and slipped away. She breathed a sigh of relief as she left the library only to run into someone on their way in. Lonnie cried out and dropped all of her books. A laugh met her ears.

"Well, hello again. *Sagwa*." Alex Moon grinned at her, and she wanted to melt into the floor. He stooped down and retrieved her books, examining the titles. "China, huh?"

She grabbed the books from him. Her face burned. "Yes. I like expanding my knowledge."

"I can see that. You were being serious then, weren't you?"

She clutched the books to her chest. "Serious?"

Alex stepped away from her as someone hurried past them out the door. He continued. "About what you said the other day—that you wanted me to teach you about the Korean culture."

She kept an eye out for anyone that might be overhearing their conversation. Why had it grown so hot all of a sudden? She wanted to fan her face, but she wouldn't relinquish the hold on her books. "Of course I was serious. Why would I say something like that if I wasn't serious?"

Alex regarded her with amusement. "Not everyone says things they mean. Sometimes they say things to get out of an uncomfortable situation."

Lonnie stared wide-eyed. If only she could think of such a thing now.

His lips twitched. "Most people wouldn't bother giving me the time of day."

"Well, I would. And it's nearly five. I must be going. Goodbye."

Alex laughed, drawing a few curious faces, but stepped aside to let her pass. "Goodbye, *Sagwa*. I hope we cross paths again soon. And by the way, you're looking in the wrong place."

"What do you mean?"

"I'm from California, remember? Not China."

Lonnie scowled and stomped off in a huff of consternation. That man. How did he manage to make her feel mortified, annoyed, and fascinated all at the same time? And to call her that ridiculous name. Who gave him permission to do that? She stopped and looked back at the library. Cross paths with him indeed.

She made her way to the smaller park near the center of town and sat beneath the greenery of a large oak tree shading a wooden bench. Lonnie opened one of her books and began to read. The book was about the topography and wildlife of the Orient in general. It was interesting, but didn't tell her anything she wanted to know. The next two books weren't any more helpful. One, a history of China, was rather tedious. The other was a survey of Oriental Art. After skimming for some time, she finally closed it with a frown. She was no nearer to learning about Korea than she'd been before. She needed a better resource.

Should she ask Alex directly for more information? The whole idea was embarrassing, especially after his teasing. She'd already mentioned it once, and he hadn't offered assistance, only ridicule.

Besides, he'd think she was a nosy busybody with nothing better to occupy her time than to pry into his personal background. No, it was best she did this on her own. But who knew what would be available through the library? She wanted to know things now. What could she use as a resource in the mean time?

She checked her wristwatch. It was almost six. Her mother would need her home to help with supper. She got to her feet with a heavy heart at having wasted her afternoon.

She walked home by way of River Bluff Grocery where Tunie worked after school and on Saturdays. Lonnie pulled out the list her mother had made and scanned it, hoping they had everything.

The door's bell jingled as she walked into the small, but busy establishment. River Bluff Grocery was one of two food stores in town. The other was Simmons Grocery, and they were owned by competing brothers. Since the brothers joined up at the start of the war, their wives ran the stores and the competition wasn't friendly.

Lonnie hurried, gathering the things she needed into a basket. Spying Tunie working at the counter, she waved and went over.

"Mother sent me for a few things," she said. "How's your day been so far?"

Tunie shrugged. "All right. It's been non-stop since I got here. I just want to go home, soak in the tub, and forget about everything."

Lonnie laughed. "I know what you mean."

Tunie's eyes lit up. "Oh. You'll never guess. Grandma Chan who lives on the edge of town stopped into the store today. I think it's been a month or something since she's last come in. I wonder how she survives." Her eyes shone with delight at her gossip. She leaned forward to whisper. "Someone told me they walked by her house one night, and they swear they heard a two-way radio and her voice speaking in Chinese. They think she's communicating with the Japs."

Lonnie frowned. "That's silly. Uncle Phillip's talked to her many times, and he tells me she's a sweet, old woman. She's used to being alone so she doesn't venture out much." Lonnie tore the required ration stamps from her booklet for the sugar and put the money on the counter. "Besides, if she's Chinese, why would she want to communicate with the Japanese? Whoever told you that is a mean, old gossip."

Tunie scoffed as she took Lonnie's ration stamps and money. "You never can be too careful."

"And you can never be too careful about letting your imagination run wild." Lonnie left her sister glowering and exited the shop with her sack of groceries. It disturbed her that so many people jumped to such baseless conclusions.

She arrived home just as her mother did. Her mother's face drooped with exhaustion. "Long day at work?" Lonnie asked.

Her mother nodded. "On top of regular work, I've had to help train a whole group of new people Mr. Stanton just hired on. We're barely keeping up with orders, so I suppose it was just a matter of time. You did the shopping?"

"Yes. Tunie's off in a half hour."

"I'm going up to take a shower. Tell Marty to come in and help you."

"All right."

Lonnie called Marty in and got him busy setting the table and unloading the groceries. She consulted the meal plan she'd carefully worked up at the beginning of the month and set to work. She ran out to the garden to pull up some carrots to cook, mixed up some biscuit dough, cooked some hamburger, and made a beef biscuit roll. This she put into the oven, and by the time Tunie was home from the shop, supper was ready and on the table.

Marty sniffed the air appreciatively as he took his seat at the table. "Mmm, I love it when Lonnie cooks."

Lonnie smiled at the compliment. "How was school?"

Marty shrugged. "It was okay. Mr. Parker enlisted, so they have to combine two of our classes until they can find a replacement."

Their mother stopped picking at her beef roll and frowned. "I would've thought they've squeezed this town dry of men to enlist or draft."

"What if they lower the draft age to eighteen?" Tunie asked. "There's been talk about that. Most of the boys in the senior class are itching to go anyway. As soon as they graduate, most of them will enlist."

"Well, let's hope it doesn't come to that," Harriet said. "We can only hope the war will be over before then."

"It'll be over by the end of the year, now that our boys are in it." Marty's confidence beamed out of his youthful face. Lonnie wanted to trust in his innocent words, but there was no telling how long it was going to drag out.

After eating and cleaning up the kitchen, they retired to the living room. Marty switched on the radio to listen to one of his favorite programs. Their mother picked up some knitting, while Lonnie and Tunie started a game of checkers.

"I wasn't letting my imagination run wild, by the way." Tunie spoke up in between moves.

"About what?" Lonnie asked, eyes on the board.

"About Grandma Chan, silly. I know she's been around for ages, but why's she still here? Didn't her husband die years ago? Doesn't she want to go be with her people or something?"

Lonnie jumped one of Tunie's pieces. "She has as much right to live here as anyone else. Just because she's different doesn't mean she's guilty of something, and vicious gossip is hardly deserved either, don't you think?"

Tunie tucked a piece of hair behind her ear, her eyes defiant. "I guess so."

They continued the game without speaking, but their renewed conversation of Grandma Chan sparked an idea. Why couldn't Lonnie talk with Grandma Chan? She wasn't Korean, but she could at least tell her something about China, and she might know something about the other lands in the Orient. Lonnie smiled to herself, pleased that she had at least one place to turn. She would write the woman a letter tonight and hope for the best.

Chapter Six

LONNIE STRAINED TO hear the music wafting in from the living room radio as she methodically kneaded some dough in the kitchen. Sometimes their reception wasn't bad, but today it was horrible. It might be the weather outside, but it could be she hadn't gotten the knob turned just right.

"Marty." She turned to her brother who was working on a model airplane at the table. "Could you fiddle with the knob a bit? I can barely hear the music."

It was a few seconds before he replied. "I'm busy, Lonnie." He eyed his airplane closely as he carefully glued a piece in place, his tongue bit between his teeth.

She blew a stray strand of hair out of her face. "Well, I can hardly do it myself, now can I? Go on."

Marty huffed in exasperation. "Oh, all right." He was gone for a minute. The music came in a little more clearly than before. He reappeared and sat back down. "Happy?"

"Yes, thank you." She continued kneading. "What are you working on?"

"It's a . . ." He squinted in concentration. "It's a Heinkel He 111 German bomber."

Lonnie smiled politely, though she had no idea what that meant. She could barely tell one airplane apart from another.

"Oh," she said. "That sounds exciting." She plumped the dough, put it in the greased loaf pan, covered it with a cloth, and set it to rise. She tidied up and went to sit with her brother.

His materials were spread over an entire half of the table—dozens of thin pieces of wood with the blueprint of the airplane pieces yet to be cut out, wood scraps, a blade, pungent-smelling glue, paints, brushes, and cutting board. Upon seeing the last item, Lonnie cried out.

"So that's where that cutting board went. I thought it had sprouted legs and joined the army."

Marty spared her a skeptical eye. "Really? I'm pretty sure I told you I was borrowing it."

"Well, borrowing and keeping for weeks at a time are a bit different, wouldn't you agree?"

"No." He turned his attention back to his gluing.

Lonnie laughed and ruffled his hair, making him shout in annoyance. "You nearly made me break the starboard wing. For Pete's sake, Lonnie." He was very serious about his plane models, spending weeks finishing one to be an exact replica of the actual plane. Then he'd send it to the military for them to use in training their pilots. He took great pride in it, especially amongst his friends who were absorbed in the same hobby.

She offered a sincere apology as someone knocked at the front door. Lonnie pulled it open to see Gladys looking stunning in a mauve bolero jacket dress with a matching hat, clutching her purse.

"Lonnie, dear. I'm so glad you're home."

Lonnie led her into the living room where they sat. "How are you?"

"Oh, the same." Gladys appraised her, an expertly sculpted eyebrow raised. "You're looking rather domestic today."

Lonnie laughed in embarrassment and hurried to brush some offending flour away. "I was making bread." Why did she always have to feel so homely with Gladys around? She hadn't even put on any lipstick. "Is there anything you wanted?"

"Oh . . ." Gladys picked at an imaginary thread on her flawless skirt. "I felt bad about what I said at Rose's house and wanted to apologize. About you and that Jap. Teddy and Rose were right. I was jealous you knew more than me. It was stupid." She shrugged. "I don't know why I say things like that. You've always been so kind to me, even when I was the dumpy, buck-toothed girl in braids. I've never forgotten that, you know. So even though I seek attention in the worst possible ways, I'd hate to lose you as my friend. Will you forgive me?" Gladys finally met her eyes.

Lonnie stared at her friend who was far from being dumpy and buck-toothed. Finally, she smiled. "Of course I forgive you."

Gladys exhaled in a great rush. "That's a relief." She flashed her white teeth. "You're such a sweetheart. I don't deserve you."

Lonnie laughed. "No. You don't."

Gladys giggled. "I was going into town to do some shopping. Would you care to join me?"

"Well, I just set the bread to rise . . ." Lonnie said. "And I've got Marty."

Gladys batted the air. "Oh, we don't have to be long. And Marty can come with, though he might have more fun at a friend's house."

"That's true. Can you wait ten minutes? I'd like to change."

"Of course."

With Marty at his friend's house, Lonnie and Gladys strode down the sidewalk toward town, arm in arm. Even though she'd changed into her nicest dress, Lonnie still felt shabby beside her friend. Their situations were very different. Gladys only had an older sister who was married and living up north in Bloomington. Gladys kept most of the money she earned; her father had a good job with the bank, and her mother took care of things at home. And while Lonnie knew all this, she still couldn't help the twinge of envy that accompanied every encounter with her friend.

"Penny for your thoughts?" Gladys asked.

"Oh, nothing really."

"You seem down. It doesn't happen to have anything to do with a certain Mr. Moon, would it?"

Lonnie gasped. "Gladys, how can you still joke about that? No, I wasn't thinking of him at all. In fact, I've successfully managed to avoid thinking of him all day until now, thanks to you."

Gladys laughed gaily. "I'm sorry. I couldn't help myself. He's quite the mystery isn't he?"

"I don't want to talk about him."

"Hmm." Gladys hid a smile. "Well, I know just the thing to cheer you up." She pulled Lonnie into Wickett's Department Store, a shop full of a wide variety of things including ready-made dresses cut in the latest fashion, dozens of shoes, and counters with powders and lipsticks. Gladys, bursting with enthusiasm, pulled her over to the counter and consulted with the woman employee.

Twenty minutes later, Lonnie had a new tube of lipstick in a shade she'd never pick for herself in a million years and a tiny bottle of the most delicious perfume.

"Gladys, you didn't have to do this. I can't take these."

"Of course, you will, silly. I wanted to do it. Consider it my penance."

"Penance? That's absurd."

Her friend stuck her nose in the air. "It's too late. I can't take it back. Now, did you need to go anywhere?"

"I do need to stop in at the grocery. I was just there yesterday, but I forgot a few things."

"Lead on."

The bell tinkled above their heads when they stepped into the busy Simmons Grocery. Gladys followed behind her as Lonnie took a basket and filled it with cereal, gelatin, flour, and a few other staples. She nodded to people she recognized while they made their way to the front. They ran into a small crowd at the checkout counter. Craning her neck, Lonnie recognized the person at the center of disgruntled customers. He was tall, with shiny black hair.

Lonnie and Gladys gasped at the same time.

"That's not Alex Moon, is it?" Gladys whispered loudly.

It was clear he was uncomfortable as he addressed the scowling owner of the store, Joan Simmons. "Are you saying you won't take my money? I just want to buy some food."

"And I told you to take your money elsewhere. I wouldn't touch it if I was dead broke. Now, get out of my store, you filthy Jap." The small crowd of shoppers whispered and murmured.

A muscle in Alex's jaw worked as he clenched his teeth. Lonnie felt an unexpected anger rise in her, and before she considered the action, she pushed her way through the crowd of chattering women. Bursting through the final knot of bodies, she ignored Alex's stunned expression and fumbled in her purse, trying desperately to distract herself from the dozens of watching eyes.

Lonnie laid some cash on the counter and met the storeowner's bulging stare. "Will you take my money, Mrs. Simmons?"

The graying woman took a step back. "Well . . . well, of course, Miss Hamilton. You're a good customer."

"Thank you. Good day." She left her full basket on the floor and hurried out. On the sidewalk, she gazed glassy-eyed at the traffic on Main Street, unseeing. Gladys caught up to her.

"Lonnie, I can't believe you. And what about all your groceries? Do you want me to go back in and get them for you?"

"It doesn't matter." Lonnie scrambled to make sense of what she'd just done.

"What possessed you to do such a thing? What's everyone going to think?"

"I said it doesn't matter." She frowned. "I suppose I'm not surprised, but there was something about the tone of her voice—I just couldn't stand by."

Gladys laughed and touched her shoulder. "Of course not. That's just like you isn't it? Always doing the charitable thing."

Lonnie brushed her off. "It wasn't charitable, Gladys. It was human. A person has to eat, don't they?"

"Sure, but did you have to stand up for him in front of the town's biggest gossips?"

Lonnie eyed her sharply. "You're not going to gossip are you?"

Gladys widened her eyes, all innocence. "Not if you don't want me to."

Lonnie's laugh came out in a single sarcastic burst. "Of course I don't."

"All right, I won't." Gladys turned her head. "Don't look now, but the man you just rescued is heading our way."

Lonnie didn't have time to react before Alex was in front of her glaring. He shoved out his fist.

"Take your money. I don't want it."

Lonnie turned crimson and reluctantly took the wad of money he'd try to pay with. His gaze was withering. Gladys didn't bother hiding her delighted grin.

Alex persisted. "You didn't have to interfere."

"I have to go." Lonnie dashed down the sidewalk.

"I don't need your charity either!" Alex shouted after her.

Lonnie was already too far away, or she would've come up with some snappy return comment. She immediately regretted leaving Gladys behind. Who knew what her friend would say to Alex in her absence?

She fumed. What had possessed her to take his side anyway? Why did she have to butt into Alex Moon's business at all? It's true she couldn't stand by and watch someone be unjustly humiliated. What difference did it make who the money came from? Money was money.

So Alex was angry. She didn't care. He had no interest in being nice to her, and she'd just been fulfilling her Christian duty. He could be grateful or not, it made no difference.

When she got home, a thick parcel addressed to her was sitting on their front porch. Bringing it inside, she opened it to find a torn and dirty jacket and a pair of equally soiled and torn trousers. They were oddly familiar. She unfolded the paper note and read.

Dear Lonnie,

I was wondering if you could do a kind service on my behalf. These articles of clothing belong to Alex Moon. Might you be willing to clean and mend them? He isn't aware of me asking you, but I felt you were the right one for the task.

And before you ask why I didn't ask Mrs. Godfrey, who is a superior seamstress to be sure, I have no intention of asking her for any favors and giving her the wrong ideas.

Much love,

Uncle Phillip

Lonnie's hand dropped in her lap with a crinkle of paper. Of all the things to ask her to do. Uncle Phillip knew her sewing talents didn't extend past sewing on a button. Even Tunie was a far better seamstress.

She lifted the clothing to survey the damage more closely and sighed. There was no way she'd be able to do a passable job and they still be fit enough for him to wear. Even if she did try to patch them up, it would take her ages. Didn't he need the clothing right away? And really, what was so wrong about asking Mrs. Godfrey? She wouldn't assume anything about Uncle Phillip asking her a favor, would she? A second later, Lonnie changed her mind. No, her uncle was right. Mrs. Godfrey would read into it, but surely, there were dozens of capable seamstresses in town.

She frowned at the clothes, faced with yet another charitable act of service for Mr. Moon. "Will there be no end?" She asked the question of God, but got the uncomfortable impression He was laughing at her.

Lonnie took the packet upstairs and shoved it under her bed. She'd decide what to do about it later.

***

Alex walked home, torn between burning humiliation and dazed gratitude. Going to the grocery when it was so busy had been a mistake. Being rescued by Lonnie Hamilton was downright embarrassing. Being accosted and gushed at by her chatty friend Gladys while he watched Lonnie disappear down the block was even worse.

Regret at losing his temper nagged him. He surveyed his pitiful sack of food—a few cans of soup, a box of crackers, coffee, and oatmeal. The only reason he was walking home with food for dinner was because of her.

To see Lonnie march up, pushing her way through the crowd to intermediate like some feisty, golden-haired angel—it had done something to him. His heart palpitated, and he trembled a little in fear. Who was she? On the outside, she seemed demure, almost shy, but that belied the brave, benevolent young woman underneath. Or perhaps she was just foolish. It was obvious there was more to this girl than he originally believed.

Alex squirmed with the indebtedness that hung over him. He'd have to pay her back somehow, and that made him the most uncomfortable of all.

Chapter Seven

ALEX FINGERED THE money in his hand—his first month's pay. It was the only time he'd been able to call his earnings his own; his father wasn't standing over him, expecting him to pull his weight. He was free to spend or save it as he wished.

He wanted to feel elated. He wanted to celebrate, but his duty nagged at him like a cat expecting to be fed. Saving for a ticket to his uncle's house was the obvious purpose for this money. But that wasn't what consistently bothered him.

Everyone Alex knew bought war bonds religiously with every paycheck to support the war effort. But he'd never bought one. Not once. Not even when his mother urged him to support the war after his father's tactics of persuasion had failed. The whole war was a bitter taste in his mouth. It filled him with loathing.

He strolled into town and walked past the post office where a large poster hung in the window. It pictured children playing, a swastika overshadowing them with the phrase "Don't Let That Shadow Touch Them—Buy War Bonds". He clutched the money in his pocket and walked faster, stopping in at the five and ten store next door instead. A minute later he came out, the new issue of *Popular Science* tucked under his arm and headed back down the street.

He stepped into Marelli's, the corner drug store at the center of town. The place was busy for a weeknight. A good half of its round tables and wooden chairs were occupied. The black and white tiled floor was scuffed from use, but clean. The walls were hung with pictures of what Alex assumed were folk from around town, a few of them posing with prominent-looking people. One entire wall at the end of the soda fountain counter was dedicated to photos of hometown boys serving in the war, including a few young women in uniforms. A small banner hanging near the ceiling read, "Go Get 'em, Boys!" A little cartoon of Hitler getting his backside kicked graced the bottom.

The hum of chatter lulled a moment when he walked in. He got a few curious glances and a few dark looks with accompanying cold shoulders, but the chatter picked up again and he allowed himself to relax. Now that he was clean and presentable with money in his pocket, he wasn't refused service.

He went to the counter and ordered a sundae from a friendly, brunette woman. Alex found an empty table and waited, thumbing through his new magazine.

***

Lonnie and Tunie walked along the sidewalk, taking in the early evening air.

"Thanks for treating me out," Tunie said. "It's been ages since we've been to Marelli's."

"It has been a while since we've gone out just the two of us." Lonnie smiled at her little sister.

"Why aren't you going out with Teddy Stanton? He likes you."

"No, he doesn't. We're only friends. Besides, this is to congratulate you on getting an A on your history paper. We don't need Teddy for that."

"I suppose so."

At the drug store, Tunie chose a table. Lonnie, however, lagged behind, her attention diverted to a small table in the corner. Alex sat alone, slowly eating some ice cream. He seemed to be off in his own world, absorbed in reading a magazine, undisturbed by the bustle and noise around him. She was relieved to see him eating in peace without anyone accosting him.

Her body tensed without warning, her heart galloping at top speed. She wanted to talk to him, but should she? She wanted to explain what had possessed her to stand up for him at the grocery store. With a thick swallow, Lonnie whispered to Tunie. "I'll be right back." She drifted over to his table. Alex looked up as she approached, but his expression was impossible to read.

"Hello," she said.

He studied her, making her breathless with anticipation. "Would you care to join me?" He gestured to the chair across from him. His eyebrow was cocked with sarcasm. It was plain he didn't expect her to take him up on his offer.

Lonnie sat promptly, eliciting a gasp from Tunie halfway across the room. She stared into her lap.

Alex leaned forward, amused. "I don't think your sister approves."

"I'm not here on approval." She jerked her chin up, almost in defiance of his words. Encouraged by the surprising gentleness in his eyes, she said, "A-about the grocery store. I—"

"Thank you." His tone was reluctant.

"What?"

"Thank you for what you did. That couldn't have been easy."

"Oh." Lonnie clenched her gloved hands in her lap. "I wasn't really thinking—I mean I couldn't stand by and watch . . ." The words she wanted to say weren't forming, and she gave up. "You're welcome."

Alex cleared his throat. "And I'm sorry for the way I reacted. You were only trying to be kind." He paused. "Please let me make it up to you. I feel I owe you something for your kindness."

"No," she cried, appalled. "No, you don't need to worry. I don't need anything."

"Still, I must insist. I wouldn't feel comfortable otherwise."

"Really, there's no need." Her voice was small, her protest weakening. There was something about him that made her want to give in to his every request. She trembled at the revelation.

"Do you really want to know?" Alex asked.

"Know what?"

"About my family's culture. The Korean culture."

She inhaled sharply at this surprise. "Yes, I really do."

He searched her face. Finally, he nodded, pulling out a pen from his pocket and the paper napkin from beneath his empty dish. He bent over the table as he wrote, and Lonnie unconsciously leaned in closer. Odd characters began to fill the napkin, all lines and circles. It was the strangest thing she'd ever seen.

Alex finally finished writing and his eyes flicked up, their faces inches apart. Lonnie jerked back. Unperturbed, he held the napkin out to her.

"Here. I've given you the alphabet to memorize with the letters' sounds and a short phrase to decipher."

Timidly, she took the napkin. "You're—you're teaching me Korean?"

"It's as good a place to start as any. Do you not want to? I can teach you something else."

Lonnie clutched the napkin tightly, afraid he might take it back. "No. This is perfect. Thank you."

A small grin worked its way onto his face. It was only half the radiance of the one he'd shown that time at Aunt Millie's. Nevertheless, her chest filled with a fluttering like a hummingbird. He stood and the fluttering died.

"I should go. I look forward to seeing how you do. Good day, Miss Hamilton."

She must've said goodbye as he left, but she didn't remember until she found herself alone. It was hard to describe the feelings that overwhelmed her. He was going to teach her? He was going to tell her about his culture? She glanced down at the napkin again with a little thrill before carefully folding it and sliding it into her purse. The excitement emanating from within was impossible to suppress.

Lonnie rejoined Tunie, whose face was a threatening thundercloud. An explanation would be in order. Her insides were all quivery as if she was about to deliver some important speech where every word would matter. And indeed, she had an audience. Out of the corners of her eyes, others nearby were trying to discreetly listen in.

"Are you crazy?" Tunie hissed. "How could you speak to that Jap again?"

"His name is Alex Moon," Lonnie said, keeping her voice low. "I already told you, he's not Japanese. He's Korean. Uncle Phillip likes him, so you don't need to get all hot under the collar."

Her words didn't make a dent in Tunie's mood, and they ate in awkward silence. About a half hour later, Lonnie and her sister walked back home.

"Slow down, will you?" Tunie grumped.

Lonnie slowed her pace. "What's wrong?"

"What do you mean what's wrong? How could you keep something like that from me?"

"Something like what?"

"Don't play dumb, Lonnie."

"Oh, all right. I didn't mean to keep it from you. It never came up. And what was there to tell anyway? You were the first one I told about meeting him at the jail with Uncle Phillip. What else do you want?"

"Like how did you go from meeting him at the jail to being all friendly at the drug store?"

"I wasn't being friendly; I was being polite. It's not like he knows many people in town, and it's not likely anyone else was going out of their way to be nice."

Tunie snorted. "I'm sure they all have good reasons. Why don't you?"

"I think he's interesting, and besides, like I said, Uncle Phillip vouches for him. Isn't that enough?"

"And what about Mother? What's she going to say when she finds out you're fraternizing with the enemy?"

Lonnie stopped. "Oh, don't, Tunie. Why bring Mother into this?"

"Why shouldn't I?" She crossed her arms over her chest. "Maybe she'd talk some sense into you."

"Please don't. Mother wouldn't understand. I'm only being charitable. Don't make more of this."

Tunie scowled. "Fine. But I think you're being stupid. You shouldn't get tangled up with this man. You don't know anything about him. It isn't safe."

Lonnie couldn't help but smile a little. "I've never known you to care so much about my safety."

They continued walking and after a while, Tunie softened enough to link her arm through Lonnie's.

"He's a stranger, Lonnie. And he's different. Doesn't that scare you?"

Lonnie pictured his warm eyes, his bright smile. How could he be scary? "Not really."

"I don't understand you sometimes," Tunie said.

When Tunie was engrossed in wrapping her hair into curlers at her vanity, Lonnie sat at their desk and rummaged in her purse for Alex's napkin. She smoothed it flat, and under the golden circular glow of her desk lamp, studied the carefully drawn characters filling the napkin clear to the edges. No doubt, his lesson was going to be challenging, but she wasn't intimidated. She'd been a top student in school. If anything, she'd give her new teacher a run for his money. With a little laugh, she set to work.

Chapter Eight

A FEW DAYS later, Alex was finishing work for the day when Reverend Hicks stopped by the shop. Alex wiped his hands and stepped forward to shake the man's hand.

"It's good to see you again, sir."

"And you, Alex. How are things working out for you?"

"I've been well, thank you. Mr. Hardy's been fair, and he gives me challenging work. There's quite a bit of it too."

"Yes, I understand parts and tires are difficult to come by these days."

"We're doing everything we can to patch them, but there's only so much we can do."

"I can imagine. Oh, before I forget, a letter came for you." He pulled it out of his pocket and held it out.

Alex took the letter with some reluctance. If it was from his father, like he suspected, it couldn't bode anything but guilt. "Thank you. I appreciate you letting me use your address."

"Of course. Well, I'll be on my way. I just wanted to see how you were and drop the letter by. I'll see you on Saturday for the yard work?"

"Yes. I'll be there early."

"Great. I'll see you then." Reverend Hicks took his leave, and Alex climbed the steep flight of stairs to his room. He washed, changed clothes, and made himself a simple dinner on the hot plate Mike had loaned him.

Alex was unhurried as he ate, eyeing the letter on the tiny card table. He dreaded what was inside. He'd told his parents he met with some difficulty in his journey, but was taking care of the problem on his own. He doubted that had gone over well with his father. He ate even more slowly until his soup was cold and unpleasant.

He continued to eat anyway until his spoon finally scraped bottom. He cleaned his dishes and put them away. After that, he ran out of excuses to procrastinate. With resignation, he sank onto his bed, ripped open the letter, and drew out the sheet of paper.

He scanned his father's firm and unwavering print, his heart sinking. It was just as he feared. His father was more disappointed, more angry, and more condescending than ever. *Why can't you be more like your brother—how he fights and serves the American army with the hope of eventually freeing Korea? Why can't you focus on your duty? You should feel shameful of your actions.* His knuckles turned white from gripping the paper, but he read the letter to the harsh and bitter end.

Alex breathed with difficulty. All of this started when his older brother, Henry, had joined up at the start of the war. How their father's eyes had shone with pride only to have them harden when Alex refused to follow suit. *You dishonor your entire family. I'm ashamed to call you my son.*

With sudden fury, Alex viciously crumpled up the paper and threw it across the room. "Damn you, Henry, and your saintly patriotism!" Alex clutched at his hair, fighting tears and wishing his pain would stop. If only he could hear his mother's voice again, calming him, reassuring him.

Filled with a sudden hope, Alex went back to retrieve the paper and smoothed it out. Flipping the letter over, a flicker of warmth fanned his cold, aching heart. His mother had penned a few words—bright, loving, and encouraging. He sank back onto his bed, his eyes feeding on the spare words hungrily. His father never would have allowed her to do such a thing—undermining his reprimand. The only explanation could be that she'd quickly written him this little note before she put it into the post, his father none the wiser.

Alex let the letter fall to his lap, stunned from the juxtaposition of words from his parents—loathing and love, anger and understanding, sternness and patience. His eyes stung with frustrated confusion. His parents' attitudes were symbolic of the bigger picture.

This whole patriotism thing was a major part of his problem. Whose side was he supposed to be on? His father taught him everything was for Korea and freeing it from Japanese tyranny. America taught him it was for Uncle Sam and fighting the evil Axis. What was he supposed to think?

For his father, Alex's refusal to volunteer for the military was an utter betrayal. Resentment still burned hotly in Alex's heart for being yanked out of college and sent from home like an unwelcome burden. What awaited him living with his politically active uncle was an apprenticeship not only in his restaurant but in what it truly meant to be Korean.

Alex got wearily to his feet, the letter fluttering to the floor. His head was heavy. Intent on getting some fresh air, he left his room by way of the outdoor staircase. He walked around the side of the house to the sidewalk, contemplating a walk in the park on the bluff, but was distracted by a young boy struggling with mowing Mrs. Godfrey's yard.

Something came over Alex as he watched the boy straining through the thick grass with the push mower, hair plastered to his forehead, face red from exertion. The boy's effort was so genuine. He was trying so hard, and it didn't seem to matter how much strength he used, he made so little progress. Alex commiserated with the boy, but also envied him. The work was hard, but his youthful face was determined. That kid was never going to give up.

All the anger and fight dissolved right out of Alex, as if a stormy sky swiftly cleared, allowing the blue skies to show again. His lips twitched in a smile, and he went back to the garage, rummaging up a can of oil, a file, and an old rag. The boy was still hard at it when Alex approached him.

"Can I give you a hand with that?"

The boy wiped beads of sweat off his brow. "This is my job, mister. I gotta do it myself, or I don't earn the money." He glanced nervously at the house where the living room curtain twitched. Mrs. Godfrey was no doubt checking the progress of her lawn.

Alex nodded. "I can respect that." He held up the can of oil and the file. "How about we get that thing oiled and sharpened? You'll be done mowing in half the time."

The boy's brown eyes lit up. "That would be swell, mister. Thanks."

Alex grinned. "Well, sure. What are neighbors for?"

***

With Reverend Hicks's energetic explanations of Isaiah finished, the echoes of the chorus emptied the rafters, and the last prayer was said. Alex rose from his seat near the back. He'd kept well away from Lonnie this time, allowing her to have her pew back. He turned to head out the side door when he heard his name being called.

"Alex, how are you?" Lonnie walked up to him, brother and sister in tandem.

"Hello." His heart did an unanticipated flop. She was especially pretty today, wearing a green dress, with her blonde hair curled on the ends and swept back with a bow. It was a little hard to believe her sweet smile was aimed at him. After their first few negative encounters, his giving her lessons was the peace offering they'd needed. He was amazed how different she looked to him now that they were on better terms.

Lonnie turned to her siblings. "Alex, I don't think I've ever introduced you. This is my younger sister Tunie and our brother Marty. Tunie, Marty, this is Alex Moon."

Tunie's face remained warily passive. "How do you do?"

Marty pushed to the front. "Wow, hi. Lonnie told me not to say anything about it, but have you ever seen any Japs in person? I know you're not a Jap because Lonnie told me you weren't, but I've *really* wanted to meet you. I've been working on this model of a Jap fighter plane, and if you know anything about them, I'd love to hear about it. Really, I would."

Alex blinked a few times, trying to get a grip on what the kid was saying, and finally burst out laughing. "It's nice to meet you, Marty. No, I haven't seen any Japanese fighter planes, but I've seen a few American fighters. In California, my friends and I would go down to the beach and see the planes from the naval base flying overhead."

Marty's eyes grew round with amazement. Lonnie tried to steer her brother toward the exit. "Let's go outside, shall we? I'm sure you have some friends looking for you, Marty."

"Who cares? I wanna talk to Alex."

"Let's go, Marty." Tunie pushed him ahead of her out of the church.

At that moment, Gladys appeared, dragging a tall, stoic young man with broad shoulders and a limp.

"Gladys, what are you doing here?" Lonnie asked.

"Lonnie, you doll. You disappeared so quickly, I—oh. It's you." Gladys batted her long eyelashes as she pretended surprise at seeing Alex. He wanted to roll his eyes, but managed a bland smile.

"Gladys, isn't it? How good to see you again."

She grinned. "I can definitely say the same about you. I didn't know you attended church here."

Lonnie narrowed her eyes. "I told you that just the other day. And what are you doing here? You've never been keen about coming to church when I've invited you."

Gladys forced a bright laugh. "Oh, Lonnie, what a silly thing to say. I adore church immensely. Walter here has been feeling especially religious lately and suggested we attend today. I thought, well, why not? You never know who you're going to meet at church." She flicked Lonnie a meaningful glance.

Alex watched the exchange with raised eyebrows. Out of the corner of his eye, Walter scowled, unmoving. Just as Alex was contemplating excusing himself from this awkward conversation, a lanky young man with blonde hair and glasses approached them with a casual, confident air, flanked by an older couple. They paused at their little group, and Lonnie became flustered.

"Mr. and Mrs. Stanton, h-how are you?" She nodded at the young man. "Teddy."

The older woman smiled. "Lonnie, my dear. How have you been? Teddy insisted we come over and say hello." She radiated her adoration for her son, whose hands were in his pockets, surveying Alex coolly.

"Oh?" Lonnie said, her voice weak. "Did he?" A smile flickered on her lips. There was a brief lull and Alex wondered what Lonnie would do now. It seemed as if her group of friends was waiting for something. His gaze slid around the circle. They were all staring at him.

Lonnie seemed to sense their desire for a formal introduction, for she finally gestured toward him. "This is Alex Moon. Alex, Mr. and Mrs. Stanton, Teddy Stanton their son, Walter Chase, and you already know Gladys Marshall."

Alex cleared his throat and inclined his head. "Nice to meet you all." Though, he didn't find it nice at all to be the object of their blatant curiosity. Only Gladys beamed.

Mrs. Stanton piped up, her voice wavering. "I'd heard Reverend Hicks met a Ja—an—an Oriental. Are you long in town?"

Alex clenched his fists, but he hid them behind his back. "Yes, ma'am. I'm here for the foreseeable future."

"Oh." Mrs. Stanton's cheeks grew rosy.

Mr. Stanton clearly didn't wish to add to the conversation. He cleared his throat. "Let's leave the young people to talk, Amelia." They moved off, leaving Teddy behind who hadn't taken his gaze off Alex.

"Alex Moon," Teddy drawled when his parents had gone. His stance was nonchalant, but his eyes flashed. "So you're the dirty Jap rat they had in jail. How fascinating."

Lonnie gasped. "Teddy!"

Walter finally came alive, turning on Alex with a growl. "I can't imagine why they'd let a traitor like you walk our streets. Don't expect us to leave you alone."

Lonnie gaped in open-mouthed horror.

Gladys laughed, placing a gentle hand on Walter's arm. "Boys, boys. There's no need for that kind of talk. We're in a church, need I remind you?" She grinned round at them. "We must remember to be charitable, mustn't we? Lonnie sets such a wonderful example for us all, don't you, dear? Just recently, she rescued poor Alex from the terrifying clutches of Mrs. Simmons when she refused to take his money. Lonnie's heroics were quite breathtaking."

It was Alex's turn to gape. He was too astonished to do anything else.

"Gladys, please," Lonnie said, voice low. "You're embarrassing me. And Alex as well."

Gladys grabbed Walter and Teddy by the crooks of their arms. "Well, I know Alex never really got a chance to thank you, Lonnie, so we'll be going now. Didn't you say we could stop by for Sunday brunch at your house sometime, Teddy?" She dragged them away, Walter still glowering like a dog whose prize had been yanked from his teeth, and Teddy shooting Alex icy daggers of mysterious warning.

"I must apologize for my friends," Lonnie said, hands pressed to her ruddy cheeks. "I know Gladys likes to tease, but I never know what she's going to say. It's like facing into a storm not knowing whether you're going to get hailstones, twisters, or just a sprinkling."

The corner of Alex's mouth twitched. He rather liked how unsettled she was. "I feel as if we've just experienced all three, don't you?"

Lonnie laughed. "Yes."

"You don't have to keep sticking up for me, you know. I can defend myself."

The brightness faded from her face. "Oh."

He grinned to reassure her. "I just don't want to put you in a difficult position with your friends. And I don't want to put you to any trouble on my account."

"It wasn't any trouble . . ."

"So," Alex burst out. "How's the lesson going?"

Her face relaxed into a smile. "I've nearly finished what you gave me."

His eyes widened. "Really? Already? Have you figured out the phrase yet?"

"No, not yet, but I'm close."

"It's not too complicated?"

"Oh no," she assured him. "It's perfect."

Her enthusiasm was astounding. Why would someone like her be so excited to learn about Korean? It gave him a surprising thrill, and he couldn't help the happiness that filled him from how her eyes lit up talking about it.

Chapter Nine

THE NEXT DAY at work, Lonnie had an unexpected surprise from her boss. She liked working for Mr. Pickering, but sometimes he could be overwhelming. Like this morning. She'd barely gotten settled at her desk when he burst out of his office, waving a thick manila envelope.

"Miss Hamilton." His boom caused her to jump. "So glad to see you here, right on time as usual. I need this delivered pronto."

"Isn't Mary here?" Mary was a young woman who acted as their delivery boy. Before the war, Billy had delivered for them, but he turned eighteen a month after the bombing of Pearl Harbor and had gone off and enlisted that same day.

"She's visiting her sick mother today, I'm afraid."

"Well, what about my duties here?"

"Oh, don't worry." He laughed. "I don't think we'll have a rush on insurance claims this morning, do you?"

She chuckled. "No, sir. Probably not. Where does it need to be delivered?"

"Stanton Glass Works. I know it's on the opposite end of town. Would you feel comfortable riding Mary's delivery bike?"

"Of course."

She pinned her hat back on and slipped her hands into her gloves once more. Taking the envelope, she walked to the back entrance of the office building where the bike was stored in a little shed. She placed the envelope in the delivery satchel on the back of the bike and shoved off, emerging out of the shadows of the alley and into the sunny street.

She grinned as buildings, parked cars, and people rushed by, the wind streaming her hair behind her. How deliciously free and swift it was to be coasting along when she was used to walking everywhere. She pedaled diligently, enjoying the fresh, warm air as cotton candy clouds sailed along. She raced with the cloud shadows until she was nearly out of breath. Before she knew it, the smokestacks of Stanton Glass Works loomed ahead of her.

She approached the gate to the fenced grounds and found the ramshackle gatehouse where an older man snoozed inside.

Wheeling the bike along with her, Lonnie stepped up and cleared her throat. He startled awake and straightened up, red-faced.

"How can I help you, ma'am?"

She hid her smile. "My name is Lonnie Hamilton from Pickering Insurance Company. I have a packet of papers to deliver to Mr. Stanton."

The man picked up the receiver of a black telephone, waited, and repeated what she'd said to the person on the other end. He hung up and said, "You can find Mr. Stanton in his office. It's in the main building straight ahead. You can't miss it."

She nodded, taking in the imposing brick buildings. It was funny she'd never been to visit the factory before now. Not even when Teddy first started coming into the office with his father when he turned sixteen.

"You can leave your bike here," the guard offered kindly. "I'll keep an eye on it for you."

"Thank you." Lonnie went in through the gate and surveyed her surroundings as she walked toward the main building. The entire yard was enormous and was covered in fine gravel. To her left a railroad track dead-ended into a large, wooden-sided warehouse. A few smaller buildings were scattered around, mysterious in their function, but the main building ahead was made of brick, the large smokestacks rising into the air like smoking, rusty fingers pointing to the sky.

Lonnie felt the warmth emanating as she drew near the main brick building. A pair of large double doors leading inside were closed and locked. To the side of them was a smaller single door. She opened it and stepped inside. Two swinging doors led to the main factory, and a flight of stairs led up toward what she assumed were the offices. She climbed the steel stairs to the second floor, opened another door, and walked down a narrow hallway lined with several glass-windowed doors. Several offices had lights on inside and one was slightly ajar. As she approached, the neatly lettered words on the glass came into view—*Charles Stanton – Manager*. Lonnie knocked.

"Come in." A deep voice called out.

Lonnie stepped inside, her eyes widening in surprise. "Teddy."

Teddy's neatly combed and oiled blonde hair gleamed in the lamplight. His head jerked up from his paper-strewn desk at her astonished reply. A smile spread across his face. "Lonnie, what are you doing here?" He unfolded his tall frame and straightened his wire-rimmed glasses.

Her lips tilted up in return. "I had something to deliver to Mr. Stanton." She held up the manila envelope.

Teddy grinned. "That would be me. My father's out of town on some business." He came from around his desk, took her envelope, and gestured. "You've never been to visit me at work. Should I give you a tour?"

"Can you do that?"

"Sure. I'm pretty much boss until Dad gets back." He stood a little taller, puffing out his chest slightly. She wanted to giggle, but discretely held it back.

"I'd love a tour, but I don't have much time. I need to get back to the office."

"Aw, Mr. Pickering can spare you for another twenty minutes, can't he?"

"I suppose."

"Great. Let's go." She took the crooked arm he offered. "Let me know if the heat is too much, though," he added with concern. "If you're not used to it, it can be overwhelming." He led her down the hall and stairs and through the double doors. They were met with a blast of hot air. "You all right?"

"I'm fine for now, but doesn't it bother your lungs?"

He shook his head. "I'm used to it, and actually the hot, moist air does wonders. I'm like a different man in here." And indeed his cheeks had a healthy color, and he breathed easily.

"I'm glad."

Teddy led her around the main workroom where several groups of large furnaces glowed red with an intense, blinding heat. Dozens of employees worked methodically, seemingly oblivious to the waves of heat radiating from the furnaces.

"The glass is melted in these continuous tanks." He shouted to be heard above the steady roar of the furnaces. "Because they're constantly going, we're better able to keep up output to meet the contract demands, which are really high since the war started." He kept her well away from the bulk of the labor force and led her around the inside perimeter of the vast building to view the six enormous furnaces and equipment for the machinery-produced glass.

"Do you only make one color of glass?" Lonnie asked.

"No, we make a number of colors, but right now we're mostly on government contract work. We make what they ask, which usually doesn't involve anything that exciting."

"What kinds of things are you making?"

"Headlight covers for army vehicles. Things like that."

She gazed around the bustling factory in amazement. "How interesting. And you have so many workers. Have this many people always worked here?"

"No. We've hired more people recently, many of which have come from surrounding counties, a few from neighboring states. We're having difficulty finding enough places for the new workers to live. They're planning on building some housing on this side of town, but it takes time and supplies are hard to come by."

Lonnie nodded. "I hadn't considered that. I can see why that would be a problem, but it's good to see so many people have jobs."

"Yes." Teddy smiled ruefully. "As callous as it sounds, the war has been great for business. But it's also good knowing we're helping our boys out there." Wistfulness passed over his face. "This wasn't my first choice of a way to help the war effort, you know, but it's something, I guess." He studied his hands.

Lonnie remembered the day Teddy had tried to enlist, even knowing his health condition. He told her they'd barely even acknowledged him, just turned him away after a quick look over his medical records. They'd told him to get a desk job. It had taken him several weeks to get over that humiliation.

She placed a comforting hand on his arm. "What you're doing here is wonderful, Teddy. Someone has to make these things, and I know you're indispensible to your father. Your mother is proud of you too. Whenever I see her in town, she just gushes about how you help to handle the business—you have a talent for it."

Teddy nodded, placing his hand over hers. "Thanks. You're right. It's hard not being able to do what you want because your health is holding you back. And when we get letters from Eugene it's even worse." He met her eyes and his countenance lit with a grin. "I just need to stop feeling sorry for myself. Especially since I'm here with you." The silence between them lingered for a moment.

Lonnie blushed and gently removed her hand.

The moment broken, Teddy led her back to the exit door. As they passed one furnace, a worker caught her eye. They were checking the temperature on one of the furnaces, pulling out a sample of glass, then putting it back in. When they turned away from the furnace and removed their protective helmet, Lonnie was startled to see her mother. Her face glistened with sweat, her hair plastered to her forehead. She addressed another worker who wrote something down on a clipboard.

"Come on," Teddy said loudly over the noise. She followed after him, and they passed back through the double doors. Instantly the temperature cooled. Teddy offered her his handkerchief. She took it gratefully, delicately dabbing her face and neck.

"I have to say I'm impressed," Teddy said. "I thought you might faint from the heat, but you handled it remarkably well."

"I was busy being impressed myself. It's incredible the work you and your father do here. I had no idea."

Teddy's grin quickly shifted to something more nervous, his brow crinkled into deep furrows. "Say, Lonnie. There's a new movie showing this Saturday. I was wondering if you might want to go with me."

"Oh." Lonnie felt warm all over again. Was Tunie right? Did he like her? His expression was tense with anticipation. What should she do? They'd known each other since they were children, but she'd never considered him in a romantic way. She did like spending time with him though. What harm could a movie do?

"I'd love to."

His face radiated happiness, and she wondered if she'd made the right choice.

She gathered her bicycle from the gatekeeper with a smile of thanks and hurried back to work. As she rode, her visit to the factory ran through her mind. She knew her mother spent long hours at her job, but she'd never stopped to think about what conditions her mother worked in or how strenuous it was. Guilt weighed heavily on her for thinking too harshly about her mother who was often cranky and sensitive when she got home. How grateful she was for her mother's hard work to keep a roof over their heads and food in their mouths.

Lonnie's bike crossed over the railroad tracks with a *clickety-clack*, and her mind switched to her conversation with Teddy. Now that she considered it, his face always lit up when he saw her. Had she really missed all the signs of fondness? How long had he liked her?

This development was worrying. She cared a great deal for him, but a romance with Theodore Stanton, or with anyone else for that matter, was not in her plans. It was doubtful there was anything that would change her mind.

***

Later that day, Lonnie was in the kitchen getting started on preparations for dinner.

"I'm home," Marty called. He entered the kitchen, dumping his schoolbooks on the floor. "The mail came. Didn't you see it?" He dropped the letters on the table.

"No, I didn't." Lonnie brought him a glass of milk and some cookies. He ate hungrily as she rifled through the small packet of letters to her mother, a couple bills, and an envelope addressed to her. The handwriting didn't look familiar and the cancellation stamp was for in town.

She opened the envelope. While unfolding the thin slip of paper, a delighted smile spread across her face. It was from Grandma Chan. In thin, spidery script the woman thanked her for her note and invited her for tea the following Sunday afternoon.

Going to the small desk in the living room, Lonnie dashed off a quick note of acceptance, stuffed it into an envelope and addressed it, thinking she'd post it on her way to work in the morning. The only thing left was to figure out how she'd explain her absence to her mother.

Chapter Ten

TEDDY ARRIVED AT her house promptly at seven o'clock on Saturday. Tunie answered the door and shouted his arrival up the stairs.

"I'll be down in a minute." Lonnie sat at her vanity putting in the last of her hairpins. Her sister had helped her with a new style, and she smiled at the result. It was definitely different than what she was used to, but the gentle waves and the way her hair swept up made her seem older.

She slipped into her green striped dress. While it wasn't new by any means, it was flattering. She surveyed herself in the mirror and gave herself an encouraging smile. Tunie came into the room.

"You look pretty. I'm sure Teddy will approve, though I bet he wouldn't care what you were wearing, even if it was some old rags." She winked.

Lonnie scoffed. "Such nonsense. We're only going out to a movie. And remember, we're just friends."

Tunie laughed. "Of course you are."

Lonnie grabbed her purse. "You'll look after Marty? I think Mother has somewhere to go this evening."

"Yes, I know. I'll even take the little tyke out to get some candy if it'll keep him out of my hair. Bye now. Have a good time." Tunie waved, her smile overly sweet.

Lonnie made a face at her and met Teddy, who was talking to her mother in the living room. She was seated in her usual chair by the large cabinet radio, smoking a cigarette.

Teddy was dressed smartly with a snappy blue tie, vest, and linen jacket. His slacks were ironed sharply, his shoes shined. His eyes widened in appreciation at seeing Lonnie. "Wow, you look fantastic."

She blushed. "Thank you. You look very nice yourself."

"I was just telling your mother about the movie we're going to see—'Mrs. Miniver'. I've heard good things about it. Right, well, it's been nice talking to you, Mrs. Hamilton."

Harriet offered a rare smile. "And you too, Teddy. Be sure to bring her back at a reasonable time."

"Of course." Teddy offered Lonnie his arm, and she waved goodbye to her mother.

They headed downtown to the movie theatre. It was a bit silly going down the sidewalk arm in arm when not too long ago they were walking normally as they'd always done as friends. It would be rude to extricate her arm, so she left it crooked in his, anxiety about his feelings for her mounting. She kept reminding herself this was just a date. There was nothing behind it but friendship. The sick feeling in her stomach, however, told her otherwise.

They reached the theater and waited in line to buy tickets. Once inside, Teddy bought a box of popcorn, and they followed the stream of people entering the theater. He chose seats in the middle. How many times had she come to the movies with Teddy and her other friends? Not once had she come alone with him though. She hadn't gone alone to the movies with anyone. She found this monumental moment in her life more uncomfortable than expected.

She stole a glance at Teddy. His glasses gleamed in the dim light, his profile etched in fine white lines. At last, her face relaxed into a smile. If she was going to share a new moment like this, she was glad at least it was with a friend.

He caught her studying him. "Do I have something on my face?"

"Oh. No." She turned away, flushing. The room darkened and the movie screen flickered to life. They munched on the popcorn, and Lonnie was whisked away into another world of London and its first years in the throes of war. She was mesmerized. The newsreel after the movie was like watching the film all over again. The screen filled with army troops, tanks, guns, and explosions. She shifted uncomfortably in her seat. Those poor people in England and France. She wanted to learn about and see new places and lands, but war was a terrible thing. Her heart was sore for what they were going through while she went to bed feeling safe every night.

After the movie, Teddy walked her home. The early evening was fine with a pearly blue sky, though large clouds threatened some rain on the outskirts of the horizon. Lonnie walked, lost in contemplation. The movie still weighed on her emotions.

"You're awfully quiet," Teddy said, breaking into her thoughts. "How did you like the movie?"

"It was good."

He cocked an eyebrow. "You don't sound very convincing."

"To be honest, I'm sad and jealous at the same time."

"How's that?"

"I envy my cousin David, fighting overseas in England. He's getting to see the world first hand, even if it's terrible what the British are going through. How much I wish I could help them. How I'd love to visit England, or just anywhere really. Sometimes I get so tired of this town."

Teddy stopped walking. "I never knew you wanted something like that. I mean, not really. You're always talking about going off to see the world, but I always thought they were just some far-fetched dreams."

"They are. There's no point in even dreaming about it. How could I leave? My mother, Marty, and Tunie depend so much on me. How can I shirk that responsibility? And with father . . ." Her voice tapered away, and they stood quietly for a minute.

Lonnie lifted her head. "Besides, there are still some interesting people to meet here, and there are changes going on around town with your factory hiring more workers. Our town is bound to perk up in fascination."

Teddy stared at her. "Interesting people . . ." he said slowly. "Like that Jap?"

"He's not—"

Teddy cut her off with a sharp gesture, his face contorted in a deep scowl. "He's not a Jap. Okay, so you've told us. Do you really think talking to him will do you any favors? Befriending him is a bad idea, Lonnie. It's best if you ignore him from now on. Someone needs to make that guy leave town. We don't need his kind around here."

Lonnie's jaw tightened, her heart raced with the shock of his words. She turned and continued to walk toward home.

"Lonnie, wait." He quickly caught up to her and grabbed her arm, coughing slightly from the exertion. She stopped and gritted her teeth as he caught his breath. "You have to know I'm only saying this for your own good. Walter, Gladys, Rose, and I—all of us feel this way. We only want to protect you."

She turned on him, eyes flashing in anger. "Protect me from what, Teddy? What? Go on and say it."

Teddy spluttered. "He's—he's a stranger. Who knows what his intentions are?"

The meaning behind his words hit her hard, and her anger blazed. "His *intentions*? You don't know anything about him, Theodore Stanton. How can you make absurd statements about someone you don't know?" Tears pricked at her eyes.

"Exactly. I don't know him. That's why I'm worried." Teddy reached forward to gently grasp her shoulders. "We've known each other our entire lives, Lonnie. We *know* each other. But—but this guy is a total unknown. He's shifty. He just showed up from out of nowhere. Why is he sticking around? I don't trust him and neither should you."

Lonnie yanked herself from his grasp. "Don't tell me whom I should or shouldn't trust, Theodore Stanton. It's obvious I can't trust you." She turned and ran, leaving Teddy, who couldn't and shouldn't run, far behind.

***

After work on Saturday and a simple dinner, Alex lay back on his bed, enjoying some moments of peace. He didn't mind solitude. He found it refreshing to be alone for a while without anyone butting in on his thoughts. It was at times like this he liked to delve into books.

He rolled out of bed and pulled his suitcase out, flipping open the lid to sift through the small collection of well-worn books he'd brought with him. All his favorites were there—*The Time Machine*, *The War of the Worlds* by H.G. Wells, and *Journey to the Center of the Earth* by Jules Verne. Henry had given them to him as a set as well as *The Hounds of the Baskervilles* by Arthur Canon Doyle. There was a complete and wonderfully detailed set of Audel's mechanical engineering books a friend had given him as a parting gift. It contributed to most of the weight in the heavy case and they reminded him how long it had been since he'd studied. A few of his favorite issues of *Popular Science* magazine were in there, and a small, dog-eared book of Korean poems his mother had given him when he'd turned twelve. This last book he pulled out and lounged on his bed to read. His hand gently smoothed the worn cover. The gold-leafed title in *hangul* was faded from many readings. He knew most of the poems by heart.

Opening the book, he began to read aloud, the familiar language of his childhood flowing from his lips. It was wonderful to speak the words again. His voice filled the small, cluttered space, surrounding him like a comfortable cocoon. The sound and cadence of the Korean words eased the ache of homesickness in his heart.

As he turned the page to keep reading, a small tickle of worry at being overheard by Mike bothered him—what might he think? He continued to read, but after a time, the syllables became distorted, the feel of the words in his mouth warping into something foreign. His voice faltered, and he was suddenly overtaken by a rush of despondency.

Korean was so much a part of him; in many ways it was the anchor of his identity. And yet . . . and yet it was the part that separated him from everyone else around him. If he went out on the street right now and began speaking his family's language, they'd all think he'd gone raving mad or was speaking some secret code language of the enemy.

Sighing, he set the book aside, no longer gleaning comfort from its pages. A familiar emotion stole over him—doubt. Doubt in himself, in the culture he'd always known, and in his ability to keep up what he increasingly felt was a ruse.

He was torn. Stuck between two countries, two cultures, two selves. He *was* Korean. He *was* American. Couldn't he be both? He was born in this country, sounded like everyone else, only he didn't look like everyone else. He found it ironic that while the Americans were fighting against a prejudiced, fascist leader, they had yet to identify and eradicate their own prejudices against those that were different from them. A country of immigrants who wanted everyone to be the same.

Disgust twisted inside him. When his father had pressured him especially hard, he'd deliberated about the possibility of joining up. At the time, the internment camps had been reason enough to refuse. But even now, he couldn't bring himself to do it. Why should he fight for a country that hated him so much for something he wasn't even guilty of? He was sick of the glares, the vicious comments said to his face and behind his back, the avoidance. The other day while walking in town, a mother with her young children crossed the street to avoid his path. What could he say to people like that?

He kicked his suitcase viciously, sending it sliding a few feet across the floor. His toe immediately jabbed with a sharp pain, and he cursed loudly. He wanted to curse the whole world. Even more frustrated than before, Alex yanked on his socks, jammed his feet into his shoes, and left the little room above the garage by the outside stairs.

He blindly sped in deep strides down the mostly deserted sidewalk, ignoring everything around him—bent on expelling his pent up emotion. The night darkened, the moon slowly rose above the horizon, and he still walked.

He turned a corner to go up a side street when someone collided with him. He cried out and stepped back.

"I'm sorry. Are you all right?" he asked.

The young woman was out of breath, and when she looked up, her wet eyes glimmered.

"Alex!" she exclaimed.

"Lonnie!" He appraised her in astonishment. "You're crying." How stupid to state the obvious, but further words evaded him.

She hastily wiped her cheeks. "I was."

Alex cleared his throat. "I'm surprised to run into you," he finally said. "I would think you'd be home by now." The moon had slid into view from behind the rooftops, etching her face with an icy glow.

She didn't say anything for a minute, and he could tell she was contemplating an answer. "I was on a date that didn't end so well," she said, shrugging. "I didn't want to go home right away because I was so upset. I guess I lost track of the time."

A date? She'd been on a date? With whom? A dense knot churned in the pit of his stomach. "Uh, do you know where we are?" he blurted out. He swiveled his head to take in the street. "I wasn't paying attention to where I was going."

Lonnie lifted her chin. "Yes. Should I show you the way back to Mr. Hardy's?"

"Oh. No. You really shouldn't be out alone after dark. If I walk you home, I'd know how to get back from there." His heart thumped in his chest. What an idiot. He made it sound like he stalked her. If she were the least bit suspicious, she'd reject his offer.

She turned slightly. "I'd like that. It's this way."

They set off walking. Somewhere a dog barked, a door slammed, a baby cried. All the regular, familiar nighttime sounds of the town floated on the air. It was such a stark difference from the noisy bustle of Los Angeles. And the vigilant air raid drills. And the blackouts. Memories of the madness from the so-called "air battle over Los Angeles" were still fresh. The whole thing had supposedly been a false alarm, but it left everyone shaken by the very real Japanese threat to the west coast.

They walked past a few businesses—a dry cleaner's and a tavern. The lights from the tavern glared out into the soft darkness as the door opened. A man stumbled out yelling and cursing. Instinctively, Alex grabbed Lonnie's arm, walking a little faster.

"Hey," the man shouted. "Hey, you." His shrill catcall filled the street. "Nice pair o' legs you got there, honey." Lonnie stiffened, and Alex bristled in anger.

The door to the tavern opened again, and a second man emerged. "What're you doin' out here, Homer?" he said loudly. "They just started another game."

Alex stopped and his skin crawled. He knew that voice. Lonnie stopped beside him.

"Aww, just admirin' the scenery," Homer said, his voice echoing out into the night. He must've indicated the both of them, because the other man whistled.

"I see what you mean."

To Alex's horror, their footsteps approached. He glanced back to see the two men advancing on them.

"Hey, sweetie," the man called. "Fancy a drink with ol' Jake?"

Alex's blood began to boil. He half-turned around, hoping his face was in shadow. "Excuse me, gentleman, but this young woman is with me. Now if you'll excuse us—"

The man called Jake stopped, swinging out his arm to keep from stumbling into his drunkard companion. "Hold on . . ."

Before he could finish his thought, Alex grabbed Lonnie's hand and frantically whispered, "Run!" He dashed off, her hand tightly grasped in his as she struggled to keep up with his long legs.

"Hey, get back here!" Jake shouted. "Homer, go get the other guys. It's that Jap."

Alex ran with Lonnie, zigzagging through alleyways between businesses and houses. A few dogs barked at them as they raced past. Heavy footsteps followed at a distance and shouts punctured the night.

He heard Lonnie gasping for breath as he continued to pull her along. His own lungs felt like bursting, and yet he continued to run. The men chasing them weren't gaining much ground, but they weren't falling far behind either. Alex hated to think what might happen if they caught up. He'd protect Lonnie and himself if he had to, of course, but it was something he'd rather not get into again. The last thing he wanted was to land back in jail.

Finally, he found a pile of sloppily stacked crates leaning against a brick building in a dark alley. He crouched in the silky black shadow of the crates and pulled Lonnie down next to him, his arm around her shoulders to keep her tight against his side in the darkness. The moonlight shone strongly, giving everything a sharp contrast.

Lonnie sagged into him, trying to catch her breath. He tilted his head back against the rough wall, closing his eyes. All that could be heard was the sound of their breathing and a radio playing somewhere nearby.

"Do you think we lost them?" she asked.

Her face was so close to his that goose bumps prickled over his skin. He quickly removed his arm and leaned forward to peer around the crates. He listened. There were distant shouts and running footsteps, but they didn't come any closer. "Yeah, I think so. To be safe, though, we should wait a bit longer."

She sighed and relaxed against the building. "Who were those men? How do you know them?"

Alex swallowed nervously. He didn't want to tell her, but after dragging her all over, she deserved to know. "They're the men that attacked me at the train station when I first came here. I got out of the train to stretch my legs while we waited for a military train to pass. They saw me, assumed I was Japanese, and tried to do their worst. I fought back, but . . ." He shrugged. "It was a huge mess. The police were summoned and arrested us all. That's why I was in jail when you met me."

"Oh," she said in a small voice.

They listened for another long while and not hearing anything, Alex straightened, helping Lonnie to her feet. "You should get home. Your mother's probably wondering where you are."

Lonnie grabbed his arm, her brows furrowed. "I think what they did to you was terrible, Alex. I'm so sorry."

He gazed into her face. Her eyes were filled with sincerity, her lips curving down. He swallowed thickly as he battled with a strange, new sensation. His hand itched to reach up and brush a fallen lock of hair off her cheek. The hair moved slightly in a delicate breeze, but he kept his hand firmly clenched and hitched up a smile. "No need to apologize, *Sagwa*. You weren't involved."

To his surprise, she didn't retaliate about the nickname, but only nodded. He led the way out onto the street. The walk to her house was blissfully uneventful. They approached her gate where he was going to watch her go inside, when she turned to him, her eyes imploring.

"Can you do me a favor?"

Her words made him wary. "I guess so. I think I owe you one after the craziness back there."

"Can you pretend to be Teddy for me?"

He cocked an eyebrow. "Teddy?"

She smiled, pleading. "Yeah. My date. Remember?"

"Ah." That same roiling tension in his stomach started back up again. *Teddy.* So that's whom her date had been with. He frowned. "I don't exactly look—"

"Oh, I know," she hastily broke in. "I just need you to stand on the porch so I can say goodnight to you. You're about the same height, so seeing your silhouette should be fine."

Alex's eyes slid over to her house. A light was on in the front room as well as the porch light. "It seems kind of risky. What if someone was to spot me? How would we explain that?"

"Please?" she begged, grasping his arm. "If I don't do something, Mother will be suspicious, and if she finds out I left him over an hour ago and wandered the streets alone at night, she'll be furious."

Alex remembered she'd said the date hadn't ended well. The tension in his stomach instantly eased, and he fought the temptation to grin with wicked pleasure. *Such a shame*, he thought with sarcasm. "All right. Let's go."

Lonnie led him through the gate, up the path, and onto her porch. The front door was slightly ajar. She turned to him. "Thank you, Teddy," she said, more loudly than necessary in their close proximity. "I had a wonderful time."

Her eyes widened in expectation.

"What?" he mouthed. She wanted him to say something? He sighed. "Uh, you're welcome. I hope we can do it again sometime," he said, shaking his head in disbelief.

She only grinned back. "I'll see you later."

"Goodnight," he mumbled, grouchy about the whole situation.

To his utter amazement, she stood on tiptoe and placed a delicate kiss on his cheek. "Thank you," she whispered. She went inside and shut the door with a soft click.

Alex was stunned. Why did she do that? His fingers found the spot her lips had brushed. The skin still tingled.

After a moment, he roused himself and made his way home amidst churning seas of emotion. Was she crazy?

Because of the panic that seized him, he tripped on a crack, but caught himself. Rooted to the sidewalk, he stared wide-eyed at the moon. He gripped his shirt where his thudding heart wanted to leap out of its place. His breath came in short gasps.

Why did he feel this way?

***

When Lonnie went inside, her heart still thrilled from the unexpected adventure with Alex. She was relieved her mother didn't seem the least suspicious.

"How was your evening?" Harriet asked from her customary chair in the front room. She was working on some knitting.

"It was good, and the movie was nice. Greer Garson was lovely."

Her mother smiled, fine wrinkles crinkling at the corners of her eyes and mouth. Lonnie was slightly taken aback. She couldn't remember the last time her mother had smiled at her. When had those wrinkles developed?

"I'm glad you had a good time," Harriet said. "Teddy's a wonderful, promising young man. I hope he asks you out again."

This comment surprised Lonnie. Her mother had never talked to her much about her dating life, probably because she didn't really have one. But for her to show an interest was strange. Lonnie had a sneaking suspicion it had less to do with her daughter's happiness and more to do with who Teddy's father was. Still, it was a nice change hearing something positive coming from her mother.

Lonnie bade her goodnight and climbed the stairs to her room. Guilt for the deception about how her night had ended gnawed at her. She knew she shouldn't lie, but she also didn't want to talk about the argument with Teddy, especially with her mother so obviously fond of him. And the frightening, yet exciting episode with Alex was definitely under wraps.

Lonnie's mind wandered as she got ready for bed amidst her sister's chatter about her day. She did feel bad about her fight with her long time friend. He was acting so strange lately, and it seemed he'd purposely created a moment where he could talk to her about her association with Alex. She stopped brushing her hair at a sudden thought. What if he didn't have a crush on her at all, but was just trying to keep tabs on her? What if the whole date idea had been concocted by Teddy and her other friends as a way of tying up her time to keep her from spending it with Alex? Or to use her to spy on him?

She shook her head. It was too convoluted, but she wouldn't put it entirely past them. Well, they *weren't* going to stop her. She was going to continue to get lessons from Alex about his culture, *and* she was going to Grandma Chan's house tomorrow.

How she would pull it off though, she had yet to figure out.

Chapter Eleven

AS IT TURNED out, Aunt Millie asked her over after church on Sunday so they could talk about the volunteer opportunities she'd alluded to at her dinner party. Lonnie was delighted, because she'd be able to slip over to Grandma Chan's before heading home, and no one would be the wiser. She sent Tunie and Marty home with the message of her spending the afternoon with Aunt Millie, and after a brief wave to Alex, she hurried after her aunt.

The walk was long, but the weather was pleasant. It was no wonder Aunt Millie was able to keep so fit with how far she walked to church every Sunday. Her car was in storage in their garage, and she'd vowed not to get it out until the rationing on gasoline and rubber was over.

"I want to keep the car in the same shape as when George left it," she'd explained when Lonnie asked.

They walked side by side, enjoying each other's company. Lonnie had always loved Aunt Millie. She liked how bubbly, open-minded, and matter of fact she was—quite the stark contrast to her mother. If it weren't for how much they resembled each other, Lonnie would've had a hard time believing they were sisters. In fact, sometimes she found herself wishing Aunt Millie were her mother instead. Going to her home was always a breath of fresh air, and Lonnie was relieved stepping into her house knowing she didn't have to walk on eggshells.

As soon as they reached her home, Aunt Millie put on an apron and prepared their lunch. Lonnie found a spare apron, got out the bread, and sliced it.

"How's your job going?" Aunt Millie asked as she mixed up a sandwich filling of cottage cheese and cucumbers.

"Oh, it's all right. Mr. Pickering keeps me pretty busy."

"Do you like being a secretary?"

Lonnie shrugged. "I don't know. It's work. Why do you ask?"

Her aunt was thoughtful. "Oh, I just see you doing something else, that's all."

They brought their food to the table and started eating.

Lonnie swallowed a mouthful. "Something else? What do you mean?"

Her aunt smiled. "You're a quiet one, but I've watched you since you were a little thing. Your eyes were so big; they just took in everything. You were forever asking questions. 'What is this?' 'Why is it like that?' Oh, they just never stopped. Your mother, Phillip, and I thought our heads would never stop spinning from your questions."

Lonnie laughed. "I didn't know I was like that."

"Oh, yes." Aunt Millie laughed too. "What I mean is you were so curious about the world. I still see that hunger in your eyes. You have a special, deeper understanding of things that's different from other folks. You have something bigger to do, something more to give. Which is why I think you helping with our town's new chapter of the American Women's Volunteer Service would be a wonderful fit."

"I see." Lonnie flushed. "I didn't realize all of that was a sales pitch."

Aunt Millie laughed. "Oh, dear. I didn't mean for it to come off like that." She fidgeted with her napkin. "I think we both know tact has never been my strong suit. How do I rephrase . . ."

"No, it's fine. I know what you meant." Lonnie paused, trying to put it into words. "I have a way of looking at things in a more open and thoughtful way, and because of those skills you feel that I can help others by teaching and explaining how to better approach the war effort. Is that right?"

Aunt Millie looked relieved. "Yes. That's it exactly. You see what I mean? We need a bright young thing like you to connect to the younger women in the community so they can help in their own homes to make a difference. You'd only be required to come to occasional meetings. Since Christmas isn't too far off, we were hoping you might teach a class on baking cookies for sending to soldiers, with sugar rationing in mind of course. You've always been so clever in the kitchen; I just know you'd be a huge asset. What do you say?"

Lonnie considered a moment. "I think I could do that."

"Wonderful." Aunt Millie glowed.

They ate in silence for a few mouthfuls before her aunt spoke again. "Now about the War Bond Fundraiser dance . . ."

***

An hour later, Lonnie was finally able to make her escape. Aunt Millie had not only secured her services for the AWVS, but also for helping at the refreshment table at the fund-raising dance and distributing flyers to advertise for the event.

Lonnie hurried to the edge of town, breathless from the sense of overwhelm. She didn't know where she was going to fit in this extra time, and she had no idea what her mother would say about it. She hated to let her aunt down though.

The biggest reason she agreed was because she liked knowing she was doing more for the war effort. There was so little she could do besides the humdrum saving waste fats and buying war bonds. It was a little exciting to anticipate teaching other young women about cooking. Only sugar was being rationed currently, but if this war didn't end, she was sure not only sugar would need ration coupons.

Lonnie pulled the scrap of paper out of her pocket where she'd scribbled the directions to Grandma Chan's house. She wasn't too surprised when she found herself on a dirt road leading out into the country.

As she walked, she grew warm from her exercise; the road was dusty and hot. By the time she reached the tidy, white house with red shutters, she was thirsty and damp with perspiration. Using the window by the front door to tidy her hair the best she could, Lonnie finally knocked and waited.

She took in a trim front yard with well-manicured shrubs and beautiful yellow rose bushes. A tall maple tree waved its branches in the front yard. In the quiet of the countryside, Lonnie heard the lowing of cows in the distance and closer, the clucking of chickens. She was startled when something rubbed against her ankles. A gray-striped cat mewed for attention, and Lonnie bent down to pet it a few strokes.

The door opened, and Lonnie straightened to greet a short, smiling Chinese woman. Her silver hair, streaked with bits of black, was neatly tied back into a bun.

"Hello. May I help you?" Her voice wavered slightly, and it was as soft and gentle as the woman's hands looked.

Lonnie smiled in return. "Hello. I'm Lonnie. I sent you a letter about coming to visit."

"Of course. Please come in." The woman held the door open. Lonnie found herself in a cool, tiny front room with a couch, a sitting chair, and a side table with a little radio. The only decorations were a few pictures on the wall and some trinkets and photos on the mantle of a stone fireplace.

On the side table with the radio sat a beautiful white teapot and two tiny cups. "I've been expecting you." Grandma Chan gestured to a chair. "Please, sit down."

Lonnie took a seat. The woman positioned herself across from her and began the ritual of pouring the tea. Lonnie watched her for a minute before saying, "I'm Lonnie Hamilton, though you knew that from my letter. I just thought I should formally introduce myself."

The woman's face wrinkled like delicate paper in a broad smile. "And I'm Grandma Chan. At least that's what everyone always calls me." Her black eyes twinkled, and she leaned forward conspiratorially. "My name is really Xiao Lin Chan." She paused chuckling a little. "You look like you wanted to know."

Lonnie blinked. "Oh." She laughed too. "Well, I suppose I should tell you my real name is Appalone, but I dread anyone calling me that. The teasing would never stop."

Grandma Chan nodded, handing her the teacup, which strangely didn't have any handle. "Such an interesting name. It's a shame our beautiful names should stay hidden, isn't it?"

Lonnie sipped the tea. The green liquid was fragrant and exotic. "Yes, it is a shame."

Grandma Chan sipped her own tea. "I know we've just met, but shall we use our given names as friends do? I promise I won't tease." Lonnie believed her despite the mischievous twitch of the old woman's mouth.

"I think that's a wonderful idea," Lonnie said, smiling. She loved how instantly comfortable she felt in this woman's presence and sensed she'd discovered a new friend.

***

Lonnie was content as she walked home. Her belly was full of the delicious prune nut cake Xiao Lin had served with the tea, and her mind was full of all the amazing things the woman had shared about her homeland of China. To Lonnie's delight, Xiao Lin had explained she was a quarter Korean on her mother's side. Lonnie had then excitedly told her all about Alex and their growing friendship, explaining how much she wanted to learn about his culture.

Xiao Lin agreed happily to share what she knew, even offering to teach her what Korean recipes she could cook in exchange for Lonnie helping with her chickens and garden. Lonnie was thrilled with the success of her visit and with the anticipation of visiting

Xiao Lin again, as soon as she found a good enough excuse to disappear for a few hours.

It was nearly dinnertime when she walked in the door. She was confronted by her mother who, with fists on bony hips, glared at her from the foyer. Lonnie's heart sank as she waited for the impending scolding. Her siblings peered down from the top of the staircase as if they too could sense what was coming.

"Where have you been?" Her mother's voice had a sharp edge, and it cut the air.

"I was at Aunt Millie's."

"No, I mean after that. I called Millie two hours ago to see where you were, and she said you'd already left. Mrs. Rogers said she saw you walking toward the edge of town. We both know that's in the opposite direction of home."

Lonnie couldn't make eye contact with her mother. She'd never been good at evading her mother's sixth sense of when her children were lying. She wouldn't get out of this by making something up.

"I went out to visit someone."

"And who might that be, Appalone?"

Lonnie took a deep, shuddering breath. "Grandma Chan."

Her mother's eyes bulged. "What? Why in the world would you visit that old Chink?" Lonnie flinched at the harsh tone. "You know, I don't care why you felt you needed to go there. What's more important is you lied to me. I never knew you could be so conniving and deceitful."

Harriet's voice rose, and she jabbed her finger at Lonnie. "You disgust me. With all the freedom I give you, with all the responsibility you have and the example you are to your siblings, I would've thought better of you. You're such a disappointment. For the next month you're confined to the house."

Lonnie gasped, her jaw dropping. "But . . . but I'm nineteen, Mother. I'm not a child to be kept at home."

Harriet's eyes flashed. "You are when you're under my roof, young lady."

Lonnie wanted to stamp her foot like a child, but knew it would only make things worse. "I have a job. I can't be confined to the house."

"You can go to work and straight back home. Tunie and Marty will have to run any errands you normally take care of."

Lonnie furiously blinked tears away. "And church? Can I go to church?"

Harriet's nostril's flared in anger. "If I had my way, none of you would go to that ludicrous church of Phillip's. Ever."

"Please?" Lonnie pled.

Harriet was quiet a moment. "You can go if you have your sister with you. Besides work, you can't leave home without her if you're allowed to leave at all."

Tunie's moan echoed down the stairwell. Lonnie pressed her lips together and nodded in resignation. Being babysat by her younger sister? It was beyond humiliating. She turned and sped up the stairs, pushing past her brother and sister, who regarded her with pity. In her bedroom, Lonnie flung herself onto her bed and wept. She was glad Tunie didn't come in until after she'd calmed down and dried her tears. Even then, she refused to talk, preferring the company of the papered wall.

The month of punishment yawned out ahead of Lonnie. She didn't regret going to see Xiao Lin, though. And she wasn't going to stop going to see her. She'd just have to be more careful in the future. Maybe, now that her mother knew about Xiao Lin, she wouldn't mind so much if she knew in advance Lonnie was going.

***

Sunday passed without a sighting of Lonnie, and Alex was relieved he wouldn't have to come up with conversation after their confusing parting. Work kept him busy with having to invent ways to make parts when metal was scarce. Less time to venture out in town meant less of a chance he'd run into her which suited him just fine.

On Friday, when Mike asked him if he'd run to the store and pick up groceries, he reluctantly agreed. He hadn't returned to Simmons Grocery since that first incident. It was a relief Mrs. Eileen Simmons at River Bluff Grocery didn't mind him coming in.

Alex walked across town with a grocery list and a few dollars in his pocket. The weather was turning chilly, and he shrugged his shoulders up to block some of the wind. On days like this it was hard not to close his eyes and think wistfully of palm trees swaying in balmy breezes and beaches burnished in golden sun. The changing seasons were appealing though. The normally green leaves had gilded their edges in crimson and orange. The sky was paling, setting off the deep, golden fields of grain on the outskirts of town.

He reached the store without any unwelcome incident and went inside. He grabbed a basket and went down his shopping list as he walked the aisles. When he was finished, he saw Tunie was working at the counter.

"You." She glared.

He nodded. "Yep. It's me."

She took his items out of the basket, banging them on the counter. He wisely kept his mouth shut.

"It's your fault, you know." The cash register *pinged* its little bell as she viciously punched keys.

"What's my fault?"

"If it wasn't for you, Lonnie wouldn't have had any reason to lie."

"Lie?"

"She's confined to the house for a month. She just *had* to go out to Grandma Chan's house and not tell anyone. You're the one that gives her these crazy ideas. I know it."

Alex's mouth dropped open. That must've been why she'd been scarce on Sunday.

"Look, I'm sorry she's being punished, but I don't see what that's got to do with me. I didn't get her to do anything."

"You're such a coward, you creep." Tunie jabbed a finger, stopping short of his chest by a few inches. Her gray eyes were like ice, the complete opposite of Lonnie's warm, blue ones. "Everything was going fine in her life until you came along. I've never seen Mother so angry. Lonnie's never lied to her before." She narrowed her eyes and finished ringing him up. "Two dollars and thirty-five cents."

Wordlessly, Alex handed her the money. The register opened with a loud *ching*. She pulled the change out, shut the drawer with a bang, and slammed his change on the counter. "Just stay away from my sister, buddy. The last thing she needs is someone like you messing up her life."

She folded her arms across her chest and scowled some more. It was obvious he was dismissed. He nodded politely, picked up his sack of food, and walked out of the store.

Walking home, his ears burned from the girl's harsh words. Half of what she said didn't make any sense. "How can any of that be my fault?"

He pitied Lonnie being punished like that, especially at her age. If it were him, he'd be completely humiliated. He frowned, swallowing back bitterness. He already, in fact, had experienced that. The only reason he was out here was because he was being punished. In some ways, Lonnie was getting off easy. His punishment was indefinite—unless he could push it off even longer by remaining in River Bluff. He was close enough to his uncle in Washington DC to feel slightly uncomfortable, but far enough away it was like he was hiding.

He sighed. Tunie was right. He *was* a coward. He couldn't even face his own punishment.

When he got home, a letter waited from his uncle, as if thinking about him had conjured up the correspondence.

We were so worried for you when you didn't show up at the train station. I would come and bring you home now if I wasn't so busy with the business and the activities to free Korea. With the heating up of the war, things are getting more difficult. I am gaining audience with a few congressmen, but things are slow. There seems to be some suspicion about the loyalty of Koreans to the United States, which I'm working hard to correct. In the meantime, I suggest you take some time to reflect on your position and what your father feels is best for you. I will come for you just as soon as I can get away. You seem to have your basic needs met and are in good hands until that time.

Alex folded the letter and shoved it into his pocket, his heart becoming a hardened rock in his chest. He loved his uncle, but he knew he was just acting in proxy for his brother, Alex's father. In essence, Uncle Harry was telling him to cool off before continuing on and performing his filial duty. But he didn't want to cool off. He didn't want to be tied to such a duty. His life was a mess. Alex kicked a stray metal pipe on the floor, and it clattered across the garage, catching Mike's attention.

"Sorry," Alex mumbled and returned to his work.

***

That evening after work, Alex decided to head to the library. The strange scolding from Tunie had left a bad taste in his mouth, and he needed something to take his mind off of it.

He walked into the library and took a deep breath in relief at the sight of the aisles upon aisles of books. He wandered up and down the aisles, trying to lose himself. He ran his fingers along the spines, relishing their varied look and feel.

He found the aisle that held the fiction and browsed happily, wondering which book he should escape into. The late afternoon sunlight streamed through the line of windows. As he turned the corner, a familiar figure with golden hair caught his eye. She could've been browsing like himself, except she was leaning against the shelf of books, staring off into space. Her shoulders rose and fell with a deep sigh.

"Lonnie?"

She jumped. Seeing him, her face relaxed. "Hi, Alex."

"Have any books you'd recommend? I'm hunting for something new to read." He could tell she was putting on a brave face as a weak smile wobbled into view.

"I—I don't know." She glanced furtively around. "I really shouldn't even be here. I was just on my way home from work." She pressed her lips together.

"I heard about what happened from Tunie. I'm sorry."

At his statement, her face crumpled and tears dripped down her cheeks. "I suppose I deserved it. I did lie, but I only wanted to visit her. Is there something so wrong in that? What if my friends find out the real reason why they can't see me for a month? I'll be mortified." She inhaled sharply, her eyes red-rimmed and wild. "But that's not really what makes me so angry. I think she's doing it on purpose. Mother never likes to see me happy. It's only ever about her control over me. There's nothing I can do, and she takes every chance to rub in my face what a failure I am!" With that, she burst into full-on tears, covering her face with her hands.

For a second, Alex froze in shock. Not knowing what else to do, he placed a hesitant hand gently on her shoulder in comfort. That was all he'd truly intended to do. Then without thinking, he was pulling her to him, wrapping her in an embrace, her body heaving in sobs against him.

His heart raced. *What the hell are you doing, Alex?* He knew he should pull away; any sane man in his position would run for the hills. But she'd completely melted into his arms, grasping onto his shoulders as she cried. A fierce desire to protect her welled up inside of him from out of nowhere. Nothing in the world would have induced him to let her go in that moment . . .

The feeling alarmed him so much that he jerked back, pushing her away. "I—I am *so* sorry. I hope you don't think—my intention wasn't . . ." He trembled thinking of what had just happened. If someone should've seen . . . He swiveled his head in desperation. The coast was clear, but that didn't help the panic restricting his lungs.

Lonnie's sobs quieted to noisy sniffles. She pulled out a handkerchief and busily wiped at her tears. "No, I'm the one who's sorry. I didn't mean to break down like that in front of you."

She took a deep, shuddering breath. "I should go." She smiled at him, her eyes still watery. "Thank you. It helps to have a shoulder to cry on now and then."

She hurried away but stopped at the end of the aisle. "I'd appreciate it if you'd forget everything that just happened." She laughed a little. Ducking her head, she went.

Alex stared after her, feeling weak in the knees, knowing with the full and glaring knowledge that he would never forget.

Chapter Twelve

LONNIE WAS USING her forced time at home to catch up on things. She tried to keep the resentment at bay by keeping busy, starting with the repairs on Alex's clothing. She held up the trousers to survey the extent of the damage. She'd done her best to wash out all the stains, and was pleased she couldn't find them anymore. The mending was another matter. She pulled out her needle and dark brown thread.

Sewing up the torn fabric went faster than she expected, but after tying the thread off and cutting it, she grimaced at how big and sloppy her stitches were. Frowning, she ripped the stitches out with her small scissors.

She began again and took her time. With each painstaking stitch, she thought about how these were Alex's trousers, and how he'd looked in them the day she'd seen him at the jail. He'd been a little scary at first, especially with the sunlight streaming in the windows, making his hair gleam and his eyes flash. His wounds had been especially bad.

Thinking of him in jail got her thinking about how unjust her own punishment was. She'd been pleased to see Alex at the library during her stolen moment of rebellion. Lonnie blushed as she remembered how, to her astonishment, his arms had gone around her in comfort. Why had it felt so natural to be in his embrace? A shiver ran down her spine.

She cleared her throat and shifted in her seat, trying to shake the images in her mind. The whole thing was ridiculous. Why had he done such a forward thing, especially when she'd been so vulnerable? She sewed with more diligence, trying to keep on task, but like a stubborn wad of chewing gum stuck to the bottom of her shoe, the images wouldn't go away. The tenderness of his embrace, the solidarity of his chest, how close his face had been to hers . . .

"Ouch!" She jerked her finger free of the fabric to see a little bead of blood where the needle had left its mark. She frowned and sucked on her tiny wound. She'd get nowhere at this rate. Setting the mending inside its box, she pushed it under her bed out of sight and went downstairs to check if the mail had come.

A pile of letters lay at the foot of the door in the foyer. Lonnie picked them up and rifled through. One letter was addressed to her, and she gasped as she recognized the handwriting. Tossing the rest of the mail on the hall table, she dashed upstairs to flop onto her bed and tore the envelope open. The familiar handwriting flowed beautifully across the paper.

My Dearest Lonnie,

Thank you for your letter. It always cheers me to receive something from you, even if it's just a line or two. Your poem was wonderful. It made me laugh out loud! The other men in the barracks looked over to see what the fun was, and I hope you don't mind, my dear, but I read it to them. They all enjoyed it immensely. Your poems have become quite the popular form of entertainment here. A few are so delightfully written that the men have requested I read them multiple times. It may not seem much to you, but as I read, the men and I are able to forget, for just a moment, the horrors of this war. Keep them coming, my girl. They're pretty much expected now.

Thank you for your update on Tunie and Marty. I'm glad to hear they're doing well in school and that Tunie is liking her job. If you could send a photograph of the three of you I would love that. I know it might be hard to manage, but please do try. It helps me to see how healthy and strong you all are. I can hardly imagine how tall Marty has grown.

Now, my sweet Lonnie girl, even though you don't say so directly in your letters, I know how hard you work to help your mother and care for your siblings. I worry for you, with your job at the office and the time you volunteer for Uncle Phillip and Aunt Millie. You take on so much for someone so young. Take care and remember to take time for yourself. I don't want the days to pass only for you to regret all the things you wish you'd seen or done. I wish you to live with happiness and contentment.

Well, never mind the ramblings of your old man. Your letters keep me going even on the hardest days. It does my heart good to know you think of me. Take care and write again soon.

With love,
Father

P.S. I've enclosed letters for Tunie and Marty. Could you see that they get them?

Lonnie sniffled. It had been two months since she'd heard from her father. She clutched the papers to her chest. Every word was precious. She read through the letter again, smiling at the mention of her poem. Since her father had joined the war, she'd started writing him humorous little musings for fun. It made her happy that so many soldiers enjoyed them too.

Just as she was beginning a new letter to her father, the doorbell rang. Lonnie went down and pulled open the door, beaming at seeing Rose. Her friend had her purse slung over one shoulder, her ruddy hair cascading around her collar in graceful waves.

Rose smiled. "Can I come in?"

"Of course." Lonnie led her into the living room and made a quick detour to the kitchen for some water and a small plate of cookies.

"How have you been?" Rose asked as she took position on the couch. "I haven't seen you in ages."

Lonnie hitched a smile onto her face, trying to keep the sadness from her voice. "I've been busy at work and here at home catching up on chores and things."

Rose regarded her kindly, and Lonnie suspected her friend knew the real reason. "Well, I've missed you."

"I've missed you too. How is everyone? Walter and Gladys?" She paused. "Teddy?" The embarrassment must have shown on her face because Rose sighed.

"I think his pride is a bit wounded. He won't even talk about your date. I know it's been a while, but what happened?"

Lonnie shrugged. "Overall the date was nice, but at the end we argued."

"What about? I really can't see—" Rose stopped. "Oh, Lonnie, I'm sorry. I shouldn't have pried. It's really none of my business."

Lonnie pursed her lips. Out of all her friends, Rose was the most kind and understanding, but when it came to Alex, how would she react?

"Rose," Lonnie began.

"Yes?"

"What do you think of Alex Moon?"

Rose thought. "Well, I don't know. My sisters and I ran into him at the park. He helped fix my sister's roller skate. He seemed nice and was interested that I was your friend. Other than that, I only know what I hear about him."

Lonnie straightened up at this. "What do you hear about him?"

Rose's cheeks flamed red. "Oh, well . . ."

"What do you hear?" Lonnie persisted.

Rose gestured helplessly. "You know, Lonnie. He's different, and he looks like a Jap. What do you think they're saying?"

Lonnie pondered for a few moments. The air was thick with awkwardness. After a time, she resigned herself to the facts.

"I know I shouldn't be surprised. I know not everyone thinks like me. I asked what you think of him because that's what Teddy and I argued about. He seems to think I should have nothing to do with Alex and that he'll ruin my life." She surveyed her friend's reaction to her words. Rose was as pink-cheeked as ever.

"Do you feel the same way?"

Slowly, her friend nodded. "Lonnie, I don't want to argue with you. I didn't come here for that. I've missed you. Honestly, I have."

Lonnie finally smiled. "I know. Let's talk about something else." They changed the subject and chatted some more, but Lonnie couldn't dispel the feeling of unease from Rose's revealed feelings. If Rose, who was the sweetest girl she knew, wouldn't accept Alex, then who would?

***

Alex was working steadily, his head under the hood of a car, when someone asked for him. He paused to listen to Mike's exchange. The voice was young—like a kid. Curious, Alex set down his wrench and emerged. A familiar-looking boy with light brown hair and bright blue eyes turned at his movement. His face lit up at seeing Alex.

"Hi, Mr. Moon." The boy came forward. "I'm Marty Hamilton. Do you remember me? I'm Lonnie's brother."

Alex extended his hand. "Of course I remember you. And please, call me Alex." They shook hands. There was something about this kid with his big, goofy grin that made him want to ruffle his hair.

"Sorry. I have to call you Mr. Moon. My sister said she'd box my ears if I called you Alex."

Alex's eyebrows shot up. "She did?"

Marty laughed. "Tunie did. Not Lonnie."

"Oh." That made a whole lot more sense. He didn't doubt Tunie would box *his* ears if she could. "How can I help you, Marty?"

Marty pulled an envelope out of his pocket and handed it to Alex. "Lonnie said to deliver this to you."

He took the envelope and put it in his pocket. "Thanks."

Marty studied the floor and shuffled his feet.

"Was there anything else you needed?"

Marty glanced up with hope shining in his eyes. "Do you have any metal scrap? There's a contest in our school to see who can collect the most out of all the other schools around. I thought this might be a good place to ask."

Alex crossed his arms and frowned. "Oh, I don't know. Spare metal is pretty scarce around here." His face relaxed into a smile. "But for you, I'll see what we can do."

Marty grinned. "Thanks, Mr. Moon."

"Hey, Mike?" Alex called to his boss who was going over some paperwork at his desk.

"Yeah?"

"Do we have any scrap metal Marty here could haul away?"

"We got some in a box in the back."

Alex turned to Marty. "It's your lucky day. You going to carry it back home on your own or do you need help?"

Marty leapt into action. "Nope, I brought my wagon." He raced out the garage door and returned quickly with his beat up Radio Flyer wagon bumping along behind him.

"Enterprising little tyke," Mike mumbled.

Alex led Marty out back and helped him load the metal up. The scrap hadn't looked like much in the box, but it filled the boy's small wagon to brimming.

"I guess we had more than I thought." Alex smiled. "Good luck with your competition."

Marty grinned. "Thanks. Now, I'm sure I'm way ahead of anyone."

Alex couldn't help but laugh at his eagerness. "You want a drink before you head back? The sun's pretty hot today."

"Yes, sir. That'd be swell."

Alex led him inside through the kitchen door. He poured some milk and pulled some cookies Mrs. Godfrey had brought by yesterday out of a crock on the counter. He handed everything over. "There you go."

Alex watched the kid eat and drink eagerly. The boy's eyes forcefully reminded him of Lonnie. He cleared his throat to clear his mind of any dangerous thoughts.

As Marty finished drinking his milk, his gaze wandered. Catching a glimpse of the map in the living room, his eyes grew wide. Setting down his glass and sporting a milky mustached upper lip, he gravitated into the other room.

"Wow, look at that. He's got the whole Pacific theater mapped out."

Alarm bells went off in Alex's head. They shouldn't be in there. He'd avoided going into the living room since the first time seeing the map. In his mind, that area was a sacred shrine he should bow in respect to, only it would be crazy considering his situation. Mike hadn't shown any anger or bitterness towards him, but Alex was still waiting for that moment to break.

"Come on, Marty. We should go."

"All right." Marty caught one last wistful glance as they left the room.

Once Marty was on his way with his loaded wagon, Alex walked back into the garage to continue his work.

"You guilty 'bout something?" Mike studied him with narrowed eyes. "You've got the look on your face."

"What? No." Alex tried to keep calm. He wasn't guilty of anything. But why did he feel like he was?

"Hmm." Mike frowned and turned back to his desk but continued grumbling. "I raised three boys. I know that look when I see it."

Alex was increasingly confused. He knew Mike must trust him on some level since he sent him on regular errands to the grocery store with cash. He even left him alone working in the shop. But he also kept him at a distance, as if he didn't want to get too close. And if he thought Alex was guilty of something, it was only a matter of time before he brought up the glaringly obvious questions.

Part of him just wanted to have it out already. Mike wasn't the most talkative person, so Alex didn't see that happening anytime soon. Grabbing his wrench and a rag, he ducked back under the car's hood.

It wasn't until he was getting ready for bed that Alex found the letter from Lonnie in his pocket. Sitting on his bed, he opened it. It was only a few lines long written in a pretty cursive.

Dear Alex,

I've finished your lesson and would like to meet with you to discuss it. Could we meet at Harrison Park this coming Sunday afternoon at two? (It's the park at the bluff overlooking the river.)

Sincerely,

Lonnie

The formality of the letter hitched up the side of his mouth into a half grin. She was actually following through.

With a start, he realized he should make up another lesson to give her when they met. And he had to write a note in reply as well. How was he going to get it to her? He mentally kicked himself for not reading the note right away and sending back a reply with Marty. But it was okay. He'd stop in at her office first thing in the morning and tell her himself. Already planning his next lesson, he scrambled around hunting for some paper.

Chapter Thirteen

LONNIE WAS SETTLED into the first of her typed reports at the office when in strode Alex. He brought with him the chill of impending autumn, but his infectious smile warmed her like the sun.

"Alex, what brings you here?" She stood to greet him and noticed out of the corner of her eye that her words had drawn the attention of Mr. Pickering through the open door of his office.

"I brought a reply to the note you sent yesterday. I wasn't thinking when I could've sent it back with your brother."

"Oh, yes." Her palms grew damp. She needed to keep his visit short. "Would that time be agreeable, Mr. Moon?"

His brow furrowed in confusion. Mr. Pickering had gotten up from his desk and was at his doorway listening.

"Yes." Alex answered slowly. She flicked her eyes to her boss's door, hoping he'd catch on that they had an eavesdropper. His eyes followed and noticed the man standing there. He nodded.

"I'll inform my uncle then," Lonnie stated stiffly. "He'll be delighted to have your help. Good day." Lonnie walked from around her desk and ushered him outside. Before he walked away, she placed a hand on his arm and whispered, "I'm sorry. You have no idea how stuffy Mr. Pickering can be. I'll see you on Sunday."

"See you then." He waved before leaving.

Lonnie deflated with a sigh of relief. What a shock to see Alex come to her place of work. When she'd sent the note, she hadn't considered he might reply at her office, in person.

Mr. Pickering emerged. "Miss Hamilton, who was that young man? Isn't he that Jap that's been wandering around town disturbing the peace?"

Her heart pounded. What she said now could have a ripple effect. "No, sir, he's not."

He frowned. "Do you mean to tell me he's not the man they had in jail back in August?"

"He is that man, but—"

"And you mean to say that you know him? Do you think it's wise to fraternize with someone like that, Miss Hamilton?"

"Well, he's not—"

"I'm surprised at you, young lady. You've always struck me as intelligent and levelheaded. That's one reason why I hired you on above the other young women who applied. I'm shocked beyond words. Beyond words."

Lonnie fought the urge to roll her eyes. *He's hardly beyond words,* she thought.

"Furthermore," he continued, "I hope we won't be seeing the likes of him in the office again. This business has a long and prestigious reputation to uphold. There's no sense in bringing all that crashing down because of one disagreeable troublemaker. I hope you take my meaning, Miss Hamilton." He eyed her sternly.

She gulped and nodded. "Yes, sir."

Once he'd gone back into his office, Lonnie plopped down in front of her typewriter. His words seared into her mind. How could someone be capable of such dislike for a person they knew nothing about?

Her fingers trembled as they took up typing. The rhythmic clacking of the keys eventually soothed her, but her mind had trouble focusing on typing such civil replies to inquiries when she was boiling inside.

After work, Lonnie stopped at Simmons' Grocery to pick up a few things. She was grateful her punishment had finally been lifted so she could go back to moving about freely and without the reluctant shadow of Tunie. The doorbell jangled wildly as she entered the store. Lonnie nodded to Mrs. Simmons at the counter, grabbed a basket, and pulled out her list.

She stopped to survey the contents of Mrs. Simmon's freezer case—her pride and joy. She was the only grocer in town to rent a freezer case, which was stocked with frozen fruits and vegetables and, before the war, frozen beef. Today the case seemed unusually well stocked with white butcher-paper wrapped parcels each labeled neatly with their contents. They weren't the usual Birdseye brand.

"Mrs. Simmons, did you get a delivery recently? You have a wonderful supply here."

Mrs. Simmons's face lit up from where she was tidying a shelf. "Why, yes, I did. We have frozen peas, sweet corn, and even some late strawberries. Oh, and there's fish as well. These are a fraction of the cost of Birdseye's. Would you like me to select some for you?"

"Yes, thank you," Lonnie said and continued her browsing.

Some other women hurried into the shop to make last minute purchases for dinner. Their chatter filled the store and by the time she'd finished her shopping and made her way to the front, a small line had formed at the counter.

"I couldn't believe it. There he was, just striding through town as bold as brass, his nose in the air. He nearly knocked me over."

Mrs. Simmons gasped conciliatorily. "Well, I never."

Another woman spoke up. "I took our car over to Hardy's Garage like I usually do for an oil change, and I couldn't believe he'd hired that heathen on. I nearly fainted to the floor with shock. I've known Mike Hardy for years, but I honestly thought he had more sense than that, especially since every single one of his boys were killed by those nasty Japs. I don't know what that man is thinking."

Lonnie, who'd been trying to ignore the gossip, looked up at this last bit. They definitely had to be talking about Alex.

Mrs. Simmons frowned and shook her head slowly. "I don't know either, Susan. A few weeks back, that Jap came in here and expected me to sell him some food, but I turned him right out. Our boys are fighting so hard against the enemy, why should I serve one? The fact that there's one on our very doorstep is beyond me. What are the police officers doing in this town?"

The women all murmured their agreements, and it was all Lonnie could do to keep her mouth shut. Mrs. Simmons was finally ringing up Lonnie's things, but the women, all finished with their purchases, were lingering to talk.

"And what do you think of all this?"

Lonnie was startled that Mrs. Simmons directed the question at her. Her purchase was all finished now, and Lonnie clutched the sack nervously in her hands.

"Me?"

"Yes, what do you think of this Jap that's been hanging around? You took his side when he came in to shop before. I figured you were just being charitable, but surely you agree he doesn't belong here."

The women stared at her. If she dared say what was really on her mind . . .

"Didn't my Ernest see you with him at the drug store a while back?" one woman said, her eyes narrowing suspiciously.

"What?" Lonnie's breathing became more labored.

"Well?" Mrs. Simmons insisted.

She ignored the other women and turned to Mrs. Simmons. "F-first Timothy. Five thirteen."

Mrs. Simmons frowned. "What's that?"

Lonnie tried to calm her racing pulse. "And withal they learn to be idle, wandering about from house to house; and not only idle, but tattlers also and busybodies, speaking things which they ought not." She then bolted out of the store, pushing past the women, and hurried away from their spluttering indignation.

Lonnie nearly ran all the way home, but her grocery sack was slipping and her lungs were bursting. She stopped to catch her breath only to find herself laughing uncontrollably. How had that scripture come to her at that moment? Remembering the women's shocked expressions only made her laugh harder, but the fury boiling back up turned her mirth into hot tears. She leaned against a fence as she slid to crouch down on the sidewalk, huddling with her arms wrapped around her.

"Lonnie? Are you all right?" She hastily dried her face as Gladys approached. She reached out and helped Lonnie to stand. "What is it? Are you hurt?"

Lonnie shook her head. "No. I'm fine. Just shaken up a little."

Gladys smiled in sympathy. "Here, let me help carry your things. I'll walk you home."

Lonnie nodded, though being in the company of yet another gossip set her a little on edge.

After a moment, Gladys said, "Are you sure you're all right?"

Lonnie shrugged. "Oh, it's nothing. Where were you headed?"

"I was just on my way home from work myself. I was in a bit of a hurry, but I can spare a few extra minutes to walk with you."

"Thank you, I—"

"This is going to be such fun." Gladys's eyes shone, her cheeks plumping with unsuppressed glee as she linked arms with Lonnie. "Now, about that date with Teddy."

***

Alex arrived early to church on Sunday to help Reverend Hicks with a few things. He was surprised to see someone already in the pews near the front. Her head was bowed as if in prayer. He walked quietly around the perimeter toward the reverend's office to avoid disturbing her, but then she tilted her face to the colors of light streaming in through the windows.

It was Lonnie. He paused to stare at her. Her face was brightly illuminated, etched in glowing ruby, sapphire, and emerald, making her look for all the world like she was a part of the stained glass herself.

He didn't realize his mouth was gaping open until he heard a voice at his side. "The light is quite beautiful this time of morning, isn't it?"

Alex gulped. "Reverend Hicks. I—I was just coming in to see you."

The older man smiled, though his gleam of knowledge left Alex feeling queasy. "My niece occasionally comes here to commune with God. There are times that this is the only place that offers any peace or solitude."

Alex nodded, hoping he'd let the matter of his gaping drop. He hadn't *meant* to gape. She'd just taken him by surprise. Alex followed him into his office. Reverend Hicks took his place at his book and paper-strewn desk.

"I'll be the first to proudly admit my niece is a beautiful young woman."

"I didn't say—"

"You didn't need to say it, my friend. I saw it written all over your face." He leaned forward, his seat creaking. His face furrowed into stern lines, though it wasn't unkind. "You do remember the warning I gave you? To take care?"

Frowning, Alex nodded.

"Whatever your friendship with my niece, whatever your feelings—don't let them get carried away. Don't put her reputation in danger."

Alex's eyes widened at the man's implication. "Sir, I would never dream of such a thing."

Reverend Hicks settled back into his chair. "I apologize. That wasn't my meaning. I'm afraid your very association with my niece has already made some question her character. And her judgment. I know you're a decent young man with a good head on your shoulders, but others don't know or don't care to know that for themselves. To them, you . . ." He spread his hands wide in defeat. "Are the enemy."

The reverend's words stung and Alex felt small. "But I'm not," he answered, voice soft. "I'm as much an American as any of them. Is it my fault I look Japanese to everyone else? They can't even tell the difference between Japanese and Korean. What else can I do to convince these people?" His voice started rising. "I keep my head down. I treat everyone I meet with courtesy despite their disgust. I keep my mouth shut when I hear their comments, their whisperings behind my back. I didn't ask to come here, and I didn't ask to stay here. I'm only still here because I don't have a choice. If I had my way, and if I somehow found all that money I lost, I'd be long gone!" His breath came in deep heaves as he struggled to reign in his anger.

Reverend Hicks' face sagged with sorrow. "Alex, I'm sorry. I didn't mean to bring you in here to lecture you. I'm well aware of the difficulties you face." He leaned forward. "I'm going to make this a matter of prayer and contemplation. The only thing I can say is you are here for God's purpose, and it's up to you to find out what that is and make the most of things as they are. It's through trials that God makes us stronger."

Alex turned his head as a sound came from the doorway behind him. The door to the office had been wide open for their entire conversation, and now Lonnie was there. He wanted to moan in misery. No doubt, his raised voice had carried out into the chapel.

Alex rose to his feet as Lonnie spoke. "Uncle, I'm not feeling well. You'll forgive me if I don't stay for the service later."

Reverend Hicks nodded. "I understand. Get some rest. I know Millie's been running you ragged with her different charities."

She offered a small smile and left. Without caring how it would appear, Alex scrambled out of his chair and hurried after her.

"Lonnie, wait." His voice echoed loudly in the cavernous space. Her pace slowed, and she turned to face him.

He stopped short with a few feet between them. "Did you happen to hear . . . ?"

Her firmly pursed lips answered his question.

"Please don't misunderstand. The only good things about being here are the kindness of your uncle and—and you." To admit this gave him a great wrench of astonishment.

"But you want to leave." Her tone was short.

"Well." He gestured helplessly. "I wasn't meant to end up here, was I? I'm only around because I have no other means to leave except for what I'm saving now. I was supposed to be in Washington." This last thing he said quietly.

Lonnie stared at him with her large blue eyes. He tried to comprehend what he saw there. She opened her mouth to say something.

The organist, Mrs. Raisor, bustled in, interrupting her. "Good morning." She sang to no one in particular.

Lonnie began to turn away, and Alex nearly leapt forward to stop her, catching himself just in time. "Will you still meet me? At two?"

She nodded, only a sliver of her face visible. It was impossible to see what she was thinking. She disappeared out the door, and Alex was left to wonder what she'd been about to say.

***

Alex waited anxiously on the bench. The soothing vista over the river did nothing to calm him. He glanced at his watch. It was ten past two. Had she given up on meeting him? He couldn't blame her after overhearing his conversation with the reverend. How incredibly stupid he'd been for losing his temper. He'd managed to offend and worry the only two people who were friendly toward him in this town.

He was about to walk dejectedly back to his apartment when he saw her approaching him on the park path. Someone else accompanied her, and as they got closer, he realized it was Tunie. A tense knot worked its way between his shoulders. Why did she have to come?

Lonnie waved.

"Hi, Lonnie." He nodded. "Tunie."

Tunie merely offered him a withering stare accompanied by an unladylike snort and stomped off to stand at a far distance, though she kept an eye on them.

Lonnie smiled in apology. "Don't mind my sister. She insisted on coming."

"I can't imagine why." His voice was hard with sarcasm. He started when Lonnie's hand touched his arm.

"Please, don't mind her."

He sank onto the bench, and she settled comfortably beside him. That morning at the church seemed forgotten as she pulled his paper out of her pocket and unfolded it.

"I enjoyed your lesson. It took me some time to work out the alphabet, but I found it so fascinating. You put a note here that said the written language came about from the king sending experts into the country to record how the people spoke, and they based the writing on where in the mouth the sound was made. That's so incredible."

Alex warmed from the excitement in her eyes, the animated way in which she gestured. It was hard to believe she loved learning what he knew.

"Yes, it's a unique thing about the Korean language. I hope I didn't make it too hard. *Hangul* is quite different from English. Did you work out the phrase?"

Lonnie blushed. "Yes, I think so, but I've no idea what it means."

"Well, let's hear it. I'll tell you what it means in a minute."

She cleared her throat, nervousness plain on her face. "An-yang-ha-say-yo." She took a deep breath and continued. "Son-sang-neem?" Her expression was tentative. "Did I completely butcher it? It was horrible wasn't it?"

Alex laughed loudly, drawing Tunie's scowl. "It was quite good, actually. I'm impressed. Let me say it for you. *Anyanghaseao, seonsaengnim.* It means, 'Hello, teacher.'"

It was Lonnie's turn to laugh. "Oh, does it? The way you say it sounds so much nicer."

"Say it again," he demanded. She repeated the phrase and pronounced it much better the second time. She laughed again, cheeks pink.

Alex grinned, loving the sight of her face as she laughed. "It was a little hard, but you managed it well. You're proving to be a very good student."

"That's nice of you to say." Her blush deepened, but she didn't look away.

He pulled out another paper and handed it to her. "Your next lesson. You did want another one, didn't you?"

She took it happily. "Yes. Thank you." She was quiet a moment. "I'm sorry you feel so unhappy here."

He shook his head. "I shouldn't have said those things. I'm even more sorry you had to hear them. I never meant to hurt your feelings."

They gazed out over the river and let the silence linger between them. It was a comfortable pause—at least mostly. Tunie's distant monitoring was like a little black cloud hovering on Alex's otherwise peaceful horizon.

"My father used to love bringing me here," Lonnie said.

"Is he serving in the war?"

She nodded. "He left home when I was twelve though. I never knew all the reasons why, but I think it was something that passed between him and my mother. Neither of them talk about it."

"Do you hear from him at all? If—if you don't mind me asking." Alex regretted asking such a personal question, but it had just slipped out.

Her eyes gleamed. "I've been writing him secretly since I was fourteen. Mother has never known, and I don't plan on telling her." She giggled, and Alex was astonished at seeing this deceitful side of her. He never would've guessed she'd be capable of something like that. He instantly admired her for her rebellion. He liked thinking of her as a fellow rebel.

"You must miss him a lot."

She nodded. "I do. I miss him terribly. I just got a letter from him recently." She paused. "Do you miss your parents? They must be sad you're so far away."

Alex let his gaze wander back out to the view, but in his mind's eye, images of his home with its tall cypress trees gracing the front came to block what really lay before him. "I miss my mother. And my little sister June, though maybe not my older brother and sister. We didn't always get along. My father on the other hand . . ." He shrugged. "Let's just say he's the reason I'm here and not there."

"Oh." She smiled, but didn't pry.

He wanted to tell her more. He wanted to tell her everything, to let it all come pouring out, but to open up like that to someone he barely knew . . . Besides, the sun was sinking, and he knew he shouldn't keep her.

He got to his feet. "We should probably head home. Thank you for meeting me. And for understanding."

She joined him at his side. "I've enjoyed our visit. It's selfish, I know, but it'll be a sad day for me when you continue on to where you were meant to go."

He swallowed thickly at her words, looking down into her eyes. *Where he was meant to go.* Where *was* he meant to go?

His heart pounded as he considered a new thought. Was it possible he was meant to end up here?

Chapter Fourteen

FOR THE NEXT couple of weeks, Lonnie worked hard in her spare time helping Aunt Millie prepare for the fundraising dance. She had no time to devote to working on Alex's next lesson, and she hadn't even had the chance to look at it. She was relieved when the week of the dance finally arrived, and she could anticipate the end of her commitment.

She did, however, find spare bits of private time to work on Alex's mending. As she sewed, she debated back and forth about inviting him to the dance. If she considered only her own feelings, she'd invite him in a minute. But considering the way everyone else in town felt about him, she worried it might cause more trouble.

Animosity toward Alex seemed to have quieted down. Perhaps it wouldn't be as bad as she feared. Lonnie didn't know what Alex did in all his free time, but he sure must want for something a little more exciting than a night of reading books or listening to the radio. Besides, the dance was for a good cause—raising money for war defense bonds. Every ticket helped.

By the time she finished her mending for the day, she'd determined to ask him on Sunday. She'd just put away her needle and thread when the telephone rang. "I'll get it," Marty bellowed from downstairs. A moment later he shouted, "Lonnie, it's for you."

She went down to the hall and took the phone from her brother. "It's *Teddy*." He made a face. She frowned and waved him away.

"Hello?"

"Hi, Lonnie. I would've stopped by, but I've been tied up at the factory all day."

"Is everything all right?"

"I wanted to ask you before it got too late—would you like to go to the dance on Saturday with me?" He paused. Even the static over the line sounded awkward. "I know our last date didn't end very well, but I'd like to try again. Will you go with me?"

Her heart sank, but it wasn't with disappointment. "Oh, Teddy, I wish I could, but it's not really possible for me to go with a date. I'm going early to help my Aunt Millie, and it's quite likely that I'll stay after to help clean up. It wouldn't be fair to you."

"I see."

Lonnie gripped the phone cord. "I don't think Rose has been asked yet."

"Really? All right. Well, I guess I'll see you there. Save me a dance, will ya?"

He hung up before she could respond. She set the receiver back in its cradle with a sigh. It was with relief, not guilt. She was glad he wanted to make up, but was she ready to? She hadn't changed her mind, and it was doubtful he had. The idea of spending an evening with him was uncomfortable, and it was a good thing she had volunteer work as an excuse.

***

Sunday morning, Lonnie took extra care in getting ready for church, trying not to think Alex was the reason for her motivation. She tried her hair in a new style she'd seen in a make-over magazine article. When she went to put on her lipstick, she was dismayed to remember she'd used the last of it and forgotten to buy a new tube.

Tunie was downstairs taking her time finishing breakfast, so Lonnie went over to her sister's vanity and rummaged in the drawers. Make up, nail polish, photographs, notes, ribbons, dance cards. It was a jumbled mess, and Lonnie impatiently pawed through the contents.

"I know I saw her put her lipstick in here."

She pulled the drawer out as far as it would go, still hunting, but something at the back caused her to stop. It was a bundle of money. Curious, Lonnie picked it up and unfolded it. She gasped as she quickly counted. One hundred dollars. Where had Tunie gotten this much money? But ten and five dollar bills weren't the only things there. A paper note popped out of its own accord and Lonnie opened it. The color drained from her face.

The note resembled a code, all lines and circles and slashes. Only, Lonnie knew this wasn't a code. And she knew the handwriting.

"What are you doing?" Tunie strode into the room. Her face darkened as her eyes traveled to Lonnie's hand. "Why are you going through my things?"

Lonnie faced her sister. "I was searching for some lipstick because I'm out. Why do you have this? Do you know what this is?"

Tunie stomped up to the drawer and yanked out her tube of lipstick. It had been hidden under the money. "Here's the lipstick.

And yes, of course I know what it is. It's a hundred dollars. I found it, and it's mine."

"Where did you find it?"

Tunie tried to grab the money, but Lonnie jerked it out of her reach. "Answer me."

"Phyllis and I went to the train station after we heard about the Jap in jail. We wanted to ask the stationmaster about it. I dropped something and found the money under the bench. Finders keepers. Satisfied?"

"No, I'm not. This isn't yours."

"It is," she protested. "No one's put up any notices about it."

"Tunie, this is Alex Moon's money."

Tunie stared at her. "That's crazy. No, it isn't. You're just saying that."

She crushed the money in her fist. "I'm not."

"You can't prove it."

"Yes, I can." She fumbled to pull out the note. "See this? This is Korean. I know because I've seen it, and better yet, *this* is Alex's handwriting. If you need further proof, I can show you other examples. You can't keep this. We have to return it."

"No." Tunie stomped her foot. "I was saving it, Lonnie. For once, I wanted a decent Christmas. I wanted to send Daddy a box as big as his head stuffed with all of his favorite cookies and socks and books. We could get Marty new clothes and us new dresses. Just think of it. We could even buy some war bonds." Her eyes were pleading, begging. Neither of them had seen this much cash in one place. Her suggestions were tempting, but . . .

"Tunie, we can't. Alex is stuck in this town because he lost this money, don't you see? We have to give it back. It isn't ours." She turned and stuffed the bills into a little pocket inside her purse. Grabbing Tunie's lipstick, she glided it over her lips and handed it back. "Thanks. You should get ready for church. We'll be late."

Lonnie turned to leave the room and narrowly missed being hit by a flying hairbrush. "I hate you, Lonnie!" Tunie shouted. "You're a terrible sister. You don't care anything for any of us. You just care about stupid Alex Moony."

Marty stayed well ahead of them as they walked to church. He always steered clear when she and Tunie fought, and she didn't blame him. It was never pretty, especially with Tunie's temper. All the way there, she stomped, and huffed, and glared. It was all

Lonnie could do to keep her composure. She was relieved to finally see the spire of the church come into view, the chime of the bells marking the hour, welcoming her.

While she was relieved to have the distraction of Uncle Phillip's sermons, her mind wandered anxiously. His words floated over her head, acting as a background noise to her thoughts. The discovery of Alex's money made everything more difficult. She needed to give it back as soon as possible. Today after church, she determined.

And then there was the dance. She debated back and forth in her mind how she might present the dance to Alex that might sound the most enticing. What if he said no? Her stomach knotted queasily. In reality, she didn't have a right to ask him to come, did she? Inviting him to the dance would be asking him to make a spectacle of himself, even placing him in the dangerous position of being everyone's target of hostility again. She couldn't do that to him, could she? But then she knew he'd enjoy the music. Perhaps they'd get to dance. And if she gave him the money now, would he leave before the dance? Oh, why did it have to be so complicated? She wrung her hands until her finger joints ached.

When the final prayer was said, Lonnie nearly leapt out of her seat. She stood on tiptoe to see over the crowd of rising parishioners leaving the chapel, but to her consternation, she didn't see Alex anywhere.

"You're looking for Moony aren't you?" Tunie folded her arms across her chest, glowering.

Lonnie ignored her sister and walked down the aisle to talk with her uncle.

In between saying farewell to members of the congregation, she managed to squeeze in. "Have you seen Alex today?"

Uncle Phillip shook his head. "I'm afraid not."

"Oh." Her heart sank.

"I'm a little concerned I haven't seen him, actually," he said. "He told me he'd be here. It's possible he could be ill. Or perhaps he didn't feel like coming." He studied Lonnie sternly. "You aren't thinking of seeking him out, are you? And I hope you most certainly aren't thinking of going to his apartment alone."

Lonnie blushed fiercely, revealing she'd been thinking that very thing.

Uncle Phillip frowned. "You have more sense than that, Appalone." He glanced around. "Let me finish up here, and I'll walk over with you myself. I was contemplating a visit anyway."

She sighed with relief. "Thank you." She wound her way back through the remaining people to Tunie and Marty, both of them frowning.

"Can we go home yet?" Marty whined.

"Tunie, why don't you and Marty go? I'll be going with Uncle Phillip somewhere. Don't expect me for lunch. I'll be home in an hour or two."

Tunie scowled, stepping closer, not bothering to lower her voice. "You've found a way to meet with *Moony*, haven't you?" Marty snorted in laughter, but stopped instantly at Lonnie's glare.

"His name is Alex *Moon*, and you just mind your own business," Lonnie retorted.

Her sister stomped off with Marty in tow. Lonnie watched them go with a wary relief, hoping Tunie wouldn't say anything to their mother.

Twenty minutes later, Lonnie walked beside her uncle on their way to Alex's house. They climbed the outside staircase of Mr. Hardy's garage and knocked on the screen door. After a long moment, the door opened.

Alex was in striped pajama bottoms and a white undershirt, his hair disheveled and his eyes squinting from the bright light streaming into his face from the open door.

Lonnie's face burned, and she quickly turned away.

"Lonnie." The warning in Uncle Phillip's voice was enough to send her right back down the stairs to wait at the bottom. The image of him barefoot, sleepy, with his hair sticking out returned, and she erupted into giggles. Her uncle closed the screen door and descended the stairs.

"It appears Alex has a bad cold," Uncle Phillip said. "He felt he should sleep so he'd be fit for work tomorrow. But he's touched we came all this way and said he'll be out in a moment to have a word. I tried to insist he stay in bed, but knowing you were here, no doubt, was motivation enough."

Lonnie colored at her uncle's comment. "I didn't want to disturb him. We should come back another time perhaps?" Again, her eyes traveled up to his door. She didn't really want that at all. She wanted to talk to him now.

After a few minutes, a properly dressed and hastily groomed Alex appeared. "I'm sorry. I had no idea you'd worry about me. And I had no idea it was so late in the day." His voice was raspy, and Lonnie immediately repented her selfishness.

"I'm sorry, Alex. We really should've tried to call or something."

He shook his head. "I don't have a telephone. It's all right. I'm glad to see you."

Uncle Phillip cleared his throat. "I'm going to take a walk to the end of the lane. Mr. Rhodes's mums have just come into bloom, and they're quite breathtaking. I've been meaning to go see them. You won't mind if I take a peek will you?"

Lonnie smiled in gratitude. She could tell he was leaving reluctantly, but at least he was willing to make himself scarce for a few minutes. After watching her uncle disappear down the sidewalk, Lonnie turned back to find Alex watching her.

She blushed under his unswerving gaze and then the nicely arranged speech she had in her head went to pieces. Her attention was caught by Alex wrapping his arms around himself. Even though he wore a cardigan, he trembled with cold.

"I shouldn't keep you. Look at you. You really should be warm in bed."

His hand shot out and gently grabbed her arm. "No. Please don't leave. I'm fine." He pulled his hand away and went back to hugging himself.

Silence lingered for a time, and the money seemed to beckon from its hiding place. She needed to give it to him. Right now.

She fumbled inside her purse as thoughts squeezed in, building the pressure in her head. He'd be grateful to have his money back. He might stay one or two more days, maybe a week, to finish things up, then leave town. She'd never see him again.

Her fingers found and grasped the money. Breathing became a trial, as if she had to draw each breath through thick jelly. This was for the best, and it was the right thing to do. It was.

Blood pounded through her veins, throbbing in her temples.

She made the mistake of glancing up at Alex. The sun made amber glints appear in his eyes, and his lips curved up in a patient smile. He spoke, and she knew she'd lost the battle.

"I heard there was a dance coming up. You're helping your aunt, aren't you?"

She gasped from holding her breath, and her heart fluttered. Perhaps . . . after the dance might be a better time to give it back.

"Yes." She cleared her throat and relinquished the hold on the paper bills, clasping her hands behind her back. "Alex, I wanted to ask you . . ."

Alex's mouth cocked in a grin, no doubt entertained by her nervousness. "Whatever the question is, the answer is yes." He was teasing her.

"But I haven't even told you yet." She frowned but dove right in. "Do you want to come to the fundraising dance on Saturday? Not necessarily with me because I have to go early to help Aunt Millie, but would you come? We've got a fantastic band lined up. It might be nice to get out for some dancing. I just thought, even though you don't know many people, you'd at least enjoy the music and—and I'll be there." She was relieved it had all come spilling out, though her stomach churned from *what* had spilled out. And she felt like she'd betrayed him somehow.

The grin hadn't left his face. "Sounds great." Something caught in his throat, and he hacked out a grating cough. "I'll be there if I can beat this cold, that is."

Lonnie managed a weak smile. "I hope you feel better."

He nodded. "Thanks. So do I." He glanced down the sidewalk and drew her gaze. Uncle Phillip was returning. "I'll see you on Saturday then."

As Uncle Phillip reached them, they bade each other farewell. She watched Alex go back up the stairs, his shivering much more pronounced.

On the way back to her house, guilt nagged at her for dragging him out of bed, and she berated herself for being so determined at his expense. Besides that, the money still remained stubbornly in her purse, though she couldn't help the relief that he'd be around for a little while longer.

When she got home, her mother was at the table with three of her friends playing Euchre. She'd forgotten today was her mother's day to host. Tunie and Marty were no doubt upstairs staying occupied in their rooms as they usually did on Euchre days. Lonnie entered the kitchen.

"I'm home, Mother."

"There you are," her mother said, still focusing on her cards.

"Lonnie, dear. How are you?" Mrs. Cooper from next door glanced up from her cards, her reading glasses perched precariously on her long, straight nose.

Lonnie nodded cordially in greeting. "I'm fine. And you?"

"Not so well, I'm afraid."

"Yes, that last round wasn't so kind to us." Mrs. Alice Marshall sighed. She was a fifty-year old version of her daughter Gladys—beautiful and fashionable with perfectly set, shining brown hair, manicured nails, and glowing skin.

Harriet's partner was Mrs. Simmons from the Simmons Grocery. She was new to the group of women since their last member moved away to work at the RCA factory in Bloomington. Having her here made Lonnie squirm with self-consciousness. There was no way the woman had already forgotten Lonnie's recent public demonstrations at her store with Alex and the group of gossipy women.

"I'm just glad I'm finally figuring out the rules," Mrs. Simmons admitted.

"You're doing fine." Harriet smiled.

"Lonnie, dear," Mrs. Marshall said. "Your mother tells me you've got a beau—Teddy Stanton? He's a fine catch."

"Well, he—he isn't exactly my beau," Lonnie stuttered in surprise.

Mrs. Cooper laughed. "I've seen him trailing after you like a lost puppy, Lonnie. He's certainly besotted with *you*."

Lonnie's face burned. She wished she could make an easy escape. "I don't know about that. He's just an old friend."

"Well, Teddy is a far better friend than that what's-his-name Moon fellow," Mrs. Simmons said, her face all prim and self-righteous. "I really don't see how you can have such an acquaintance, Lonnie. Think of your reputation."

The women turned to stare at her, waiting for her reply. Lonnie's eyes darted to her mother, and the cold clutch of fear made her head swim from what she saw there.

Her mother broke out into a light laugh. "Really, Joan, I think you're overreacting. You know how she helps my brother with charity work. That's all it is. She's being charitable out of the kindness of her own heart, and there's nothing to read into."

Mrs. Simmons sniffed, and the others went back to their card hands. "If you say so."

"Well," Mrs. Marshall said, "I think you and Teddy make a wonderful match. You'd better not let that one go, Lonnie, dear."

Her mother was quick to speak up. "He's such a responsible young man too, and fair. He does a fine job running the factory when his father's away on business."

Mrs. Cooper frowned. "It's a shame he's not fit to join up for the war. I think he'd make a wonderful soldier, but I suppose he does his bit in his own way."

"He does." Lonnie spoke loudly, relieved the topic had turned. "It isn't his fault his health is what it is, but he works hard just like the rest of us. There's more than one way to fight for your country. So we have no reason to pity him."

"Well said." Mrs. Cooper and the other women nodded their heads.

Mrs. Marshall, however, batted her eyelashes in a slow, sly way. "I think it's obvious where Lonnie's affections lie." The woman tittered in laughter, and her mother radiated elation.

Lonnie plastered on a smile and excused herself. Once upstairs in her room, she shut her door and kicked her bed in frustration. "Those women. They're enough to make me scream!"

Tunie looked up from painting her nails a dark pink. "Why?"

"Oh, never mind." Lonnie plopped down on her bed and removed her shoes. After a moment she said, "Did you tell Mother where I went with Uncle Phillip?"

Tunie screwed up her face and stuck out her tongue. "I've got better things to do with my time than worry about what stupid things you get up to."

Lonnie turned away and jammed her pillow over her head. Shutting out the whole miserable world seemed the only logical thing to do at this point.

Chapter Fifteen

LONNIE MADE UP with Tunie just in time for the dance. The money was still a tender issue, though Tunie had stopped being resentful about it. Their disagreements usually didn't last very long. Lonnie was always relieved when the tension blew over and they could happily exist together again.

She sat with Tunie, crowding around the mirror of Tunie's small vanity, applying make-up. They were dressed in slips and stockings, their hair up in rollers. Three magazines were splayed open on the vanity for them to study.

"Well, look at her eyes, Lonnie. They're demure, yet mysterious. I think if I add a bit up here, I could get the same effect . . ." Lonnie held still as her sister applied the eye make-up. She rarely put on more than a little blush and lipstick, but for the fundraiser dance, more was definitely called for.

"There." Tunie moved back to survey her work. "What do you think?"

Lonnie leaned forward to study the effect. "It's odd."

"That's because you're not used to it. Here, let me do the other side."

Lonnie froze as Tunie worked on her other eye. "Who are you looking forward to dancing with?" Lonnie asked, trying hard not to blink.

"Oh, I don't know. I'll just be grateful to dance with anyone under the age of thirty."

Lonnie laughed, and Tunie cried out. "Watch it. I almost gouged your eye."

"Sorry."

"Is Alex coming?" Tunie's tone was guarded.

"He said he was."

"Are you going to dance with him?"

"I was planning on it. Why?"

"Oh, nothing. I needed to know to prepare myself."

"For what?"

"For any resulting spectacle." Tunie studied her work. "There. It's perfect. Now, don't touch it."

Lonnie turned to face her sister. "What do you mean—spectacle?"

Tunie shook her head in disbelief. "Lonnie, you're so blind. Can't you see Teddy is wildly jealous of how much attention you pay to Alex? Of all people, why did you have to make friends with *him*?"

Lonnie frowned. "Well, why not? I dare you to get to know him, Tunie. He's not a crazy Japanese spy like you and everyone else think." She closed her eyes briefly. "Let's talk about something else. I don't want to argue with you about this again. Can't we just have fun and be civil to one another?"

Tunie smiled. "Oh, all right. How about this? In honor of the charity dance, I promise to have charitable feelings towards Alex—at least for today."

Lonnie instantly cheered. "Would you?"

Tunie nodded. "And speaking of charity . . ." She went over to their closet, rummaged around and turned to reveal a beautiful, red floral-patterned dress. "I took pity on you and got you this dress."

Lonnie stood with a gasp. "Oh, Tunie. It's gorgeous. Where in the world did you get it?"

Tunie shrugged. "I've been saving up some money, some *different* money, and when I saw this dress on sale I bought it. I had to take it in a bit, but it wasn't hard. It's made of that rayon fabric everyone loves so much. You haven't had a new dress for ages, and I couldn't stand the thought of you going to this dance wearing the same old thing."

Lonnie took the dress, relishing its cool, silky feel. She turned to the mirror and held it up to her shoulders. The neckline crisscrossed in the front and was held together with a pretty pin. The sleeves were short and the length of the skirt hit just below her knees. She turned to Tunie, tears glistening in her eyes, and hugged her tightly. "Thank you. I love it."

Tunie sniffled and wiped her nose. "Well, try it on. I've been dying to see you wear it."

Lonnie slipped on the dress. She marveled at her sister's handiwork for it fit perfectly. Admiring the dress in the mirror, she turned back and forth. "You don't think it's too form fitting do you?" she asked tentatively.

"No."

"I just don't want to make the boys go *too* wild." Lonnie grinned, feeling daring and saucy.

Tunie laughed.

***

The strains of jazzy music reached Alex even before he got to the doors of the high school gymnasium. He lingered in the shadows and relished the cold night air before going inside.

He didn't like to admit it, but he was a little scared. It wasn't that he'd never been the minority in a crowd before. And it wasn't even that he knew how much people in this town disliked him. What made his palms damp and his heart palpitate was Lonnie. He'd already made an idiot of himself showing up at her office and gawking at her with Reverend Hicks as witness. There was something unnerving about her that made him throw his common sense out the window. But to do that in the middle of a potentially hostile crowd? Was it really worth it? Could he muster the self-control?

The doors to the building opened and shut as more people arrived, the music wavering between loud and muffled with every swing of the door. Alex closed his eyes and focused on the rhythm of the drums to steady his heart.

Decision made, he squared his shoulders, stepped out of the shadows, and went in. His stomach dropped. A sign boldly advertised that all ticket sales raised money for war defense bonds. Why was he surprised? Of course, something like this would support the war effort.

He gritted his teeth, but paid for and claimed his ticket from the skeptical-looking girl at the table in the foyer. The wail of the clarinets, blare of the trumpets, and beat of the bass drum hit him full force as he entered the gym. For the first time Alex relaxed. He had to resist tapping his feet and snapping his fingers. A smile slid onto his face. He'd forgotten how much he missed dancing.

Alex surveyed the dancing couples spinning around the room. Everyone appeared so happy and carefree. He scanned the throng for people he recognized. Deep down, though, he only had eyes for Lonnie.

The room was dim with strings of lights hung along with festive red, white, and blue streamers. A large banner proudly stating "River Bluff Victory Dance" hung at one end of the room where the live band played an upbeat number on the decorated stage. The dance floor was nearly full while little knots of people along the fringes talked and enjoyed refreshments.

Out of the crowd, he picked out Tunie on the dance floor. He spotted Gladys and Rose, who were talking animatedly with Walter. Other than that, he didn't see any people he recognized right away. Discouragement started creeping up on him. To keep it at bay, he wandered, getting glares and questioning annoyance as always. He thought he'd been in town long enough for the curiosity to wear off, but apparently not.

His eyes found the refreshment table, and he froze. There was Lonnie looking a vision in a flattering red dress. She was so incredibly beautiful, beaming and nodding at people enjoying the refreshments. He knew he was done for. Her eyes sparkled, her motions were graceful. He swallowed with difficulty. He might as well go straight back home, because he was going to behave like a total idiot.

He was about to turn tail when a young man he recognized as Lonnie's friend, Teddy, walked right across his path heading for the drinks table. Teddy spoke with Lonnie, apparently asking her for a dance. She smiled, but shook her head, gesturing at the table. Teddy turned away, his face crushed in disappointment. This startled Alex, but it gave way to smug satisfaction. She turned him down?

After Teddy was well away, Alex approached the table. She was back to filling cups with punch. It was a minute before she noticed him.

"Alex, you came." She looked pleased to see him which gave him a surge of happiness.

"I did." He glanced back over his shoulder. "Did Teddy ask you to dance?"

"Teddy? Yes, he did, but I'm so busy here helping my aunt, I don't feel right in leaving just now."

"That was stupid."

She blinked in surprise. "Pardon?"

"Teddy. Not you. He just left the most beautiful girl in the room standing here. If he'd wanted to dance with you that badly he should've been more determined."

Reaching forward, he grabbed her hand and led her from around the table.

"What are you doing? I know I told you I'd save you a dance, but it's still so early yet. Aunt Millie is desperate for my help."

"I'm sure she expects you to dance some of the time." He pulled her to the dance floor.

"Well, I really don't think I should yet. She needs me."

"And I need a partner for this next dance."

"There are plenty of other girls—" she protested.

"Yes, but they're not you."

Her cheeks flamed red, but she gave in. His arm went around her waist, and they danced to the new, slower strains of the band playing "Hang Out the Stars in Indiana."

Her hair brushed his cheek. For a moment, Alex closed his eyes, allowing himself to enjoy the light scent of her sweet-smelling perfume. With that action, he was filled with a sensation that could only be described as an ache. It tugged from a recess of his heart he'd never been aware of until now. He realized it had been building up over time and wondered when it had started.

This woman he held in his arms was too perplexing to comprehend. She talked to him as an equal, laughed easily in his presence, didn't balk at their touch. She'd planted a kiss on his cheek, for heaven's sake. She allowed him to pull her close and hold her in his arms.

He was reminded of the time at the library. His holding her then had been unintentional, but he knew he'd never take that moment back for anything. And now he had a legitimate excuse to hold her, however finite—just to the end of the song. His grip tightened slightly on her hand, he inched her body closer to his.

They stepped easily to the music as they moved around the room. It was wonderful to blend into the crowd in the dimness, for once not being noticed or ridiculed. Holding her felt so natural, which overwhelmed him with all sorts of frightening questions he didn't want to ask himself.

After a moment of dancing in silence, Lonnie spoke up. "Teddy's not stupid, you know."

"I know. I'm sorry."

"Oh," she mumbled. "Well, as long as you're sorry."

"I am, but I'm not."

"What?"

"I know I shouldn't have called him stupid. I'm sorry. But I'm not sorry he didn't get to dance with you."

She turned her face away, but not before he caught her discreet little smile. "You're just infuriatingly persistent."

Alex laughed. "Now who's calling names?"

She opened her mouth to retort, but a shadow loomed over them, and someone tapped his shoulder. Alex stopped dancing. An annoyed-looking Walter was leaning forward in an intimidating way. "I'd like to cut in, if you don't mind."

To avoid causing a scene, Alex stepped away to accommodate. He was surprised to feel Lonnie's hand tighten the grip on his.

"I don't want you to cut in, Walter," Lonnie said firmly.

Alex felt as taken back as Walter looked. "You don't?"

"No."

Walter spluttered. "But—"

"I see Gladys over there talking to Mr. Avery." Lonnie jerked her chin in that direction. "He seems completely enamored. I'd cut in over there if I were you."

Walter did a double take, and with a scowl, he left.

Alex continued to stare in wonder at Lonnie. He finally took her back in his arms.

He was curious. "Why didn't you want to dance with Walter?"

"I never dance with him. He's a terrible dancer, and I'm slightly vain about my feet."

Alex tried to hide his grin. "Is that the only reason?"

Lonnie paused. "No."

"Well?"

"Frankly, I didn't like how he was talking to you."

"Isn't he your friend, though? Surely friends are entitled to dance together."

"Yes, we're friends, but I never dance with Walter, remember?"

Alex decided to lay off, strangely pleased and annoyed she'd stuck up for him yet again. The conflicting emotions clashed inside of him like cymbals from the band.

Lonnie met his gaze. "Besides, we're friends too, aren't we?"

"Are we?" He furrowed his brow.

Her cheeks flamed. "I would hope so and that I'm not just presuming."

At last, he laughed and relief passed over her face.

"I'm sorry," he said. "Yes. I'd like to be able to call you my friend."

She nodded. "Then you may. But I hope that means teasing will be kept to a strict minimum."

"I don't know if that'll be possible. I love how easy you are to tease." He grinned as she shook her head in disapproval.

The dance ended and everyone clapped. The time had passed too quickly.

"I really should get back to help my aunt," Lonnie said.

"She won't miss you for another three dances at least."

"Alex, I promised her. We can dance again later."

"All right, fine. Then I'm helping too."

"Suit yourself," Lonnie replied. He followed her to where Aunt Millie was red-faced and bustling, trying to keep up with the demand for food and drink.

"Oh, there you are, Lonnie. I'd wondered where you'd gone."

"Alex stole me away for a dance," she replied with an imperious glance in his direction. He smirked in return.

Aunt Millie finally saw him and smiled. "Why, Alex, I didn't know you were here. Good for you, getting her out to dance. I've told her she should take a break to have a good time, but when she makes herself so indispensible, how can I send her away?"

"I wish I could answer that, Mrs. Smithfield. However, if you're in need of more help, I'm here to offer my services."

"Why, thank you. That would be wonderful. I'm going to see if the next bowl of punch is ready. Could you put these cookies out? And these sandwiches need to be arranged. And more cups of punch need to be ladled. Oh dear, we're nearly out."

"Don't worry, Aunt Millie. We'll take care of it."

They kept busy after that. Lonnie arranged the food, and Alex scooped out the remaining punch. When a couple came up for some refreshment, they glared at Alex with wrinkled noses and exchanged whispers. They avoided the punch bowl, but took a few cookies and left. Alex didn't think much of it until it happened a half dozen times more. His anger began to smolder beneath the surface.

Lonnie must have sensed something, because after the last avoidance of his drink offerings, she reached out and touched his forearm. "Are you all right?"

He gritted his teeth and nodded. Aunt Millie arrived with the new bowl of punch wheeled in on a cart. Alex helped her move it to the table, and she left again with the empty bowl. He began working to fill more cups, but this time he kept to his task and didn't try to meet anyone's eyes when they approached.

After another fifteen minutes of snubbing, Alex was fed up. He wanted to spend time with Lonnie, but not like this.

"I'm going out for some air."

"Okay." Her voice was reluctant, worried.

Trying to keep his face passive for her sake, Alex made his way through the crowd and outside. The door banged shut behind him, and he took a deep breath. His stress left his limbs in a rush, and he propped himself against the trunk of a nearby tree.

He wasn't alone for long.

"Hey, Jap."

Alex didn't bother to turn around.

"Hey! Face me when I'm talking to you." A hand on his shoulder jerked him around. A scowling Teddy stood before him.

"What do you want?" Alex tried to keep his voice even, though his anger was mounting again.

Teddy shoved his fists into his pocket. "I wanted to have a word. About Lonnie."

"What about her?" The tension pressed in on him like a balloon waiting to pop.

"Stay away from her. She's my girl, and she's worth a whole lot more than a nasty Jap like you."

"And what if I say no?"

A wavering uncertainty passed over Teddy's face. It was quickly replaced with a glare. "I'd have to teach you a lesson, of course."

Alex shrugged. "All right. But first, let's set something straight."

"What's that?" Teddy asked, stepping closer, threatening him.

"I'm not Japanese." Alex drew back his fist and punched him hard, full in the face. It connected with a crack.

Teddy stumbled back, while holding his bleeding nose and cursing. He lunged forward wildly and tackled Alex from the side. Wrestling, they fell to the ground and pummeled each other. Alex managed to break away and get to his feet, but he didn't flee. He wiped his mouth and found blood on his hand. He waited for Teddy to stagger up, and they were at it again, throwing punches and growling curses.

Alex was so busy taking out his anger on Teddy, he hardly noticed the small crowd that had gathered. No one stopped them. After some time, they were both heaving and tiring, but they kept lunging at each other, insults and hits flying as fast as they could manage.

"I hate you, you stinkin' yellow Jap." Teddy snarled, aiming another blow at Alex's head.

Alex fought back with a viciousness he didn't know he had. "I'm Korean American, you bastard!" He landed more punches, his knuckles aching and bloody. "You ignorant lowlifes can't even tell the difference."

Teddy slammed him against the wall of the building and pinned him to the brick. His breath was hot on Alex's face. "You'll never be an American, no matter how hard you try." His whisper was harsh, grating. "Just go back to your own country where you belong."

Alex roared and lashed out again, his fury freshly kindled. He was slipping further and further out of control as he battled with Teddy. From beyond the commotion they made with their scuffling, Lonnie's gasp and frantic shouting burst painfully through Alex's brain. "Stop it. Both of you, just stop!"

Walter pushed his way through the crowd, grabbed Alex's collar and separated him from Teddy. Walter managed a vicious kick to Alex's stomach, making him groan and swing out in defense. He missed. Walter was much bigger, and Alex was worn out.

Lonnie's shocked and hurt face swam into his view, which made Alex's rage come screeching to a halt. His arms fell to his sides, and he wrenched his collar away from Walter. He and Teddy took deep breaths. They almost simultaneously started coughing as they got their wind. Thanks to the leftovers of his recent cold, coughing caused painful, sharp jabs to his lungs.

Mrs. Smithfield arrived with her face full of fury. He cringed away from it. "A fine pair of fools you are. I can't believe this. You realize you've ruined this evening for everyone, don't you?" Her voice cut through the air like a well-sharpened knife. "I would've thought better of you. If only you could see yourselves." She scoffed. "I'm ashamed for you both."

She put her hands on her hips. "Both of you should go home. Now." She turned away. "All right, everyone. It's all over." She gestured, shooing everyone back into the building. "Please go back inside. There's nothing to see anymore. Walter, you too. Inside."

Everyone obeyed without a word. Everyone but Lonnie.

Teddy spoke up. "Lonnie, I can explain."

"Just shut up, Teddy Stanton," she snapped. "I don't want to hear it."

Her eyes found Alex, and he trembled with shame.

Teddy glanced back and forth between them, scowled, and skulked away into the shadows. Alex didn't move. He was frozen with the depths of his humiliation. What had his actions just cost him?

She approached him, her lips turned down into a frown, her eyes filled with sadness. He stared at her, not knowing what to do or say. He had no excuses. No explanations. He weakly hoped she'd just somehow know and understand.

She stood in front of him, and then to his astonishment, she reached up and gently touched his lip. He jerked back in surprise.

"You're bleeding." Her words were simple, but they overwhelmed him.

"I'm sorry," he whispered, his eyes never leaving her face.

She pressed her lips together and nodded. "I know." She paused and reached for his hand. "Come on. Come with me."

He followed her without question, too ashamed to do anything different.

***

Once she was alone with Alex, she took in his bloodied, bruising face. This was all her fault. Guilt and remorse blossomed inside Lonnie. If she said it aloud, he'd probably deny it had anything to do with her, but she knew if she'd never invited him to come in the first place he would've stayed well away on his own.

The least she could do was take care of him after putting him into that situation. Taking his hand, she led him home. She was glad he didn't try to stop her.

Just as she pushed through her gate, his hand pulled back. "I don't think—"

"It's fine. Mother goes to bed early, and Marty's been asleep for ages. No one will bother you here."

He gave in and followed her inside. Lonnie ignored the nervousness gnawing at her. It was the first time he'd been inside her house. She switched on a light in the kitchen and led him to a chair at the table. "Wait here."

She went upstairs to the tiny closet in the bathroom. Rummaging around, she found some antiseptic, bandages, and gauze. When she returned and sat in front of him, Alex looked so contrite she had trouble hiding her smile. Though once she began working on his cuts, her solemn mood returned.

She worked in silence, the quiet of the kitchen broken only by Alex's occasional hiss of pain. With each dab of the alcohol-soaked gauze, she felt the pain of the cut as if it were her own, deepening her guilt and sorrow over what had transpired.

Lonnie was also overwhelmed and frightened of being so near him—alone. She was mere inches away. Every detail of his face was plain to see—the strong curve of his jaw, his lightly tanned skin, the shine of his black hair, normally so perfectly combed, but now tousled from his fight. She wanted to smooth back his hair, she wanted to take his clean-shaven face in her hands . . .

Her hands trembled as she struggled to smother these thoughts. It wasn't right. She shouldn't be thinking such things. She couldn't have these feelings for Alex Moon—it would only put him in danger, and no one would accept them anyway.

Near the end of her work, she bowed her head, fighting back the burning in her eyes.

"I don't want you to pity me." Alex's tenor voice filled the room, startling her.

"I don't." She paused, trying to hide the unsteadiness in her voice. "It's—it's me I pity."

Alex frowned. "You? Why?"

Lonnie stood, her heartbeat galloping. She needed to get away from him. "I've done the best I can. You should probably go home now."

Alex got to his feet as well. "I still don't understand."

She smiled sadly and walked him to the front door. "I'm a pitiful creature, that's all. Goodnight, Alex."

He gripped the doorknob tightly as if he might stay if she asked him. But she didn't.

Once he was gone, she closed the door and wept.

Chapter Sixteen

LONNIE SAT AT the kitchen table picking at her oatmeal. Marty chattered away to their mother who sipped her tea and read the morning paper. Tunie finished making the scrambled eggs and toast. She settled next to Lonnie, placing the steaming plate on the table.

"What's wrong with you?" Tunie asked. "You've been quiet all morning."

Lonnie shook her head.

"Still mooning after *Moony*?" she asked with a glance in their mother's direction.

Lonnie frowned. "Will you stop that? I'm not mooning after anyone. I'm just upset about the fight last night. If anything, it's my fault the whole thing happened."

Tunie shook her head. "What did I tell you before about there being a spectacle?" She paused before adding, "Look, Lonnie. Don't blame yourself for what those two dummies got themselves into."

"But I was the one who invited Alex to come," Lonnie said, trying to keep her voice low. "If it wasn't for me, they wouldn't have fought."

Tunie snorted and whispered. "I seriously doubt it. That fight was bound to happen sometime. It's not like you twisted his arm. Alex made the choice to come. He made the choice to fight with Teddy. That's all there is to it."

"Now you're making it sound like it's all Alex's fault."

Tunie rolled her eyes. "I'm not blaming anyone. I'm only saying you shouldn't be blaming yourself."

Her sister turned away to get herself a drink, and Lonnie scowled, stabbing a particularly large lump of tan oatmeal. "But you still think Alex is to blame, don't you?" she mumbled darkly.

She took her bowl to the sink. "Mother, I'm leaving. I'm going to see Mrs. Chan. I'll be back after lunch."

Harriet frowned. "I don't recall saying you could go back there. I don't like the idea of you visiting that old Chink."

"Please, Mother. She hardly gets any visitors, and I promised Uncle Phillip I'd keep an eye on her. She's getting so old."

"Oh, all right." Harriet huffed. "So long as you're back before dinner. And don't forget about getting your chores done. I shouldn't have to nag you all the time."

"I know. Thank you." Lonnie went upstairs, pulled on her sweater and left the house. The bite of the morning air was bracing, and it was just enough to set her thoughts to tumbling over and around in her mind.

The image of Alex, blood smeared on his face, the regret in his eyes, dominated her mind. As did the defiance in Teddy's face, his expression of loathing aimed toward Alex. She burned with anger at the whole situation. Why had she been so selfish in wanting Alex to be at the dance? Had it really been so important he be there? She wondered what had passed between Teddy and Alex that had brought on the fight. Had Teddy teased or insulted him?

Lonnie stopped walking long enough to stamp her foot. Why had Alex fought with Teddy anyway? She began walking again, faster, her thoughts jumping to a different track. Didn't Alex have enough sense to keep out of trouble? He could've just walked away. He could have chosen not to fight. Why did he have to be so reckless?

By the time she reached Xiao Lin's house, Lonnie was out of breath, her throat constricting painfully from suppressed tears. Xiao Lin opened the door. "Appalone, what is it? Are you all right?" She let Lonnie in and led her to a chair. The tears fell as soon as she sat, though she tried to resist. She'd had her cry the night before, but these new tears were not for pitying herself.

Xiao Lin let Lonnie collect herself. Finally, she spoke up. "I'm sorry. Something upsetting has happened, and I'm still trying to sort it all out."

Xiao Lin nodded, but she didn't ask questions. After a few minutes, she reached for Lonnie's hand. "Come with me. I find my frustrations are best worked out in the kitchen."

Lonnie followed her and was amazed to see the table was taken up by bowls of long, white quartered cabbages, their leaf tips green and wrinkly. "Your timing couldn't have been better. I just pulled out a few of my mother's old recipes and came across hers for Korean *kimchi*."

"*Kimchi?*" Lonnie repeated the word, curious. "What is that?"

Xiao Lin's face wrinkled in a smile. "*Kimchi* is a type of pickled cabbage."

"Like sauerkraut?"

"Not exactly. It's a staple of the Korean diet though. I'd forgotten how nice it is to have help when you make it. I got in a little over my head. Look at all this cabbage." She laughed.

"I'd love to help." Lonnie washed her hands and tied on the apron offered to her. "Do you cook it? Or eat it raw?"

"You ferment it. So it does take a few days before it's ready. I've already quartered the cabbage heads, salted them, and let them sit to draw out the juices. Now we rinse them and make the *kimchi sok*. It's what gives *kimchi* its distinct taste along with dried, crushed red peppers and homemade fish sauce."

The women worked in silence. Once the cabbages were rinsed, Xiao Lin set her to slicing carrots, radish, and green onions. They combined the thinly sliced vegetables in the rich, crimson mixture.

"Now," Xiao Lin instructed, "we coat each leaf of cabbage with the paste. This is what takes a while." She smiled as if in apology, and they both sat at the low table. Pulling on clean rubber gloves, they got to work.

Lonnie's tumultuous thoughts returned, and her mental defenses began to break down. With each leaf she coated in red, her frustration leaked out. She thought about everything her friends had ever said about Alex. She thought of Tunie's animosity, Mr. Pickering's unjustified prejudice, those women's vicious gossip at the grocery store, her mother's friends' snide comments—how she felt so powerless to change anything.

Wasn't this war they were fighting supposed to be about change? About protecting the freedom of the civilized world? She thought about the sight of Alex and Teddy's violence toward one another—their own miniaturized world war. She thought shamefully of how she'd gotten him into that mess in the first place. And then the guilt came crashing down. How utterly selfish she'd been keeping him here. Alex was, in effect, her prisoner. He'd left one jail cell only to step right into another one of her making.

Lonnie bowed her head. Tears escaped and dripped one by one. She wiped her arm across her eyes and turned away, drawing Xiao Lin's attention.

"Appalone? What is it? Did you try a piece? I should have warned you it's very spicy." She studied her face.

Lonnie shook her head. "It isn't that."

Xiao Lin's mouth spread in sudden understanding. "Have you sorted everything out?"

Tears streaming, Lonnie nodded and broke down into full-out sobs. She sagged against the table, relying on its strength. Xiao Lin removed her gloves and slowly rubbed her back and waited for Lonnie's crying to fade to occasional hiccups.

"Oh, Xiao Lin," Lonnie sighed, removing her own rubber gloves and wiping her cheeks with a handkerchief she dug out of her pocket. "I've been such a selfish fool." She crumpled the fabric in her hands, wishing she could as easily crush the dreadful shame that threatened to suffocate her.

"Are you any worse of a fool than anyone else? We all do things we regret. Even me." The old woman's eyes smiled, and Lonnie's pain eased a fraction.

"I guess not, but I've done something horrible, and I can't forgive myself."

Xiao Lin didn't say anything, only waited. Lonnie appreciated how she didn't pry, didn't judge. But Lonnie needed to speak the words aloud—to acknowledge what she'd done wrong. Only then would her burden ease.

Lonnie stared down at the wad of pink fabric, creased and stained with bitter tears. "When Alex first came, my sister found some money at the train station. She didn't know who it belonged to, and so she kept it. I only discovered this about a week ago. It . . . it had a note inside. Written in Korean." Lonnie looked up at her friend who nodded silently, encouraging her to go on.

"I knew right away it was Alex's money, and I determined to give it back to him, but I decided to wait until after the dance. I wanted him to come, and I was afraid he'd leave if I gave it to him before."

She told Xiao Lin about the fight between Alex and Teddy at the dance. "His fight last night with Teddy was my fault. Because of my selfishness he's been hurt; he's been subjected to even more prejudice and hatred. It's not even just the money. I shouldn't have invited him in the first place. And now this has happened. For all I know he could lose his job because of Teddy. He could be forced out of town." She gasped. He'd have nowhere to go. What had she done?

Xiao Lin's hand gently rested on Lonnie's arm. Lonnie's panic was arrested as she waited for the woman to speak. The small clock chimed on the mantle in the living room and continued ticking relentlessly, serving as the heartbeat to Lonnie's anticipation.

Finally, Xiao Lin spoke. "This prejudice and hate you describe is not something he can escape from, Appalone, and it isn't something of your making."

Lonnie listened, the words sinking deep.

"Alex needs to learn to face this part of his life. He needs to learn what to do with it and how to overcome his personal battles. This isn't something you can do for him, Appalone, but it is something you can help him with."

Lonnie hung her head again. "But do I even have that right anymore? After what I've withheld from him?"

Xiao Lin smiled. "It isn't too late. Perhaps the best route would be to tell him what you've done and then allow him to decide. I know I haven't met him yet, but from what I can tell, you're a special friend to him. If he's wise, he won't let go of that so easily."

Lonnie was still troubled, but her heart was lighter after getting everything out. She nodded, determined. "You're right. I need to tell him, but I can't say I'm not afraid."

Xiao Lin smiled. "Fear can work to your advantage, Appalone, but don't let it conquer you. Making things right wasn't meant to be easy, but you'll never regret the effort."

Lonnie took her hand in gratitude and squeezed it. "Thank you."

***

A long moan escaped Alex's lips as he pushed himself up to sit on the edge of his bed. He clutched his side and winced, but even that action sent splintering needles of pain shooting through him. It felt like he'd been run over by a milk truck. He slowly stood, testing his balance, and hobbled over to the small mirror atop his dresser.

He moaned again at seeing his reflection, not in pain, but in dismay. A bruise had spread across his cheekbone, and his lip was swollen where it had been cut. Other than a few more cuts, it wasn't *too* bad, though he couldn't vouch for the rest of his body. No doubt, Teddy looked worse. Alex laughed at this thought, but it morphed quickly into a cry of pain. He pulled up his shirt to see an ugly bruise across the side of his chest. He felt it gingerly, hoping he didn't have a cracked rib.

He took his time dressing, and after a quick bite to eat, headed downstairs to the garage. Mike was just coming through the door. Upon seeing Alex, he let out a low whistle.

"What happened to *you*?"

Alex gave a half-hearted smile. "Let's just say Teddy Stanton and I didn't see eye to eye on a few things."

Mike nodded. "Mrs. Godfrey mentioned something about a scuffle at the charity dance." He paused, mouth curving down. "Fighting with Stanton wasn't a good idea, Alex. You know who his father is, don't you?"

Alex nodded. "He owns the glass factory on the edge of town."

"He's an influential businessman in these parts. If he were to look into it, you might very well be sent packing."

Inside, Alex's heart seized with fear. What would he do if that happened? He'd be forced to go to his uncle's then, because where else could he go? What else could he do? His hands were tied. Being without money made him powerless.

Alex looked up when the weight of a hand fell on his shoulder. Mike gazed at him with earnest. "You know I wouldn't do that to you, son. Not without good cause."

Alex pulled gently away. "It wouldn't be hard to find a good cause."

Mike grunted. "Why? You done somethin' wrong?"

"No."

"Then why?"

Alex shrugged. "I'm just saying it's easy to find an excuse to accuse someone like me."

Mike narrowed his eyes. "What was this fight between the two of you about anyway? Was it because he insulted your pride? Called you a dirty Jap?"

Alex stared at the man, his stomach clenching. *This was it.* The time when Mike would give it to him. He swallowed nervously. "Yeah, but I'm not—I'm not Japanese."

Mike's laugh was short. "I know that."

Alex's mouth hung open. "You do? But how?"

"The reverend told me."

All of the tension melted out of Alex, and he laughed, grabbing his side from the pain. He shook his head. "All this time I didn't know what you really thought of me. Your sons . . . they were killed. You have every reason to hate someone that looks like me."

Mike clapped Alex on the shoulder, making him wince. "Let's get you inside, and I'll see what I have for the bruises." Alex followed Mike into the house and watched as the man broke ice cubes out of his ice tray and filled a small towel with them. "Put this on that lip to start with and follow me."

Alex obeyed and went after Mike into the living room. For the first time he was able to face this memorial to Mike Hardy's sons without feeling like an imposter. They stood gazing at the map scattered with dozens of pins, the proud faces of his sons staring forever out at them from behind glass.

Mike's shoulders heaved with a heavy sigh. He turned to Alex. "My boys died fighting for a country and a cause they loved. But I'm no one special for sending them off. Countless parents around the world have done the same—watching their sons dress in uniforms, saying goodbye at a train station, not knowing if they'll ever see them again, waiting anxiously for a letter . . . or the worst possible news." He frowned. "War is an ugly thing and the boys who fight are nothing but pawns to do the dirty work. I've seen it myself in the Great War. After that, I had my fill of fighting and have never had the desire to fight a man again. No matter who they were."

He gestured for Alex to take a seat, and they perched across from each other in Mike's miss-matching armchairs. "You wonder why I took you on?" For the first time in the conversation, Mike smiled. "Before the Great War, I had the opportunity to travel to the Orient as a young man. My grandfather was a successful businessman and traveled to Shanghai quite a bit. He allowed me to come with him on one trip, and it was the most remarkable experience of my life." A faraway look came over him. It was some time before he spoke again. "I grew to love those people. They were intelligent, respectful, and dignified. It's where I met Xiao Lin Chang. Have you met her?"

Alex shook his head. "Who is she?"

"She's a Chinese woman who lives on the outskirts of town. One of the reasons she came here with her husband was because of their connection with my grandfather."

Alex nodded. He'd be interested in meeting this woman.

"When Pearl Harbor happened, it broke my heart. Not only because of what it meant, but also because I knew all those Orientals living here in America would go through a hard time. I know how people think in wartime." Mike leaned forward. "When Reverend Hicks told me about you, I wanted to give you a chance.

You haven't had an easy time of it here, I know, but by God, it wasn't going to be because of me."

Alex clenched his teeth together, deeply moved by the man's words. "I don't know what to say," he mumbled. "But thank you."

Mike nodded. "Enough jabbering. I have work to do. You," he jabbed his finger toward Alex, "are to take the day off."

Alex half-rose to his feet. "I can't do that. I can work."

Mike laughed. "Have you seen yourself, son? Do yourself a favor and take a day to recuperate. You'll be no good to me in that state anyway." Having had his final say, Mike left the room.

Alex sat alone for some time, the ice starting to melt against his lip, trickling down to drip on his arm. Mike's words replayed in his mind, and Alex couldn't help but feel a deep sense of gratitude and good fortune. Of all the people to give him a job . . . The knowledge that there were people like Mike and Reverend Hicks in this world gave him hope—hope that someday in the future there'd be change and maybe even less prejudice.

Alex rose to his feet and approached the map wall and the three photographs of Mike Hardy's boys. He read their names—Michael, Thomas, and Paul. He examined their faces, young and proud, appreciating how much they resembled Mike. They'd given their lives fighting against greed, power, and hate. They'd given everything.

And then, even though it hurt him enough to take his breath away, Alex, his arms at his side, bowed low in deep and humble respect.

Chapter Seventeen

ALEX DIDN'T VENTURE out into public for a week. The swelling had gone down on his lip, but the idea of going into town or to church looking like he'd been pounded to a pulp hurt his pride. Not only that, but he didn't want to put his face on display as an example of the discord he brought to their town.

When he finally did make a trip to the library, he knew he should've stayed home even longer. He passed a woman carrying her shopping in a bulging knitted bag. She shot him a dirty look as she passed and mumbled a rude comment. He frowned but crossed the street. He walked past the shops busy with morning shoppers and workers. The wind was brisk, and he turned up his coat collar, but it didn't chill him nearly as much as the numberless scowls and barely muffled insults.

Alex's anger continued to rise, but he stared ahead as he walked, determined not to be provoked. He was relieved when he saw the limestone library building come into view. He hurried his pace, passing by an older gentleman, when his feet caught on something and Alex tripped, falling painfully to his hands and knees. He took a moment to gather himself, eyes pricking from the shock of the injury. He turned to see the old man shake his cane at him and growl.

"Serves you right, you dirty Jap. I hope you burn in hell."

Alex got to his feet, brushing off his knees. He nodded curtly to the man and continued on his way. He burned with resentment. Now he was being tripped by old men? Why did he have to put up with this?

He finally entered the warm stillness of the library and escaped into the furthest reaches of the stacks. Alex selected a book at random and found a seat, but instead of reading, he stared off into space.

The old man's words still stung, but the throbbing in his knees was nothing compared to his frustration. He didn't want to hurt anymore; didn't want to be hated anymore. Had he ever done anything to anyone in this town? What right did they have to treat him like this? He wanted to scream to the world he was no more an enemy than they were.

Alex finally looked at the title of the book in his hands—*A Mortal Storm*. He laughed out loud at the irony. He *was* in a storm, and he was nowhere even close to reaching the eye. He tossed the book aside, leaning his head back to rest on the back of the seat. He closed his eyes and attempted to focus on something that would calm him.

He struggled to bring his mother's image to mind, but somehow remembering the warmth of her smile was fading like a dying fire. She felt so far away—too far away to be a comfort anymore. His heart ached with regret. He'd wanted to be a good son. He'd tried his hardest, but it had never been good enough for his father. His mother could do little to alter her husband's determination in sending him away. What he would give to feel her loving arms around him, her words of whispered encouragement in his ear, her smile like a beam of light piecing the black clouds surrounding him.

"*Eomma.*" It was more like a moan, pleading for his mother.

"I'm sorry, sir. You can't sleep here."

Alex was startled by the voice of the librarian at his elbow.

He sat up straight, striving to regain his composure without success. "I—I wasn't sleeping. I was reading . . ." He searched around for the book, but couldn't see where it had landed. He clenched his jaw. "Never mind." He stood and brushed past to avoid the woman's incredulous eye.

It was even colder when he emerged onto the sidewalk, as if the weather was conspiring against him too. Alex shoved his hands deep into his pockets and walked fast, not caring where he went or whom he met. He was in such a reckless mood he feared he wouldn't be able to control his actions at one more provocation.

Alex crossed the street without even looking. A car's horn blared. He ignored it. He walked back past the shops, passing the police station, the train station, and on into the surrounding neighborhoods. He lost track of how long he walked, but by the time he got back to Mike's, he was cold, worn out, and on edge.

Mike glanced up when Alex entered the garage. "There you are. Reverend Hicks called ten minutes ago. He said he needed you to stop by as soon as you could."

"Okay, thanks." Alex stepped out into the cold again with a sigh and set off.

Alex arrived at the church to find Reverend Hicks in his office with the door slightly ajar. Alex knocked.

The reverend's voice echoed thinly into the chapel. "Come in."

Alex pushed open the door to see Reverend Hicks grinning broadly and a man seated across from him, his back to Alex. The man's hair was as black and straight as his own. He was seated stiffly, though it seemed more out of pride than discomfort.

As Alex stepped through and shut the door, the man turned around and smiled. Standing, he said, "Yeong Su! How long it's been."

Alex stared, open-mouthed. "*S-Samchon.*"

His Uncle Harry was there before him. He was a younger version of Alex's father, but his face was softer, kinder, and his eyes always held a delightful sense of mischievousness. It had been years since Uncle Harry had moved from California out to Washington DC. A flash of memory came to him—of getting a piggy-back ride from Uncle Harry and laughing hysterically. He'd been about five. He remembered it because it was the first time he loved his uncle more than his own father.

Alex recovered himself enough to bow in respect. "*Anyanghaseao, Samchon.*" His stomach knotted at the thought he might be forced to leave with him.

Uncle Harry laughed. "No, no, my dear boy. Come here. It's been too long for only that in greeting."

Alex embraced him. His uncle clasped Alex's shoulders, searching his face. "My goodness. Look at what a handsome man you've become. Your mother must be proud." Alex swallowed and nodded wordlessly. Uncle Harry had chosen his expression with tact, making no mention of Alex's wounds. For that, he was grateful.

"And how tall you are. You were always such a shrimpy thing. I worried you'd never grow."

Alex's face warmed. "Uncle, please."

Uncle Harry laughed. "Come, sit down. Reverend Hicks has been telling me about your time here."

Alex sank into a chair, eyeing the reverend. What kinds of things had he said?

As if in answer to his silent question, Reverend Hicks leaned forward. "I was just telling him of your irreplaceable help to me here at the church as well as your excellent work over at the auto garage."

Alex nodded.

Reverend Hicks pursed his lips, but kept going. "I also was telling him about the friends you've made here and how fond we've become of you."

Alex took in what the man said. "Wait. You sound as if you're sending me away."

Reverend Hicks leaned back in his chair. "Isn't that why your uncle has come? To take you with him to Washington? I know you were unable to leave before because of lack of funds, but his being here solves that, doesn't it?"

Alex briefly closed his eyes against his feelings of confusion. What was he supposed to say? How had he come to feel this way—that no matter what, he didn't want to leave? He stood. "I'm sorry. I'm going to need some time to think."

Uncle Harry got to his feet. "Why don't you walk me back to my lodging?" He turned and bowed to Reverend Hicks. "It was an honor to meet you. Thank you so much for your hospitality and for caring for my nephew. If there's anything I can do in return, please ask."

Alex followed his uncle outside, and they strode down the sidewalk together. For some reason, it was uncomfortable walking with him. Just having himself in town was bad enough, but *two* Koreans? Would the town be able to handle it? They barely knew what to do with him. How had Uncle Harry managed to secure a room at the town's only hotel in the first place?

"You don't want to come with me?" Uncle Harry broke their silence, but now he spoke in Korean. "You know it's your father's wish."

Alex ground his teeth. "Yes, *Samchon*. I know."

"I apologize it took me so long to come out. I had no idea you were in such circumstances. Your father was worried and sent me the last address they had for you with Reverend Hicks. Why didn't you contact me? You've had a hard time here."

Alex shrugged, not wanting to commit to the conversation.

His uncle continued. "I really see no reason for you to stay. Your aunt's been busy in the kitchen for weeks, preparing *meet banchan* until it's coming out our ears. Your arrival is greatly anticipated." He laughed and Alex couldn't help but smile a little, his mouth watering. His mind filled with memories of all the familiar side dishes. How he missed Korean food.

"You'll have a bit of time to settle before I show you the business. We even happen to know an eligible young Korean woman whom your aunt has set her sights on for you. You'll need to work hard, but soon you'll be able to approach her family."

Alex stopped abruptly. "No." His voice came out sharper than he intended. He lowered his gaze, finding he couldn't face his uncle's eyes after such disrespect. "*Joesonghamnida, Samchon,*" he apologized and bowed.

A hand landed lightly on his shoulder. "Yeong Su, I know things haven't been easy for you. My older brother can be harsh, but he does have your best interests at heart. Think how he must feel: disappointment that you've let him down and displeasure you haven't fulfilled his wishes. It's very frustrating as a parent."

Alex tried to pull away, but his uncle's grip suddenly became like iron. "You probably can't see it now, Yeong Su *joka*, but someday you'll understand. When you are in his shoes."

Alex's temper blazed, and his head snapped up. "I *never* want to be in his shoes. *Never.*"

Uncle Harry's hand dropped. There was sadness in his eyes, though his jaw clenched in anger. "You need some time to think. Is that what you need? I would've thought you've had plenty of time to think and come to grips with your duty the past couple months. Now, it's time for action. You'll be coming with me tomorrow morning on the train. I'll meet you at the station promptly at nine-thirty. Do you understand?"

Alex wanted to rage. He wanted to shout at the top of his lungs and destroy everything in sight. This wasn't fair. Had he no say in his own life? When would he be free to do as he wished? Without making eye contact, he finally nodded, though it took all his power of control to do so.

Satisfied, Uncle Harry smiled, the anger gone. "I'll see you tomorrow." He turned on his heel to leave, but Alex reached out and touched his arm.

"Please, *Samchon*, try to understand. I have responsibilities. There are people here who are counting on me." With his mouth he meant Mike Hardy and Reverend Hicks, but it was Lonnie who sprang to his mind. Beautiful, sweet Lonnie. He flushed and balled his fists, feeling even more confused than before. Did his feelings really run deeper than he realized? Was she the true meaning behind wanting to stay?

His uncle cut into his thoughts. "I appreciate your position, but you must remember that the responsibility to your family always comes first. I'm sure your friends will be able to respect that." He clapped Alex on the shoulder with a grim smile and left.

As Alex stared after him, emptiness and turmoil ate away at him from the inside. He finally turned and strode away with a long and agitated gate. With hands shoved into his pockets, he walked, too angry to see, too helpless to care where he headed.

His fate was finally sealed. His uncle had come to claim him— for Alex to fulfill his responsibility as a dutiful son at last. He didn't want to go. He didn't want to be dragged away from his life again. As frustrating as this town could be, River Bluff had become a home to him. It was something he'd built himself, something he was proud of accomplishing. How could his uncle just take all that away without a second thought? Without any consideration for what *he* wanted?

Alex lifted his head to cross the street when she drew his eye. Lonnie. On the opposite sidewalk, she laughed, her arm linked with the girl he recognized as her friend Rose. He drank the sight of Lonnie in, his mind spinning.

Without warning, she met his gaze, and her face brightened. Her rosy lips curved into a delighted smile, and she raised her hand in a small wave. Without thinking, he raised his hand in response, then let it drop. It was as if the whole world ground to a halt in a single second. All Alex could hear was the pounding of his pulse, and his breath escaping his lungs in loud puffs.

He was never going to see her again.

His heart wrenched. He couldn't face leaving, but now he had no choice. He'd never had a choice.

In a sudden rush of anger, he began running. People, automobiles, and buildings all melted into a blur. He hardly acknowledged their existence. He ran until his lungs seared with pain and his muscles ached, running as far out as the park at the bluff and finally collapsing onto the grass. The wind blew stronger here and his cheeks stung with cold.

Reaching up, he was surprised to wipe away tears.

***

The door opened a few seconds after Lonnie knocked. The tall, thin woman who resembled Teddy so much answered the door.

"Lonnie, how lovely to see you." She swung the door open wide with a bright smile.

"Hello, Mrs. Stanton. It's good to see you too."

"Please, come in. How can I help you?"

Lonnie stepped into the airy foyer of the Stanton home. It was a large, old gothic house with beautiful stained glass windows letting in fractured beams of color. She smiled as she took it all in.

"I didn't realize how long it's been since I last visited. Nothing's changed."

Mrs. Stanton nodded. "Yes, it's been a long time. Not since yours and Teddy's senior year. Has it been two years already?"

"I suppose it has. Speaking of Teddy, I was wondering if he was home. I wanted to see him."

The woman's eyes sparkled, though with what meaning, Lonnie couldn't guess. "Yes, he's home. I'll call him down. Why don't you take a seat in the parlor?" She bustled up the stairs, and Lonnie went to take a seat on the plush blue couch.

The parlor was spotless and stylishly decorated with the latest style in drapery and finely upholstered couch and armchairs. Envy gave her a little stab. The Stantons did so well. She didn't begrudge them any of their finery, of course. They'd certainly worked hard enough for it, but it definitely helped their situation that both of Teddy's parents were around. She tried to shake the creeping pity for herself but wasn't entirely successful.

A moment later, Teddy strode into the room. His face was like a ray of sunshine upon seeing her. She gasped softly as he took a seat beside her. Being so close to him, she saw what a number Alex had done to his face. Bruises were turning from purple to yellow, especially over the bridge of his nose, and his jaw sported a small bandage.

"I have to admit, I was surprised when my mother said you were here," Teddy said.

Lonnie clasped her hands in her lap, mustering her courage.

"I came to talk to you about what happened at the dance."

Teddy's cheerful face fell. At that moment, his mother came in with a tray of coffee and cake and slipped out again.

Once she was safely gone, Teddy avoided Lonnie's gaze. "Something told me your visit might be about that, but I was hoping it wasn't."

"I was rude to you after your fight with Alex, and I wanted to apologize. But there was no excuse for you getting into that mess. I expected better from you."

He sighed in exasperation. "I don't know why. I've never liked him. I've made that pretty clear, haven't I?"

"I'm not asking you to like him, Teddy. I'm asking you to be civil at least. He's never done anything to anyone. Hardly a soul has taken the trouble to get to know him, and if they did, their silly, false conclusions would go away."

Teddy pounded his fist into the arm of the couch. "Why do you always take his side? What do you even see in him? Are you sweet on him or something?"

"No!" Lonnie flushed hotly. "He's—he's my friend. And you're my friend. Why can't you just get along?" Tears threatened, and she swallowed them back.

Teddy shut his eyes for a moment. "Lonnie, I don't want to argue with you again. It's not going to get us anywhere." He met her eyes. "I'll try my darndest to be civil to him—for you. Though I fully admit it'll be like torture. I'd do anything for you, you know. I like you a lot." He paused. "No. I love you. I *love* you." He scooted closer until their knees were touching, and he took her hands gently in his. She trembled.

"I hadn't planned on it being like this, but I don't know when else I'll have a chance to say it. Lonnie, I want you to be my wife."

She nearly choked. "What?"

"I want to marry you." His gaze was so intense, she couldn't look away.

Lonnie pulled her hands from his grasp, frantic. "But when did you start to feel this way? We've only ever been good friends." She scrambled to think of times he'd given her some clue. The recent date was the only thing that came to mind.

Teddy raised an eyebrow in question. "I've only ever loved you since the sixth grade when you accidentally tripped me, and I fell and broke my arm. You came every day to see how I was doing until the cast came off. Do you remember?"

She riveted her gaze on the lamp, avoiding his eyes. Of course she remembered. The humiliation and guilt were still a residue from the past in her mind. "I was going through an awkward phase." It always had been a feeble excuse.

Teddy laughed. "I was so smitten with you that I begged the doctor to let me keep the cast on a week longer." He reached up and gently turned her face towards him. "You've always been so kind and so beautiful. You mean the world to me, Appalone. Please say you'll be my wife. Everyone knows we've always been meant for each other. I only hope you can see that."

Being so near him made her uncomfortably warm. She stood slowly. "I'm going to need some time."

Teddy frowned, but he nodded his understanding. He walked her to the door. "Don't wait too long. I feel like we haven't a moment to waste."

She smiled, though she was puzzled by his statement. "I promise. It won't be too long."

Before she could turn away, he grasped her by the shoulders and pressed his lips to hers. She inhaled sharply. His lips were warm and sweet. While it was nice, the action also felt terribly wrong, as if she was kissing a brother. The sensation made her shudder.

He finally released her, and Lonnie gasped out a "goodbye" before hurrying away. She welcomed the chilly afternoon air to whisk the heat from her cheeks. Her lips tingled, almost as if in embarrassment. She certainly burned with embarrassment.

What had just happened? She'd only gone there to clear the air with Teddy and somehow she'd left with a marriage proposal. How had things gone so horribly in the wrong direction? She was going to have to open the topic again to give him her answer. She dreaded facing him more than anything.

She didn't have to think very hard about what her answer was, though. Her mother expected their marital union, all of their friends expected it, and probably half the town thought the same. It made sense on the outside, but she'd been friends with him long enough to know they weren't suited for one another. Teddy was perfectly content to stay in River Bluff until he died, running his father's factory and being a leader in the community. She understood that. But she wanted to go away. She wanted to see new places and do incredible things. There would be no chance of that if she were to become Mrs. Theodore Stanton.

No, she wasn't going to marry him. She knew that without a doubt. What remained was convincing everyone else.

Chapter Eighteen

ALEX SLID OPEN the window next to his seat across from Uncle Harry, craning his neck to search the platform. The memories from that fateful day when he'd been attacked crowded into his mind, but he pushed them away, like so many shadows of the past. There was no sense in dwelling on that now. He desperately wanted to see Lonnie, but he knew she wouldn't be there. Not when he hadn't told her he was leaving.

By the time he'd left the park yesterday, he'd resigned himself to his uncle's request. It was futile to resist. He'd been uneasy about the decision, trying to convince himself everything would be fine when he knew perfectly well it wouldn't.

The next morning he'd risked stopping by Lonnie's house to tell her he was leaving, but no one was home. When he went by her work, her boss had informed him, with a disapproving sniff, that she was out on some errands and wouldn't be back until after his train had gone.

Alex left her office without any respite from his desperation. He'd left a note with Reverend Hicks and said a hasty, grateful farewell to Mike Hardy who was sad to see him go. But to the very end, all Alex could think about was Lonnie. She completely consumed him, and there was no way to bridle the fearsome thoughts he was just now beginning to acknowledge.

Alex tried to tell himself it didn't matter—Lonnie didn't care that much for him. He could always send her a letter or a telegram. He could always come back . . .

The train whistled and jerked as it pulled away from the platform. The River Bluff station disappeared from view and with each turn of the wheels, the turbulent and painful memories of his time in the little town started to fall away.

He settled back into his wooden seat and resigned himself to the beginning of his new life, but his heart refused to be at peace.

He got out one of his books, but he barely noticed the words on the page. River Bluff hadn't been all bad. Far from it. He'd made some good friends there. Reverend Hicks. Mike Hardy. Even little Marty Hamilton.

And Lonnie. Always Lonnie—constant, sweet, and so many times protective, however maddening it was. Images of holding her in his arms flashed before him. He remembered how soft her hair had been, how intoxicating her perfume was, the way her lips curved up into a smile, and his heart squeezed bitterly with his regret.

How would she feel about him going away, particularly after leaving her only one hastily written note? She'd probably be a little disappointed. *He* was disappointed he'd never get to see how she did with his second lesson.

He shifted uncomfortably. Surely, she was better off without him. He'd caused her enough grief and heartache already, especially after getting into the fight with Teddy. He was being wise in leaving for his own health and safety. He hadn't exactly been popular. Teddy Stanton was right in a way. He'd never belonged in that town and was better off with his own family, with his own people. The thought made him sick.

He studied the blur of autumn colors speeding by his window and his lips curled with disgust. Those were the kinds of things his father would say to him. Stubbornness welled up inside as he pictured his father's stern face.

Alex remembered sitting with Lonnie at the park and being struck with the thought that maybe he was meant to turn up in River Bluff all along. That was still true. If anything, he felt more certain about it than before. He didn't feel like he really belonged in that town, but when he was with Lonnie . . .

His eyes shifted from the distorted landscape to focus on his own reflection in the soot-soiled window. When he was with Lonnie, all the confusion, all the self-doubt, and all the frustration melted away. When in her presence, he was so sure of himself—he could do anything. With her, he belonged anywhere.

His breath caught in his throat; his heart pounded until it became a roar in his ears. He couldn't leave now. For heaven's sake, why hadn't he seen it before?

He loved her.

He, Alexander Moon, loved Lonnie Hamilton.

Alex was thrilled at this epiphany and petrified at the same time. Was there any remote possibility she'd ever feel the same way? It was crazy to think a romantic relationship would even be permitted. He trembled at the idea of broaching the subject with

Reverend Hicks. But he could no longer keep still. Whatever the consequences, he needed to find out.

His thoughts tumbled over themselves, fighting for recognition. But what could he do? Here he was, on a train hurtling to a life he hadn't chosen and didn't want. It would be a life devoid of the woman he'd come to love. What was he doing?

The conductor came through the train car announcing the next stop. They'd passed two stations already. Alex turned urgently to his uncle.

"*Samchon.*"

"Yeh?" Uncle Harry looked up from his newspaper.

"I'm sorry, but I'm going to be getting off at the next stop. I'm going back to River Bluff."

His uncle sat straighter and stared at Alex in alarm. "Why? Did you forget something?"

Alex took a deep breath. "It's not that I forgot something, but I did leave something behind."

Uncle Harry frowned. "Surely, Reverend Hicks could send it to you."

Alex shook his head. "It's not like that. I—I've left some*one* behind. I can't leave now. Not without her knowing how I feel."

Realization quickly dawned, and his uncle's face grew sober. "Do you hear what you're saying? Yeong Su, this is madness."

The train slowed, and Alex pulled down his suitcase. "I know it may seem that way, Uncle, but if you knew her, you'd understand."

Uncle Harry stood. "You're young. It's easy to make rash decisions, especially where a pretty face is concerned. Think for one moment about what you're about to do. A relationship with someone so different is unwise. How could you ever bring her home to your parents? The consequences would tear your relationship apart. No." He spoke firmly. "You will forget this foolish notion. I've selected a young Korean woman that is far more suitable."

Alex turned to face his uncle. "I have thought about it. I'd regret it for the rest of my life if I didn't go back. Please try to understand." The brakes squealed as the train came into the station. "Please tell *sookmo* I'm sorry I won't get to see her, but I'll come to visit as soon as I can."

"Please don't do this, Yeong Su," Uncle Harry pled. "Think of what your father wants for you. Think of your future. If you think society will leave you alone, you're grossly mistaken. Remember what's already been done to you. You would be bringing that down on both your heads."

Alex squared his shoulders, ignoring his uncle's advice. "I'm sorry. I have to do this. This is the decision I've made. For once in my life *I'm* making the choice for myself."

The train came to a stop, and Alex bowed respectfully. "Goodbye, *Samchon*." He grabbed him in a quick hug, took his suitcase, and hopped off the train. The train chugged away and Alex waved. His uncle remained where Alex had left him, face sagging with sorrow.

A distinct pang of guilt stabbed at Alex, but he had no problem burying it under the euphoria pumping through his veins. He turned to face the direction from which they had come. He was going back to River Bluff.

And this time it was because he chose to go.

***

Lonnie was thrilled to see Alex in church again. She looked furtively around and finally spotted him in the back when she should've been paying attention to the sermon.

Later, she stole another peek and found his eyes on her. She hastily turned back, suppressing a grin. Then she caught herself and frowned. He's a *friend*, and you're not a little school girl, she chided. With sudden forcefulness, the memory of Teddy kissing her, with his glasses fogging from their breath, loomed in her mind, and she stifled a gasp. The same image had plagued her the entire evening yesterday and this morning. It was a stubborn stain, that no matter how hard she scrubbed, refused to go away.

What had possessed him to confess so suddenly—without warning or hint as to his intentions? Had he already spoken to Uncle Phillip?

She studied her uncle as he delivered his sermon on the Beatitudes. He was passionate, filled with such conviction and concern for his parishioners. There was no indication of such a conversation. There were no meaningful glances or frowns of displeasure that she had such an eager suitor. Surely, he would've said something. Or perhaps he was planning to tell her later? Would he have readily given Teddy his consent? Without even asking her? Her hands twisted in her lap as she contemplated the possibilities.

By the time the service was finished, she was a bundle of nerves. She jumped several inches when Alex touched her shoulder. His eyes, curved into little half moons by his broad smile, faded as he saw her face. Her heart sank as they disappeared. The way his face transformed when he smiled was something she was beginning to find so endearing.

"Are you all right?" he asked.

"Yes. Yes, I'm fine." She pushed a reluctant smile onto her face.

"How has my latest lesson been going? Have you made much progress?"

"Yes, I've finished it actually."

He grinned. "That was fast. You're quite clever, you know that?"

She laughed, letting the action carry away some of her distress. "Would you like to meet at the park to go over it?"

Alex's lips turned down into a small frown. "It's cold today, and it's pretty windy there, isn't it?"

She nodded. "Well, perhaps we could go to my aunt's."

"Are you sure she wouldn't mind?"

"Oh, no. She wouldn't mind in the slightest. I'm supposed to join her for lunch today anyway." Lonnie smiled her encouragement.

"All right. You're sure she won't mind having an extra mouth to feed? I could stop by Mike's and grab something."

She led him to the side door. "Don't even think about it. My aunt lives to care for others. She'd be mortified to think you'd eaten before you came."

Twenty chilled and blustery minutes later, they arrived at Aunt Millie's door. "Lonnie, I didn't know you were bringing Alex along. How wonderful. Come in from the cold, you two."

They were soon seated at the dining room table, sipping steaming bowls of soup and dipping crusty bread. They talked lightly of the weather, the most recent news of the war, and Aunt Millie's latest charitable work. After they'd finished eating, Alex and Lonnie insisted on clearing up. Aunt Millie went to put her feet up and read in the living room.

Lonnie filled the sink with soapy water, but Alex gently moved her aside. "I'll wash."

She stepped out of the way. "I won't put up a fight about that."

He winked, rolled up his sleeves, and plunged his hands into the water. The clatter of dishes and sloshing water filled the space between them until he spoke. "Tell me about the lesson. What did you learn?"

She pursed her lips, nervous. The sounds of the Korean language still felt strange in her mouth. She was afraid of making a fool of herself. "I've learned the alphabet by heart and most of their sounds; a few of the sound blends too."

Alex nodded. "Good. Did you figure out what I wrote in *hangul*? It was a lot shorter than the last phrase."

"Yes. I suspect you were taking it easier on me. I did figure it out, but once again, I don't know what it means."

His eyes twinkled with expectation. "Well?" He handed her a dripping dish.

She took it and wiped it with a towel. "Yong soo." She cringed. "Was that right?"

Alex grinned. "Yeong Su. Very good."

"What does it mean?"

"It's . . . my name."

Lonnie's eyes grew round. "Your name? But isn't your name Alex?"

He handed her the last dish with a small smile. "Alexander is my American name. Because we were born here, my mother wanted my siblings and me to fit in. But Yeong Su is my Korean name."

Lonnie set down the dried dish and the towel and turned to him. Sharing his Korean name with her was intimate and incredibly personal. She sensed he didn't share it with just anyone. Gratitude that he trusted her this much overwhelmed her. She touched his arm.

"Thank you," she said. "Yeong Su."

He glanced up quickly. "Say that again."

"Thank you?" She laughed a little and retrieved her hand, but he caught it in his.

"No, my name."

She blinked, her heart racing. "Yeong Su." She said it in a voice of wonder. For some reason, in this moment, he was a new person, someone she was discovering for the first time. It was as if something in his countenance had changed—a barrier had come down. Relief showed plainly on his face.

Lonnie studied him, that feeling of attraction toward him swelling inside as it had after the dance. She tried to distract herself from the strength and warmth of his hand still holding hers. "Is it good hearing your name again? You don't really get to use it here, do you? I mean, I can imagine it would make you homesick. I know it would make me feel that way." She laughed weakly, but Alex didn't say anything.

He only smiled at her, eyes shining, leaving her breathless.

Chapter Nineteen

WHEN LONNIE ARRIVED home from Aunt Millie's, she found her mother in the front room reading the newspaper. Lonnie hung up her coat and scarf and approached her mother whose fists clenched the paper tightly.

She watched her a moment before speaking. "I'm home, Mother."

Harriet dropped the paper in her lap with a loud crinkle and sighed. "This horrible war. Why doesn't it just stop?"

Lonnie sank onto the couch. "I don't know."

Her mother kneaded her forehead, and Lonnie wondered why she was so distressed. She seemed worried about something, though she was afraid to broach the subject. With a start, Lonnie realized her mother wasn't even supposed to be here.

"What happened to Euchre? Isn't that going on right now?"

"Two of them had sick children, so we put it off until next week." Harriet looked up. "Where did you go after church?"

"I went to Aunt Millie's for lunch."

Her mother frowned but nodded. Lonnie wished she wasn't so stubborn towards Aunt Millie and Uncle Phillip. Aunt Millie had powers of cheering that always seemed to make her feel better when she was feeling down. But what could cheer her mother?

Lonnie grinned, struck with an idea. "Do you still want to play Euchre?"

"What?"

"Just a minute." Lonnie ran upstairs. She found Tunie laying on her bed on her stomach, her friend Phyllis next to her. They were both flipping through magazines and laughing about something. "Is Marty here?"

Tunie's head bobbed up. "No. He's playing next door. Why?"

"I need you two for a bit. Come on." She beckoned. Tunie and Phyllis gave her quizzical looks but came downstairs with her.

"Your Euchre party has arrived," Lonnie sang cheerfully. When she walked in, her mother had been back at her newspaper, but seeing them, she broke into a rare laugh.

"What?" Tunie complained. "Euchre? Gosh, Lonnie, you could've said. I don't want to play Euchre."

"Oh, come on. It'll be fun." Lonnie cleared the kitchen table while her mother got the cards. "Phyllis, do you know how to play?"

Phyllis, a freckly girl with shoulder-length curly brown hair, nodded. "Of course."

"Great. Do you want to pair up with me?"

The four of them began the game. After a while, Lonnie rummaged around for snacks of some late apples and leftover orange honey loaf from the previous day. The four of them ate and laughed, moaning at rotten hands and opposing teams' successes.

After some time, the conversation turned to school and boys. "Did you see Roger during football practice yesterday?" Phyllis asked, laying down a card.

"No. I was at work," Tunie said absentmindedly. "Why?"

"He's so dreamy, that's why. It's no wonder the coach finally made him quarterback."

Lonnie laughed. "Because he's so dreamy?"

Tunie snorted with unladylike laughter, and Phyllis scowled playfully. "No, silly. Because he's so talented."

"So, Lonnie." Tunie eyed Lonnie slyly. "How's Teddy these days?"

At the mention of Teddy, Harriet looked up from her hand. "Yes, I haven't seen him come around in a while. Is everything all right between you two?"

Lonnie's throat constricted in fear. She could shake Tunie for bringing it up. She swallowed with some difficulty before responding. "I saw him the other day, actually. He's good. We've both been busy, so . . ."

"You should invite him for dinner next weekend." By the tone of her voice, her mother made it sound more like a demand than a friendly suggestion.

Lonnie gripped her cards tighter, reigning in her consternation. "Yes, Mother. I'll talk to him tomorrow." She would rather have jumped into the river from the top of the bluff than talk to Teddy again so soon—he'd think she was offering him an answer to his proposal.

They finished one last round before putting the game away. Lonnie was about to go upstairs to read, but her mother stopped her with a hand on her arm.

"Thank you," she said with grudging.

Lonnie smiled. "For what?"

"For the game. You were being thoughtful, and I appreciate that."

A warm feeling started in Lonnie's chest and spread out like she was being submerged in a fresh bath. She couldn't keep the grin from her face. "You're welcome."

Harriet nodded. "I also wanted to see how things were going with Teddy. You looked uncomfortable when he came up."

The warm feeling rushed out of her. "Teddy?" That haunting image of Teddy's kiss returned, and she flinched. "Does it really matter?"

Her mother's face clouded. "Of course it matters, Appalone. It matters a great deal."

Lonnie's palms prickled with sweat. "I—I'll admit we had a falling out a while ago, but we've patched things up."

An angry wrinkle appeared above her mother's nose. "You had a falling out? Why? Was it something you said? Was it something you did?"

Lonnie took a step back at the assault of accusations. "Why must it be my fault?"

"Don't ruin this chance for your future, Appalone. He's the *best* thing that will ever happen to you. The Stantons are the most respected family in town. Your life can only be improved by attaching yourself to him." She took an intimidating step toward Lonnie. "Whatever it is that passed between you, make sure it's resolved absolutely. Do you understand?" Her voice was low, threatening.

Lonnie nodded silently.

"Good."

Her mother turned and disappeared into her bedroom. Once the door clicked shut, Lonnie slumped against the wall, pressing her hand to her mouth to keep the sob from escaping. She was trapped—like a cornered squirrel trembling before a vicious, barking dog.

What was she to do? She'd planned to refuse Teddy without a second thought, but now her mother was making it so difficult. If her mother knew he'd proposed . . . She closed her eyes, tears coursing down her cheeks. The feeling of being utterly at a loss frightened her, threatening to overcome her.

Lonnie pulled on her coat and left the house, striding out toward town. She hastily wiped her tears and walked briskly to keep warm. Soon the comforting spire of her uncle's church came into view. She hurried inside, wrapped in a cocoon of silence and space. Without bothering to remove her coat, Lonnie slid into a pew, pulled out the padded stool, and knelt to pray.

She let the tears flow, whispering words of gratitude and of pleading. A measure of peace fell over her, but her listlessness remained.

It wasn't until her knees started to throb that she noticed her uncle observing her. Meeting his eyes, she rose, and he approached.

"Is everything all right?"

At his words, her last defenses fell. "Oh, Uncle Phillip." She threw herself into his arms and cried bitterly. He patted her back in mute comfort and waited until her tears had subsided into hiccups before they sat together on a bench.

Lonnie's head bowed in defeat as she dabbed at her swollen eyes.

"Is it about your mother?"

She nodded.

"Do you want to talk about it? You don't have to, but I'm willing to listen."

Lonnie lifted her head to see his kind face, the fine wrinkles at the corners of his eyes crinkling in an understanding smile, and she let it all come spilling out.

"Teddy Stanton proposed to me. Mother doesn't know, but she expects things to happen between us. He took me out on one date, and it ended horribly, only she doesn't know that either. I went over to his house recently to patch up things from what happened at the dance with Alex. And somehow, he proposed to me. Did he say anything to you? I feel like it's come up out of the blue."

Her uncle shook his head, brow furrowed in concern. "Not a word." Lonnie frowned, and her uncle spoke again. "Do you love him?"

Without hesitation she shook her head. "Not like that. We've been friends for ages, but that's all I've ever seen him as—a friend. I suppose lately he's been hinting at feeling something more, but marriage is the last thing I would've thought."

"Is it that you love someone else?" Uncle Phillip asked tentatively.

Lonnie colored. "No. It's not that. And it's not that I don't care for Teddy. I just don't want to be stuck here as Mrs.

Theodore Stanton. I have other plans for my life—things I want to go and do."

Uncle Phillip nodded. "I understand."

Her lip quivered again. "But if Mother knew . . . she'd be livid if she finds out I've rejected him. I don't know what to do."

"Have you given him your answer yet?"

She shook her head. "Not yet. I'm dreading it."

"Don't make him wait, Lonnie. It isn't kind. If you already know your answer you should tell him."

She stared at her clasped hands. "You're right, but what about Mother?" Her eyes filled with tears again. "She'll be so furious."

Uncle Phillip leaned back, thinking. "I don't know. I'll make it a matter of prayer, but let me deal with your mother. You need to focus on telling Teddy, all right?" He patted her hand. "I know it may seem difficult now, but God will strengthen you through your trials. He is the source of peace and hope. Never forget that. And never despair."

Lonnie nodded and offered him a watery smile. "You're right. Thank you, Uncle Phillip." She gave him a hug and left the chapel, finally at peace.

***

Alex was grateful Mike had welcomed him back with open arms as if he'd never left. In fact, when Alex had shown up, suitcase in hand and a sheepish expression on his face, Mike had grunted. "I had a feeling you'd turn back up." The smile curving his lips contradicted his gruffness.

Alex was grateful to have his job and something to keep him occupied, but spending stretches of time alone, working on cars, and Mike's normally silent nature didn't help at all. His thoughts obsessed over Lonnie until he thought he'd go crazy. He tried to wrestle his feelings into something more reasonable, but they resisted. He wanted to shout to the world that he loved her. He wanted to take her in his arms and—

Alex dropped his wrench and shook his head roughly. No. He couldn't think of that. He refused to allow himself that liberty. He stooped to pick up his wrench only to find Mike appraising him.

"What?"

"You got your head in the clouds, boy?"

Alex shrugged. "I don't know. Maybe."

Mike narrowed his eyes. "Why did you come back, anyway? You seemed pretty decided about leaving."

Alex shrugged again. "Things have changed."

"Does it have to do with your uncle?"

"Yes and no." He took a deep breath and let it out in a rush. "But there's no going back now. I can't take back what I've done."

Mike frowned. "It's never too late to fix a mistake. Especially with family."

Alex shook his head. "No. Not with mine. Besides, I don't want to go back. I'm here to stay. I want to be here."

Mike didn't say anything after that, leaving Alex to himself. He could only hope things would work out the way he hoped. Otherwise, what else did he have left?

Later that afternoon, a shadow fell across him as he filed a scrap of metal he was hoping to fashion into a new part. He looked up. Teddy Stanton was standing before him, his face a mask of petulance.

"You need to talk with Mike?"

"No, I came to talk with you." Teddy scowled as if it pained him to say it.

Alex's eyebrows shot up. "Really? Okay."

"Not here though. I thought we could go out for drinks and clear the air."

Alex clenched his teeth. He was suspicious of what Teddy's definition of "clear the air" meant, but he wasn't going to let his suspicions show. "Sure. I get off in about ten minutes. Give me a few minutes to get changed."

Teddy nodded. "I'll be back."

By the time Alex had changed and reemerged, Teddy was waiting for him again.

"Let's head down to the pub over on White Street."

Alex paled. That was where he and Lonnie had run away from Homer and Jake. "How about the Red Rock Tavern on Main Street?" he suggested. "I like the atmosphere there better."

Teddy shrugged. "Suit yourself." They walked in silence the entire way. Small talk was too much of an annoyance. Alex couldn't think of anything to say anyway. Even if he could think of something, it wouldn't be anything friendly. It seemed the feeling was mutual since Teddy also remained tight-lipped until they walked into the dimly lit tavern.

The place was filled with richly stained and gleaming wood beams and panels. Globe lamps glowed dully; the air was hazy with cigarette smoke. A dozen men were already occupying barstools and tables nursing mugs of beer and talking in low murmuring voices.

Teddy and Alex approached the bar, and Teddy hailed the bartender. "Afternoon, Milton. Two pints of the house ale."

Milton stared pointedly at Alex. He'd once attempted to get a drink here, but it had been made obvious he wasn't welcome. Apparently, Milton remembered too.

Teddy noticed the silent exchange. "It's all right. He's with me."

The man grunted and slid two mugs of golden ale down to Teddy who grabbed them and led the way to a back corner table away from most of the other patrons. It was quieter there and the setting sun shone in fractured amber beams through the plate glass window and smoke.

They sat across from each other and drank in silence for a few minutes until Alex couldn't stand it anymore.

"So, what was it you wanted to talk with me about?"

"Lonnie." Teddy's eyes shone resolutely from behind his glasses.

No surprise there. "What about her?" Alex asked, trying to remain calm. Already he felt his temper simmering, and they hadn't even gotten started into the conversation.

"I don't know what you fancy your relationship to be with Lonnie, but I wanted to let you know what my intentions were so you don't get any stupid ideas."

Alex seethed. "Stupid ideas? To what ideas would you be referring?"

Teddy leaned forward with a scowl. "You damn well know what ideas I'm talking about. I see the way you talk with her, the way you seek her out. She's too nice to push you away or put you in your place, so it's about time somebody did."

"And you think you're the one to do it?"

Teddy nodded, a smug smile sliding onto his face. "Absolutely."

"And how exactly do you plan on 'putting me in my place' as you say? I wasn't aware I was out of place."

Teddy scoffed. "You just have to look in a mirror to see how out of place you are. Isn't it obvious you don't belong here? You have no place next to Lonnie as a friend and most certainly not as anything else."

Alex didn't realize he'd been clenching his fist until he brought it sharply down on the table, making the mugs jump. "I don't see what business it is of yours to decide who Lonnie's friends are and with whom she chooses to speak." His temper was boiling, and he had to take a deep breath to keep from knocking the glasses from Teddy's face.

"It will soon be my decision to make. I've asked Lonnie to marry me."

Alex's jaw dropped. "W-What?"

Teddy grinned in triumph and took a swig of his ale.

"Marrying you is the *last* thing Lonnie Hamilton would ever think of doing."

Teddy laughed. "Don't be so sure. Her mother is very fond of me. I don't know if you know Harriet Hamilton very well, but she's not someone to be reckoned with. She has Lonnie right under her thumb."

Alex shot to his feet. Reigning in his temper took every last fiber of self-control he had. "I think we're done here."

Teddy held up a hand. "Not quite yet. I have something else to say: a word of warning. Stay away from Lonnie. You'll regret it if you don't."

Alex narrowed his eyes. "You're threatening me?"

At that moment, a hulking figure loomed over their table.

"Oh, hello, Walter," Teddy said cheerfully. "Join us."

"Hey, Teddy. I didn't expect to see you here." Walter's head swung around, and it took him a second to register Alex. He glowered in confusion. "What are you doing hanging out with the Jap?"

Alex's hands balled into fists, and he nearly exploded, but Teddy pushed between them. "He's not a Jap, Walt. Why don't you take a seat? Alex and I were just having a friendly chat, weren't we? Sit back down, Alex. I wasn't finished."

"Oh, we're finished."

"Don't flip your wig. Just sit down and finish your drink."

It was the last thing Alex wanted to do, but a small part of him was curious about what else Teddy had to say.

As soon as he reclaimed his seat, Teddy smiled, though his smugness was gone. "Now that the unpleasant part is out of the way . . . I wanted to tell you I promised Lonnie I was going to be civil to you, and I'm going to keep my word. I wanted to apologize for fighting with you at the dance and express my hope that it won't happen again."

Alex gaped at his sudden change of attitude, and Walter nearly choked on his beer. "What? You're apologizing to that scum? If anything, he deserved it."

"Come now, Walter. Let's be civil. Alex is living here in this town for the unforeseeable future, and we should work to keep the peace. There's enough war going on in this world. There's no need to bring it down on our own heads."

Alex's eyebrows shot up, and he took a sip of his drink. "I think that's the first reasonable thing I've ever heard you say."

Walter grunted. "*I* didn't make that promise to Lonnie." He jabbed a finger at Alex. "You better watch your back, Moon."

Alex stood again, pulled some money out of his pocket and slapped it on the table. "Let's just keep out of each other's way, and I think we'll be able to keep the peace just fine, hmm?"

He walked out of the pub without looking back, though a dozen pairs of eyes pierced his back on the way. Alex wished he could hope for peace where he was concerned, but he wasn't a fool. It wasn't going to be that easy—one reason being that staying away from Lonnie Hamilton was the last thing he intended to do.

Chapter Twenty

LONNIE WAS GRATEFUL for some spare time to slip into the library before heading home from work. She welcomed the warm stillness after the brisk autumn air. Unwinding her scarf, Lonnie tucked it over her arm and walked her favorite aisles, skimming book spines for a promising title. She was just rounding another bookshelf when one of the librarians approached her with a small yellow volume in her hand.

"Miss Hamilton?"

"Yes?"

"A while back you placed a request for some books on Korea. Is that right?"

"Yes." She was surprised. Had they actually found something?

The dark haired woman cast a furtive look around and took a step closer, lowering her voice. "We weren't able to find anything for you, I'm afraid. It's a limited subject unless you were to go to Indianapolis and look at the library there or at the university."

Lonnie's heart sank, but she nodded. "I understand. Thank you."

The woman reached out and touched her arm. "I think I know why you want to learn more about Korea. It's that young man isn't it? The Oriental one?"

The heat rose in Lonnie's cheeks. "What do you mean?"

The woman smiled in understanding. "I happened to be walking past when he embraced you. Just over there." She pointed.

"Oh!" Lonnie's face was now completely red. "It wasn't what it looked like."

"Don't worry. I won't say anything. The thing is, my mother runs our family's bookshop here in town. The Crooked Spine—do you know the place?"

Lonnie nodded. "I've been there a few times. You sell old books, right?"

The woman nodded. "That's right. I was helping my mother straighten the shelves, and I found a book that might interest you. It was written about twenty years ago. It's set in China, but it still might prove helpful. I read it and found it quite good. Sweet, but sad. Then I remembered your request and how little we have about the Orient. So I asked my mother if I could give it to you." She held out the book in her hands.

A rush of gratitude filled Lonnie as she accepted the unexpected gift. "How thoughtful. Thank you. May I know your name?"

The woman smiled. "It's Florence. Florence Williamson."

"Thank you, Florence." Lonnie inspected the yellow cover and smoothed her hand over the title. *The Vintage of Yon Yee*. Even the letters were written in a kind of Chinese-style script.

She left the library and after a hurried journey, she pushed open her front door, a little out of breath. "I'm home," she announced.

"We're in here." Marty's voice came from the kitchen. Lonnie went in and stopped short at seeing Alex sitting at the table with her little brother.

"Alex. What are you doing here?"

His face brightened. "I came by to drop something off for you. Tunie saw me and invited me in. She said you'd be home any minute." His eyes held a hint of worry.

"Where's Tunie?" Lonnie asked. She was amazed her sister would think to be so nice to him after all her sour words.

"I'm in here," her sister called from the front room. "Don't worry. Mother has to work some extra hours tonight."

Relief allowed Lonnie to relax until she noticed Alex gazing in open surprise at her hands. "What is it?"

"That book. Have you read it before?"

"No, I haven't. I just got it." She paused. "Have you read it?"

He was oddly guarded. "Yes."

"How did you like it?"

He shrugged. "It was okay. The ending was a bit disappointing, but you might find the storyline interesting. You'll have to let me know what you think."

Lonnie was confused by his cryptic opinion. "All right, I will." She left to remove her coat and scarf and set down her things. By the time she came back to the kitchen, Marty and Alex were leaning back over his math homework.

Marty stuck his tongue between his teeth as he scribbled with his pencil. He looked to Alex. "Is that right?"

Alex shook his head. "I'm afraid not."

Marty threw down his pencil. "I don't get it. What am I doing wrong?"

Alex and Lonnie exchanged a knowing smile. "Why don't you get your pencil, and I'll explain it to you."

As Marty dutifully obeyed, Lonnie checked the cookie tin and found it empty. Figuring they'd want a snack after all their hard work, she got busy making some oatmeal drop cookies. She listened to Alex explain the problem.

"You see, you're getting the order wrong. If you do the problem in the wrong order you're going to end up with the wrong answer."

Marty frowned. "I still don't get it. What difference should it make which order I do it in?"

"Okay, let's try this," Alex said. "Let's say you have a squadron of twelve fighter planes, each with two engines—"

"What kind of dual-engine fighter planes?" Marty interrupted. Lonnie smothered a laugh as Alex contemplated.

"Let's see . . . How about Douglas A-20 Havocs?"

Marty nodded his approval.

"They're out on a night patrol when out of nowhere some German fighter planes come zooming in—"

"What kind of German fighters?" Marty interrupted again.

Alex sighed in exasperation. "We don't know, because it's dark."

Marty's mouth hung open. "Oh. Okay."

"They zoom from out of nowhere and shoot down three of our boys."

Marty nearly leapt out of his seat. "Why those, dirty rotten—"

"Marty . . ." The warning in Lonnie's voice stopped him mid-sentence. He resumed his seat, grinning sheepishly.

"Now, we get down to the problem," Alex continued. "How many American engines are left?"

Marty calculated for a few moments. "Eighteen."

Alex grinned. "Don't look now, but you just solved your problem."

"I did?"

"When you factored six engines minus two engines and multiplied by twelve the answer was completely different. Follow the correct order and you get it right. You see?"

Marty's face lit up as if a light bulb had turned on. "Oh, I get it now. Thanks, Alex."

Alex whistled in relief and then joined Lonnie as she dropped cookie dough onto a baking sheet.

She smiled but didn't meet his eyes. His kindness and patience toward her brother made her heart swell. She was almost afraid to speak.

"That kid." Alex laughed and crossed his arms over his chest as he leaned against the counter. "I always liked math, but when you're stumped it's good to have someone explain it in a way you can understand."

She finally met his eyes. "He really admires you. Thank you for helping him. It means a lot."

"No problem." Alex shrugged, eyeing the cookie dough hopefully. His eyes lit up. "I nearly forgot the whole reason why I came." He pulled a paper from his pocket and held it out to her. "It's your next lesson."

Lonnie put the pan of cookies in the oven to bake and took the paper, flushing happily. "Can I look at it now?"

He shrugged. "Sure."

She unfolded the paper and skimmed it, scrunching up her nose as she concentrated. "Well, I can't read much of it right away, but from the numbers I might guess this is a recipe. Am I right?"

Alex laughed. "You *are* right. It's a Korean recipe my mother made me memorize before I left home, because she knew it was my favorite. But I'm not going to tell you what it is. That's for you to figure out."

Lonnie narrowed her eyes suspiciously, a mischievous smile twitching the corners of her mouth. "This isn't some round-about way of you getting me to make this recipe for you is it?"

Alex gaped, and then it was his turn to blush.

Lonnie laughed. "I'm right, aren't I?"

"Cooking isn't something—I mean, I don't . . ."

"It's all right." She placed a hand on his arm, amusement still playing on her lips. "I don't mind making it for you. As long as it doesn't have any impossible to find ingredients, we should be fine."

"It's fairly basic."

Soon after, Lonnie pulled the fragrant oatmeal drop cookies out of the oven, and Tunie joined them for their snack including cups of hot cocoa.

Tunie didn't say much, but Lonnie noticed the grudging admiration she directed towards Alex. She smiled smugly to herself, itching to tell her sister 'I told you so' when they had a moment alone. Watching Alex eating and joking around with Marty, he was the most relaxed and happy she'd ever seen him.

All four of them froze mid-sentence when the front door opened and shut. Lonnie's gaze darted to Tunie whose widened, terrified eyes mirrored her own. There was no time to do anything else before their mother walked into the kitchen.

"You're all in here, are you?" Harriet asked, unloading her coat and purse onto a chair. "It turns out they didn't need me working late after all." Then she saw Alex. Lonnie's heart leapt in her chest as if it wanted to run away. Her mother's eyes narrowed. "What is he doing here?"

Lonnie swayed slightly, her mind a blur. What should she say? How could she explain in a way her mother would understand? What could she do to keep her mother from exploding?

Alex took a small step forward. "Hello, Mrs. Hamilton. I'm a friend of Lonnie's, Alex Moon."

Lonnie closed her eyes briefly as if shutting out the scene would make it go away.

"I know who you are." Harriet's voice was low and as cold as ice. "I asked what you were doing here."

Please don't get angry, Lonnie begged silently. Please don't lose your temper. Not now. Not in front of Alex.

"He was just leaving, Mother." Tunie stepped forward. "He was running an errand for Uncle Phillip. Alex helps him over at the church." She quickly bundled up some of the cookies in wax paper and shoved them into Alex's hands before pulling him toward the door. "These are some of Uncle's favorites. You'll make sure you get them to him right away? They're best when they're fresh."

"Of course." Alex's eyebrows were knit in confusion, but he didn't ask for an explanation. "Goodbye. Thank you for the cookies, Lonnie."

She couldn't bring herself to look at him as he left, and Tunie shut the door behind him. Lonnie leaned against the wall, waiting for the barrage of angry shouting. To her surprise it didn't come. Her mother's back was to them all, and they waited. Finally, she faced them, her face contorted into a scowl. "Who invited that filthy traitor here?"

"No one invited him, Mother," Tunie said, folding her arms in front of her. "He was just running an errand. Lonnie had made cookies and we offered him some. That's all." Marty gratefully remained silent. He only watched with round eyes.

Harriet approached Lonnie, eyes narrowed. "He said he was your friend. Is that true?"

Lonnie swallowed. "Yes." Her answer was a breath, so soft it was barely audible.

"Let me make this clear to you all. That Jap isn't welcome in this house. Not ever. I can hardly believe you. Here I go to work for endless hours every week, working to not only put a roof over your heads but to make sure we win this awful war. Your own father is fighting overseas, and you have the gall to invite the enemy under our very roof." Her voice rose steadily. Lonnie felt a sharp jab at the mention of her father. "Don't be fooled into thinking he's your friend, Appalone Hamilton. He only wants to take advantage, and I won't permit that. I forbid you from having him in this house again, do you understand me?"

Lonnie bowed her head, nodding ever so slightly, devastated.

"Oh, Mother," Tunie cut in, her voice light. "He's not even Japanese. That was some silly rumor that got started. Alex is Korean."

Harriet grunted. "The Koreans are as good as enemies with the Japanese as their dictators. Who knows what kinds of things they're doing to brainwash those people? For all we know he could be a spy. What if he's a Jap posing as a Korean? How do we know? He could be getting up to all sorts of trouble behind your back. No. I'm not taking the risk." She stared pointedly at Lonnie. "You're old enough that I'm not going to tell you who your friends should be, but you're not to bring that man into this house again, understand?"

"Yes, Mother."

At long last, Harriet went to her bedroom. Lonnie stumbled after Tunie up the stairs to their room. Once the door was shut, she sank onto her bed.

"Thank you," she whispered. "I didn't know you would stand up for him. I honestly don't know what I would've done without you."

Tunie plopped onto the bed beside her and laughed. "It wasn't for *Alex*, it was for you. Besides, Mother can be so unbelievable sometimes. I get so sick of it."

Lonnie reached over and gave her a big squeeze. "How did I get so lucky to have you as a sister?"

"It beats me." Tunie giggled, then raised an eyebrow. "Don't think I've given up keeping an eye on that guy. I still think it's a bit fishy how he keeps hanging around you. If I didn't know better, I'd think he was sweet on you."

Lonnie gasped and swatted her sister's shoulder. "Don't be a goose. That's absolutely not true. We're only friends." She laughed, but the possibility of her sister's words was unsettling. She shook her head.

Tunie shrugged, getting up. "Suit yourself. I'm just telling you what I see. I'm only an innocent, high school junior, though. What would I know?" She winked and left the room leaving Lonnie to stare after her in bafflement.

***

Alex left the Hamilton home in a state of confusion, but it didn't take him long to work things out. It was obvious Lonnie's mother didn't approve of him. He recalled Teddy's words that Lonnie was under her thumb. That alone made him depressed. Her uncle would never approve, and now her mother?

The image of a terrified Lonnie jumped into his mind. He knew what it was like to have a domineering parent, but where he had his mother in the home to deflect much of his father's harshness, Lonnie had no one. No, he corrected himself. She had Tunie, who seemed to act as her protector. And she had her uncle and aunt. But being under a different roof made a big difference. No one could possibly see everything that went on behind closed doors.

Alex gritted his teeth together in consternation as he shivered with cold. He hunched his shoulders against the piercing wind and shoved his hands deeper into his coat. The one pocket containing the still-warm cookies helped ward off the chill somewhat. He missed the mild winters of California. The coldest it ever got was sixty degrees or so, colder if you went down to the beach on a gloomy day. He was completely unprepared for the harsher winters of the Midwest, and he wondered how he was going to afford a thicker coat and warmer underclothing. His last pairs of socks were wearing thin in the heels too. They'd just have to last, that's all. Either that or learn how to darn. That idea made him laugh.

Alex arrived at the reverend's house and knocked. After a moment, Reverend Hicks answered.

"Alex, come in, please. November is already being a bit harsh, isn't it?"

"Yes, it is. Thank you." Alex stepped into the wonderfully warm front room. He held his hands up to the little fire in the fireplace and sighed as the wavering heat penetrated his stiff fingers. After a few minutes of thawing himself out, Alex remembered the cookies.

"Tunie said I should bring these to you." He pulled them out of his pocket and lamented their crushed state. "I'm sorry they're a little worse for the wear."

Reverend Hicks laughed. "I can see they served a more useful purpose for your hands on the way over."

Alex laughed in return. "I'm sorry. I should get myself a pair of gloves."

"Not to worry." Reverend Hicks took them into the kitchen and returned with them on a plate and two cups. "I just brewed some coffee. Now that they've started rationing that too, I have to savor it. I was just about to enjoy my last cup for the day. Would you like some?"

"Yes, please. Anything hot would be most welcome."

The two men sipped their coffee, enjoying the broken, crumbled cookies.

"Reverend?" Alex spoke up after a while. "Is Lonnie afraid of her mother?"

Reverend Hicks' cup rattled in its saucer. His face paled. "What do you mean?"

"Well, I met Mrs. Hamilton for the first time today. She didn't seem that fond of me. I suppose it's understandable, but I can't forget Lonnie's expression. She looked as if she was about to faint from fright."

Reverend Hicks sighed and set down his cup. "My sister Harriet is a difficult person, but I don't like going around airing our family's dirty laundry, you know."

Alex persisted. "I realize that, but I'd never speak of it with anyone. Lonnie is my friend. I just want to understand." Some uncomfortable heat rose in his face from the fib. She was much more to him than a friend.

The man frowned, but conceded. "No, I don't imagine you would speak of it with anyone. And there's not much I'm at liberty to tell you, but I will say this. My sister is an extremely angry and bitter person. Much of it comes from unfortunate circumstances in the past, some of it has to do with Lonnie's father Martin, and the rest . . ." Reverend Hicks cleared his throat and his shoulders slumped. "The rest has to do with me, I'm afraid."

"Oh." Alex didn't know what else to say. What things from the past could leave a person so bitter and spiteful? And toward her own children? And what had Lonnie's father done? What had Reverend Hicks done? He knew it would be crossing the line to ask any of these questions aloud, and so he kept them to himself.

"I worry about Appalone." Reverend Hicks's brow wrinkled. "She's a wonderful young woman, and I worry her living in that home is doing more harm than good. Lonnie fancies she's protecting her siblings from her mother's unpredictable temper by taking the brunt of it, but in all honesty, it's almost always focused entirely at Lonnie."

Alex straightened up at this. "It is? But why?"

Reverend Hicks stood abruptly. "More coffee?" He rushed to collect their cups and disappeared into the kitchen.

Alex picked at the cuff of his coat, thinking. What could Lonnie possibly have done to deserve all of her mother's anger? Why would it only be focused toward her to begin with? It didn't make any sense. He knew from his own father's anger, it was bent toward any child that was disobedient or disrespectful. True, that person was usually himself, but he'd seen his siblings get into trouble plenty of times before.

When the reverend came back into the room, Alex got up. "Thank you. I should head home. I apologize if I've overstayed my welcome."

"Oh, certainly not. Thank you for stopping by to deliver the cookies." He paused. "And Alex, please keep what we've talked about in confidence. While Lonnie is living under her mother's roof, there's not a lot you or I can do. The best we can offer is our prayers of faith."

Alex nodded. "Yes, of course. I'll remember that."

He walked home, so consumed in his thoughts that he nearly didn't feel the cold. As he lay in bed that night, the wind howling around the corners of the house, Alex thought of Lonnie still, of the fear shading her face. The image tormented him because he didn't know how to help her. How desperately he wanted to protect her. He wanted to pull her close, shield her ears with his hands, lock her eyes with his own, and together they'd completely disregard the world of malice that swirled around them.

Chapter Twenty-One

DESPITE THE TINY space heater which Mike gave him to use, Alex awoke the next morning to his breath puffing out in clouds of fog. The windows were frosted over and a blanket of chill permeated the room. He shivered and burrowed himself deeper under his covers. He couldn't help but think of the beaming, warm sun and the fresh tang of a balmy sea breeze. He moaned. He was beginning to hate the cold.

There was a knock on the door that led out into the garage. Alex waited a moment to brace himself before throwing off the covers and shuffling to the door.

Mike whistled at Alex whose arms were wrapped around his torso, shivering. "I suspected it was this cold up here. Why didn't you say anything? Come on." He beckoned Alex to come downstairs. Alex grabbed his coat and stuffed his threadbare stocking feet into his shoes before following after him.

The heady warmth of the house enveloped Alex like a cloud, and his shivers instantly eased.

Mike shoved a cup of hot coffee into his hands. "Drink this and come in here. I've got something for you."

Sipping the black liquid, Alex relished the heat sliding down his throat and warming his belly. He trailed after Mike into the living room to see a large mound of clothing occupying the couch.

"I pulled out everything I figured would fit you. Thomas was more your size, I think. Luckily, he took better care of his things than my other two."

Alex's eyes slid over to the picture of Thomas on the wall. Mike was giving him his dead son's clothes? Something in his chest constricted. He opened his mouth to protest, but Mike beat him to it.

"I know what you're going to say, son." Mike turned to face him, his voice coming out low and gravelly. "But these clothes don't do any good gathering dust in a closet or a box, especially when you're freezing to death. It's only going to get colder, you know. And the wind off the river is something fierce." He paused, studying Alex's face. "Don't think of it as charity, either. This is part of your wage. Understand?"

Alex nodded slowly, overcome. "Thank you."

Mike left to go into the kitchen, but turned back. "Oh, and another thing. You're to stay in the house from now on. I can't afford the extra fuel running that space heater up there." He disappeared into the kitchen, leaving Alex to stare after him.

He was asking him to stay in the house? A strange mix of emotions engulfed him—surprise, gratitude, humility. He stepped forward and picked up a sweater, fingering its thickness. It was a handsome, blue knitted wool. Had Mrs. Hardy made this? His eyes roved over the rest of the clothing. There were piles of socks, underclothes, pants, shirts, sweaters and vests, a few sets of flannel pajamas, a couple jackets, ties, even a modest, stylish hat. Winter gloves, scarves, a wool coat and a warm, knitted wool cap lay right on top.

Without warning, hot, sharp tears formed in Alex's eyes. He looked at Thomas' picture again. "Thank you," he whispered. For the briefest of moments Alex could've sworn Thomas's grin had widened, his eyes blinking in receipt of the gratitude. But then the moment was gone, and Alex quickly swiped away the tears as the smells of eggs and sausage wafted into the living room. His stomach growled, and he followed the smell to join Mike in the kitchen for breakfast.

After a full day of work, Alex moved his things down into Thomas's bedroom. It was small, but cozy, with a chest of drawers, mirror, a closet with a door, and a much more comfortable bed than the one in the garage apartment. Mike had put on a fresh set of sheets and aired out an old quilt for the bed. Alex was touched Mike was allowing him so much into his life, treating him almost as another son. It was a tentative feeling between them that was difficult to interpret. He was incredibly grateful to Mike, but he didn't want to be pushing himself in, replacing Mike's boys.

After refreshing himself with a shower, Alex changed into some of the new clothes Mike had given him and surveyed himself in the mirror. He was amazed. He had no idea how shabby he'd looked before—not until he put on Thomas's gently used clothing. He turned to admire the clean figure he now cut. He definitely felt more like himself now that he could view himself in the mirror with more dignity. All that was left was a haircut.

Satisfied, Alex began folding and putting away clothing. He opened the closet, which Mike had cleaned out for him, and as he hung up a shirt, a drawing in the back caught his eye. He stepped in to take a closer look. It was a heart with Tommy H + Rose E written inside. Alex's lips tilted a little, touching the heart with his fingertips. He wondered how long ago Thomas had drawn it. He drew his eyebrows together. Was Lonnie's friend Rose the girl who'd been the object of Thomas's affections?

With a sudden idea, Alex grinned. He rummaged in his things for a pen and returned to the closet. A few inches from Thomas's heart Alex drew his own heart. He sketched busily, frowning in concentration to ensure he was drawing it evenly. Once the heart was drawn, he wrote in the middle Alex + Lonnie.

He finally stood back to survey his work and laughed. Satisfied, he continued to hang clothing in the closet. He was happy and content, as if he officially belonged there now. He wasn't claiming the room from Thomas, but was only adding to its history—tattoos of boyish dreams and desires. Alex somehow sensed Thomas wouldn't mind. He hung the last shirt in the closet. Now that the closet was full, the graffiti was hidden from view. It was a secret between Thomas and himself—just as it should be.

***

The sun had set a few hours ago. With nothing else to do, Alex sat in bed studying in one of his engineering books. While it was interesting, he kept putting it down to think about Lonnie. He couldn't forget that book she'd had in her hands when she came home and he'd been waiting for her. *The Vintage of Yon Yee*. Why would she be reading that? He remembered as a teenager borrowing it from his older sister, Esther, and being a bit disgusted by how sappy it was. The descriptions had been good, the characters somewhat interesting, but it was the storyline that had been fascinating, almost scandalous for his young mind—a Chinese man and a British man and their mutual struggle with their love for a young woman of mixed British and Chinese parentage.

But why was Lonnie reading a book like that? Perhaps she didn't know what it was about. What would she think about the romantic elements of the story? If she knew how he felt, would she be as repulsed as the British man had been at first, or would she react more favorably as the Chinese man had? He needed to know what she thought. Depending on which side she related to more, it would be his guide in how to pursue their relationship.

Giving up on his book, Alex set it aside and pulled out a dresser drawer to find a set of pajamas. He was excited to wear a warm pair for a change. He pulled out what he needed and was about to close the drawer when a flat corner of white in the back caught his attention. He tugged it out.

It was an envelope. Written in even print was a name—Rose Everett. The envelope wasn't opened and with growing unease he realized this letter was probably written by Thomas before he left home as a soldier only to be killed overseas. The feeling made him sick. If this Rose was indeed Lonnie's friend, shouldn't she have this letter?

"A letter from the dead," Alex murmured aloud. Would he wish to receive a letter like this? Without hesitation, he knew he would, however painful it was. Pulling on a robe, Alex left his room in search of Mike, letter in hand. He found him reading the afternoon paper in the living room.

"Mike?"

"Hmm?"

"I found this in one of the dresser drawers. I think it's something Thomas meant to have delivered."

At his words, Mike looked up sharply and took the envelope. His face paled slightly. "Rose Everett."

"Is she a girl in town?"

Mike nodded. "Thomas was sweet on her, but could never get up the courage to tell her. He must've written this—" His voice caught, but after a moment he continued. "He must've written this before he shipped out."

"Do you think we should give it to her?"

Mike shrugged, handing the letter back. "I wouldn't have the heart to."

Alex paused. "If it's the Rose I'm thinking of, she's a friend of Lonnie Hamilton. I could give it to Lonnie. She might be a better person to deliver it anyway. Would that be all right?"

Mike nodded, returning to his paper. "That might be best, but I don't see what good it would do. Go ahead if you've a mind to do it."

Alex returned to his room and tucked the letter into his coat pocket. There was no way he'd stop by her house or workplace to deliver it. He'd have to wait until he crossed paths with her again.

***

It took Lonnie an entire day of anxiously wading through a pile of typed reports and correspondence to work up the nerve to speak with Teddy again. The steady clacking of the typewriter keys helped pace her tumbling thoughts and reservations. With every new sheet of paper she cranked through the roller, she wavered between "Yes, I'm going to speak with Teddy tonight" to "No, I can put it off another day." As it turned out, the last sheet of paper ended on a "Yes" and she sighed, accepting her fate.

She bundled up after bidding farewell to Mr. Pickering and trudged through a freshly fallen skiff of snow, the first of the season. The entire town was blanketed in glittering white, except where the shadows of the buildings cast by the setting sun left the snow a dull and lifeless gray.

She allowed herself to enjoy making new tracks on the edges of the sidewalk where others had avoided stepping. It helped keep her mind off her unpleasant task ahead. She kept her head down and didn't look anyone in the eye, afraid if she did, they'd see her trepidation and ask if she was all right.

Of course she wasn't all right. Everything was all wrong. Teddy had proposed out of the blue, her mother had forbidden Alex from ever coming to their home again, and on top of that, she felt a cold coming on. As if to emphasize the point, she sneezed and fumbled in her pocket for her handkerchief. A fine day this was turning out to be.

Teddy's house loomed far too soon for Lonnie's liking. She loitered on the walk just outside and allowed her eyes to travel up its imposing edifice. Was it really so bad to think of being mistress of such a home some day? She'd promised Teddy she'd think about it, and yet she hadn't even done that much for him. She could be a fine figure in the town—the wife of a prominent factory owner. No doubt, they'd drive a fancy car and maybe even visit the capitol now and then by train. They'd have a servant to help with the cleaning, even a cook. Her weary bones ached after the idea, especially since she had to think of dinner as soon as she got back home.

She shook her head. There was no sense in daydreaming when she knew very well she'd be unhappy married to Teddy, grand home and oodles of the latest fashions or not. Having a dry and dull life, hearing endlessly about factory work, talking about whether she had a good day at home doing who knew what, sharing details about her latest charity function, and taking care of the baby. It was too much to bear.

She blushed as she considered a baby. She wanted children, of course. But Teddy as the father of her children? It was unfair, she knew, but what if they inherited his poor lungs? She'd be taxed with the burden of worrying after them all her days. And even if they didn't, to have Teddy as a father? What kind of father would he be? She and Teddy had been friends for ages, but she had yet to discover all the intimate details about his life and personality.

Besides, she didn't want children right away. She wanted a chance to leave this town, to be her own person, to make decisions for herself, and only for herself, without walking on eggshells or being dictated to.

At long last, Lonnie squared her shoulders and marched up to the front door. She knocked resolutely and waited. Mrs. Stanton answered.

"Why, Lonnie. What a pleasure to see you again so soon. Do come in out of the cold."

Lonnie stepped inside. "Is Teddy home yet? I wanted to speak with him."

Mrs. Stanton's face fell. "He is, but I'm afraid he's ill. He couldn't even manage to go into the office today with his father."

Lonnie's confidence deflated. "I should come back another time." She wanted to curse.

Mrs. Stanton reached out to touch her shoulder. "Actually, Lonnie. Would you mind terribly if you went up to see him? He'd be so upset if he knew he'd missed you. He could use some cheering up. You know how down he gets with these ill spells."

Lonnie's heart thumped in her chest. This was not going the way she'd planned. How could she say what she'd come to say to a sick man? "All right. If you think I should."

Mrs. Stanton brightened. "Wonderful. Just follow me."

She led Lonnie up the glorious, winding staircase to a door at the end of the landing. "Just in here. I'll leave you then." She disappeared quickly, and Lonnie was left to wonder if Mrs. Stanton had orchestrated something she had yet to discover.

Lonnie turned the knob and entered the bedroom. Teddy was propped up in his bed, the only light coming from a golden globe lamp on his bedside table. He was reading a book, his glasses shining in the light. She approached softly. As she got closer, she saw that Teddy was actually asleep, his head resting against his headboard, the book held open by his lifeless hands.

She pulled up the chair Mrs. Stanton had no doubt occupied earlier and watched him sleep, his chest rising and falling peacefully. It reminded her of when she'd sat by his bedside during one of his bad days, regaling him with events at school or reading to him from a favorite book. She was fond of those memories and treasured them. His boyish smile and hopeless jokes were always good for a laugh, and her heart warmed, recalling them. He'd seemed handsome to her then, but in a way that made her feel proud he was her friend. Nothing ever romantic.

Right now, though, his hair was disheveled, his face was unshaven, and he snored gently, but she allowed that he was handsome as a man—in his own way.

She sighed, her shoulders slumping as she studied her hands. She knew she was being shallow. There was far more to a relationship than attraction, despite what Cary Grant or Gene Kelly might make the world think. But it certainly was an important part, wasn't it? Yes, she argued silently, but there was also kindness, compassion, and service. Laughter and the sharing of disappointments and pain. It was counseling together and solving problems. Could she see herself doing all of those things with Theodore Stanton?

She removed Teddy's book, setting it on the nightstand. She gently pulled the covers up. He stirred and woke, startling her. Her face was close enough to feel his warm breath on her skin. A smile reached his sleepy eyes.

"Lonnie." His voice was soft and gentle. "Am I still dreaming? Have you really come?" He began coughing. She pulled away, but his hand on her arm stopped her. He finally recovered. "Please, don't go. I'm so glad you came. I've been longing to see you."

She pulled the chair closer to his bedside and studied her hands, now grasping together, reflecting the agony that ate away inside. "You wouldn't be so glad if you knew why I'd come."

He watched her, but ignored what she said. "It's remarkable, but I'm taken back to when you used to sit by my bed when I missed school. We always had such fun."

Lonnie allowed herself a small smile. "Yes. I was thinking the same thing." She sighed. "But, Teddy . . ." Could she bring herself to finally say it?

He reached out to grab her hand. "Why can't it still be the same? What happened to those times? Why can't you love me now?"

Unexpected tears sprang to her eyes, whether it was from her own emotion or Teddy's heart-wrenching pleas she didn't know. "We were children then. We've grown up. Grown apart. We're meant for different paths." She couldn't meet his eyes. Somehow she knew if she did, the image would haunt her for a long time.

"No." His voice was raspy, and he coughed again. "No. I want you, Lonnie. I *need* you. I've only ever loved you. Surely you'll grow to love me as I do you?"

Her jaw ached from clenching it. She wanted to cry out, to shout at him and to wound him. If only to make his pleading stop. She turned her head away and took deep breaths, her heart skipping unpleasantly in her chest.

"You—you love someone else. That's it, isn't it?"

Lonnie's head whipped around at this accusation. "What?"

Teddy's face was full of shock and hurt. "It's him . . . isn't it?" he said. "Alex Moon."

Lonnie was suddenly filled with dread. "No. That's not true." She stood. "Please, let's not drag anyone else into this. I came to say I can't marry you, Teddy. You've been a dear friend for so long, but I can't be your wife."

She walked away, but he shouted angrily after her. "I won't accept it, Lonnie. I won't let him take you from me. So help me, I won't!"

She paused, but then continued out the door and out of the house, his words ringing painfully in her ears.

***

When Lonnie wearily opened her front door, her mother was home early and in the kitchen preparing supper. "Teddy's having one of his ill spells and won't be able to come to dinner," Lonnie announced without ceremony.

"I'm sorry to hear that. Perhaps when he's feeling better?"

Lonnie shrugged, and without saying anything else, she drifted upstairs and lay down on her bed. She pulled the covers up to her chin, hoping their warmth would ease away her sadness. Her friendship with Teddy was never going to be the same again. She'd only ever be able to gaze back through it like a locked window and see herself and those childhood memories she shared with Teddy, never to touch them again.

She covered her head with the blanket and cried herself to sleep.

Chapter Twenty-Two

LONNIE WOKE TO a wintery dim. The smell of food had faded, telling her dinner was over. No one had come to get her to eat. Where was everyone? She sat up, and her head pounded. Her nose tickled and she sneezed, her body reminding her she was getting sick. She fumbled for a tissue, blew her nose, and lay back down. Her stomach was hollow, but she didn't feel like eating. She lay in the semi-darkness and tried not to think of anything.

Her door was slightly ajar, letting weak light pour in from downstairs. After a few moments, she registered voices. One of them was deep. It piqued her interest. Who was visiting? At first, their voices were only mumbles of sound, but they grew quickly in volume. It was an argument.

"See common sense, Harriet."

"I don't see how any of this is your business, Phillip."

Lonnie propped herself up, ignoring her aching head. Uncle Phillip was here? Her breath caught in her throat. Was he here to speak to her mother about Teddy? A wave of relief washed over her, but it wasn't enough to dispel the equal measure of trepidation that seized her.

"Lonnie isn't ready to marry. She doesn't want to be pushed at a man she doesn't love."

Her mother scoffed loudly. "Love? *Love?*"

"Yes. It's a concept you've shunned in recent years."

"Don't lecture *me*, Phillip Hicks. I won't have it in my own house." There was a pause. "I think it's time you left."

"You may push me out, but it's my responsibility to see after Lonnie's welfare in matters such as courtship and marriage. It was Martin's wish." More silence. Uncle Phillip continued in a quieter voice, and Lonnie had to strain to hear. "We each have our own ways of making up for past mistakes. This is mine." The front door opened and shut, her uncle gone.

What could he possibly mean by making up past mistakes? What mistakes? She had the sinking suspicion it had something to do with her, but she couldn't imagine how. Regardless, she was grateful to her uncle for taking the courage to speak on her behalf.

Lonnie changed into a nightgown and crawled into bed, feeling safe under her uncle's watch care, but also a little anxious. What would her mother say when she knew she'd rejected Teddy's marriage offer? Would she be sent over the edge? What would be the result? She eventually fell asleep, deciding to leave those questions for another day.

***

Alex was surprised to see Lonnie at church, but only because she looked so terrible. Her face was pale, her eyes had dark circles underneath them, and her nose was red.

He watched Lonnie make her way down the aisle after church, leaning on Tunie for support. She spoke with her uncle, who frowned at seeing her, placed his hand on her shoulder, and spoke words that were drowned out by the other parishioners' chatter.

Garnering dark comments and annoyed stares, Alex pushed his way toward Lonnie as politely as he could. He reached her side just as Reverend Hicks said, "I really don't think you should be walking home in this state, Appalone. It's a miracle you managed to walk all the way here."

"I told her that," Tunie chimed in. "But she wouldn't listen."

"I'll admit I didn't account for how weak I would feel by the end, but I was simply too cooped up at home. I needed fresh air." Lonnie coughed and leaned on Tunie more heavily.

"Well, you won't be getting it on a walk home if I have anything to do with it," Reverend Hicks stated. "Why don't you go on over to my house and wait until my duties here are done? I can drive you back in the car."

Lonnie opened her mouth to protest, but Tunie interrupted. "That's a wonderful idea, Uncle Phillip. Marty and I have to get back home to work on homework, and I promised Phyllis I'd come over this afternoon . . ."

Alex stepped forward. "I can take her over to your house and wait with her, Reverend Hicks."

The reverend looked back and forth between Alex and Lonnie and finally nodded. "All right, I suppose. I'll be over as soon as I can."

Tunie beamed gratefully at Alex—her attitude had softened considerably towards him since the last time he'd seen her—and dragged Marty, who waved at Alex in farewell, down the sidewalk.

Alex offered Lonnie his arm, and she took it, leaning against him as they made their way down the sidewalk to the reverend's house. Once inside, he settled her in a chair near the fireplace and started a fire. Then, he rummaged in the kitchen and prepared a pot of tea.

When he finally came back with a pair of steaming mugs, Lonnie was asleep. Sinking into a chair, he regarded her, his heart filled with worry. How long had she been sick?

After a few moments, she stirred, and her cheeks flushed when she met his eyes. "I'm sorry. I must've fallen asleep."

"Don't apologize. I'm not surprised." He offered her one of the mugs, which she accepted gratefully. He watched her sip it, and she seemed to relax even more.

"I needed to get out of the house." She shut her eyes, but it wasn't in sleep. She looked pained.

"Is everything all right?"

Her eyes opened slightly. "I'll be fine." She took another sip. "This tea is nice."

The ticking of the mantle clock filled the comfortable space between them. Alex remembered the letter in his coat pocket, and he pulled it out.

"Lonnie," he began. "Is Rose Everett a friend of yours?"

She sat up a little straighter. "Yes, why?"

He squeezed the letter in his hands, wondering if the timing was good to bring this up. But since he'd already started . . .

"I have a letter for her. I was wondering if you'd deliver it."

"A letter? For Rose?" Her voice halted.

He laughed a little. "It's not from me. You see, Mr. Hardy had me move into the house where it's warmer, and he put me in his son Thomas's room. I found this letter in the dresser drawer addressed to Rose Everett."

Alex didn't think it possible, but Lonnie's face grew even paler than it was before. "Thomas? Tommy Hardy?"

"Yes. I know he died not too long ago. I asked Mr. Hardy, and we both thought Rose should have the letter. Do you think that's right?"

Lonnie nodded weakly. "Y-yes. She should have it. Oh, Rose!" Her hands flew to her face, and she starting weeping.

Alarmed, Alex sprang from his chair to kneel at her side. "I'm sorry. I shouldn't have brought it up now—not when you're so sick. Please forgive me."

At that moment, Reverend Hicks walked through the door. "Forgive you for what?" His voice was stern.

Alex scrambled to his feet, face flaming with embarrassment. Of all the moments for him to walk in.

"Why is she crying? What's happened?" Reverend Hicks quickly removed his scarf and overcoat to come to his niece's aid.

"I only told her about a letter I'd found that belongs to one of her friends."

Lonnie wiped her cheeks. "It's all right, Uncle Phillip. His news was surprising that's all, and in my state, I think anything would set me off." She smiled kindly at Alex.

"I see," Reverend Hicks conceded. He turned to Alex. "I'm afraid Lonnie isn't the only one on edge today." He disappeared into the kitchen, and Alex turned back to Lonnie.

"I'm so sorry. I didn't mean to distress you."

"Don't be sorry. It's just that Rose was so heartbroken by what happened to Tommy. She's still getting over him."

Alex sank back into his chair. "Would it be too difficult to deliver to her? I could go with you if you'd like." He paused. "I know this might sound funny, but I feel I owe it to him—to Thomas."

"I don't think it sounds funny, even if I don't understand exactly what you mean. It's very kind of you making sure she gets his letter. Thank you."

Alex nodded and got up as Reverend Hicks came back into the living room. "I think I'll leave now. I hope you feel better, Lonnie." Saying goodbye, he went outside. The snow dazzled his eyes in the bright sunlight. The air was clean and crisp. The beautiful day was a juxtaposition of how he was feeling.

Alex kicked at a clump of snow, scowling at himself. What had he been thinking by bringing up the letter from a man who hadn't been dead a year, especially when she was feeling so sick? He stomped home with his hands shoved in his coat pockets. How could he have been so thoughtless?

He arrived back at Mike's house and removed his winter coat and scarf. Hanging them in the closet, he plopped down in a chair, slouching as he did so.

Mike was in his regular chair reading one of Alex's *Popular Science* magazines he'd left laying out.

"Bad sermon?" he asked, a note of amusement in his voice.

"No."

"It was a good sermon then, only you've realized what a sinner you are."

Alex's eyes slid over to Mike. "You're laughing at me, aren't you?"

Mike rested the magazine in his lap. "Not exactly. You seem to be in a foul mood. I'm only guessing why."

"I'm just an unfeeling idiot. Is that something I can repent of?" He was being sarcastic, but Mike scratched his chin in contemplation.

"I'd like to think so. You're a decent man, Alex. It can't have been all that bad."

Alex grunted. "I suppose not. It still smarts though. I guess I'll get over it eventually." He straightened. "Do you want me to fix us some lunch?"

Mike nodded in appreciation. "That would be fine. See? You're already making amends. Unfeeling idiots don't offer to make others lunch."

Alex laughed and went to the kitchen.

***

Late that night, Alex turned fitfully in his bed. He flopped over on his back in a huff. The image of Lonnie bursting into tears wouldn't leave him. It was the first time he'd made her cry, and while it had been on someone else's behalf, it still made him uncomfortable. It broke his heart to see her shedding tears; and worse still, it made him feel helpless.

Finally, he sat up in resignation. Throwing off his warm covers, he pulled on his robe and shuffled into the chilly kitchen. He opened the fridge, grabbed the bottle of milk and a small pot, and began heating some of the milk on the stove. While he waited, Alex leaned against the counter and yawned. Once the milk began to simmer, Alex turned off the burner, poured the hot milk into a mug and waited for it to cool.

He was yawning for the third time when a crash came from behind the house, outside the garage. Alex jumped in surprise and then froze to listen, his heart pounding loudly in his ears. There was the crunch of running feet on snow, some muffled voices, and another crash.

Alex leapt into action. He yanked open the door that led into the garage. The unmistakable smell of gasoline and oil met his nostrils, but there was something else—a smell that didn't belong. A flickering orange light drew his eyes to the upstairs apartment. The room was on fire!

Alex sped back into the house and down the hall to Mike's room. He pounded on the door. "Mike!" he shouted. "Mike, there's a fire. Mike!"

Mike opened the door, pulling a sweater over his pajamas. "Where is it?"

"It's in the apartment over the garage."

"Call the fire department. I'll get the hose." Mike stopped and cursed. "The outside pipes are probably frozen. Just call the firemen!" He disappeared outside.

Alex picked up the phone receiver and shouted at the operator to get the fire department. He raced outside to join Mike who had gotten the hose to work after all. It wasn't long enough, and Mike only succeeded in spraying water on the door of the apartment. Alex searched outside for the people who belonged to the voices he'd heard, but they were long gone.

Ten minutes later the fire engine arrived, and the firemen took over. They doused the fire using a hose hooked up to the hydrant on the street, and they had it under control in less than an hour.

By that time, neighbors had gathered in coats and bedclothes. Mike's shoulders sagged as Mrs. Godfrey comforted him. Alex trembled from shock, fatigue, and cold. Who could've done this? Why did they attack the apartment above the garage? There wasn't anything of value there.

With a jolt it came to him—they'd been after *him*. They'd been seeking to harm *him*. Alex grew numb as he leaned against the building. At that moment, Reverend Hicks appeared, hastily dressed and out of breath.

"Alex." He propped himself against the wall to catch his wind. "I just heard. Is everyone all right? Where's Mike?"

Alex nodded in the direction of the house. "He's inside with some neighbors. I think they're making him some coffee."

Reverend Hicks took Alex's arm. "You must be freezing. Let's get you inside."

He allowed himself to be steered to a chair in the crowded kitchen. Voices were hushed and all eyes seemed to follow him. A mug of coffee was shoved into his hands, and he drank without thinking. He coughed roughly, finding his coffee had been spiked with something far stronger than milk. Warmth sped through his limbs and slowly his trembling stopped.

Even so, as he stared into space, the people surrounding him faded into a blur as if they were an out of focus photograph. This was far more than a warning. Someone wanted him gone. If Mike hadn't asked him to live inside the house, he'd be dead or seriously injured. He didn't need a very vivid imagination to figure out why. The question was who.

His mind immediately turned to Teddy Stanton and Walter Chase. Hadn't Walter threatened him to watch his back? And while he couldn't see Teddy doing anything personal on this level, he certainly could've helped orchestrate something. There was also Jake and Homer, the men who'd attacked him at the train station. Who knew how many other people were out to get him for their own personal reasons? Whoever it had been, they'd tried to kill him. Why else would they have specifically set fire to the apartment? The idea made him sick.

It wasn't only him though. They'd tried to destroy such a good, honest man's home and livelihood. It was unforgivable.

Alex came out of his daze as Reverend Hicks ushered the well-meaning neighbors out of the house. When the last of them had gone, he turned to Alex and Mike. "I'll organize a group of folks to help clean up in the morning. In the meantime, why don't you two get to bed? I'll make sure to tidy up and lock the door before I leave. Are you both going to be all right?"

Alex nodded and he and Mike stood.

"Thank you, Reverend," Mike said gruffly. "You're a true friend. I especially appreciate you chasing out the old busybodies."

The reverend laughed. "You're welcome. Alex?" He turned to him. "Are you going to be okay? When I heard the garage apartment was on fire, I feared the worst. I had no idea you'd moved into the house. Thank the Lord for that."

Alex nodded mutely, and Mike clapped him on the shoulder. "Get yourself to bed, son. Things will look better in the morning."

"I'm sorry," Alex spoke. His voice came out like a croak, his throat raw from smoke and cold. "I'm so sorry. It's all because of me. If I'd never come here—"

"Now, you stop right there, young man," Mike interrupted, grabbing his arm. "There's no use in going down that road. You can't take the blame on yourself for something a handful of stupid hooligans decided to do."

"Agreed," Reverend Hicks added with a decisive nod.

"But they were aiming for *me*." Alex yanked his arm out of Mike's grasp. "I should be dead. Don't you see?" He flung out his arm, encompassing the entire town. "This is never going to stop.

Never. I might as well give them what they want, because I can't bear to bring this kind of hatred down on your head too."

"Stop it!" Mike roared, making Alex flinch and cringe back. The man continued in a low voice, his anger simmering. "You can't let *their* hate ruin *your* life, boy. You've got to face it like a man—look them in the eye with dignity and defy their hatred." He jabbed his finger at Alex's chest for emphasis. "You can't hide. You can't give in. You have to accept this and become strong by it, or it'll eat you alive. Your life will become an empty, miserable shell." Mike's voice growled with a hidden viciousness. The experience in his words pierced Alex to the core.

Mike turned on his heel and left the room. A moment later, his bedroom door slammed shut. Alex sank back into his chair, and Reverend Hicks sat beside him. Silence permeated the air. Alex's trembling had returned, but this time it was from raw terror. How could he face this? How could he conquer these people's hatred towards him?

He sagged forward, burying his face in his hands. To his relief, Reverend Hicks didn't say anything. Alex's mind was in a whirlwind. The irony didn't escape him—he'd had his chance to leave this town behind. He would've been tucked safely in bed, no doubt sharing it with a cousin or two, but he would've been where he belonged with people who looked like him and spoke Korean. People who loved and accepted him.

But he'd chosen to stay—for a girl he loved, and he had no idea if she'd ever return the feeling.

Chapter Twenty-Three

MONDAY ARRIVED, AND Lonnie took her uncle's stern advice to stay in bed. Tunie had forbidden her from leaving the house, and Lonnie took comfort in their concern for her. It had been nice to have Alex care for her too. He'd been so attentive, thinking of it made her smile.

With Alex on her mind, Lonnie was reminded of her new book—*The Vintage of Yon Yee*. Eagerly, she retrieved it from the top of her dresser. Snuggled beneath her blankets, she began reading.

It didn't take long for Lonnie to be filled with a growing sense of alarm at the topic of the book. Two male characters were openly discussing whether the main character, Lois Ellingham, who was half-Chinese and half-British, would take a white or a yellow suitor. Lonnie gaped at how frank they were about it.

The book progressed to where a British man struggled with and eventually gave in to his feelings for Lois, but Lonnie was uncomfortable with his reasoning. And further into the book when Lois attracted a Chinese man as a suitor, even he struggled with her being half-British, though it didn't stop him from expressing his deep love for her.

Lonnie read all day, only stopping to warm and eat some soup leftover from last night's dinner. By the time she finished, she was astounded. Why had Florence recommended this book to her? What must she think of Lonnie's relationship with Alex?

Lonnie gasped. What must Alex think of her reading it? Had she unknowingly sent him certain signals by reading a book about a mixed romance? He'd read it and would know everything. Tunie's words returned to Lonnie with full force. Was Alex sweet on her? Did he really care for her in a romantic way?

To her surprise, the idea didn't bother her, and she was amazed by this revelation. She certainly found him interesting and enjoyed his companionable friendship. His intelligent eyes glinted beautifully of the deepest amber, the curve of his jaw was strong, his face handsome. She imagined the press of his lips against hers . . .

Lonnie tossed the book across her bed in a sudden fit of frustration. "Stop it!" She covered her face with her hands. Why was she feeling this way? She couldn't possibly dream of anything happening between them, so why was she so tormented?

Her fretting was interrupted by the front door being flung open and slammed shut. Footsteps pounded up the stairs, and a distraught Marty burst through her door.

"Lonnie. Lonnie!" His cheeks were wet with tears. She bolted up in alarm.

"What is it? Has something happened?"

He ran to her side and clung to her hand. "It's Alex. Everyone at school is saying horrible things like he's been burnt to a crisp and 'It serves that dirty Jap right'. He's *not* a dirty Jap. He's not."

"What?" Lonnie frantically tried to make out what her brother was saying. "What do they mean he's been burnt to a crisp? What do they mean?"

It took him a moment to catch his breath. "There was a fire last night. At Mr. Hardy's garage. Someone set Alex's apartment on fire. Oh, Lonnie. What if he's dead?" He began crying and Lonnie scrambled out of bed. She squeezed him in a hug, fighting down her own panic.

"It's going to be fine, Marty. Just take a deep breath. Could you run and fetch my coat? I'm going to get dressed." She hurried over to her closet and pulled out a warm skirt and sweater.

"But what about staying in bed like Tunie said? You're still sick."

"Never mind that," Lonnie cried. "Now, hurry."

She dressed quickly, and soon she and Marty were speeding down the sidewalk toward Mr. Hardy's house. Thoughts raced through her mind, outstripping her stride by a mile. It couldn't be true. Alex couldn't be dead. How could anyone think of doing such a horrible thing? She knew rumors could quickly grow out of proportion. Surely, there was another explanation. It had to have been an accident.

The image of Alex burned to death gripped her with fear and . . . anguish. She could barely comprehend losing him. The remembrance of his money still in her purse forced its way to the front of her mind. This was her fault. If only she'd given him the money, he would have been free to go. To escape this terrible fate. Oh, what had she done?

Her morose thoughts spiraled out of control. By the time they reached Hardy's Garage, she was on the verge of tears. The garage doors were open, and the place was a hub of activity as people trekked up and down the stairs to the apartment, removing charred remains of furniture and crates.

Lonnie's eyes widened at the scene until Marty burst out in delight. "Alex!" He flew into the crowd.

Lonnie ran after him, stopping short at seeing Alex, his face one of happy surprise. His hands rested on Marty's shoulders. Marty was blabbering incoherently about "those blockheads at school." But the fact that he stood there, alive and whole, caused Lonnie's whole frame to flood with such relief, she nearly sank to the floor.

Alex gently freed himself of Marty's grasp and came to her side. "Let's get you inside," he said. Taking her by the elbow, he guided her to the living room couch. She was grateful that Marty was with them. If he hadn't flung himself into Alex's arms at first sight, she would've done so instead.

Marty started chattering again about all the horrible things children at school had said about the fire. His voice became a mumble to Lonnie as Alex's eyes found hers and locked onto them. It was difficult to tell what he was thinking from the expression on his face, but she didn't want to look away. She drank in the sight of him, soot-smudged face and all. Her heart yearned for him, her body ached to be in his arms. The longer he held her in his gaze, the more breathless she became. Alex was all right. He was alive.

Something in his eyes shifted, and she saw gratitude there, and something else . . .

He broke their mutual silence and interrupted Marty. "Well, as you can see, I haven't burned to a crisp as everyone's been saying. You needn't worry anymore, but it's touching you were so worried." He smiled. "Come to think of it, I have something for you, Marty. Wait right here."

Marty bounced on the couch for a second as he waited for Alex and bounded right back up to take a closer look at the map on the wall. He gaped at it until Alex returned, a small box in his hand.

"I know this isn't much, but I saw it at the five and dime and thought you might like it."

Eyes wide, Marty took the box from his hand. It was a small toy tank with pivoting turret and working treads. Two army men went with it. "Wow," he breathed. "Thanks, Alex."

"Why don't you run along and play outside, but don't get in anyone's way while they're cleaning up, all right?"

Marty grinned and took off running out the door. As soon as her brother was out of sight, Alex reached down for her hand, pulled her to her feet, and wrapped her in a gentle hug. She stiffened in surprise, but then she softened, her arms going around him in relief. She buried her face in his shoulder and finally gave in to the tears.

He held her for a long time until she whispered, "I thought you'd been killed."

"I know, *Sagwa*," he murmured. "I could see it in your face."

"I hate it when I'm sick. I miss out on everything."

His laugh rumbled in his chest. "I'll say."

She tightened her grip on him before finally letting go. Before she could reach into her coat pocket for her handkerchief, his was out. She accepted it with a smile.

"Is it true someone tried to kill you?"

He hesitated, then nodded. "I heard them outside. They were aiming specifically for where I'd been staying. Luckily, I moved into the house a few days ago."

At this Lonnie's mouth dropped open. "Oh. I remember you telling me that now. At my uncle's house yesterday. I feel so foolish." She laughed weakly. "If I'd only remembered, I wouldn't have rushed down here so frantically."

He touched her arm. "It means a lot you care that much about me."

Lonnie blushed at this, wondering how much he really knew.

"The whole thing is terrible, Alex. Who would do such a thing?"

He shrugged. "Who knows? Does it really matter? Most of the town feels the same way. I doubt anything will be done."

"Well, something should be done," she replied hotly. "It could happen again and be worse. You could be seriously injured or even killed next time—others could be hurt. Why don't people have any sense?"

"If everyone had as much sense and compassion as you, this world would be a different place, Lonnie." His eyes were tender as he spoke. "We wouldn't be fighting a world war for a start. Unfortunately, we don't live in that world. This is the world we live in—where people do things such as setting apartments on fire to get rid of someone who's different, someone they can't or won't try to understand."

"It's wrong, either way, and someone should do something about it." She scowled.

"Well, if your uncle has anything to do with it, that just might happen. We'll have to wait and see. I don't like how much of a burden I've become."

"You're not a burden," she blurted. "I—" She gulped back the words that nearly came out, mortified at what she'd almost accidentally confessed. "Y-you're a friend." Her mouth stumbled on the makeshift words.

Alex's lips twitched with a smile. "Thank you." He didn't turn away from her, and their eyes remained fixed for a moment more. "I should walk you home. I'm pretty sure you still shouldn't be out of bed."

Lonnie pressed her lips together. "Well, there was an important matter I needed to attend to."

"Yes, well, now that the matter is taken care of, it's back to being on the mend for you. Let's go."

She allowed herself to be led once again by Alex, but she relished his touch, his firmness in caring for her. It made him feel much more real after her scare.

***

Alex fell back on his bed. He was surprised by all the help that had gathered that morning to clean up the apartment. Luckily, it hadn't been too damaged by the fire—the roof needed some work, but most of it was still sound. Cleaning up from the water was a larger task that would take a week or more. The biggest worry would be finding the construction materials they needed. People had come to help for Mike's sake. Alex was glad for that. Part of him had doubted anyone would want to help because he was involved. Thankfully, that hadn't been the case.

An even greater surprise was how many of the neighbors asked him how he himself was faring. They offered concern and support. His heart warmed when he realized that things weren't as bleak as he feared.

Lonnie's expression of tremendous relief at seeing him in one piece was worth more than all the comforting words and gestures of the neighbors combined. He closed his eyes, reliving his chance to hold her again, savoring the feel of her arms going around him in return. How complete he felt with her cradled in his embrace. He wanted to hold her for the rest of his life.

Even being sick, she'd pushed her own welfare aside out of concern for him. His feelings trembled on a ledge of uncertainty. What did her actions mean? She'd called him her friend, but was there more to it? She'd willingly let him hold her, where other girls in town would have pushed him away in horror because of what he was. Surely, this meant *something*. Didn't it?

Chapter Twenty-Four

THINGS QUIETED DOWN significantly leading up to Thanksgiving. Alex missed Lonnie a great deal. Only seeing her on Sundays from the back of the chapel with a short hello afterward wasn't enough for him anymore. He wanted to see her every day, but she was busy helping her aunt with charity work and her uncle with seeing to the needs of his congregation as the holidays approached. Alex didn't have much to keep his mind occupied besides studying, and even that was a poor distraction.

With work slowed, Alex and Mike spent more time finding ways to fashion new car parts from the scraps they had available to them. The weather turned even colder, and Alex was grateful for his warmer clothing. The strong winds blowing off the river whisked the last of the leaves off the trees and scattered them across town in a splattering of lifeless color.

Thanksgiving Day was a quiet affair. Mike purchased a small turkey, which he cooked and basted with the loving care of a father over his small child. Alex made some mashed potatoes and boiled a can of green beans. Mrs. Godfrey brought them hot buttered rolls and pumpkin pie. The crowning glory was a can of jellied cranberry sauce. Alex regarded the cylinder-shaped jiggling mass with uncertainty. He'd never had cranberry sauce. It didn't look too appetizing, but Mike swore it was delicious, especially with a spot of cream.

Together they sat, and Mike said a prayer of thanks.

"Dear Lord, on this day of Thanksgiving we thank you for our health, our strength, and this meal before us. We're grateful for our friends and our family. Please bless all our boys away from their families, who've sacrificed so much to protect this great country and who fight for our safety. Look out for them, Lord. Protect them and all those who fight against the powers that would seek to harm for the sake of power and revenge. You have truly given us everything, for which we are forever thankful. Amen."

"Amen," Alex echoed. He would have started eating, but his eyes were on Mike. He never knew Mike to be a religious man, but his words had been heartfelt, and Alex felt his feelings for this fathomless man deepen. He was crusty, no doubt, but he was fair, kind, and honest.

It struck him then. Not all fathers were like his father. It was something he knew before, but he felt it now in a painful, longing way. How would his life have been different if he'd had a father like Mike?

Mike carved the small turkey and dished it up. They dug into their modest Thanksgiving meal with enthusiasm. The cranberry sauce was surprisingly tart, but delicious, and Alex and Mike finished it off easily.

As they ate, Alex wondered what his family was doing at that moment. They were probably sitting down to their own Thanksgiving dinner. His family celebrated all the American holidays, but they were definitely Korean influenced. They also observed traditional Korean holidays like Korean Thanksgiving *Chuseok*. His mouth watered as he thought of his mother's *kimchi* stew and the *songpyeon* rice cakes filled with red bean, chestnuts, or sesame seeds she made especially for *Chuseok*.

He longed to see his family again—to be instantly known and understood without any explanation or justification for him being there. To speak Korean and eat Korean food. He'd never missed his home as much as he did now. He'd never missed being Korean as much as he did now. When he'd been home, there were times he wanted to leave his identity behind—to be as American as he could make himself.

Slowly, this was changing. And without a doubt, Lonnie was the reason. For the first time in a long time, he was excited sharing his heritage, sharing his ancestor's language. For the first time in a long time, parts of himself made sense. There was a clarity gradually filling his view like a fogged glass being wiped clean. He was starting to truly see himself for the first time.

After a while, Alex caught Mike eyeing him. "You're surprisingly quiet. I know you're not much of a talker anyway, but you've been contemplating those mashed potatoes for a really long time."

Alex set down his fork. "I've got a lot on my mind, I guess."

"You miss your family?"

He stared at Mike, who always seemed to be able to read his mind. "I was thinking about them, yes."

Mike nodded in understanding. "The holidays are a natural time to miss your family. If it wasn't such an expense, I'd gladly let you call them."

"It's all right. I do miss my mother and my little sister June. Even my older, irritating sister Esther." Alex shrugged. "But my brother Henry and my father . . . it's hard to find it in myself to feel anything for them but loathing and resentment." He stopped, stunned that the words, his private torment, had found their way out.

Hearing them out loud, they sounded unreasonable. *He* had been the one to disobey his father. *He* had been the one to defy him, to refuse to do what needed to be done—his duty to his family and his heritage. He hung his head as the shame settled around him like a leaden shroud.

Mike cleared his throat. "Son, I don't know what water has gone under the bridge between you and your father and brother. But I can tell you this: no one is perfect. Being a father is no picnic, and a family is a messy affair—full of flying fists, black eyes, curses, and name-calling between siblings; as well as hardheaded kids who won't listen. Sound advice just goes in one ear and out the other." Mike chuckled and Alex joined in, recalling some tussles with Henry that had ended in a few black eyes.

Mike continued, his voice growing rough. "There were countless times I thought I'd go stark raving mad. I've lost hair and gone white from my boys, but I loved them fiercely. I'd do anything for them." He swallowed. "I know I'm not the most polished of men, but what I'm trying to say is, I can tell even without meeting him that your father loves you just as fiercely. You may not understand his reasons for doing things, but he's doing it in the best way he knows how.

"Now, your brother on the other hand—that's something you'll have to sort out between the two of you. I wouldn't know what to say. I have five sisters."

Alex grinned. "Five?"

Mike stood to clear his place. "Yeah. They all live in Ft. Wayne on the opposite end of the state. They're five good reasons why nearly two-hundred miles separate us." With that, he winked and took his dishes to the sink, leaving Alex busting out with laughter.

After clearing the table, Alex insisted on cleaning up while Mike listened to the radio and dozed in the living room. He felt a tentative peace settle over him as he thought back over what Mike had to say. He could understand how his father's actions were a form of him showing Alex he loved him. It was a harsh kind of love, but knowing his Korean upbringing, it wasn't unheard of. If anything, Alex could see how helpless his father might feel raising a Korean son, only to see him slipping into the unfamiliar and unacceptable American culture where Korea was only a hazy, far-off place that didn't mean anything.

Alex finished drying the last dish and hung up the damp towel. Weeks ago, Uncle Harry had asked him to put himself in his father's shoes, and so Alex finally tried. If he had a son, would he want him to turn his back on his culture, to forget the foundation his life was built on just because he lived in a different country?

He wandered to his room and sat on his bed while he pictured this imaginary son. As a father, would he do everything in his power to set him on the path he felt was the most right? Would he argue, threaten, and punish to get him to listen?

Alex leaned forward to pull the picture of his family off his dresser. Clad in *hanbok*, the traditional Korean dress, their familiar faces peered up at him, even his own young, defiant face. His heart swelled. He loved them. Even Henry. And even his father.

As a father with that fierce love for his son, would he fight to protect him, even if it meant sending him away to learn the lesson for himself?

His breath shortened, his chest tightened with knowing.

Yes. Yes he would.

***

Lonnie used the time between Thanksgiving and Christmas to make Christmas presents and work feverishly on finishing her mending of Alex's clothing. She was nearly finished, and she couldn't wait to give them back.

As Christmas drew near, Aunt Millie approached her about helping with her annual Christmas party. She insisted that, wartime or no, she was going to be throwing her party. "It's tradition," she said with a sniff. Lonnie didn't like to think about what had happened last year at her aunt's party and no doubt, Aunt Millie was trying hard not to think about it either.

That year of 1941, she'd held it early in the month on Saturday, December 6th. They'd all had such a wonderful time, and the party had gone late. The next day, news came of the Japanese bombing Pearl Harbor. Their lives had never been the same since, and they felt sick with how just the day before they'd been celebrating.

As if in repentance for the previous year's party, Aunt Millie was holding her party December 12th. Lonnie helped plan the decorations and the recipe ideas. Her aunt coordinated with the invited guests about potluck dishes.

A few days before the party, Lonnie pulled out the letter Alex had given her for Rose. It was another thing she'd been putting off. She had a Christmas present for her friend and missed how they hadn't spent much time together lately. She really owed her a visit.

After dinner, Lonnie bundled up and walked across town to Rose's house. When she arrived, one of Rose's three little sisters answered the door. "Hi, Lonnie." She grabbed Lonnie's hand and pulled her inside. "You must be frozen."

"I'm not too bad. My goodness, you've grown tall, Betsy."

Betsy laughed. "Yes, that's what Rose keeps telling me. I'll go get her."

Lonnie pulled off her hat and gloves and smiled wide when Rose entered the room. "I'm sorry for just stopping by, but I haven't seen you for so long."

Rose rushed over and hugged her. "Gosh, I've missed you. How've you been? Let's sit in the front room."

Another sister, Mary, was drawing by the fire. She greeted Lonnie with a smile. Rose showed them to two chairs by the front window.

Without ceremony, Lonnie handed her a wrapped parcel. "I couldn't wait to give you my Christmas gift, so here it is."

"I haven't even gotten yours, silly." Rose laughed. "But I won't stand on ceremony." She pulled off the ribbon and opening the box, she gasped. She lifted out a delicate chain with a small gold locket dangling from it. "It's beautiful. Oh, Lonnie, you didn't have to get me anything like this. A bar of chocolate or even some fancy soap would've been enough."

Lonnie shook her head. "I gave you chocolate last year. Besides, I saw that and thought of you. It wasn't too expensive, so don't worry."

Rose's cheeks were pink with pleasure. "Thank you. I love it." She promptly put it around her neck, fingering it happily.

"I'm glad you like it." After that, words failed Lonnie. The letter weighed heavily in her pocket, and her resolve weakened.

"How's Teddy?" Rose asked tentatively, taking Lonnie by surprise. "The last time I saw him, he wouldn't even look at me. I asked him about all of us getting together again, but he said he was busy and hurried off."

Lonnie fidgeted with her skirt. She hadn't planned on their conversation venturing into this territory. Before she could speak, Rose turned to her sister. "Mary, could you give us some privacy?"

Her sister hid a smile but left the room. Rose gestured for Lonnie to speak.

She swallowed thickly. "Well . . . Teddy proposed to me, and I turned him down." Lonnie cringed at her friend's shocked expression.

"What? Why would he do that?"

"Propose to me?"

"Well, yes. Just before the dance, he confided to me that he liked you a great deal, but he never gave me any indication he was planning something like that. I mean, he just took you out on your first date together."

Lonnie frowned. "I know. I don't understand it either. He was upset by my refusal and turned everything around to me loving someone else."

"Well, that's understandable if he was so upset, but—" She regarded Lonnie with curiosity. "Is that really the reason? Do you love someone else?"

Lonnie didn't want to answer. She wasn't sure what would come out.

"Oh, Lonnie. Is it—do you like Alex?"

Lonnie's head shot up. "Why does everyone assume that? Have I said anything to indicate my feelings? Has there been anything in my actions that has it spelled out for everyone?" She gripped the arms of her chair, her temper rising. "Can't he just be my friend and leave it at that?"

"I'm sorry. Please don't get upset. A lot of people have seen you spending time with him or talking with him. They start to assume things. There's so many who are concerned for you, myself included. I just don't want to see you get hurt."

Lonnie clenched her teeth, trying to reign in her frustration. Reaching into her coat pocket, she pulled out the letter. "I don't think you realize what kind of a man Alex is. He's good and kind and far better than many a man in this town, Teddy included." She thrust the envelope at her friend. "This is for you."

Rose took it. "What is this?"

"It's a letter. Alex is staying with Mike Hardy in Tommy's old bedroom. Alex found it in the dresser drawer. He felt it was important you got this letter and said he owed it to Tommy. He didn't say this, but if it wasn't for Alex, I'm sure there's no way this letter would be in your hands now."

Rose's face went white, her red hair stark against her skin. Trembling, she opened the letter and painstakingly unfolded its pages. As she read, tears fell, dripping onto the paper. At last, the letter fell into her lap, and she covered her face with her hands.

Immediately repenting her harshness, Lonnie knelt at her friend's feet and reached around to hug her. Rose sobbed into her shoulder. Lonnie squeezed her friend tighter, tears pricking their way to the surface of her own eyes.

"Oh, Lonnie," Rose whispered after a time. "I knew he loved me. Why did he never say anything? Why didn't he just tell me?"

Lonnie patted her on the back. "I don't know, darling. I don't know."

Once Rose's tears had slowed, Lonnie regained her seat. "I'm sorry. I shouldn't have been so angry at you. It isn't your fault for the way others feel."

Rose shook her head. "You were right to feel angry. Ever since I told you how I felt about Alex, I've been uncomfortable, as if I'd judged him unfairly. Alex wanting me to get this letter proves it." She took Lonnie's hands in her own. "I really did have your best interests at heart, but it seems your instincts are better than mine. I've misjudged him, and I'm sorry. I've seen how kindly he treats you and how respectful he is. A month or so ago, I saw an old man trip him in the street. Alex didn't retaliate, he just got up, nodded to the man and kept walking. I'll admit I was very moved. He must have an extraordinary character to maintain such composure in the face of so much ill feeling."

"Thank you." Lonnie was stunned by her friend's speech. Alex had never said a thing to her about it.

Rose stood. "Alex is your friend. I'd like another chance to meet him and get to know him."

Lonnie got up and embraced her. "You're a wonderful friend, Rose. Yes, we'll all get together soon."

She left her friend's house in a more pensive mood. The fire a few weeks ago had been shocking. Even with an investigation, the police were never able to find enough evidence to figure out who had done it. Besides, she'd never considered how Alex had to deal with people's reaction to him on a daily basis. How bad was it? How much was he being put through?

She paused on the sidewalk to shut her eyes against the agonizing guilt that washed over her. She was keeping him here. She was putting him through this. She remembered her agreement with Xiao Lin that she should tell Alex. She was going to have to get up the courage and give him back his money. That's all there was to it.

She started walking again, striding with more determination, but her heart still shuddered with dread.

Chapter Twenty-Five

APPALONE, DEAR." AUNT Millie bustled up to her, setting a basket of eggs on the counter. Lonnie, assisted by Rose, was just putting the finishing touches on a plate of gingerbread cookies, mincemeat tarts, and praline cookies in her aunt's kitchen.

"The Millers dropped off the eggs from their chickens. You won't mind mixing up the eggnog, will you? The recipe is in that new Health for Victory magazine over there. And do hurry. The guests will be arriving in half an hour." And then she was gone.

Lonnie sighed. "Of course not, Aunt Millie. I'd love to."

Rose giggled and winked. "Your aunt is the regular drill sergeant, isn't she? I can finish these up if you like."

"That would be nice, thank you. I know she's been preparing for this party for days, but I think the lack of sleep is starting to show."

"It's too bad Gladys and Walter couldn't come."

Lonnie nodded as she separated eggs. "It is a shame, but weren't they going to a dance? I can see that being more Gladys's cup of tea."

"Yes, but not for poor Walter."

Lonnie was grateful Rose didn't bring up Teddy. She would've hated to admit she'd begged her aunt not to invite the Stantons. After some investigation, Aunt Millie said they had plans anyway.

Christmas music played on the Victrola, and the girls sang along as they worked. By the time Lonnie finished making the eggnog, the first guests arrived, bringing with them cheery voices and a draft of December chill. Besides inviting Lonnie, Harriet (who declined to come), and Uncle Phillip, Aunt Millie invited practically the whole street, and her friends from her charity work. Almost everyone accepted, so Lonnie was warned to expect a full house.

She removed the apron covering her festive red velvet dress to help Aunt Millie welcome the guests. She took their coats into David's room to put them on his bed, while Rose took dishes of warm and fragrant food for the potluck to the kitchen. Presents for the white elephant gift exchange piled up under the sparkling

Christmas tree. Lonnie greeted the familiar faces she knew and Aunt Millie introduced her to those people she didn't.

Aunt Millie's house was full to near bursting when Alex arrived. His face became strained, instantly uncomfortable at the crowd. Lonnie could guess why. Half the people there were neighbors whom he didn't know, a good portion were people who'd made it clear they didn't like him, and those that were left were busily occupied. She herself was crammed into a corner by the kitchen, helping her aunt to replenish the platters of food, pulling out new ones the guests brought and arranging them on the dining room table. Rose was near the door and greeted him cheerfully, taking his coat.

Lonnie raised her arm and waved, catching his eye. Seeing her, his face relaxed. He mouthed a hello with a small wave, but couldn't do much about moving closer to speak with her. Nearly every inch of floor was taken up by groups of talking people, a few couples trying to dance to the lively Christmas music, and older folks grouped together, talking and eating.

Lonnie hurried with her task. Finally gesturing to him, they made their way over to meet at the Christmas tree, which was brightly lit with colorful electric Christmas lights, glittering tinsel, a few sparse candy canes, popcorn chains, and glass and paper ornaments with a delicate angel of lace at the top.

"You made it," Lonnie said just as Alex reached her and said, "You look wonderful."

"Oh!" Lonnie exclaimed, and they both laughed. She blushed a little and smoothed the front of her dress. "Thank you. You look nice as well." Saying the words, she knew they were a bit of an understatement. Everything about him was supremely well groomed from his shined mahogany-colored shoes to his carefully combed hair.

Alex held up the glass in his hand. It was half-full of the eggnog she'd made earlier. "By the way, what is this drink?"

Her eyebrows shot up in surprise. "It's eggnog. Haven't you had it before?"

"No. We grew up celebrating Christmas, of course, but it definitely had more of a Korean flair." He grinned.

"Do you like it?"

He took a sip with a thoughtful expression. "I think so. The rum is a bit strong."

"Rum?" Lonnie gasped. "But I didn't put any rum in it." She frowned over at her aunt who was chatting with a group of her friends from her charity organization.

Alex laughed, and she joined him. They stared at each other, allowing the voices and the music to permeate their little bubble for a brief moment.

He broke their silence first. "Did you finish that book?"

Lonnie froze. "What book?"

"The Vintage of Yon Yee."

"Oh." The word squeaked out, and she gulped. "Yes."

"Well, what did you think?"

She grasped at what she could say. "It was . . . unexpected. I—I liked it though."

Mirth played at the corners of his mouth, his eyes crinkling. He was laughing at her. Of all the nerve.

"I have a gift for you," she said in a rush to change the topic. She hadn't planned on giving it to him then, but she was willing to do anything to distract him from any further conversation about the book. She reached under the tree, found the bulky, paper-wrapped package, and gave it to him with embarrassment. Some present. If it wasn't for all the finger-numbing hours of mending she'd put in, she'd want to kick herself for giving his own clothing back to him for Christmas.

He took the gift from her. "Thank you. Should I open it now?"

Mortified, Lonnie blanched. "Heavens, no." She quickly checked herself. "I mean. No. Please wait. I'd be really embarrassed. Here." She grabbed the present back, worried he'd try to open it anyway. "I'll put it with your coat."

"Okay," he said, amusement playing on his face.

Lonnie worked her way through the crowd to her cousin's bedroom where the coats were lying in a large heap on his bed. She found Alex's coat and moved it with the package over to the desk.

On an impulse, she paused, holding the coat in her hands. The dark wool was scratchy to her fingers and it still held a bit of his warmth. Holding it out, she could picture the coat on Alex, framing his shoulders and height. She slowly brought it up to her face, closed her eyes and deeply breathed in his scent. It was spicy and complex mixed with the earthiness of the wool. The smell made her giddy.

Realizing what she was doing, she quickly dropped the coat and hurried out of the room, her pulse racing. She nearly ran into Alex, who was waiting at the end of the hallway for her.

"It's a bit less crowded over here."

"Yes." She had a hard time meeting his eyes. She didn't know what to say to him, as if she'd crossed some invisible line of intimacy, only he'd yet to discover it.

Just then, there was a commotion and Aunt Millie came pushing through the crowd, waving her hands and laughing with delight. "Oh, you lucky ducks. You've found it!"

Alex turned to meet the oncoming Aunt Millie. "Found what?"

"Why, the mistletoe, of course. We all know what that means," she sang and laughed again, clapping her hands. She was joined by many of the others near enough to see what was going on. Out of the corner of her eyes, Lonnie saw Rose squeeze her way to the front, her eyes big as saucers.

Lonnie's gaze flicked up to see the offending mistletoe, and the blood drained from her face. How had she missed where her aunt hung the mistletoe? She wanted to kick herself for not being more cautious.

Alex looked into Lonnie's face. "What *does* it mean?" he asked her, his brows furrowed with his question.

Lonnie's throat felt very dry. "It—it means you're supposed to kiss me." Her insides trembled, her heart threatened to pound itself to pieces, and all she wanted to do was run away.

Strangely, Alex didn't seem fazed by it at all. Nor did he seem to mind the crowd of expectant people watching them. His eyes stayed riveted to her face, and he was as dignified as ever. Lonnie almost hated him for it.

"Do you want me to kiss you?" Alex asked.

"Come now," Aunt Millie interrupted cheerfully. "You don't have a choice, you two. We're all waiting." Her singsong voice filled the entire house.

Alex only had eyes for Lonnie. "Do you?"

She stared at him, scrambling to make her brain work. "I—I . . ."

He didn't wait for her to finish. He leaned down and kissed her gently on the cheek. The pressure of his lips against her skin sent a shower of sparks trickling down her spine, and she gasped.

A cheer went up from the party and soon their attention was diverted back to their conversations, though a few of the guests wore stony expressions.

"Sorry," Alex said, his face still close to hers. "I figured ending it quickly was better than dragging it out."

"Excuse me." She brushed past him and Rose, whose mouth gaped open, before pushing her way through the party to hide in the kitchen. This sanctuary was taken up by a few of Aunt Millie's friends getting together more drinks.

She sighed in exasperation and slipped out the back door onto the icy patio. Instantly, her warmth was whisked away, and she wrapped herself in her arms, rubbing to keep warm. The frigid evening breeze cooled her flushed cheeks. She breathed deeply, each exhale coming out in long streams of fog.

Her head whirled with what had just happened. She cursed the mistletoe. *Why* did she have to be the first to discover it? And with Alex no less? Her face started to burn all over again.

Lonnie's toes were beginning to go numb when the door opened and Alex joined her on the patio.

"I thought you'd want to disappear. I brought your coat." He draped it around her shoulders. She clutched it to her desperately, touched by his kindness.

"How d-did you kn-know?" Her words stuttered out of her through chattering teeth.

"I know you better than anyone else in this town."

His words stunned her. "Y-you do?"

Alex smiled, shoving his hands into his pockets. He shivered. "Wow. It's cold." He turned to look at her in admiration. "You are one stubborn woman to have been out here as long as you have. It's been fifteen minutes."

"Th-thank you," she stammered, trembling violently.

He laughed. "Was my kiss that bad?"

"Y-yes. I m-mean, no. N-no. It was j-just all those p-people."

Alex laughed again. "We should get you inside before you catch cold. Come on."

She nodded, and he led her back inside. In less than a minute, he'd cleared a seat for her over by the fireplace, tucked a warm blanket around her, and stuck a mug of hot wassail in her hands. Alex left her then, and while she was a little disappointed not to have his company, she was grateful too. She really didn't want to talk to anyone. Even Rose had made herself scarce. Had she been as scandalized as everyone else?

Lonnie sipped her drink, feeling its heat seep into her body. She watched the people enjoying themselves: laughing, talking, eating, drinking, dancing. It was so wonderfully happy and for a time they were forgetting the war and all its frustration and gloom. For now they were just good friends celebrating Christmas together.

A warm bubble of happiness crept into her chest and she finally relaxed. After a few minutes, her eyelids drooped. She'd rest her eyes for just a moment . . .

***

Alex left Lonnie to warm up by the fire and found his way over to grab another drink. He'd abandoned the spiked eggnog for a glass of fruit punch instead. Now that he didn't have Lonnie to talk to, it was obvious how out of place he was. No one took an interest in him; in fact, they seemed to be outright ignoring him. He set down his drink.

He'd use the bathroom and then leave. There was no sense in staying where he wasn't wanted. He went along the hallway toward the vacant bathroom when voices came from the bedroom behind him, its door slightly ajar.

"I don't see why you're so hot under the collar about it, Phillip. It was just a bit of fun."

"Yes, but Alex and *Lonnie?*"

Hearing his name, he inched closer to the door.

"Don't blame me." Millie's voice was testy. "Anyone could've been the first to stand under the mistletoe. It just happened to be them. I don't see what the problem is. It's a festive tradition. And I have to say he was a gentleman about it too. He only kissed her cheek."

"That's not the point," Phillip hissed. "You seem to be perfectly, if not intentionally, oblivious to what is going on and how people feel about Alex. You should've seen some of your guests' expressions and heard their comments after Alex kissed her. I've tried endlessly to convince people that he's harmless, that he's not the enemy; he's just another hardworking American, but most people refuse to believe me. They'd rather see him quit this town than find out if what I say is true. Putting him in a spot like that, and with our niece may I remind you, is not only uncomfortable for them both, but it's dangerous. Just look at what happened with the fire at Mike Hardy's place."

Millie laughed derisively. "Oh, don't be so overdramatic, Phillip. There's nothing dangerous about that young man, except maybe his smile." She laughed again, but this time it was lighter, in fun.

Alex couldn't help but grin at that revelation.

"Besides," Millie continued, "Lonnie is fond of him. I haven't seen her so happy in a long time. I think their friendship is a good thing, and I don't want to discourage it."

"You're not taking me seriously," Phillip said. "I'm warning you, Millie. Throwing those two together will only bring heartache. I like Alex as much as you do, and I realize Lonnie is fond of him, but what then? What if they—"

"Nothing is going to happen, Phillip," Millie interrupted, imperious. "Now, if you don't mind, I need to get back to my guests."

Alex jerked away from the door and slid into the bathroom, shutting the door without sound. He switched on the light and leaned against the door, going over their conversation in his mind.

His feelings were so distorted—as if they couldn't decide whether to be pleased, worried, or angry. He knew what people thought of him, and it did his heart good to know some people liked him.

But the fact that Lonnie's uncle didn't like the idea of anything happening between them was discouraging. He loved Lonnie. He wanted to know her even better than he did now, but he hardly dared to hope she'd have the same type of feelings for him. Why would she? He was Korean. She wasn't. Relationships like that just didn't happen and if they did, there were consequences; he didn't like to think of subjecting Lonnie to those consequences. The whole situation felt impossible.

Besides, he knew what he really was to Lonnie—a passing fascination to liven up her life in this dull backcountry town. There was no way her family would give their consent to anything more than friendship. He already knew her mother wanted him to drop over the edge of the bluff.

He pushed himself away from the door with a soft growl of frustration. He turned on the sink and splashed cold water on his face, trying to wash away the pain and confusion he felt. When he finally felt he could leave without his anger boiling over, he grabbed his coat and the parcel Lonnie had given him, and made his way through the crowd.

Glancing over at Lonnie, he could see she'd fallen asleep despite the noisy chatter and loud music. The curve of her face was etched with flickering gold from the firelight. She was so beautiful. Her lines of distress had been replaced by the smooth peacefulness of slumber. Guilt tugged at him that he'd been part of the cause of her distress.

He pulled a small box out of his pocket—the gift he'd gotten for Lonnie. How could he give it to her now?

At that moment, Rose approached him. "You're not leaving are you?"

"I am. I thought it would be best if I slipped out while I had the chance."

"Lonnie will be disappointed."

"Are you sure about that? She was pretty humiliated."

Rose frowned. "Well, that wasn't your fault." She bit at her thumbnail, guilt written all over her face. "I'll admit I knew where the mistletoe was. I saw Mrs. Smithfield hang it. I really should've given Lonnie warning. Sorry."

Alex shook his head. "There's not much we can do about it now. I only worry how it'll affect Lonnie."

"Look, Alex." Rose took a step toward him, taking him in confidence. "I never got to thank you for Tommy's letter. It meant a great deal to me that you made sure I got it. Thank you." Her eyes glimmered with the beginnings of a tear, but it didn't fall. "I know a lot of people don't like you, but I do. I'm glad you're Lonnie's friend."

Alex's heart eased a fraction from her words. "Thank you."

Without stopping to think, he held out the little box. "Would you give this to Lonnie for me?"

"You're really not going to stay?"

"No, I don't think so. Please tell her I'm sorry."

She accepted the box. "I understand. I'll be sure she gets it."

He thanked her then made his way over to Lonnie's aunt. "Thank you for inviting me, Mrs. Smithfield. I'm going to head home now."

She turned, her face falling with honest disappointment. "So soon? We haven't even started the white elephant gift exchange yet."

He smiled. "It's all right. I didn't bring anything anyway. Give my regards to Reverend Hicks."

"All right, if you insist." She grabbed his hands and squeezed them with a smile. "I'm so glad you came."

"Thanks. I'll see you again." He waved farewell and headed out into the frigid night.

***

Lonnie awoke to shouts of laughter from the crowd by the Christmas tree. It took a moment to gain her bearings. Rose was standing nearby, clapping her hands with enthusiasm. Lonnie removed the blanket from her lap, catching Rose's attention.

"Oh, good. You're awake." She stepped closer and spoke over the chatter. "They're doing the gift exchange. Mr. Richardson just opened one. It was the most hideous woman's dressing gown and matching cap you've ever seen, which he just tried on." She giggled.

Lonnie stretched. "How long was I asleep? I had no idea I was so tired."

"Not long, and I'm not surprised. Your aunt's been running you ragged since six this morning."

Lonnie swiveled her head, trying to spot the familiar head of black hair. "Where's Alex?"

Her friend regarded her with sympathy. "He left maybe a half hour ago." She grabbed a little box off the mantle. "He wanted me to tell you he was sorry and give you this." Rose rubbed her shoulder. "It's almost my turn." She winked and moved over to the Christmas tree, leaving Lonnie alone.

The box was crisply wrapped in colorfully striped paper. There was no note on the outside. Curious, she unwrapped it, removing the lid. A smile spread slowly across her face.

She lifted out a delicate glass apple ornament. Its ruby surface gleamed in the firelight. A piece of paper sticking out of the padding caught her eye. Carefully nestling the ornament back in its box, she unfolded the note. There were five Korean characters written. Her brow furrowed as she worked it out.

"Sss–ah–g–wah. Sagwa." She burst out laughing at his mischievousness. Alex had managed to gift her not only with a pretty ornament, but with a lesson as well. "*Sagwa*," she said again and twirled the ornament on its string with a smile.

***

By the time Alex reached Mike's house, his face was frozen, and he could no longer feel his toes. As soon as he'd shut his bedroom door, he stripped off his clothes and bundled into a pair of flannel pajamas and wool socks. He sat on his bed and pulled Lonnie's package onto his lap. What could be inside such a large bundle? He pulled the twine off and folded back the paper to see a jacket and pair of trousers. He stared at them in surprise, wondering why she would given them to him. Though the closer he looked, he realized they were a little familiar . . .

With a start, he recognized them as his own jacket and trousers from when he'd first arrived in River Bluff. It was ages ago that Reverend Hicks had taken them to have them cleaned and repaired. He must've given them to Lonnie. It's funny she'd never said anything.

He lifted up the jacket and examined the spots where there had been tears on the elbow and shoulder. The tiny stitches and patches she'd sewn in were barely noticeable. His admiration for her grew. He knew it wasn't an easy task from watching his mother do the family mending.

He brought the coat closer and breathed in. The faint smell of her perfume enveloped him. He closed his eyes, drinking in her scent. But then his hand fell with a crinkle into his paper-strewn lap. With a scowl, he threw the coat across the room, shoved the paper and trousers to the floor and flung himself back on his bed. She was everywhere. In his thoughts, in his dreams, even in his clothing. If he couldn't have her, then why couldn't he just forget her?

Chapter Twenty-Six

NOW THAT LONNIE had finished the mending on Alex's clothing, she found her hands were too idle in her spare time. She didn't feel like reading, especially after *that book*. There was a lull in any charity work on her aunt's front until February. The New Year had swept in bringing icy temperatures and more snow and freezing rain. The trees groaned and crackled with it. Normally, Lonnie would've gone for a walk when she was feeling fitful; in fact, she owed a visit to Xiao Lin, but she doubted the pitted country roads were safe.

She wandered the quiet house one Saturday afternoon. Mother was working overtime hours at the factory, Marty was next door at his friend's house, and Tunie was at work at the grocers. Lonnie longed for someone to talk to, someone to distract her from her muddled thoughts. In every spare moment, the Christmas party replayed over and over in her mind—her stupid give and take with Alex's pitiful present, her silly instinct to hold his coat and breathe in his scent, and that moment underneath the mistletoe. She could still feel the soft press of his lips against her cheek. She touched the place with her fingers, remembering. It filled her with an unquenchable yearning.

What was it about him that drew her in? Why didn't any other boys she knew from town attract her? She'd never even been the least bit tempted by them. Why had she always felt like she never truly fit in, always hovering on the edge of acceptance by others for her ways of thinking? Why was she so different?

Maybe she took after Aunt Millie. She certainly had a wild view of the world, bordering on scandalous—at least according to the word about town. Aunt Millie commanded respect though, in her manner and warm personality. Lonnie on the other hand . . .

She shook her head. No, that wasn't the point. Alex was the issue here. Until he'd come, she'd never been so stirred up, so excited about knowing anyone. And it wasn't that she was in increasing awe of how handsome he was, but he was so comfortable to be with. Her true self was emerging, crawling out from the tiny cupboard of fear she'd built for herself over the years. And it was wonderful.

She paced back and forth in the hallway leading from the front door to the kitchen. Yes, having a wonderful, intellectually stimulating friend was one thing, but to feel romantic towards him was something entirely different. There was no sense in ruining the friendship they'd built by being silly about emotions.

Head nodding in decisiveness, Lonnie turned to go upstairs when someone knocked at the front door. She opened it to find Gladys looking as lovely and made up as she always did, her lips curving upward in greeting.

"Boy, am I glad to have a distraction," Lonnie said. "What are you doing out in this weather?" She ushered her friend into the living room. "You've caught me at the best time. I have absolutely nothing to do, and it's driving me nuts."

Gladys removed her gloves, her perfectly sculpted eyebrow arched in skepticism. "You? Having nothing to do? You're always a whirlwind of charity work, caring for someone or another."

Lonnie smiled. "How about you? I haven't seen you in so long. What have you been up to?"

"I've been back and forth between my job here and helping my aunt with her children up in Bloomington. I've managed to fit in a few dances chock full of military boys as well, and let me tell you, that was ten times more fun than any dance this dinky little town could put on."

"Well, no wonder I haven't seen you. You sound busier than me."

"Tell me about it. In fact, I've actually stopped by to say goodbye."

Lonnie gasped. "Goodbye? Where are you going? Are you joining up?" Her stomach gnawed with jealousy.

Gladys laughed. "No, silly. I quit my job at the telephone company. I'm moving up to live with my aunt full time to care for my nieces and nephews. I'll get room and board and a little extra on the side. Aunt Penny started her new job at the RCA factory, and it's a nightmare trying to find someone to care for the kids for the hours they have her working."

"Don't you want to work at the factory too? I've heard they pay really well."

Gladys laughed again, only louder. "Heavens, no. Whatever they're doing there is top secret, and everyone knows I can't keep a secret to save my life."

Lonnie joined her in laughter because it was the complete truth.

"No," Gladys continued, "It'll be best if I stick with caring for the children. They're all little hooligans, but I can't help but love them. Besides, it'll be the easiest money I've ever made." Her face glowed. Lonnie was happy for her friend and told her so.

Gladys nodded, then examined her nails. "To be honest with you, Lonnie, I've had something I've wanted to tell you, but never got the chance before now."

"Oh?"

It was a moment before Gladys met her gaze. "I made a friend while I was visiting my aunt. Violet Won. She's half-Chinese."

Lonnie's eyebrows shot up in surprise. "Really?"

"Her mother is American, her father a Chinaman. She's a terrific gal; you'd like her. Spending time with her and even meeting her parents, it got me thinking about you and Alex."

A big lump formed in Lonnie's throat, and she struggled to swallow it down. "Me? And Alex? What do you mean?" She asked the question out of politeness, not because she wanted to know. Because she didn't.

Gladys looked at her as if she were a pitiful little child. "Oh, Lonnie, don't you see it?"

Lonnie's heart raced, her breath growing short. "See what?"

"You love him, you silly goose!" Gladys rolled her eyes in exasperation.

"No."

"Oh, yes. It's as plain as day whenever you're together. Rose has said as much to me too. It was apparent at the charity dance. The way you radiated happiness in his arms . . . you might as well have been holding up a sign. Rose also told me what happened at your aunt's Christmas party. There's no use in denying it." Gladys crossed her arms over her chest, pouting. Her face wore that steely determination Lonnie knew only too well. She wasn't leaving until she'd had her way.

"But—but I can't. I can't love him." Her protests came out in gasps.

"And why not?"

"Well, because. It's not allowed, is it? We're from two completely different worlds. He's *Korean*. As a friend that doesn't bother me in the slightest, but to be in a relationship? Think what he'd be subjected to because of me. He'd be in even more danger from people who wouldn't understand."

Gladys sighed impatiently. "I know it seems scandalous and scary, and maybe it is, but to hell with all that. All I know is what I saw of Violet's parents. They're totally devoted to one another, and somehow they make it work. Even folks in their town have grown used to them and have come to accept them in a way. The world is changing, Lonnie. They felt it, and I feel it too."

Her words seeped into Lonnie, easing her fear with a sliver of hope. Could she dare to acknowledge what had been growing in her heart these last few months? Could a relationship with Alex become a reality? Would he accept her feelings—her feelings of deep longing and fondness for him—even with all it would bring?

Gladys gazed at her with affection. "Lonnie, you're my dear friend, even if I haven't been as dear a friend to you. I couldn't leave without telling you this one last thing. Sometimes the person meant for you isn't who you expect it to be. Maybe your grand adventure won't just be to go off and travel the world or even to join up for the war. Maybe part of your grand adventure will be to spend your life at Alex's side."

Tears sprang to Lonnie's eyes. Gladys was right. There was no denying the truth when she heard it.

Gladys' face softened in a kind smile. "You do love him, don't you?"

Hesitantly, Lonnie nodded, the realization hitting her so forcefully she nearly choked on the sob escaping her. Her hand flew to her mouth to suppress it. "I—I *do* love him, Gladys. I don't even know for how long I've felt it, but I do."

Gladys pulled her into a soft hug. "I think my work here is done. Now, I'm off to report to Rose, and then I'll be taking the five o'clock train."

Lonnie's lips wavered into a smile, and she sniffled back tears. "Oh, Gladys, I'll miss you. Even if you never could keep a secret."

Her friend grinned cheekily and sighed, resting her hand on Lonnie's shoulder. "Lonnie, you doll. I almost envy you your adventure."

Gladys pulled on her gloves and fussed with them for a moment, her eyes twinkling. "Besides, I always thought Alex was quite the dreamboat." She laughed gaily, winked, and was gone.

***

After Gladys left, Lonnie drifted upstairs and sat on the window seat to stare out the frosted glass. "I love Alex," she whispered, unhurriedly tasting each word on her tongue. "I love Alex."

Her pulse skipped faster. "I love him!"

The words made the color rise in her cheeks, as if admitting it out loud shocked the bed linens, books, and window curtains. She wanted to shout it to the world, but something caught at her.

Now that she'd finally admitted the truth to herself, what was she going to do about it? Her memories surged up—going over Alex's lessons, laughing and talking with him, being in his arms dancing, feeling the safety of his embrace surround her in comfort. She was reminded of how excited she felt every time she saw him at church, of how kindly he treated Marty, and of how respectful he always was to her and to others. She thought of how much he endured people's torment without striking back..

Her heart swelled until she felt it would burst. She wanted to be with him. She wanted to see him, embrace him. But it all seemed impossible.

With her index finger, she traced out a heart on the window glass fogged from her breath. She smiled at how lopsided it was— as lopsided and unsure of itself as she felt. Her feelings were useless. What could she do about them anyway? Nothing. Alex didn't love her. Maybe he was fond of her as a friend, but he wouldn't be crazy enough to develop feelings for her. Even if he did, if anyone in town found out, they'd probably try to kill him. Her heart pricked with fear, filling her with helplessness.

What was she going to do? What *should* she do? She needed some heavenly guidance. Lonnie stood, her jaw set in determination. Snow or no snow, she was going to walk to the church and find out what her path should be—whether she should fully acknowledge and pursue these feelings or resign herself and set them aside. The decision had to be made now while her newly confessed feelings were still fresh. And if deemed unacceptable, she wouldn't hurt as much as she cast them away.

***

Alex worked hard at shoveling the sidewalks around the church in preparation for services the next day. When he was finished, he entered the chapel and removed his coat and hat. He walked to a pew midway up the aisle and sat, draping his coat over the back of the bench. He enjoyed the stillness of the empty room. The sun poured through the stained glass windows in jeweled colors, painting the lazy dust motes floating in the lofty space.

Alex's gaze finally settled on his coat pocket where the letter hid. Reverend Hicks had given it to him before he started shoveling, and he'd been amazed to see it was from his mother. He worried what it might say. Bad news only she could soften enough for him to hear? Had something happened to Henry? Had their town suffered an earthquake? Had his father died of a sudden illness?

Sick of his morose thoughts, Alex finally yanked out the letter and opened it. As he scanned the letter, his eyes widened, his breath caught. He skimmed past her pleasantries and inquiries as to his health—he'd go back over those later. It was the middle of the letter that caught his full attention. His mother and father had gotten word through their connections with their Korean political group that the U.S. Government had quietly recognized Koreans as separate from Japan.

Separate . . . Korean immigrants in America were no longer coupled as enemies with the Japanese.

He gaped in wonder at his mother's delicate *hangul* characters, his throat constricting with emotion. As he read over the words again, it finally struck him. From the very start of the war, he'd always felt as if the country he loved had betrayed him. And he could no longer ignore the guilt—he'd been left behind while his Japanese friend Danny had been taken away.

This news didn't change anything for his friend, but for Koreans, it allowed their hope to burn that much brighter. The unfortunate thing was, according to his mother, this important news hadn't made it into the newspapers. Who was going to find out about it? Hardly anyone. The victory was bittersweet.

Alex tossed the letter aside and leaned forward to rest his elbows on his knees. He hung his head and found himself praying. He hadn't prayed in ages, but right now, his heart was utterly full of gratitude, hope, and relief—for himself, for the Korean people, and for the future.

A few minutes later, the echo of footsteps coming down the aisle filled the room. He didn't need to look up. He would recognize those footsteps anywhere. They stopped at his pew, but retreated to the opposite bench. At long last, he turned his head to see Lonnie sitting quietly, regarding him with thoughtful eyes, though there was something else there too. Something he couldn't quite pinpoint.

As countless times before, Alex was overwhelmed by her loveliness. Her golden hair cascaded in gentle curls over her shoulders, her tilted navy hat brought out the blue in her eyes, and her smile would've warmed him on the coldest day in winter. Watching her smile, he was reminded of the Christmas party and how desperately he had wanted to kiss those lips, but hadn't. His feeling hadn't diminished, if anything it had grown stronger.

They regarded each other in silence, but all Alex could feel was the gaping chasm between them created by differences of birth and family. It seemed an impossible distance to bridge, and he was beginning to doubt his ability to cross it. Would she want him to?

He picked up the letter again to give his eyes and mind something to do.

"A letter from your family?" Her timid voice was made grander by the largeness of the space.

He nodded, still avoiding her gaze. "It's from my mother."

"What does she say?"

Alex took a deep breath and then gestured, trying to find the words. "I—it's hard to explain . . ." Lonnie got up and came over to his pew.

"May I?" She pointed to the spot beside him and he nodded. She joined him and her delicate cloud of perfume followed. He closed his eyes briefly, fighting the urge to take her in his arms then and there.

She held out her hand for the letter, and he let her take it. She furrowed her brow as she scanned the *hangul*, and Alex's eyebrows shot up in surprise. "Can you read it?"

She laughed lightly. "A little. Do you mind if I try?"

"No."

They leaned over the letter together. Lonnie picked out characters she knew and sounded out words quickly, turning to him for their translation. He guided her through the entire letter, and by the end, they both leaned back. He was relieved, because he really had wanted to share the news with someone, but hadn't known who. How fitting it should be Lonnie. And to hear her reading it in Korean . . . It left him light-headed with the thrill of it.

"Oh, Alex." She turned to him, her gloved hands clasped in earnest. The delight in her eyes lit up her whole countenance.

"This is wonderful news. What a relief it must be for Koreans. We should celebrate."

He grinned. "I agree."

She suddenly grew serious. "Alex, can I ask you something personal?" She rushed on to explain herself. "It's just we've become such good friends, and it's something I've been wondering about. I hope you won't be too disappointed in my prying."

Alex raised his eyebrows. "What is it?"

"Is there a reason why you haven't joined up? To fight in the war, I mean. I understand Koreans have a lot against the Japanese, but wouldn't that mean your resolve to fight them would be greater?"

He let out a long, low whistle. "That's a short question for a long answer."

Her hand fell on his arm. "Do you mind that I asked? I don't mean to pry."

"No. I figured you were bound to ask sometime anyway." He took a deep breath. "I don't even know where to begin."

"Please try."

He scuffed his shoe against the stone floor as he contemplated for another moment. "You know this letter you read? About the Koreans being recognized as separate from the Japanese?" She nodded. "Well, I suppose this letter was an answer for me."

"In what way?"

"When the Japanese bombed Pearl Harbor, while the U. S. was horrified and angry, Koreans in America were celebrating. They wept with joy, because they saw it as a long awaited chance of freedom from Japanese rule. America would go to war against Japan, and Koreans in our homeland would eventually be freed from the terrible things happening there. It was a moment of great sadness, to be sure, but also of tremendous hope." Alex leaned back, his view getting lost in shadows of the rafters as he spoke.

"I was in my second year of engineering school, so it wasn't even in my mind to volunteer to join up. My brother, Henry, signed up the day after the bombing, just like so many other boys our age did. My father was so proud. Fighting for Korean independence was always first in his mind. As time went on, my father started pressuring me to volunteer, but I resisted. My studies were more important. I think my mother helped persuade him, because for a while he left me alone. Besides, I wasn't old enough for the draft, so I thought I was off the hook.

"But then in the spring of last year, the government rounded up all of the Japanese and Japanese Americans in my town and sent them off to camps. They did that all throughout the west coast."

Lonnie nodded. "I remember reading about that in the newspaper."

"One of my best friends, Danny, who's Japanese, disappeared without even being able to say goodbye. It scared me—he was just gone. I couldn't believe they took him like that. It left a lot of us in our community unsettled, though many felt it was justified. The hatred for the Japanese is so strong among Koreans. My father was one of those that agreed they should be put in camps. Who could know which ones were the enemies? But—but I didn't feel the same way."

"You didn't?"

"No. I do despise what they're doing to the people in Korea, and I hate being mistaken for being Japanese, but many of them came here to make a better life for themselves, just like so many other immigrants have for decades. Just like my own family. So many of them were born here as I was. It angered me to think that the government could round up one group of people out of fear. What would prevent them from doing it again? How is it any different from what Hitler is doing to the Jews?"

"But they *are* the enemy, Alex," Lonnie said in a small voice.

He turned on her. "Yes, but that's not the point, Lonnie. What if the U.S. had a war with Ireland and decided to put all the Irish in internment camps? Or the Germans. Why haven't they put the Germans into camps? The Nazis are as bad as the Japanese. It would never stop, don't you see?"

Lonnie's cheeks blushed. "I—I guess I've never thought of it that way before."

Alex took a deep breath. "I refused to join up because I felt my birth country had betrayed Koreans, especially since they gave them an enemy status in Hawaii—just because Korea is under Japanese tyranny and certainly not by choice.

"My father never could see it that way, though. We argued about it. He pulled me out of college and sent me out to live with my uncle as punishment. He figured I'd gain a better appreciation of my heritage and for the Korean cause." He shrugged. "So here

I am. I didn't make it to my uncle's, but I'm glad I didn't." His face softened with a smile. Lonnie's lips curved up in reciprocation.

She gazed out over the pews. "Your mother's letter is an answer for you because the country has somehow redeemed itself. Is that it?"

Alex nodded. "Yes. Exactly. They're on their way there anyway."

Lonnie smiled. "Thank you for trusting me enough to tell me."

His heart soared. It wasn't just Lonnie. It was everything—hearing from his mother, reading her news. Perhaps it was time.

"I think . . . I think I'm ready," he said aloud.

"Ready for what?"

"To buy my first war bond stamp."

Lonnie's eyes widened. "You mean you've never bought one before? Not ever?"

Alex flushed, fully aware of how sheepish he looked. "No, not once. Well, unless you count the dance."

Her eyebrows drew together. "But Alex, just think. Your brother is out there fighting. You'd be supporting him with war bonds, helping to pay for bullets, for his protection."

He bowed his head. "That never occurred to me, I'm sorry to say. I was too mad about things." He held up the letter, then carefully tucked it into his pocket. "But after this news, I think it's time. Would you care to join me for this momentous occasion? Suddenly, I feel nervous."

Her lips curved up. "I'd be honored."

He threw on his coat and hat. Lonnie shyly threaded her hand through his arm, gazing up at him with happy, tentative eyes. His heart throbbed in surprise and at how incredible it felt to have her at his side. With a grin, he led her out of the church and into the bright day.

Chapter Twenty-Seven

ALEX NOT ONLY bought one war bond stamp, he bought six. Then, he carefully tucked his crisp new stamp booklet into the pocket next to his mother's letter. He'd finally done it. He was finally, willingly supporting the American war effort. A handful of bolts in some airplane or a few bullets in an American G. I.'s gun were funded out of his own pocket. The idea settled him in a way he never would've expected, as if his unease about the war had dissipated with the affixing of that first stamp. It was a small victory. Would his father approve?

They walked a long time after their trip to the post office, until they reached the park. A kind soul had shoveled the walking path that led round to the view of the river. With a long swipe, Alex cleared the bench of its remaining snow, then removed his outer coat and laid it down.

"With the sun and the walking, I've gotten pretty warm," he said by way of explanation. Lonnie thanked him, and they rested, taking in the landscape. The river was like a glittering olive-colored snake, cutting its way through the snowy earth. There was nothing to hold back the sun's magnificence, and it wasn't long before Alex had to turn away, his eyes too dazzled to see clearly. He watched Lonnie's face instead, her cheeks rosy from the cold, her expression content.

"You love it here, don't you?"

She nodded. "I do. More than any place I know."

A twinge stabbed him at her words. "Would you ever think of leaving?" The words were out of his mouth before he could think to stop them.

She turned to him quickly. "Oh, yes."

"Really?" Her urgency took him by surprise.

"Yes," she repeated. "There are so many incredible places to see in the world, and I feel like I'm so far behind. I mean, not too far away down in Kentucky, they just made a national park of Mammoth Cave. A friend sent me a postcard—it's incredible. And then there's New York City. To be surrounded by buildings like a forest, so tall they seem to touch the sky."

Lonnie turned toward the river. "I'd love to see the beaches and palm trees of Hawaii—even the volcanoes. To taste all those amazing tropical fruits fresh off the plants. It would be wonderful to go down into the jungles of the Amazon or to fly over the snow on a dog sled in Alaska, to see the glaciers up close, and the amazing Northern Lights."

She shifted to face Alex. "And then I'd want to travel to Europe, to see the old villages and cathedrals—far older than this country—the Roman coliseums in Italy, the Eiffel Tower in Paris, Stonehenge in England. To see the Orient; the Great Wall of China must be awe-inspiring."

Her eyes shone from her gushed revelations. There was a look on her face he'd never seen. It was complete and unbridled bliss. He stared at her in awe. She knew exactly what she wanted to do. She had it all planned out. It made him marvel, but the pit in the bottom of his stomach told him he was jealous too. Her dreams were her freedom. She only had to step one foot out of this town, and they would begin to be realized.

Alex pulled his eyes away from her, his feelings in turmoil. He realized how different their goals were: namely she had them and he didn't. What did he want in his life? He'd never had the chance to really plan much beyond school. Most of his life had been decided for him.

He knew one thing. He wanted to be with Lonnie. But even that was a hollow goal. What could he ever give her? A trip around the world? Hardly. More like a life of sorrow and suffering colored by hatred and violence. A future with him would be a useless failure.

She gazed at him, an amused expression gracing her face. Suddenly she burst out laughing, delighted peals marking the air like music.

His heart wrenched at the sound, and with a flare of determination, he tightened his jaw. No. He would not let his father's voice shadow his life anymore. He wanted to be free like Lonnie. Free to dream what he wished and do what he felt was right.

Lonnie's mirth continued. "You look so serious, Alex!" He mustered a small smile, only causing her to laugh all the more. Regaining her voice, she said, "Did I surprise you? I'm sorry it all came pouring out. My dreams are pretty wild, aren't they? If I had all the money in the world, maybe I could begin to do those things, but in the mean time, I just read books." A last giggle escaped.

Alex pursed his lips and nodded. "It's true it would be pretty expensive to travel to all those places. But going to Alaska isn't too hard."

"It isn't?"

"Nope. I can even tell you exactly what it's like there."

Her eyes widened. "You can?"

Without warning, he scooped up some snow, and threw it at her, hitting her in the neck. "It's like that."

She gasped sharply. "Alex!"

He laughed in triumph and leapt to his feet. "So how does Alaska feel?"

"It's cold," she squealed. Stooping, she retaliated with her own ball of snow. He danced out of the way, and she chased after him, shouting.

Before she could get another snowball in, he grabbed her by the hands and twirled her around, both of them laughing, the world around them a blur of blinding white and azure. In a sudden release, they both fell back into the soft wintery blanket. Motionless, Alex felt the happiness soak into him. He breathed deeply, and for a brief moment, he tasted that freedom.

***

Lonnie's steps were light as she walked home, thinking of her time with Alex. Meeting Alex at the church, she'd somehow gotten an answer to her unspoken prayer, especially when she'd gone on and on about her plans and he hadn't laughed at her or shot them down as unpractical. Well, he *had* thrown a snowball at her. She kicked a little chunk of ice and giggled as it skittered down the sidewalk.

"What are you so happy about?" The familiar skeptical tone made Lonnie freeze. Harriet crossed the street to meet her at the corner.

"Hello, Mother. Are you just now off work?" Her mother's face was weary and pale.

"I am. And where have you been?"

The heat rose in Lonnie's cheeks. "Out walking. I needed some fresh air." She joined her mother's quick gate in the direction of home and found it difficult to keep up.

"Alone?"

Lonnie's consternation burned. How did her mother know just what questions to ask to needle out the information she was trying so hard to keep hidden?

"No."

"Well, it wasn't with Teddy Stanton. He was still in his office when I left. So who was it?"

Lonnie stopped an exasperated outburst just in time. "It was Alex."

Her mother halted in her tracks and surveyed Lonnie. Her eyes glinted with anger. "You were spending time alone with that—that *yellow* man?"

Lonnie started to tremble. Her mother's voice was laced with the beginning of fury, like smoke before a fire. "Please, don't call him that. He's a friend. That's all."

Harriet narrowed her eyes until they were sharp flints. "Your uncle spoke with me not too long ago. Something about not pressuring you into a relationship with Teddy Stanton. That wouldn't happen to be because you have feelings for someone else would it?"

Lonnie's throat constricted. "No," she breathed. "No, it's not like that."

Her mother took a step closer until Lonnie could clearly see the creases lining her eyes and the sharp downward curve of her mouth. "It better not be," she said, voice brusque with restraint. "Because if I find out Teddy has set his cap for you and you turned him down, there will be hell to pay. Do you know why?"

Lonnie jerked her head in answer.

"Because only a brainless dimwit would turn down a chance like that. Do you hear me? Wasting your time with the likes of Alex Moon will only bring misery down on your head."

To Lonnie's relief, she saw Tunie turning the corner with her hands stuck in her coat pockets, whistling a jaunty tune. She waved at seeing the two of them. "Funny meeting you here. We don't usually cross paths. Is dinner ready soon? I'm starving." She linked arms with Lonnie and dragged her down the sidewalk.

Lonnie wanted to lean against her younger sister to support her weakening knees, but she forced herself to remain rigid. She refused to give in to her mother's threats. Never again. But as she marched along, her brave words echoed hollowly in her head.

***

As Lonnie worked on Alex's latest lesson Sunday after lunch, she thought about the church service earlier that day. She'd stolen several glances at Alex across the aisle. But more importantly, she'd caught him stealing his own glances, and they'd exchanged a few secret smiles. Despite her mother's warning, her lips curved up happily.

She cleared her throat and shifted in the seat at the desk in her bedroom. She focused on the *hangul* on the page. She squinted in concentration, going back over the recipe title. "*Mae . . . jak . . . gwa*. I wonder what that means."

She continued reading through the recipe. It seemed straightforward—if only she knew how to translate the ingredients. She didn't want to ask Alex for help this time, though. After his help with his mother's letter, which was a thrilling experience, Lonnie wanted to surprise him with the completed product. There was only one other person who might be able to help her.

She bundled up in her coat and hat, stuffing the folded recipe into a pocket. She ducked her head in the living room to tell Tunie she was going out and walked as quickly as she could in the direction of Xiao Lin's house.

It had been too long since her last visit. Back in November, she'd had a taste of the finished *kimchi* and helped Xiao Lin finish tidying up her garden for the winter. Had it really been almost two months since then?

"Appalone!" Xiao Lin's face dissolved into a multitude of delicate wrinkles at seeing her on the doorstep. "How wonderful. And I was just about to steep the tea."

"Perfect timing." Lonnie laughed and unwrapped herself from her coat inside the warm house.

Once they were settled with tea and some sweet rolls, Lonnie pulled out the recipe. "I have a sort of riddle I was hoping you could help me with."

"A riddle?"

"Well, more like a translation." She held out the paper and Xiao Lin took it.

"Oh." The woman frowned. "I never did learn to read Korean. I don't know if I'll be able to help you."

"Really?" Lonnie tried to keep the disappointment from her voice. "Well, I can read it, I just don't know what the words mean. And I didn't want to ask Alex. I want to keep this one a surprise."

Xiao Lin's eyes twinkled at this. "A surprise?"

Lonnie laughed. "Well, I know it's his favorite recipe. I'd like to make it and take it to him as proof I learned his lesson without any help on his front."

Xiao Lin clapped her hands lightly. "What fun. I do remember some Korean words from my mother. Read them to me, and we just might be able to put it all together."

"The title of the recipe is *Maejakgwa*." Lonnie watched her friend with hope. "Does that sound familiar?"

Immediately, Xiao Lin's face spread in a smile. "*Maejakgwa*? Why, yes. My mother loved those as a girl and made them for me on special holidays. They're a traditional Korean cookie."

"Really?" Lonnie wanted to leap in excitement. With their heads bent close, they pieced together the other ingredients, most of which Xiao Lin had on hand: flour, salt, sugar, ginger, cinnamon, and oil.

Xiao Lin sat back. "I don't have pine nuts, but I do have some peanuts we could chop and sprinkle over the top." She gestured to Lonnie and led the way into the kitchen.

The two women got to work on the cookies—mixing the dough, rolling it flat, cutting out the rectangular shapes with three slits each and curling them through the center into a ribbon. Then, they heated a small pot of melted lard to fry them in. When it came time to fry the cookies, they stood together at the stove, and Xiao Lin demonstrated how it was to be done.

With the first batch of cookies dancing in the bubbling clear fat, Lonnie turned to Xiao Lin. "You know, I'm amazed you haven't met Alex yet. You haven't seen him in town at all?"

The old woman shook her head. "No. I only go into town when I really need something, and that isn't often. I suppose people are still shy of me, even though I've lived here for forty years."

Lonnie nodded, skimming the golden crisp cookies from the pot and setting them on a towel to drain. She put the next batch in to fry. "I think Alex is really going to like these."

Xiao Lin's lips twitched in suppressed amusement. "You have a special friendship, don't you?"

"What do you mean?" The color rose in Lonnie's face. Were her feelings about him that obvious? She'd been trying to be so careful.

"I mean you've extended the hand of friendship to someone who needed a friend, and that is something special indeed." Her statement was innocent enough, but Lonnie detected a faint glimmer of knowing that made her nervous.

"Yes, well, he's a good and kind person. I value his friendship a great deal, despite what other people think of him. Unfortunately, he hasn't been treated very well. Many people still think he's Japanese."

Xiao Lin bobbed her head. "I myself would like to meet him. Would you consider bringing him by? We'd need to make a new batch, but I think he'd enjoy some *kimchi*. I still have enough cabbages in my root cellar. Would you like to help me again?"

Lonnie's face lit up. "I'd love to help."

"Should we plan a dinner?"

Lonnie wanted to clap her hands in excitement, but she was in the middle of fishing out the second batch of golden cookies. "That's a fantastic idea. Could we prepare all the Korean dishes you know? He'd love it."

Xiao Lin laughed. "Of course. I'll let you set the date. Just send me a note."

***

Lonnie walked home bearing the box of warm, crisp cookies. They glistened from the cinnamon sugar, ginger glaze. Her mouth watered for them. She'd tried a few and loved every bite. They had a delightful crunch with the perfect balance of spice. She couldn't wait to share them with Alex.

She paused at a cross street. It was dinnertime. She should've been home a half hour ago, but she also really wanted to take Alex the cookies while they were still warm. Deciding on the latter option with the excuse she'd make it a quick stop, Lonnie turned left and walked toward Mr. Hardy's house.

Mike Hardy himself answered the door. "Can I help you?"

"Is Alex here?"

A broad grin spread across the man's bristled face. "Sure, he's here. Come on in."

She stepped just inside the door, nodding her head shyly.

"I'll go fetch him." He walked over to an ashtray, stubbed out his cigarette and disappeared down the hall.

Lonnie surveyed the room, remembering it vaguely from when she'd come here after the fire. Examining it closely, she could easily tell two men lived here, because there was a huge map on the wall stuck all over with pins and flags, basic furniture, a threadbare rug, dim lamps, and it was sparse on nick-knacks or art. But it was clean and comfortable.

Mr. Hardy reappeared with Alex and the older man reclaimed his chair and magazine. Lonnie's heart raced with apprehension at having an audience. Even Alex's warm smile didn't dispel the queasiness.

"I can't really stay, but I finally finished your lesson. Here they are." She thrust out the box. Opening it, he erupted in delighted laughter.

"They look delicious." He brought the box close to his nose and breathed deeply, eyes shut. "Wow, Lonnie. That smell alone transports me back to my mother's kitchen." He gazed at her with admiration. "How did you manage to figure it out without my help to translate?"

She managed what she hoped was a mysterious smile. "I'll never tell."

He grinned and held the box out to her. "Have you tried them yet? I can't possibly enjoy these alone."

"It's all right. I've already had some. Mr. Hardy would no doubt like to try them too." She backed toward the door. "I really need to go. Mother's expecting me."

Alex followed her out to the front step. "Lonnie."

His tone made her turn around; the expression on his face made her stomach flop.

"Thank you," he said.

"You're welcome." And with one small wave, she turned and hurried home, heart soaring.

Chapter Twenty-Eight

LONNIE WAS WEARILY putting away client files when the front door opened, bringing with it a draft of frigid air. The tall, lanky form of Teddy paused before her, his spectacles fogged by the warmth of the office.

She stared at him as he pulled out a handkerchief, removed his spectacles and methodically cleaned them. After putting them back on, he walked past and knocked on Mr. Pickering's open door.

"Mr. Stanton, come in," Mr. Pickering boomed in a jolly voice. The door shut behind Teddy.

Lonnie's jaw dropped slightly at being snubbed. It had been a while since she'd been to his house to reject his proposal and hadn't seen him since. But now, at the sight of him, the aching sadness hardened into a lump in her chest coupled with a looming storm cloud. Mother had yet to learn of Teddy's proposal.

Dropping into her seat at her typewriter, she frowned. She'd been right to refuse, no matter what her mother might say. She loved Alex. Picturing him made her tension ease away. She straightened her back and cranked a fresh piece of paper into the typewriter.

Her confidence didn't help with how tired she was. She'd had a fitful night. Fragmented dreams had plagued her relentlessly, and she woke that morning feeling as if she hadn't slept at all.

She was just finishing the letter she'd dictated from Mr. Pickering earlier in the day when Teddy strode out. Lonnie tried to ignore him, but she felt his eyes on her as he lingered by her desk.

"Lonnie." His voice was soft, far from the stiff, distant one she expected. She met his eyes. His face was gentle and full of hope. "May I have a word with you?"

Did she want to speak with him? Part of her wanted to give him another chance to rescue their broken friendship.

"All right." She stepped from around her desk and led him back to a little room where they took their lunch break. It was simply furnished with a table and a few chairs. She grew uneasy when Teddy shut the door behind them. It was probably for the better to keep Mr. Pickering from overhearing what he had to say.

In three strides, Teddy came to her and wrapped her in an embrace. His heady cologne swallowed her up. She stood stiffly, her pulse throbbing in panic.

"I've missed you," he mumbled into her hair.

"Teddy." She tried to pull away. He only held her closer.

"Wait. Please." The pleading in his voice made her stop struggling. "I've missed you. I've been angry about everything, but I can't stop thinking about you."

He brought her even closer until her ear rested on his chest. His heartbeat was strong and swift. The steady thump soothed her, and she shut her eyes, hearkening back to when they'd been children. There'd been one time when they were twelve where Teddy had panicked in his sickbed, believing he was dying; he was coughing and gasping so much for air. Lonnie had pressed her ear to his chest, hearing his loud heartbeat. She'd then assured him he was going to live with a strong heart like that. He'd relaxed and finally fallen asleep, his hand in hers.

She found herself smiling. Their friendship had been so sweet and innocent. Why couldn't it have stayed that way?

Teddy spoke again, his voice rumbling loudly in her head. "I've known for a long time I wanted to spend my life with you. I feel like an idiot that I haven't spoken sooner." He gently grasped her arms and held her out to study her face. "Lonnie, please tell me I'm not too late. Can't you reconsider marrying me? I want to take care of you for the rest of my life. I love you."

Without warning, he leaned down and kissed her, pressing his lips firmly to hers. It was as if he was trying to will her to feel the same way.

She wrenched her face away. "Teddy, please." She pushed against him until he finally released her and she stumbled back. He glowered, face red. "I think you should leave."

His scowl deepened. "I could give you everything—anything you could ever want for or desire. No one else in this town could offer as much."

Lonnie set her jaw. "No, Teddy. You can't give me everything, because I already have what I want."

Teddy staggered back a step as if she'd struck him. "What? What's that supposed to mean?"

She went to the door and pulled it open. "Please leave, and I think it would be best if you didn't call on me again."

His eyes narrowed, the gentleness in his voice vanishing like smoke. "That was your last chance, Appalone Hamilton. I hope you don't regret it later." He strode past her and was gone.

Lonnie was stunned. She drifted out to her desk and sank into her chair. She reached to pull out a fresh piece of paper for her next letter only to find her hand shaking. She dropped it into her lap and looked at the clock. It was four-thirty. Weakly, she went to Mr. Pickering's office door.

"Mr. Pickering, is it all right if I go home a little early? I'm feeling ill."

He spared her a look. "Of course, if you're not feeling well. Perhaps a good night's rest will restore you."

She nodded, thanked him, and went to tidy her desk before gathering her things. The gray, wintery weather did nothing to calm her trembling. Something about Teddy frightened her. There was an angry side that simmered beneath the surface. Why had she never seen it before? She was gladder than ever she'd refused to marry him.

Her mind immediately turned to Alex. Would Teddy figure things out? He'd already suspected she had feelings for Alex. At that time, she honestly felt she didn't. Of course, now things were different. She hadn't meant to drop a clue.

Lonnie stopped walking. She didn't want to go home in this state. Any little thing might set her off. It wouldn't help to give her siblings or mother any cause to speculate. Instead, she turned her footsteps toward Harrison Park, the chilly breeze pushing her along.

The wind was stronger there, and the park was vacant of anyone. Relieved, she sank onto the bench by the edge of the bluff and let the view soothe her. The sky was low and steely, hinting at snow. The river churned on its way, deep and swift from the melting ice and snow of the last few days.

Lonnie didn't know how long she stared out at the familiar, gentle hills. The permanent fixtures of farms, trees, and winding ribbons of roadway were reassuring. They were steady and immovable, though not entirely unchanging. They were as things should be.

But she was not. Things were *not* as they should be. Her whole life was in turmoil, turned upside down ever since Alex had come. She didn't regret his coming, but it was disconcerting how his presence affected everyone else. Teddy was acting strangely, her mother was more angry at her than ever, perfect strangers were lashing out at Alex. If he hadn't shown up, would she have said yes to Teddy? Would she even be in this predicament?

Teddy's warning of her last chance rang in her ears. What had he meant? Last chance until what? The dread of what he could do stole over her. Surely, he wouldn't do anything—surely, he wouldn't say anything to her mother? He knew what Harriet Hamilton was like. Did he feel spiteful enough?

Lonnie wanted to scream and sob at the same time, but she was too cold, too numb to make the effort. Maybe it would be simpler if she just stayed here on the bench and turned to stone, forever beholding this beautiful horizon. How nice it must be to be a monument, she mused. To stand for all time, and to just *be*. No cares, no worries. No pain.

Lonnie was frozen as if in a trance. Her eyes blinked sluggishly while the rest of her body remained unmoved. The serenity of the landscape enveloped her and time stopped.

From far away came a voice speaking or calling to her. She couldn't make out what they were saying, and she frowned, trying to push the sound away. Couldn't they just leave her in peace?

***

"Lonnie? Lonnie." Alex knelt down, trying to get her to respond.

She blinked, but her eyes were glassy, looking at something far away. He touched her hand. It was like ice. How long had she been out here? She scowled at his touch and tried to pull away, but her movement was without strength.

He looked frantically around for anyone nearby, someone he could consult with about what to do, but the threatening weather had chased everyone inside. He himself would've preferred to stay inside, but his restlessness had driven him out for a walk to settle his mind.

He'd hardly expected to find Lonnie at the park—but to find her in such a state. He carefully pulled her onto his back, hitching her up, and locking her knees on either side of his hips. Her head fell weakly onto his shoulder. Where should he take her? Her house was pretty far away, but Mike's was closer.

He set out, praying he didn't run into anybody. Just seeing him walk by carrying Lonnie would send the tamest of gossips in town ringing up all the neighbors. Even before he got home, no doubt, there'd be all sorts of dangerous rumors floating around.

He almost made it to Mike's house without spotting a soul, but just as he turned the last corner, their neighbor, Mrs. Godfrey, opened the door to let the cat in. He froze as she locked gazes with him, her eyes widening. *Oh no.* What should he do? His back already ached from the effort of carrying the motionless Lonnie. There was no sense in trying to hurry away to avoid speaking with the woman.

Searching up and down the street, Mrs. Godfrey urgently gestured for him to come into the house. He quickly obeyed, and as soon as he was inside, she shut the door behind him with a sharp click.

"Lay her over there on the couch," she commanded.

Alex did so and shifted his weight between feet, unsure of what to do with himself. His worry must've shown, because Mrs. Godfrey grudgingly told him to sit. She touched her liver-spotted hand to Lonnie's forehead and snatched it back in surprise. "Good heavens, she's freezing. What happened?"

"I don't know. I walked out to the park to clear my head and saw her on the bench. I called out to her, but she didn't respond. When I tried to talk to her, it was like she didn't even see me. I have no idea how long she'd been out there in the wind."

Mrs. Godfrey frowned at his story. "I'm going to fetch a pile of blankets. Could you heat the water in the teakettle? We need to warm her up."

He nodded and hurried to the kitchen. He boiled water, rummaged around and found a mug and some tea. He tried to work without letting his mind dwell on the situation, but he couldn't help but be anxious. What must Mrs. Godfrey think? He hoped she believed him.

By the time he came back with the steaming mug, Mrs. Godfrey had spread half a dozen blankets on top of Lonnie, who had her eyes shut. She gestured for Alex to set down the mug.

"I think it's better if you leave now."

He gaped. "But Lonnie—she won't know what happened."

Mrs. Godfrey set her jaw. "Mr. Moon. I'm an unmarried woman as is Miss Hamilton. That alone is reason enough you shouldn't stay, on top of you—you being what you are . . ." She gave him a meaningful frown, and something inside him hardened. "I'll let you know when she's more awake." She turned her back to him. What she said made sense, but he didn't like it. Alex balled his fists and stalked out.

He paced in front of Mrs. Godfrey's house, fuming. After a few minutes, it sunk in how fruitless this was, and he finally walked home in defeat.

He paced the living room until Mike came to tell him supper was ready.

"What in the world?" Mike looked Alex up and down. "You look terrible."

"What?" He caught sight of himself in the window glass and started. His hair was disheveled, his eyes a bit wild.

Mike grunted. "You're acting like an expecting father."

Alex flushed at the reference. "No, I . . . Oh, never mind. I can't eat right now." He turned to pace another length of the living room, and Mike disappeared. A few moments later, he returned and shoved a large mallet into his hands.

"What's this for?"

"Follow me." Mike led the way out to the shop and into a side storage room beneath the upstairs apartment. A few dozen boxes were stacked just inside the door. Alex had never really spent much time in there and had never noticed anything special about the place. It wasn't until Mike switched on the light that he saw a large hulking shape against one wall covered in a tarp. Mike pulled the canvas off, launching a large cloud of dust into the air. They coughed as the dust settled. A large car hood leaned against the cinderblock wall. It was rusted and terribly banged up.

"What happened to it?"

Mike rubbed the hood almost lovingly with his hand. "When I got back from the war I had a lot of anger in me. There were days I would just fly off the handle for no reason. It got to the point where I was afraid I might strike out and hit my wife. So I got this old hood and took to beating it up with a mallet when the fury would take me. It saved my marriage, and I'd go as far as saying it saved my life."

Mike gazed at him with his watery blue eyes filled with understanding and sympathy. "I know you don't have anything like that going on, but you've got enough reasons to be angry. I can see it in your eyes all the time. You hold it back with a strength I admire. But, son, there's going to come a day when you won't be able to hold it back anymore. Then what?" He nodded at him. "So take that mallet and do your worst. Trust me, you'll feel better."

Mike left and Alex stared at the tool in his hand. He hefted it, testing its weight. He felt silly standing there, about to bear his soul to a hunk of metal. But if Mike said it had helped him . . .

Alex took a swing. The metal clanged loudly, and the vibration traveled up his arm. It hurt, but there was a measure of relief too. He hefted the mallet again and swung it down. Over and over again he swung. With each blow, he relived all the rude remarks, the hateful stares, the maltreatment, like he was nothing better than dirt.

He cried out as he swung, pouring all his anger into the metal until he finally stopped, gasping for breath. He stumbled back and sagged against the wall. At long last, his mind was emptied, his anger utterly spent. He was free in a way he'd never felt before. He finally understood why Mike seemed so levelheaded most of the time.

A knock came at the door, and Mike poked his head in. "There's movement next door."

Alex ran a hand through his hair and lamented the lack of a mirror. He wiped off his face with his handkerchief, hurriedly stuffed it back into his pocket and strode out of the storage room. Stepping out onto the front porch, he watched as Reverend Hicks nodded a brief thank you to Mrs. Godfrey, escorted a weak Lonnie to his car, and tucked her in with a blanket. He hesitated as Lonnie said something and indicated Alex.

To Alex's surprise, Reverend Hicks pulled the car ahead to Mike's driveway and motioned him over. He approached as Reverend Hicks rolled down the window. Alex leaned down to speak with them.

"Mrs. Godfrey told me what happened," Lonnie said. "I'm so sorry to have worried you."

He searched her over to see if she really was all right. She was pale, her face drawn, and she still shivered. "Are you sure you're okay? You were so cold."

She smiled, meeting his eyes. "I'll be fine. I just need to go home and warm up, but I wanted to stop by and let you know. And thank you for coming to my rescue."

He wanted to do more than just rescue her. He wanted to take her in his arms and hold her in a long embrace to protect her from whatever it was she was suffering from, but he was rooted to the sidewalk, wary of the look Reverend Hicks was leveling at him. "I only wish I could've done more to help."

"She'll be in good hands; have no fear," Reverend Hicks answered. "I'll drive her home and be sure she has everything she needs." The man moved to roll up the window and drive away.

"Wait," Alex said. "I have something. Please wait." He hurried to his room and snatched the folded piece of paper that contained her next lesson from off his dresser. He didn't pause to think whether giving this to her now would be a good idea or not. Coming back out, he handed it to Reverend Hicks, who passed it over. "It's time sensitive, so I wanted to get it to you in case I didn't see you for a while."

Lonnie brightened. "You've got me curious now. Thank you."

Alex ignored the reluctant curiosity that passed over her uncle's face. "You need to finish it by the end of the month. Otherwise, it won't be much good."

"Yes, *seonsaengnim*." She bobbed her head and waved.

As Reverend Hicks drove away, Alex watched the car disappear, his heart lighter than it had been all day. He went into the kitchen to find Mike about to have supper.

"Go on. Have a seat."

Alex joined him at the table and picked up his spoon. Mike had managed some kind of casserole, and Alex smiled at the older man's efforts. Alex took a bite when Mike spoke up.

"You sweet on that girl?"

Alex nearly choked, but managed to swallow his food with a little pounding to his chest. "No. We're just friends."

Mike grunted, though Alex thought it sounded more like muffled laughter. "Liar."

To prevent himself from saying anything else, especially leaking out a confession, Alex shoveled in more food and avoided the man's gaze for the rest of the meal.

Chapter Twenty-Nine

LONNIE RUSHED INSIDE her house and closed the door against the swirling flakes spitting down from the steely sky.

"There you are." Tunie came out of the kitchen, her voice revealing the depth of her relief. "We were about to go searching for you. I stopped in at your office right after I got off work, but Mr. Pickering said you'd left at four-thirty to go home."

Lonnie reluctantly removed her coat and regretted it instantly. She began to shiver uncontrollably. "I'm sorry I worried you. I was out, but Uncle Phillip dropped me off. What about supper? I lost track of time."

Tunie burst into action. "Never mind about supper. I've got it taken care of. What's wrong with you? You're shaking." She grabbed Lonnie's hand and gasped. "For heaven's sake, Lonnie, you're like an icicle. What were you doing? Rolling around in the snow without a coat on? Come on, I'm running you a hot bath."

Lonnie allowed Tunie to drag her upstairs and into the bathroom. Tunie ran the hot water and left her with the command that she not come out for at least a half hour. Lonnie slid gratefully into the water. The heat was deliciously wonderful, and it eased her shaking, though, oddly, a tiny ball of ice seemed lodged in her chest despite the steaming bath.

She tried to remember what had happened, but it was all so fuzzy. She vaguely remembered someone calling her name, even being lifted from the bench. It felt as if her brain was numb to any other memory, everything except Teddy's renewed proposal. That remained with glaring and painful clarity.

Once Lonnie was out of the tub and dressed, Tunie brought her a mug of hot cocoa and a bowl of steaming golden broth with a few triangles of beautifully toasted bread. "Get under those covers and get these in you. I'll come back to check on you later." Her sister bustled out, full of importance, and Lonnie couldn't help but smile at how serious she was taking this. She sipped obediently until both mug and bowl had been emptied, the toast reduced to crumbs. Then she snuggled beneath her covers. She definitely felt warmer, but her core remained frozen, as if nothing could ever warm it again.

She worried over this until Tunie showed up to check on her. "How are you feeling?" Her sister bent to touch her forehead. "You feel better than before."

"I do feel better, but still cold. Is there an extra blanket?" Tunie laid another blanket over her and sat on the edge of the bed.

"What happened, Lonnie? You didn't just lose track of time, did you?"

Lonnie sank back into her pillows. Should she tell Tunie the reason? Her sister's eyes were filled with sincere concern. She decided if she told someone, it might as well be Tunie. Her sister had taken such good care of her after all.

"Honestly, I did lose track of time, but I was upset. I didn't feel ready to come home and face everyone."

"Why not?"

"Because of Teddy. He asked me to marry him."

Tunie gasped. She sprang from the bed, peered up and down the hallway and then shut the door. "Mother's not back from work yet, but I don't want to risk it. Marty's downstairs working on his models."

Lonnie appreciated her sister's caution. She continued. "This isn't the first time. He proposed to me weeks ago, but I turned him down. Today he tried again, but I just can't marry him, Tunie. I can't." She didn't know if Tunie understood, but she hoped she did without explaination.

"Does Mother know?"

The familiar choking dread rose up, and Lonnie clutched at Tunie's hand. "No, and please, *please* don't tell her. I don't know what she'd do if she found out."

Tunie frowned. "I won't." She shifted to face Lonnie straight on. "But why? Why can't you marry him? I thought you were such good friends. He's always seemed so keen on you."

Lonnie clenched the edge of her blanket. "I know. Frankly, I don't think we'd make each other very happy. Something about him scares me. I've never seen it before now. Not before Alex came. Lately, Teddy's gotten so angry, and he behaves like I belong to him."

"Well, obviously he's jealous, and you've known each other for ages." Tunie's eyes narrowed. "Has he hurt you?" There was a fire in her eyes at her words, and Lonnie hurried to calm her.

"No. He's never hurt me."

Her sister relaxed. "That's good. Because if anyone lays a finger on you, they'd have to deal with my wrath." She shook her fist, and Lonnie couldn't help but laugh.

Tunie's scowl dissolved into a giggle, but she became serious again. "All of that doesn't explain why you came home feeling like an ice cube. Did you just walk around town?"

"No. I went to the park to think and just sat for a really long time; I don't know how long. Alex found me. I barely remember him carrying me to Mrs. Godfrey's house. She warmed me up with some tea and blankets, and when I was feeling better, she called Uncle Phillip to take me home."

Tunie narrowed her eyes. "Are you sure Alex didn't try anything funny?"

Lonnie sighed. "Of course not."

Her sister picked at the blanket. "You know, Lonnie, I'll admit Alex has really surprised me. I started out thinking he was the enemy—he certainly looks the part, but I can say I've never seen him behave like one." She frowned. "I still don't know how I feel about him, and I don't know if I trust him completely, but he seems to be a pretty decent guy. For a Jap, that is."

"I'm astonished to hear that coming from you. What made you change your mind?"

Tunie grinned. "He fixed the toaster. It works like a dream now."

Lonnie burst out laughing at this unexpected reply. "He fixed it? When?"

"Remember when he was over that time and helped Marty with his homework? He was here for a good hour before you finally came home. I didn't know what else to do with him. He caught me cursing the toaster and offered to fix it. I finally took it to him a few days ago. He's quite handy with a screwdriver, come to find out."

Lonnie smiled, happy in the knowledge she'd savored the toast.

Tunie moved to the door. "I'm going to let you get some sleep. No doubt, you need it. Let me know if I can get you anything else. When mother gets home, I'll just tell her you're not feeling well and you went to bed early."

Lonnie reached out and grabbed her sister's hand, squeezing it. Somehow, she knew what it had taken her sister to admit those things about Alex. Tunie—who rarely apologized or acknowledged her wrongdoing. If anything, she usually laughed it off.

"Thank you, Tunie."

"Don't mention it." She switched out the light and left the room, but ducked her head back inside. "And by the way, you owe me one." The door shut with a click, leaving Lonnie grinning in the dark.

***

By the next day, the chill had yet to leave her, and Lonnie worried she'd never get warm. She called Mr. Pickering asking for a day to recuperate to which he agreed. She was grateful her mother had left her alone and gone to work without even stopping upstairs to see her.

With Tunie and Marty at school, she had a full day with the house to herself. After another cup of broth and some toast for breakfast, from the now perfectly functioning toaster, Lonnie rested up in her bed, working on Alex's lesson. After a while, she grew tired, and she was forced to set it aside.

Lonnie snuggled under her covers and was reminded of the last time she was sick. She'd read *that book* and been left scandalized by it because she'd read it when she hadn't admitted her feelings to herself about Alex. Perhaps now it would be different.

Lonnie searched on her bookcase and located *The Vintage of Yon Yee* quickly, then got back under her covers. This time she'd read it with more of an open mind, she determined. Opening the book, she began.

She let the story transport her to Shanghai, the glittering British parties, and the mystery of the half-Chinese half-British Lois Allingham. Lonnie especially thrilled at the time Lois spent in the depths of China at her friend Chenn-yi No's home and when Lois met the young and handsome Chinese man Wên T'ien. She read hungrily, absorbing every detail of their Chinese lives. Then she came to the passage she'd been waiting for. Wen T'ien pulled Lois into his arms, and there they remained, reveling in the glory of their embrace. Wild plum blossoms perfumed the air, and the sand dunes sang while the water splashing at their feet served as cadence to their beating hearts and blissful happiness.

Lonnie let the book fall to the covers and heaved a huge, happy sigh. Almost unbidden, the image came to her of Alex holding her in such an embrace with the world singing gloriously around them. He lifted her chin and gently kissed her lips, so sweet and loving . . .

Her heart pounded, and she clutched the covers to her chest. Something in her swelled, and she burst out in a giddy squeal, throwing the covers over her head. She breathed deeply, savoring the feeling of the moment. But then she threw the covers back off, wanting to face things head on.

It was unthinkable. Wasn't it? To think Alex could kiss her— that he could dare to think of such a thing. But she longed for it. She wanted to be held tenderly in his arms like Wên T'ien held Lois.

Lonnie replayed the imagined scene over in her mind of Alex kissing her. It seemed so terrifyingly tangible. How she wished Alex could hold her now. She needed to reveal to him her feelings. But how? And when? She hugged her arms around her torso to still her eager trembling. Oh, how she loved him. She loved him!

Her heart leapt with what seemed like an electrical current coursing through her. Warmth surged to her hands and feet, burning in her chest. And it wasn't until that moment that she finally felt warm again.

Chapter Thirty

HELLO, MR. HARDY. Is Alex here?"

Alex stopped his work when he heard the familiar female voice say his name.

"Alex? Yeah, he's under the car over there. I'll get him for you." Footsteps approached. "Alex, you've got a visitor."

Alex rolled out from underneath the car and stood, wiping his hands on a stained rag. Mike turned away with a suppressed grin, which Alex chose to ignore. He was happy to see Lonnie walk up to him, the sun radiating through her hair, making it look like spun gold. She returned his smile, and they stepped outside the garage to talk.

A strange sort of suppressed excitement shone in her eyes. "I was wondering if you might come with me somewhere when you get off work today."

His eyebrows went up in surprise. "Oh? Where?"

"Can it be a surprise?"

He grinned. A surprise from Lonnie Hamilton? He couldn't miss something like that. "Sure. I get off work at five. I'll need some time to get cleaned up. So maybe five-thirty? Do you want to meet me here or should I meet you somewhere else?"

"I'll come here," she said quickly. "It's closer." She turned and walked away, and he gawked after her, mouth hitched in a grin long after she'd gone.

"She's an eye-catching girl, that one," came a voice in his ear.

"I know," Alex breathed. "Wait, what?"

Mike guffawed. "It's no use hiding it from me, boy. You look like you've been smacked upside the head with Cupid's bow." He laughed loudly again and walked off.

Alex slid back under the car and grabbed his wrench where he'd left it, mumbling darkly. Was it really that obvious? Did everyone in town know how he felt? Or only those who knew him better? The thought that his actions broadcast his feelings to the world was worrying. He should be more guarded, but with Lonnie near him, it was impossible to hide his feelings for much longer.

An hour later, Alex finished up his work, ran inside, cleaned up and changed into his nicest trousers, shirt, vest, and tie. He combed his hair carefully, grabbed his jacket and headed back outside at five-thirty on the dot. Lonnie was already there waiting. Her face broke into a smile at seeing him.

"I like how punctual you are," she said and laughed a little.

They started out, walking at a pleasant pace toward the edge of town. The weather was perfect and unseasonably warm for the fifth of February. It was edging on the middle fifties with a golden sun shining and a delicate cool breeze puffing around them.

"So, *Sagwa*, where are we headed?"

"I said it was a surprise." She raised her eyebrows at him.

"Not even one little hint?"

"No." They laughed together.

Alex removed his jacket, slinging it over his shoulder as they left town and walked out onto a country lane lined with bare trees and weed-choked fences. His curiosity piqued even more, though he was beginning to be suspicious. What was out here that she'd want to show him?

Her face was peaceful in their silence. He loved seeing her so serene and content. He wondered how she felt comfortable enough to be alone like this. His heart raced a little at this idea. They were really and truly alone, not a soul in sight. He shook his head to clear the possibilities that pushed their way in. It drew Lonnie's attention.

"Don't worry. We're nearly there."

"I wasn't worried."

A minute later they approached a white house with red shutters tucked away behind a little grove of trees, all of which was surrounded by a small, tidy lawn. A sleeping kitchen garden peeked from the back of the house, along with a naked grape arbor and a little hen house. Chickens scratched happily in their run and wild birds chirped busily at a bird feeder near the garden.

They walked up to the cleanly swept porch, and Lonnie knocked. The door opened, revealing a short, slightly hunched older Chinese woman. The smells emanating from within hit Alex full in the face, and his heart wrenched with homesickness.

The old woman's face crinkled in a big smile. "Welcome, welcome. Come in, please."

They stepped inside, and Lonnie made the introductions. "Xiao Lin, this is Moon Yeong Su. Or Alex Moon." She smiled. "Alex, this is Grandma Xiao Lin Chan."

Almost without thinking about it, he bowed in greeting murmuring, "*Anyanghaseo, halmeoni.*" She bowed in return, her laugh a pleasant tinkle.

Alex tried to figure out what was going on. This must be the Chinese woman in town Mike told him about, but what were they doing here?

Lonnie spoke up as if guessing at his thoughts. "Xiao Lin has wanted to meet you for some time, and since the lesson you gave me had to do with your New Year *Seollal*, I thought this was the perfect thing."

Alex gaped at her. She'd certainly taken liberties with his lesson. He didn't have much time to ponder before Lonnie pulled him into the living room. There were two cushions on the floor in front of a chair. Lonnie nodded to the old woman who settled happily in the chair.

Lonnie tugged on Alex's hand. "Come on. We have to do things properly. I've even been practicing." She giggled, and he continued to stare in wonder at her. But a lifetime of New Years took over, and together, he and Lonnie performed the Great Bow to honor their elder for the New Year. As he touched his head to the floor he couldn't even begin to describe the feelings choking in his throat. Everything was happening too quickly. He didn't even have to think. Lonnie's enthusiasm was a whirlwind.

They both got to their feet, and Xiao Lin beamed at them. She addressed Alex. "I know I'm not really your grandmother, but Appalone said you wouldn't mind." She grasped him by the hands. There was something so warm and familiar about her. "Are you hungry?"

He nodded and before he knew what was happening, the little woman was pulling him over to her low table. He sank down in front of the most enormous spread of steaming rice, broiled fish, rice cake soup, dumplings, marinated radish and—he nearly wept at seeing it—*kimchi!*

Lonnie seated herself next to him, and Xiao Lin served up his plate, choosing the biggest fish, piling his rice bowl to the brim with the beautiful gleaming rice, ladling into his bowl the pale, but fragrant *tteokguk* soup floating with fat, white rice cakes and green seaweed. Where she'd gotten the ingredients, he couldn't guess. All he could do was gaze helplessly at this familiar food.

"Eat, eat," Grandma Chan urged him, and with a slightly trembling hand, Alex reached out to pick up his chopsticks. The feel of them in his hand was enough to send shivers through him. He hadn't even remembered to bring a pair from California.

Lonnie smiled kindly, her hand resting lightly on his arm. "I hope you're hungry. And I hope you won't laugh at my attempts to use chopsticks. I've been practicing, but I'm still clumsy. Oh, I can't wait to try that soup." And she eagerly dipped in her spoon.

He followed suit, still confused as to why she'd gone to such lengths. But then the hot, delicious broth filled his mouth and after his first swallow, he sighed with rapture. He took a pinch of *kimchi* with his chopsticks and ate that too. The taste of it made tears spring to his eyes, not only because he'd missed eating it, but because it was spicy. It had been ages since he'd had anything so hot. He grinned at Xiao Lin and dug in with enthusiasm.

The first half of the meal was uninterrupted by talk, though he did have to laugh as Lonnie wiped away tears from eating the *kimchi*. With each bite, Alex was transported back home to his mother's kitchen, full of pots and mouth-watering smells. His mother was especially beautiful to him then, her dark brown hair curling at the edges from the steam, her eyes bright and dancing as she glided around the room in her own orchestrated symphony of stirring, tasting, seasoning.

As a small boy, those pots seemed magical. With his little mouth watering and his stomach growling anxiously, he sometimes pushed a chair near the stove to peek at the bubbling and whistling steam. His mother would sneak him a spoonful of this or a few bites of that, and then she'd chase him out to play.

She was naturally a good cook, and the fact that her cooking was a source of great pride for his father said a lot. Alex wished, with a pang, he could feel her arms around him in one of her wonderfully warm hugs, and that he could eat her cooking again. She'd told him once that watching him eat her food was one of the greatest pleasures of her life. Nothing was as good as eating food that came from her hands. Grandma Chan's food did come a close second, though.

After stuffing himself to an almost embarrassing limit, they retired to the front room. Xiao Lin brought out a pot of green tea and some almond cookies.

He sat on the couch next to Lonnie in the simple, tidy room. He wasn't sure what to say, but he looked around and saw a few old photos on the fireplace mantle, and a small Chinese painting hung on the wall. She had precious few ornaments to decorate, but there was a worn teapot next to the photos along with a tiny Celadon vase.

Xiao Lin noticed his interest and said, "There weren't many things I was able to bring with me from China when I immigrated forty years ago, but those things there. The vase was my mother's, who was from Korea, and the teapot belonged to my father's mother. Those are the only things I have left of my family." She smiled sadly. "Lonnie here tells me you're from California."

He nodded. "I'm from Los Angeles. Our community has a lot of Korean immigrants. My father met my mother there soon after he moved from Hawaii. I was born in California."

"You haven't had an easy time since coming to this town, I imagine."

"I've managed. I can say I've gained a lot of strength from friends I've made here." He winked at Lonnie and took a sip of the refreshing tea. "Was it difficult for you?"

Xiao Lin pressed her lips together as she thought. "Well, there were people who were suspicious of our family at first. After a while though, they got used to us. We also had the help of good friends." With a mischievous twinkle in her eye, she leaned forward and whispered loudly, "How did you like the *kimchi*?"

Alex's face burst into a grin. "It was fantastic; it was almost exactly like my mom's."

"Lonnie made it," the old woman said with triumph.

"Xiao Lin, you promised not to tell." Lonnie's face was crimson.

Alex turned to her in complete amazement. "Did you really?"

"Xiao Lin helped me, of course. She told me it was a staple for Koreans, and I wanted to learn how to make it."

He was speechless, and Grandma Chan just rocked in her chair, happy at her mischief.

"I'm sorry, Xiao Lin," Lonnie spoke up. "We need to be getting back. These roads get pretty dark, and I'm afraid of how cold it will be."

"Of course." The woman left briefly and came back with a paper sack. She loaded the bag with the almond cookies and shoved them into Alex's hands. "For later," she whispered, winking at him. "Thank you for coming, Appalone, Yeong Su. It was wonderful to have your company. It's always nicer to have someone to cook for." She grabbed his arm. "You come back when you need some good food, okay? I'll put you to work in my garden. Goodnight."

She waved at them until they were out onto the dirt road.

They walked some way before Alex thought to say something. His mind was racing, thinking back on the past hour and a half. Lonnie's surprise had been just that—a stunning revelation, one that touched him on a deep level. Did she even realize? Did she even know how much he needed that comfort and reminder of home? It was a part of him he hadn't realized was missing until he had the chopsticks in his hand. No one had ever done anything like this for him before in his life. No one had ever cared as much, especially in this town.

Alex was about ready to explode with everything he wanted to say. He stopped abruptly, and Lonnie followed suit.

"Is everything all right?" she asked. Her cheeks were still rosy from all the excitement.

He breathed deep and fought to find the words. "Why did you do that? What made you think to take me there?"

She took a half step back. "I don't know. You've been looking—stretched. You've been here for so long without much to remind you of home, and I thought you might be feeling homesick. I guess I wanted you to feel more at ease, especially after everything you've been through. Besides, it's *Seollal* today."

His chest heaved with the difficulty of breathing. He couldn't take it anymore. Alex dropped the paper sack. Fists balled, he turned on her.

Her happy smile faded. "What is it? Did I do something wrong?"

"Why do you care?" he asked, his voice hoarse with emotion. "I know we're friends, but why do something like *this*?"

Lonnie stiffened. She struggled to say something, and finally she managed a whisper. "I'm afraid, Alex."

"What?"

"I'm—I'm afraid of what will happen if I tell you."

"You don't have to be scared of me, Lonnie."

Her pale face was tinged with pink, her lips shone red in the setting sun. "Are you really going to make me say it?"

Alex stared down into her eyes. They seemed to plead with him and to confess things at the same time. After a long moment, it hit him.

His heart pummeled his chest. "Say it." He hardly dared to hope.

She took a step toward him until they were nearly touching. Her nearness left his head reeling. Alex tried to grasp at some thought that made sense, some way he could decipher what she was doing.

But the only thing that came to him was that whatever was about to happen, there would be no going back.

"Yeong Su . . . *Sarang hae.*" Standing on her tiptoes, she leaned against him and pressed her lips to his—sweet and soft and wonderful.

For a moment, Alex froze. What was she doing? Was he just imagining this?

But her warmth was real. Her breath was real. And she loved him. Never had Korean sounded so beautiful.

Alex's tension instantly melted. He pulled her against him, desperately kissing her back. She clung to him so closely he could feel her heart beat against his. He moved to hold her warm face in his hands, tangling his fingers in her soft hair.

Closer still, he kissed her more deeply, his heart singing. How had he missed it? All her shy smiles and gestures of kindness—they weren't only an extension of her sweet nature and generosity, but she'd been *giving* him her heart. How impossible it seemed that she could love him. His own heart ached with his feelings for her. They cut into him so deeply, entwined with every fiber of his being that it hurt.

Alex pulled away to study her face only to see tears glittering on her flushed cheeks. "What is it? What's wrong?" He gently wiped the tears away with his thumbs.

"Does this mean you feel the same way?" she asked, brows knit with worry.

Alex threw back his head and laughed. Wasn't it obvious? "Yes! Yes, of course." He stroked her hair, caressed her cheek. "I love you. I've loved you for ages." He relished her perfect lips as he kissed her again.

A minute later, she pulled back and smiled happily, but it quickly crumpled, and she burst into tears, covering her face with her hands.

"Is it so bad that I feel the same way?" Her behavior completely perplexed him.

She shook her head, hurriedly wiping her cheeks. "I guess I feel this tremendous sense of relief. I've kept it bottled up, and I wasn't able to say anything to you. I didn't know what to do."

"I know exactly how you feel. I think from the moment I first saw you I was on my way to falling for you. It's been agony this entire time not being able to do or say anything about it, not knowing if you felt the same way, afraid of what would happen if I spoke. I couldn't even begin to dream you'd grow to love me." Alex wrapped her up in another embrace, breathing deeply of her fragrance, feeling completely content, though it was tinged with sadness.

"I don't want to let you go," he murmured. "I'm afraid we'll never have another moment like this one."

Lonnie turned her face up to his. "I'm not going anywhere."

He could see she understood the true meaning behind his words. Tenderly, he ran a finger down her nose, outlined her cheek. "My beautiful little, *Sagwa*. I love you." He kissed her again.

Time slipped away, and before he knew it, the day had gone, and they were in almost complete darkness except for the last of the receding sun's rusty glow. The night had chilled considerably around them too. Alex stepped back and surveyed their situation.

"Let me walk you home. It's gotten so dark already. We should hurry before the sun—"

"No." Her voice was filled with fear. "My mother—I don't know what she'd do if she saw."

He frowned, but remained firm. "I'm going to walk you home, Lonnie. I won't come in, but I *am* walking you home. Come on." He grabbed her hand, picked up the dropped sack of cookies, and they walked down the lane as quickly as they could in the twilight, reaching the town just as the last of the sun had disappeared from the horizon. The shadows were deep as the streets succumbed to the dark.

They walked quietly, hand in hand. Things between them were comfortable and at a strange sort of peace. Alex enjoyed the feel of her small hand in his own. He was on top of the world thinking she wanted to be by his side.

The wait had been worth it.

Chapter Thirty-One

LONNIE GLOWED IN his company. Even though it was dark enough that she had trouble seeing where her feet landed, she couldn't help glancing over at Alex.

Her cheeks were still flushed from his kisses. The memory of them made her heart pound. She savored the feel of his strong hand in her own. How many times had she secretly longed to touch his hand, to feel it close around hers? Her imagined kisses were nothing compared to the truth and reality of Alex's lips on hers. His declarations soared in her heart.

Alex squeezed her hand as they reached her house, but he didn't try kissing her again. As much as Lonnie longed for him to, she was grateful in his wisdom. Reluctantly, she dropped his hand, walked up the porch, and gave him a small wave before she went inside.

Music and talking emanated from the living room. She wandered in to see her mother with her cigarette trailing smoke as she stared blankly at the wall. She swayed silently in the rocking chair as she listened to the radio.

"I'm home, Mother."

The woman nodded. Lonnie moved to go upstairs.

"You look different."

Lonnie turned back. Her mother had stopped rocking and was gazing at her.

"What do you mean?" Lonnie's heart thumped, wondering if her kiss was written all over her face.

"There's a change in you." She leaned forward a little. "Does he make you happy?" Her voice was edged in sarcasm.

Lonnie's breath caught in her throat. "Who do you mean?"

Her mother went back to rocking, laughing without much humor. "I'm not blind, Appalone. I've been watching for some time now—you and that Oriental man mooning after each other. Do you understand what a relationship with him would even mean?" She snorted. "Of course you don't. How could you? You're so naïve and innocent." She took a drag on her cigarette. "It's my fault I suppose, but I honestly never thought a man like him would show up in our backwater town."

"Stop it, Mother." Lonnie's voice came out sharp. "You've barely even met him. How could you know anything?"

Harriet stood abruptly and approached. Her face was terrifying, and Lonnie stumbled back.

"I don't need to know him. I can see as clear as day what your life will turn into in his wake."

"Stop it."

"You'll be a freak. Your children will be freaks—locked between two worlds where they won't be accepted in either. Is that what you want? To be shunned for the rest of your life? No matter where you go it will be the white girl that married the yellow man."

"Stop!" Lonnie shouted. "It won't be like that. Not everyone is as hateful as you."

Her mother slapped her so hard her vision fractured into bursts of blinding light. Lonnie cried out, tears springing to her eyes from the pain.

Harriet's face was pale and twisted. "You don't know anything," she hissed. "You're just a stupid small-town girl with her head in the clouds. I'm doing my duty to knock some sense into you, especially when you turn down a perfectly good offer of marriage from a man whom you don't even deserve."

Lonnie gasped in horror.

"That's right." Harriet sneered viciously. "I uncovered your little *secret*. When were you planning on telling me you've ruined your life? Can't you see what you could have become? You would've been married to the richest family in the county and been respected and admired by everyone. But now that chance is gone. What a waste," she spat. "What a waste his proposal was on such a worthless, pathetic excuse for a daughter as you."

Lonnie cringed away from her mother. The words cut deep. Her mother stepped closer to Lonnie until her face was inches away. With her voice deadly and calm, she said, "Don't you *ever* see that piece of trash again, Appalone Hamilton. I forbid it. And if you do, so help me, you'll pay for your disobedience."

Lonnie retreated upstairs. Tears streamed down her face, and her cheek stung painfully. She shut herself in her room to find Tunie sitting in bed. Her sister scrambled to switch on her bedside light.

"Are you all right? I've never heard Mother in such a state. What's going on?"

Lonnie ignored her and threw herself on her bed where she sobbed heavily into her pillow. After a moment, the bed dipped as Tunie sat on the edge and rubbed her back.

"I'm guessing this has to do with Alex, but you know what it really is? She just hates to see other people happy."

"Oh, Tunie," Lonnie cried. "It's more than that. Somehow, she found out about Teddy's proposal. She was just as furious as I knew she'd be. You didn't say anything? By mistake?"

"I didn't, Lonnie. I swear I didn't."

Lonnie cried some more, devastated at the turn of events. What was she going to do now? For one blissful evening she'd been light and free, but in one swift blow, she'd come crashing down under the burden of her mother's spiteful expectations and demands.

Eventually her crying slowed, and she sat up, wiping her face with the edge of her blanket. She gave her sister a watery smile. "Thank you for not telling."

Tunie's mouth curved in a sad smile, then gasped. "Lonnie, your cheek. It's bleeding."

Lonnie touched the spot and winced. It was sticky with blood. Tunie quickly went to wet a washcloth and dabbed it on Lonnie's cheek. "The cut doesn't look deep, but it's not pretty either. I don't think you need a bandage." She sat back. "There. All better."

Lonnie shook her head, staring into her lap. "It's not better, is it?"

"No, I guess not. Oh, why does she always have it out for you? Now that I think about it, she's never treated me or Marty this way. Why is she always so harsh towards you?"

Lonnie shrugged. "I don't know. Maybe it's because I'm the oldest."

Her sister shook her head, curlers bobbing crazily. "That can't be all there is to it."

"I wish I knew."

"Well, what was she going on about this time?"

Lonnie pursed her lips. "I'm not sure, but I think she saw me coming home with Alex."

Tunie gawked at her. "Well, no wonder she was so hopping mad. What were you doing out with him?"

"It was New Year's, and we went to have dinner with Grandma Chan."

She eyed Lonnie, incredulous. "New Year's was last month."

"Well, not for the Orient. They have a different New Years than us."

"Oh. Well. So he walked you home. Big deal? I suppose it was a gentlemanly thing for him to do. But being out with him after dark was a mistake on your part, you have to admit."

Lonnie sighed. Should she reveal what had transpired? It couldn't hurt now. She began slowly. "Mother said I looked different."

"Different? How so?"

"Well, *different*. Like how you feel after a kiss . . ."

Tunie gasped. "What? He *kissed* you?"

Lonnie's face flushed from her sister's reaction. "No. Well, yes, but I kissed him first."

Tunie began fanning her face with her hand. "Oh. Oh, my goodness, Lonnie. You're always so demure. I never would've dreamed you were capable of shocking me. Or that you could be so scandalous." She grinned wickedly, a hungry gleam in her eye. "Tell me everything."

Lonnie didn't end up telling her everything, but enough to make her sister clap her hands in delight. "Oh, this is delicious. To think you, of all people, confessed you loved him *and* kissed him first." She laughed. "I mean, it was obvious how he felt about you."

Lonnie blushed. "Yes, but he couldn't have done much about it."

Tunie became serious. "But isn't this a bad idea, Lonnie? What's going to happen to you when everyone finds out? Look how Mother behaved. And you know how people in town feel about Alex. Just think about that fight he had with Teddy."

Lonnie scowled, indignant. What business was it of anyone's with whom she chose to pursue a relationship? She was nineteen. She didn't need anyone telling her what to do or how she should think.

Since it was out in the open, Lonnie examined her predicament. So they loved each other. Now what? Everyone in the world knew what was expected to follow a kiss, an acknowledgement of mutual feeling and affection.

Marriage.

She hadn't considered things that far. Could she realistically imagine herself being Alex's wife? Mrs. Alexander Moon. *Appalone Moon.*

And what about children? Her mother had made the idea of bearing Alex's children something ugly and despicable, but she didn't feel that way. Not even close. She wanted to spend the rest of her life with him, to wake up and fall asleep next to him, to bear his children and grow old together. She sat straighter, a new resolve filling her.

"What is it?" Tunie asked.

"I—I think I've just realized what I need to do now."

"What?"

Lonnie knelt on the floor and rummaged beneath her bed. Grasping the handle, she pulled out a suitcase and laid it out on her bed. "I'm moving out."

Tunie jumped to her feet in shock. "What? But why?"

Lonnie pulled things out of her closet. "Because I can't live here anymore. Mother forbade me from ever seeing Alex again, but I have no intention of doing that."

Her sister watched her helplessly. "You don't have to move out on account of that, do you? You can just go on seeing him without her knowing. Besides, where will you go?"

"I'll go to Aunt Millie. She's suggested I move in with her anyway. She's been feeling lonely without Uncle George and David."

"Do you have to?" Tunie's voice was unusually small.

Lonnie smiled sadly at her sister. "Yes, sweetie, I do. Because I'm going to marry Alex, and no one, not even Mother is going to stop me."

Tunie's jaw dropped. "What, like elope?"

Lonnie continued with her packing, this time pulling out her dresser drawers. "If I have to, but I hope it won't come to that."

"But what if he won't? What if he refuses to marry you? Even if it's for fear of his own life? Mother would kill him if she found out."

Right then, Lonnie remembered Alex's money, still in her purse, a well-intentioned decision never fully realized. Trepidation stole over her like a terrible wave. She'd meant to give it to him ages ago, but had put it off and forgotten it.

Lonnie cursed herself for having delayed giving it to him, and for Tunie ever having found it in the first place. She sank down on her bed, feeling lost again. She wanted to throw the money in the river and forget she'd ever found it. He'd never know. And it wouldn't matter in the end anyway, would it?

Her stomach churned because she knew it *did* matter. She needed to tell him, and she feared the consequences. Would he be able to forgive her? Would he ever be able to trust her again?

She noticed her sister who still waited for an answer. Lonnie went to her. Wrapping her in a hug, she whispered, "I don't know, Tunie. I really don't know. But I hope he will."

***

As Alex awoke the next morning, his sleepy mind struggled to make sense of the previous evening's events. Had it really happened? He hadn't made it all up in some crazy fantasy? He sorted through his memories, reliving each moment. It couldn't have been real. It wasn't possible.

His eyes slid over to his dresser. There sat that crumpled paper bag full of almond cookies—evidence he'd gone with Lonnie to visit old Grandma Chan and of everything that transpired afterward.

Alex moaned and forced himself to roll out of bed. What was he going to do? He'd kissed her. Or more accurately, she'd kissed him.

He stalled in the middle of tying on his robe, staring off into nothingness. Oh, the memory of that kiss! He shut his eyes against its bliss, but the image persisted. How could he have let it happen? Why did she have to go and do something so unexpected and completely disarming? It was one thing to think about and long for it, but quite another to actually have it happen. He'd been completely unprepared.

He stumbled out of his room and down the hall to the kitchen. Mike was already at the table drinking his coffee and reading the morning paper. Alex collapsed into the chair across from him and dug his fingers into his hair, which reminded him of threading his fingers into Lonnie's hair as he passionately kissed her. The memory only made things worse. He moaned again.

Mike surveyed him over the rim of his coffee cup as he drank.

"Oh, Mike. Mike. I'm dead. I'm really dead this time." Alex pondered the old table, frantically seeking the answer to his predicament in its worn and scarred surface.

"What did you do this time?" Mike asked.

"I kissed her," he whispered loudly. "I kissed Lonnie Hamilton."

Mike slammed his mug down with a heavy thump. "You did what?" He eyed Alex with suspicion. "Are you just messing around or do you really care about that girl?"

Alex was shaken by Mike's response, but considered it fair. "Of course I care about her. I fully admit I love her and have for months. But what do I do now?"

Mike's eyes were hard. "You didn't think this through beforehand, did you?"

Alex laughed without humor. "Of course not. I didn't think she felt the same way, but she does. How was I to know? And besides, she kissed me first." He crossed his arms, but Mike was not impressed.

"Don't avoid your responsibility, son." He jabbed a finger at him. "You've got a duty to her now. There's no backing out."

Alex relaxed his arms. "I know. I don't intend to. But I don't know where to go from here. I didn't think anything between us was very likely. I've literally never thought beyond confessing my feelings for her. That alone was almost more than I could handle."

Mike sipped his coffee slowly, brow furrowed in contemplation. "Have you considered marrying her?"

The answer was so obvious, but it was absolutely terrifying. Marriage? He gripped the sides of the table tightly as if it was his life raft. "I—I don't want to ruin her life, Mike. I mean—look at me. Look at me!" Alex scraped back his chair and paced the kitchen.

"Calm down, Alex. You haven't ruined her life, and I doubt she feels you have."

"Well, no. Not yet." He gestured wildly. "What happens when everyone finds out? It's not like we can stroll down Main Street hand in hand for the world to see." He groaned. "What happens when Reverend Hicks finds out? When her mother finds out? They'll kill me! And then everyone else in town will kill me after them." He ran his fingers through his hair again, only to be yanked back down into his chair.

"Stop your yammering, and take a deep breath, you maniac," Mike growled.

Alex shut his mouth and obeyed. He did feel calmer after a moment, but the problem was as glaring as ever.

"Now," Mike stated slowly. "No doubt Lonnie has had some time to think about things in the new day as well. Instead of going on and on with me, your best bet would be to talk it out with her. Won't you be seeing her at church today?"

"Yes, I suppose."

"Well, go to church then, boy."

***

Alex tentatively stepped into the full chapel. For some reason the room's beautiful dominance seemed more foreboding than welcoming this time—as if he was some lost soul, a sinner and hypocrite who'd come clawing and scraping his way back. It did nothing for the helplessness that overwhelmed him.

He'd purposely arrived late to slip into the back unnoticed. When Reverend Hicks began his sermon on the evils of lies and deceit, Alex's stomach sickened. He slumped lower and lower in his seat—each word a nail in his coffin. His rational side told him he'd done nothing wrong, but the fact that her uncle didn't know—that it was the very thing he'd warned Alex about . . .

As the final hymn was sung, he straightened his back, gaining strength from its words. He would face this. He needed to speak with Reverend Hicks, whatever the consequences, but he needed to speak with Lonnie first.

Alex stood with the rest of the congregation and kept an eye out for her. She gradually approached him. Most everyone had gone by the time she reached him, and what he saw made him suck in his breath in horror.

"Your face! What happened?" A purple bruise was splashed across her right cheek accompanied by an ugly red gash.

She studied the floor. "I tried to cover it with makeup, but it didn't work." She laughed ruefully. "Now I know how you must've felt coming out into public with your face looking like this. Only worse."

Alex frowned. "This isn't funny, Lonnie. Tell me what happened."

"My mother is what happened, but let's not talk here. I've asked Uncle Phillip if we could speak at his house and he agreed."

Alex nervously glanced toward the door where Reverend Hicks was saying goodbye to the last of his parishioners. "Does he know anything?"

"I didn't say anything specific, but I think he might suspect something." She turned in the direction of the side door of the chapel. "Come on. We can talk more at Uncle Phillip's."

He followed her, all the while feeling his anger leaping to a boil. Seeing the mark on Lonnie's face made him crazy, and it was all he could do to keep himself under control. Something told him he might be paying a visit to Mike's dented piece of metal later on.

Once they were safely inside, he pulled her to the couch and they sat. Alex touched her cut cheek, examining it. "Does it hurt?"

Lonnie gently pulled his arm down and held his hand in her lap. "It's fine."

"I'm so sorry that happened to you." His voice caught in his throat. "It's because of me, isn't it?"

Lonnie shook her head. "It isn't your fault. You're not the one that needs to apologize."

"But how did it happen? Why would she strike you?"

She shrugged. "Mother somehow found out about everything—Teddy's proposal that I turned down and you. I don't know how she could've known anything. She was so angry . . ." Her voice shrunk.

"I knew you'd never agree to marry him, but I'm sorry for what you've suffered as a result."

Lonnie gaped at him. "I don't think I ever told you he proposed to me. How did you find out?"

"Teddy made the point of mentioning it, to spite me I think." Alex regarded Lonnie, who'd become somber. "And you had no reason to tell me before. It wasn't really my business. But who was it that told your mother is the real question here. Someone must've said something." He paused to think and scowled. "I bet it was Teddy himself."

Lonnie sighed. "We don't know that for sure, Alex. Either way, she's found out, and I can't go on living there anymore. She's forbidden me from seeing you again, but I'm not a child. I won't be told what to do any longer." The defiance that shone in her eyes worried him.

"What are you going to do?" It was the same question he'd been asking himself all day.

"I was thinking of moving to Aunt Millie's today. I didn't get a chance to ask her myself, so Uncle Phillip was going to speak with her about it for me."

"So he knows something at least . . ."

"Well, he did see my face." Her gaze dropped to their entwined fingers. "Oh, he was furious."

The helplessness of their situation stole over him again, and it was all Alex could do to keep from crying out in frustration. He swallowed with difficulty, loathing himself for the words about to come out of his mouth. "I—I hate to say this, Lonnie, but wouldn't it be better if we stopped this now? Before anyone else gets hurt? Before *you* get hurt again."

"No!" The word hurtled from her mouth without restraint. She grasped his hands tighter. "No, I am not giving you up, Alexander Moon. For the first time in my life I feel like someone understands me, accepts me for who I am. Someone who's my match in so many countless ways. Don't ask me to give you up. Not now." Tears spilled out from her clear, blue eyes.

His heart seized. He hadn't meant to make her cry. Alex pulled her close, resting her head on his shoulder and enfolding her in his arms. They sat that way for a long time. The moment didn't need words.

At long last, Alex smoothed back her hair and wiped away her tears. "We'll figure this out. I don't know how, but if this is meant to be, then—"

"Then God will show us the way." Her weary face brightened with her smile.

He nodded, wishing he felt half as hopeful as she looked.

He gazed down at their hands—his golden tan and hers a rosy cream—and scrambled to think of a solution. "*Sagwa.*" He met her eyes. "I don't see how anyone could come to accept us, even those who don't completely hate the sight of me. If it comes down to it, we might have to go away. Would you be willing to do that?"

"What's this about going away?" Reverend Hicks strode into the room before Lonnie could answer, his face dark with foreboding. "Alex, are you trying to convince my niece to run away with you?"

Alex instantly released Lonnie's hands and leapt to his feet, the blood draining from his face. "No, sir, that's not what I meant."

Lonnie got to her feet as well. "Please don't overreact, Uncle Phillip. You walked in on the middle of our conversation. You need to hear us out."

"Overreact? You don't want me to overreact when your face looks like *that* and a young man is asking you to run away with him?" The whites of his eyes showed round and full, and his face was on the verge of turning purple.

Alex wanted to shrink away, but maintained his ground. Lonnie took charge. "Please sit down, Uncle Phillip, before you have a stroke. Alex, could you get him a cup of tea?" He obeyed with relief, grateful she hadn't left him alone in the room with her uncle.

He returned to find Lonnie had coaxed Reverend Hicks into his favorite chair and encouraged him to loosen his collar. Without a word, Reverend Hicks took the cup from his hand and drained it in one go. Alex sat on the couch, but left a good foot between himself and Lonnie.

After waiting for him to finish his tea, Lonnie was all sweetness, as if nothing in the world was wrong. "Did you speak with Aunt Millie?"

Reverend Hicks cleared his throat. "I did. She'll send her neighbor's son to help you with your luggage."

Lonnie slid forward to the edge of the couch. "And was she in favor of the reasons why? Because of Mother's feelings towards Alex and me—"

Alex glanced back and forth between them, watching the exchange with growing concern. Things weren't going very well if the grim look on her uncle's face was any indication.

"Of course she was." Without warning, Reverend Hicks pounded his fist on his chair causing Alex to jump. "Blast it, Appalone! I knew this would all come about. I warned Millie about throwing you two together. And now see what's happened."

Alex leapt to Lonnie's defense. "But nothing's happened."

Reverend Hicks launched from his chair. "Nothing's happened? I got an earful about it from Harriet last night, saying it was all my fault Lonnie was off *alone* with you when any self-respecting young woman would be chaperoned or would be at home before dark as she should be." He pointed an accusing finger. "You crossed a line, Alex, and I'm severely disappointed." Reverend Hicks turned away, pacing the length of the room a few times before continuing. "There's far more going on here than either of you realize. And if you were wise, you'd end this immediately."

His hands were on his hips, and he was breathing heavily. Alex was floored by the Reverend's words—Reverend Hicks, who'd been his friend the longest of anyone in this town. And now Alex had let him down. He hung his head in devastation.

"I'm sorry," he murmured.

Lonnie spoke up. "What do you mean, there's far more going on than we realize? What's that supposed to mean?"

Her uncle waved her words away. "It isn't my place to say. If anything, you should ask your mother. It's about time she told you anyway."

Alex glanced at Lonnie, who frowned.

Reverend Phillips strode to the front door. "Both of you should leave. I need time to think."

Alex rose and walked shame-faced to the door with Lonnie close behind.

"Your Aunt Millie says to call her right away if you need anything," her uncle told Lonnie, his voice eerily calm. "If you don't show up by supper time, she'll come fetch you herself."

Lonnie nodded, and with a stubborn defiance, she grabbed Alex's hand and pulled him outside.

Chapter Thirty-Two

ON MONDAY, LONNIE went back to work as if nothing out of the ordinary had happened. She did her best to cover the marks on her face with makeup. She hoped it wasn't noticeable enough for Mr. Pickering to mention it. As she walked in the refreshing morning air through town, she reflected on the conversation with her aunt the day before.

She hadn't been sure what she should tell her aunt. She most certainly didn't want to tell her everything. No one, excepting Tunie, knew of her intention to marry Alex, not even Alex. In the end, she settled for revealing what her uncle already knew—that she'd been out after dark with Alex, that they cared about each other and wanted to pursue a relationship.

Aunt Millie's reaction wasn't anything Lonnie had been expecting. Her aunt was unusually calm, nodding her head after listening.

"Hmm. Yes, I suspected something might be going on."

"You did? Since when?"

"Well, the Christmas party most definitely. It was almost painful to see the longing glances he cast your way. It was sweet really. I felt so sorry for him."

Sorry? For Alex? "But . . . don't you want to try and stop us?"

Her aunt sighed. "Why should I try and stop you? Honestly, I haven't the heart. This world is sick with blood and killing. Why should I stop something as beautiful as your love and friendship?" She took a sip of her tea. "Of course I worry about you and how your life will be affected because people can be pig-headed and narrow minded. But as far as I can tell, Alexander is as decent and worthy of your affections as any young man I've met."

Tears sprang to Lonnie's eyes at her aunt's kind words, and she clutched her teacup until it burned her hands. She set it down and went to hug her aunt. "Oh, Aunt Millie. You have no idea what it means to me to hear you say those words. Thank you."

Aunt Millie patted Lonnie's back. "Now, you just stay here as long as your little heart desires." She laughed. "Or until David returns. I think he'll want his room back."

"Thank you." At last, she could breathe. She was finally free of her mother.

And indeed, her heart was lighter and filled with such hope for her future. When she'd made plans for her life, she honestly hadn't considered meeting a man and wanting to share her life with him. Her head had only been for exploring exotic far off places. To think someone as exotic and wonderful as Alex had come to her little town and sent her head spinning—it was exhilarating.

***

Alex wove his fingers into Lonnie's as they'd sat together on a bench on the patio yesterday evening. He loved that they didn't always need words to enjoy each other's company. It was comfortable and sweet. After a long time, he finally spoke up.

"I've been wondering what's happened to my shy, timid Lonnie of late. This new Lonnie is quite different."

She smiled a little. "Do you like her?"

"I admire her boldness, that's for sure."

Lonnie turned to him. "Well, she's here to stay. At least I hope so. I've always tried to be obedient and patient with my mother, but I suppose I'm stubborn too. I guess there wasn't anything I ever wanted enough to become so determined."

"You had your dreams of travel, didn't you?"

She shrugged. "Yes, but when was that really going to happen? We don't have that kind of money. There's a war going on. They were all just childish dreams; something to keep my mind occupied and to pin my hopes on. I've come to accept that reality may never happen. But none of that matters now. I have you." She turned her face up at him and without thinking twice he kissed her.

He grinned happily at the memory, until someone smacked him in the back of his head.

"Ouch." Alex whipped around to see Mike frowning at him.

"What's gotten into you, boy? I've called your name five times. You're daydreaming about that girl, aren't you?"

Alex reddened.

The man grunted. "You keep your head on your work for the rest of the day, and I'll let you off an hour early. Then you go and take that girl out on a date. You may have her affection and everlasting devotion, but you've still got to show her she's important and court her right."

Alex grinned at the unexpected offer. "Yes, sir."

He worked hard and was happy four o'clock came round so quickly. He had an idea of what he and Lonnie could do together, and he couldn't wait to see her again. He hurriedly took a shower, but took his time getting ready. He wanted to look his best.

By the time he was walking downtown, it was nearly five. He got to the steps of Lonnie's office and hesitated, remembering the last time he'd been there. He didn't want to cause an uncomfortable situation with her boss, so he slipped into the side alley of her office building to wait for her.

At five after five, Lonnie swung the door open and stepped out. She turned left to set off for home, but Alex shot an arm out, grabbed her, and pulled her into the alley. She squealed in shock, but seeing his face, her expression softened into delight.

"What are you doing here? And why are you hiding?"

He enfolded her in a hug, and she relaxed in his arms. "I missed you," he murmured into her hair.

"I missed you too. I could barely concentrate on typing. I had to restart this one letter eight times." She looked up at him and laughed.

He caressed her cheek, absorbing the sight of her smiling face. "Are you still doing all right? Your mother hasn't shown up to demand you come back home or anything?"

Lonnie shook her head. "You needn't look so worried. I'm fine."

Reluctantly, he let her go. "Let's go get something to eat. My treat. You hungry?"

"Yes, I am, but I should probably—" she paused and then laughed. "No, I don't have to get home. Not at all. What a curious sensation." Her eyes were a little sad, though, and he wondered if she was thinking of her siblings.

They walked in the direction of Marelli's, and soon they were seated in the familiar place with the black and white tile floor.

"You gave me my first Korean lesson here. Do you remember?" Lonnie smiled.

"Of course. I was really nervous. I didn't know if you'd take me seriously in the end, but I hoped you would."

Their food arrived just then, and they ate for a time.

"This is nice," Lonnie said.

"What is?"

"To be sitting here, sharing a meal with you."

Alex nodded, but swallowed uncomfortably. Lonnie's back faced the other diners, so she didn't see the stares or hear the murmurs barely concealed behind hands. He wanted to be as at ease as she looked, but even her cheer didn't do much to bolster his confidence. The worry still tainted his happiness—of what their fate would be once everyone found out how they felt about one another. They were lucky in Aunt Millie's acceptance. And from what she'd told him, they even had Rose and Gladys's support. Outside of that, what hope was there?

He pushed back his chair as soon as they finished eating. "Come on. I have somewhere else I want to take you."

She followed him, and they strode out into the dimming light. "So, where are you taking me?"

He longed to reach for her hand, but dreaded the thought of running into anyone after taking a liberty like that. He shoved his hands in his pockets to quell the temptation. "You'll see, but you have to follow my directions. All right?"

"Hmm. If you say so."

Alex was a little nervous to see a line had already started forming for tickets when they got to the theater. "Thousands Cheer" was the new film that had just come to their town, and from what he'd heard, he was sure Lonnie would like it.

He turned to her. "Stay a few places behind me in line, okay?"

Her brows drew together to match her frown. "Why?"

"Remember, you need to follow my directions."

After a moment of hesitation, she pursed her lips. "All right."

He pressed a few coins into her hand and winked. "Meet me inside, but sit a few seats away."

She nodded again with a smile that didn't quite reach her eyes.

Alex purchased his ticket and went inside to buy popcorn and candy. He entered the semi-dark theater and held his breath until the usher gave him a nod and looked the other way. Alex took a seat in the back row and a few moments later Lonnie walked in, slid into his row and sat a handful of seats away. She ignored him completely until the theater had filled, and she took advantage of more people filing into their aisle to move down next to Alex at the end.

Lonnie stared primly ahead, and Alex admired her acting. She didn't even acknowledge his existence until the lights went out and the film flickered to life. He heard her sigh and immediately reached for her hand.

"Oh, Alex," she murmured. Her voice was almost inaudible over the music of the opening credits.

He squeezed her hand. "What is it, *Sagwa?*"

"I'm not ashamed to be seen with you. I thought you would've known that by now."

His stomach squeezed with a pang of guilt, but also with irritation. He didn't like being furtive about his intentions toward her either. He wanted to kiss her in the street, to hold her hand in the open, to declare his love freely without fear. But did they really have that freedom?

He stroked the back of her hand with his thumb. "I do know that. I'm afraid of what will happen to you if you're seen with me in the way we want. What about your reputation?"

She shrugged. "I stopped worrying about that a while ago. I can't help what people say or think. I can only do what I feel is right and good." She turned her attention to the movie, grabbing a handful of popcorn in the process.

He took in her light-etched profile, and his heart swelled. He couldn't love anyone more than he loved this girl by his side. Was she really saying that being with him was right and good? He settled himself to watch the film. It seemed she had a better opinion of him than he did of himself.

***

After the newsreel finished and the lights came back on, dozens of people spilled out of the theater into the night, scattering on their ways home or to the nearest pub. Alex followed Lonnie out, trailing on the edge of the crowd. As soon as they were outside, Lonnie grabbed his hand and pulled him in the direction of her aunt's house.

"That was a wonderful film, don't you think? The music was fantastic. I love Judy Garland. Her voice is so lovely to listen to."

Alex watched as she chattered on and wanted to laugh and kiss her face. Maybe when they got to Aunt Millie's . . .

"I could've sworn I was seeing things, but apparently I wasn't."

Alex's head jerked to the familiar voice.

Teddy and Walter blocked their path, their faces half cloaked in shadow. Teddy wore a mask of hatred that twisted the part of his face Alex could see into something like a fearsome, one-eyed monster. Walter merely looked menacing, but that wasn't anything new. Instinctively, Alex gripped Lonnie's hand tighter.

Teddy spoke again, his voice calm and conversational, which set Alex on his guard. "Alex and Lonnie at the movies together. How sweet and kind of you, Lonnie. No one else would dare be alone in the dark with that piece of yellow scum. I'll hand it to you for always being the good Christian girl."

At his words, Lonnie slid her hand free of Alex's grip and stood in front of him.

"Go away, Teddy, and leave us alone. Alex has never done anything to you."

Teddy threw his head back and laughed loudly, though it was tinged with something manic.

Walter stepped forward. "Stay out of this, Lonnie, and go home. We just need to have a little chat with Alex. It doesn't need to concern you."

Alex noticed Lonnie's face pale in indignation, but he pulled her back beside him. He wasn't going to be seen hiding behind her and, for once, agreed with Walter. She needed to go home and to stay out of this. He opened his mouth to tell her so when Teddy cut in.

"Oh, my dear, beautiful, Lonnie. It's always been Alex from the beginning, hasn't it? Your mother warned me. She told me you'd been caught going out with him, but I didn't want to believe it. Not after what's passed between us." Teddy's eyes gleamed viciously, and something cold stole over Alex. What did he mean? Beside him, Lonnie stiffened.

"You never told him, did you, my love?" A humorless smile stretched across Teddy's countenance. "You never mentioned how tenderly we kissed?"

Lonnie gasped. Alex's eyes darted to her in shock. She'd kissed Teddy? When?

"That's a lie," Lonnie whispered. Her skin was deathly white.

"No, it isn't," Teddy cried. "And you say Alex has never done anything to me. He stole you from me. You would've been mine if it weren't for him. I thought with your spiteful mother's help, at least, I'd have a fair chance, but it wasn't good enough. All along, you were too big of a dunce to see what you were throwing away, and instead you walk out with him. To think I have to compete with a traitor and an enemy. It's absurd!"

Lonnie wrenched herself away from Alex and stomped up to Teddy until they were inches apart. "I never would've chosen you, Theodore Stanton. Not for all your wealth and prestige in this dinky town. You're selfish and self-centered." Her voice rose. "You think you own the world, but you don't own me."

Alex's eyes widened in horror as Teddy raised his hand and backhanded her face with a loud *smack*. She reeled backward, and Alex caught her before she sank to the ground.

"Lonnie?" He bent over her, patting her cheek. Her eyes fluttered and a red welt appeared where Teddy had struck her. "Are you all right? Say something." Panic choked him. How could Teddy have hit her?

After a few seconds, her eyes finally opened. "I'm all right," she whispered.

He smoothed her hair as he studied her eyes. They looked clear enough. He quickly removed his coat and folded it up to rest underneath her head. He left her there and rounded on Teddy, his panic melting away into a white-hot fury.

Walter had stepped back, his face a blank of shock as he gaped at Teddy. A second later, Walter was at Lonnie's side, helping her to sit and lean against him. He circled her in a protective arm.

Teddy's eyes seemed to taunt Alex. Welcoming the challenge, Alex launched himself at Teddy. They collided in curses and fists. Alex didn't think. He couldn't think beyond wanting to kill this man. He landed blow after blow and took as many himself. He didn't feel the pain, only the rage. Walter held Lonnie back as she shouted for them to stop. Her words and tears were impossible to acknowledge now.

After some moments of struggle, Teddy managed to lock him in a hold. He chuckled with difficulty, his breathing hard. "Does it make you angry, Moon? To think the girl you love has kissed another man?" He moaned, mocking. "Oh, but her lips were so deliciously sweet—"

Alex roared and broke free. He turned and pummeled Teddy. Teddy raised his arms to protect himself, no longer fighting. Out of his haze, Alex heard the whistles of police officers and then he was being dragged off Teddy. An officer delivered a sharp blow to his side and wrenched his arms behind his back. For a split second, Alex thought he'd been transported back to the attack at the train station.

The next few moments were a blur. Before he knew it, Alex found himself in a chair next to Teddy in front of an officer at the police station. Alex slumped in his chair, aching all over, his mind numb. Glancing over at Teddy, Alex noticed how Teddy sat bolt upright, despite his face and hair being a mass of blood and dirt. His glasses were missing.

The dark-haired muscular officer at the desk typed at some paperwork in an unhurried way. He smacked his lips a few times, shook his head, and continued typing.

Finally, he deigned to give them his attention. "You," he indicated Teddy. "Give me your name, age, and address."

Teddy cleared his throat. "Theodore Stanton. Twenty. 101 Stanton Avenue." He managed a smug smirk even through all the blood and bruising. Alex wanted to break his arm.

The officer raised a bushy, brown eyebrow as he typed the information. "Stanton, eh?" He nodded over at Alex. "Same for you. Name, age, and address."

"Alexander Moon. Nineteen. 403 Grand Street."

The man nodded and typed. He pursed his lips. "Moon. You've been in here before, haven't you?"

Alex scowled, not wanting to acknowledge the question. Of all the times to be reminded of how he'd come to this town in the first place.

Luckily, the officer didn't expect a reply. Instead, he sat back and surveyed them. "All right, now tell me what this was all about."

Teddy spoke up immediately. "Everyone knows what a trouble-maker this man is. It's not a secret we dislike each other. And this isn't the first time he's attacked me either. I do my part for the war while this traitor walks around town, free as a bird. I'm sure you're aware of who my father is, sir. He's expressed concern over this man being a spy, and honestly, I'd have to agree with him. His unprovoked violence toward me, a hard working member of this town, is suspicious enough. It shouldn't go unpunished."

Bushy eyebrows were raised again. "Unprovoked. Really? Is that your official statement?"

Teddy nodded. "Yes, sir, it is."

The man grunted. "That's very interesting, Mr. Stanton, but too bad, really. I have two witnesses saying *you* were the one to hit a woman and Mr. Moon here came to her defense."

Teddy's pale face grew even whiter. "T-Two witnesses?"

Alex leaned toward the officer in urgency. "Lonnie Hamilton. Where is she? Is she all right?"

"Calm down. Walter Chase escorted her home. I believe he's a friend of hers." Alex didn't know if that bit of information made him feel calm, but he wondered about the two witnesses. If Lonnie was one, who was the other? Could it really be Walter himself? That didn't make any sense. Walter hated him.

At that moment, Sheriff Wilcox walked by. Seeing the two of them, his mouth curved down into a severe frown. "Not you two again. I heard about your fight at the benefit dance. I should've known it would happen again." The man jabbed a finger in Alex's direction. "You. I want to see you in my office when Officer Jenkins is done. Got it?"

Alex sagged even lower in his chair. "Yes, sir."

Officer Jenkins turned back to them. "Now, Mr. Stanton, suppose you give me your statement again."

A half hour later, Alex was relieved to get away from Teddy, but he wasn't looking forward to his chat with the sheriff.

He sat across from him in the man's office and waited for the hailstorm of whatever was coming. But it didn't come. Sheriff Wilcox slouched. He seemed weary.

Sheriff Wilcox shook his head. "Alex. Alex, I'm disappointed in you. I like you. You know that? I was rooting for you from the start. But when you do things like this, it makes the situation really difficult. You make things harder for yourself, and you make things harder for this town."

Alex burned with embarrassment, though he didn't feel sorry in the least.

The man continued. "I understand there are some people here who will say hateful things. There are plenty of people in these parts who harbor animosity. Jake Jaworski, who went after you when you first came here? His son was a pilot. He'd just found out he was killed in an attack over the Pacific the week before. And you wonder why he wanted to pummel you to death?"

Alex opened his mouth, but the sheriff stopped him. "I know. You're not a Jap. But to folks here you look Japanese enough for them to aim their frustrations at you. If you're going to stick around here, then you're going to have to deal with it the best way you can without disturbing the peace or breaking the law. I know it's unfair. I do my best to keep people in line around here. If you feel you're being unjustly persecuted you can come to me."

Alex nodded, meeting his eyes. This man wanted to be on his side. Perhaps he wasn't so friendless. Of course, he'd never go to the sheriff for help unless he was desperate, but it felt good knowing someone would look out for him if need be.

Sheriff Wilcox sighed. "But the issue at hand is Teddy Stanton. You can press charges all you like, even Miss Hamilton can press charges for him striking her, but when it comes to him, my hands are tied."

Alex scowled, the hostility boiling his blood all over again. "But why? What he did was wrong. Striking her like that."

"I know. It was a terrible, cowardly thing to do, and I feel badly for Miss Hamilton. But because his work for the war effort is so invaluable, there isn't really anything substantial I can do. I could give him a fine, but I can't throw him in jail, not even for a day."

"So he's just going to get off?" Alex stared in disbelief.

Sheriff Wilcox pursed his lips, pushing out his bushy mustache. "I'm sorry. I'm actually hoping his father will take care of it, which, in my mind, is far worse than anything I could do. But you," he pointed a finger at Alex, "you need to stay out of his way and stay out of trouble in general. I don't want to see you in here again. Or I'm going to have to do something about it. Do you get my meaning?"

Alex frowned. "Yes, sir."

Sheriff Wilcox came from around his desk. "I'm letting you off tonight, but don't forget my warning."

Alex rose at the dismissal and managed a reluctant nod. "Yes, sir. Thank you, sir." He made his way home in the dark, though he really wanted to go to Mrs. Smithfield's house to check on Lonnie. Was she really doing okay? If it weren't so late, he'd give her a call. He'd go see her the first chance he got tomorrow.

Like a horrifying movie, the scene of Teddy raising his hand and bringing it across her face played across his mind's eye. The sickening *smack* still echoed in his ears, making him ill. Lonnie, poor Lonnie. All of this abuse she was receiving was because of him. He caused her all this pain just by being here. His worst nightmare had been realized. Uncle Harry had been right—a relationship like theirs would only bring hardship, pain, and heartbreak.

He couldn't do that to her. He couldn't bear to see her being hurt and ridiculed, taunted and shamed. It had been selfish and wrong of him to stay here and to turn her world upside down like this. The sudden regret stabbed him. He regretted his choice to stay so bitterly. He would do anything he could to keep her from being hurt again. Even if it meant he'd have to leave her for her own good. He gasped from the breath he'd been holding.

He would have to leave Lonnie. And he hated himself for it.

Chapter Thirty-Three

AUNT MILLIE ANSWERED the doorbell while Lonnie stayed in her bedroom. She hadn't been doing anything in particular. Just sitting on her bed and blankly staring at the wall, trying not to think. Her head was still dazed from last night's events.

She'd never dreamed Teddy could behave like that. Was he really so jealous as to embarrass and hurt her in such a way? More than anything, she'd been amazed at how Walter had come to her aid and stuck up for Alex, not Teddy, when they testified at the police station about what had happened.

Aunt Millie popped her head in the doorway. "Are you up for visitors? Alex is here to see you."

As Lonnie stood, her shoulders slumped as if they were no longer strong enough to carry their weight. She walked out to the living room where Aunt Millie had made herself scarce. Before she could get a look at him, Alex wrapped his arms around her, holding her tight. She took a deep breath. She let the reality of his scent fill her, and then tears leapt to her eyes.

"Let me see you," he said, holding her away. He searched her face. "I can't bear to see you like this, *Sagwa*," he whispered. "It's killing me. This is the second time someone's hit you because of me."

She shook her head quickly. "It's not your fault. Teddy was being hotheaded, and so was I. I was yelling at him too."

"That's hardly the point." His voice was low, but something about his tone made her meet his gaze.

"I don't care, Alex. What they think doesn't matter. Can't you believe me?"

He turned away from her and paced in agitation. "It's not about believing you, Lonnie. It's about protecting you. This isn't going to stop here." He halted and held her arms, catching her eyes with his desperation. It was frightening what she saw there. "Don't you see, Lonnie? This is only the beginning. By now, it will have spread around town. We'll have mobs breaking down our doors."

Lonnie stiffened. "I don't think you're giving this town enough credit. So many folks like you, and I'd like to think a lot of them like me too. They'll come to accept us by and by. Like Xiao Lin and her family. You'll see."

Alex stared at her for a moment before speaking again. "I'd like to think the same, by seeing the good in people. But you haven't seen them the way I have."

She looked away. "I know. I can't even begin to understand what it's like for you. But, you're a good man, Alex. And I know people have noticed. How could they not?"

He went back to pacing. "This conversation isn't going the way I planned."

Lonnie lips curved down. "What do you mean?"

He paced some more, unspeaking. His dark looks and agony of frustration brought a sick feeling to her stomach. It was like an impending storm looming over her head, waiting to break.

And then it did.

Alex stopped in front of her. "I'm leaving." He looked frantic, and Lonnie's heart skipped in shock.

"What?" she gasped. "But—but why?"

"Why? Because—look at your face." His voice cracked. "I did that to you."

"No, you didn't."

"Yes, I did. I've been meaning to tell you for some time that I already left—back in October. I got on a train and left this town behind without meaning to come back."

Lonnie gaped at him, hardly believing the words she was hearing. "Why didn't you tell me?"

He turned his body away as if to protect himself. He shoved his hands in his pockets and stared out the front window. "My uncle came to fetch me. I went with him because I didn't know what I wanted, why I should stay, what I could do with my life. But then all I could think about was you. I wasn't on the train long before I realized I loved you. I came back for you."

"Why didn't you tell me?" she repeated, her voice rising.

"I wanted to act as if nothing had happened, which is nuts, now that I think about it, because *everything* had changed. After yesterday though, I see now how selfish I was. My uncle was right. I *didn't* think things through. I didn't think how my caring for you would ruin your life."

"Don't you dare say that! You have *not* ruined my life."

He clenched his hands into fists, his face contorted from his distress. "If I haven't already, then I will. Oh, Lonnie, I hate myself for leaving you. I need you more than anyone or anything in this world, but it's torture for me to see you like this. I can't bear it!"

She needed to talk some sense into him. There was no way she was letting him go. "What about me? I'm not afraid, Alex. I'm not afraid of what people will say or do. And I have faith in the people of this town."

In two strides, he crossed the room and grabbed her in a fierce hug. Pinned to his chest, his heart thudded swiftly in her ear. "But I *am* afraid," he whispered. "I'll never forget you, Lonnie. And I promise to write. I've decided to go to my uncle after all. I'll be with my family where I belong."

"You belong with me." Lonnie struggled to get free to argue, but she was still crushed in his embrace.

"I'll always love you." He kissed her then. It was both longing and final. She clung to him, as if she could physically hold him there. How could he really be leaving?

Alex pulled away and left her standing in the living room. He opened the front door, but turned back. "There's something I never told you about your nickname, *Sagwa*." His eyes bored intently into hers, burning her like amber coals. "It not only means 'apple'. *Sagwa* means 'sorry' too. And I am. A thousand times over." The door shut, and he was gone.

Lonnie opened her mouth to protest, to scream in defiance of his decision, the decision he made without her, but nothing came out. Panic threatened to choke her off. She stumbled after him, but he was already out of sight.

She clung to the doorframe, wanting to sob, wanting to sink to the floor like some weak and frail heroine, but she was too enraged. It surged up out of nowhere, and she gritted her teeth against the pain of it.

This wasn't right. It wasn't right that he should leave now—not when they'd barely begun. How could he be such a coward? Was he really thinking of her now? Or was he only thinking of himself?

She seethed. She wanted to pound on him and get him to listen. She didn't care what anyone thought. She only wanted to be with him. Was that so hard for him to see? Didn't he understand she'd follow him to the ends of the earth if he asked her to?

Lonnie sucked in her breath as a thought struck her—Alex's money. She raced to her room and rummaged through her purse until she found it. She ripped out the bundle of money, and with it clasped in her fist, she bolted from her room, almost barreling into Aunt Millie.

"Oh," she gasped. "What's going on? Where did Alex go?"

"I'll be back," Lonnie shouted and ran out the door.

"Looking like that?" Aunt Millie cried in alarm. "You look like some feral child. At least comb your hair."

Her aunt's voice chased her down the street, but she didn't stop. Her anger fueled her pursuit of Alex. Fine. If he wanted to leave so badly, then she'd give him the means to do it.

She reached Mike's house in a blur of time. Alex must have just arrived, for when she knocked loudly on the door, he opened it himself, his jacket still on. Surprise that morphed into wariness passed over his face.

"Lonnie . . ." His voice bore a warning, but she paid him no heed.

She jerked her hand out with the money. "This is yours."

He frowned. "I don't want your money. Mike is giving me an advance for my ticket, and I'll be paying him back. I don't need to take anything from you."

"Shut up," she snapped, surprising even herself. His eyes widened. "This isn't mine, Alex. It's yours. It's always been yours."

It seemed that time slowed down then. Alex's face paled. He gradually reached out his hand and took the money as if it was the last thing he wanted to do. When he unfolded the worn wad of cash, the little scrap of paper filled with his own Korean handwriting sprang from its confinement. He pulled out the paper and stared at it, his complexion going ashen.

"How long have you had this?" His voice came out in a low croak, as if that too had been drawn through thickened time.

Lonnie jutted out her jaw, the heat of her feelings still fueling her bravery. "Since before the dance. Tunie found it. I knew it was yours because I recognized the characters and your handwriting from your lessons. They were the same as on the note."

His eyes connected with hers, burning coals searing her once again. "You didn't think to give it back to me? Even after you knew?"

Lonnie began to waver, but she forged on. She had to see this through to the end. "I tried to, but I couldn't bring myself to give it back. I wanted you to stay."

"Couldn't you at least have trusted me? I trusted you," he said. "But, you've been lying to me this entire time. How could—how could you do that to me? You of all people!"

"It seems you're not the only one who's selfish. I wanted to learn everything about you. You were the most interesting person to ever walk into this boring, old town. And you treated me differently than any boy I've ever known. Believe me, I wanted to tell you so many times, but I was too scared you'd leave. I couldn't see how you'd want to stay." The wrath slipped away from her, replaced by remorse. She scrabbled to muster enough fight to get herself through the conversation.

"I don't believe you." Alex stared at her as if she were a stranger. "How can I believe anything you've ever said after keeping something like this from me? You've kept me here. At times against my will."

"I know!" Lonnie shouted. "I know. But now you're free, all right? You're free to go. Go on. Go. Leave like a coward, and you'll be breaking my heart in the process. Maybe I deserve your anger, but I don't deserve that."

Lonnie stomped out the door, and the tears she'd held back began to fall. They poured down in streams as she fled down the street, racing her heartache home.

***

"I've tried to get her to talk, but she only stares at the wall. No, I don't know what happened, Phillip. She won't say anything." Aunt Millie was talking on the phone, but Lonnie couldn't comprehend the words. All she could see in her mind was the crushed look on Alex's face as she finally revealed his money. She'd waited far too long to give it back. The regret was harsh and deep as a raging river.

Tears had poured out of her until she'd wrung herself dry. Now, all she could do was lie curled up in her bed. She had no choice but to live out her life as a wilted vegetable. Nothing had meaning anymore. Nothing would be the same. Not without Alex.

"*Sagwa*," she whimpered. From the beginning, he'd taunted her with that name, only to find out he'd been apologizing to her all along. He always meant to leave, that was obvious. He never meant to stay, even when he'd promised to try and work things out together. Liar! Coward!

She wrapped her arms around herself even tighter, knowing those names were meant for her too. How could she have allowed herself to go on like that? Lying to his face, deceiving him, being afraid of letting him make the choice to stay or go. Everything she should've done was laid bare before her feet, and she wallowed in her misery.

"What do you mean you can't come? Your ecclesiastical duties?" Aunt Millie scoffed loudly. "Where have I heard that line before? Your niece is every bit as important as the other 'sheep in your flock'. Don't make the same mistake as last time. And, yes, I do mean that."

Aunt Millie slammed the phone back in its cradle and bustled into Lonnie's room, mumbling. "Sometimes I want to wring his neck, he's so clueless. Here, I've brought you some fish and potato stew. Now, there's no use refusing. You need your strength after an argument like that. I think a few of the neighbors heard it too. Even deaf old Mrs. Herbertson came outside to see what the fuss was."

"You don't need to take it out on Uncle Phillip," Lonnie whispered.

"Oh, so you *are* talking. Good, now you can tell me what all that commotion with Alex was about. Did I hear correctly that he's leaving?"

Lonnie pushed herself into a sitting position, resigned to her aunt's food. "I don't want to talk about it, Aunt Millie. Please, leave me alone."

"Of course I won't. What do you think meddling aunts are for? And I'm the champion of them all." She planted her hands on her hips like she meant business, and Lonnie couldn't help the crack of a smile that twitched her mouth.

"There we are," Aunt Millie cried with delight. "The first glimmer of the old Lonnie is coming back already. Now, you get that stew down you, and we'll talk later. I have a quick AWVS meeting to run to. Your uncle had better show up. I hope I talked enough fear of God into him to bring him to his senses." She winked. "I'll see you in a bit, love."

After the front door shut on her aunt, Lonnie dutifully ate her stew, though it was tasteless and brought her little comfort. She remembered the meal she'd shared with Alex and Xiao Lin and hot needles pricked her dry eyes. She set her bowl aside, unable to face any more food.

Not ten minutes after Aunt Millie had gone, the front door burst open. Lonnie froze to listen, then slid out of bed and hurried into the living room. The sight of her furious mother caused deep-rooted fear to claw its way up again.

"Mother, what are you doing here?"

Harriet's hair was mussed, and her eyes were red and ferocious. "I ran into Millie on my way home from work. She kept going on about your terrible state and that Alex Moon—" She paused. "Look at your face."

Lonnie found it ironic she should be talking about her face when not two weeks ago she'd marked it herself. "It looks worse than it feels."

Her mother turned purple with rage, and she flew at her, smacking her on the head, on the shoulders. Lonnie brought her arms up to protect herself.

"Stop it. Stop!" Lonnie screamed.

"How could you let this happen, you shameless girl? I warned you. I warned you he'd ruin you."

Before she could strike again, Lonnie grabbed her wrist.

"Stop," she demanded. "Don't hit me again. You can no longer punish me like you did before. I'm not a child. I can choose my friends and the man I love without your say. If father knew—"

Harriet interrupted her with a derisive laugh, yanking her arm free. "Your father," she spat. "It's time you knew the truth about yourself, Appalone." Her eyes burned with hatred, her voice cut the air with a hiss. "I suppose you really are made for each other—one a yellow bastard and the other a bastard child."

A loud gasp sounding from the front door joined Lonnie's own. Aunt Millie stepped into the room, mouth gaping. Her chest heaved with exertion. "I-I had a feeling I should turn back. Oh, Harriet. You're not . . . you're not telling her now, are you?"

Harriet ignored her sister and sneered at Lonnie. "You walk around so piously, thinking you're God's gift to this town when you're no better than the wad of gum on their shoes."

Lonnie glared at her mother. "I do *not* think that of myself. Just get to your point."

Harriet paced in front of the fireplace. "Look at you, so bold and sure of yourself. I should've told you long ago—at least you'd be easier to put in your place." She began to look crazed, her pale eyes glazing over. "Every day of your life I've had to look at you. I've had to be reminded of him in your eyes. How cruel that you should've had his eyes."

Lonnie's breathing became difficult as she struggled to understand her mother's words. Aunt Mille hovered in the background, but now she was crying. Why was she crying?

"Do you mean Father?" Lonnie asked tentatively. "What happened between you two? Why did he leave?"

Harriet laughed without humor, but didn't answer her questions. "I know what it's like to meet a handsome stranger, newly arrived in town. So kind and sweet he was. I thought we were a match made in heaven. We went on long walks, talked of everything under the sun—our hopes and dreams. My parents didn't like him, though. Oh, no. They believed he was shifty, and they didn't know his family, but I was headstrong. I didn't care what they thought. Sound familiar?"

She grinned frighteningly, and Lonnie shrunk back.

"He did odd jobs, earning money. He hinted at us being together some day. I'd hoped he was going to ask me to marry him and so I waited, biding my time. But the question never came. I pressured him about it, and he told me he loved me, but was still earning money so we could be together. What I didn't know was that he was going around stealing from folks in town. He was so charming, no one even suspected. And then—and then . . ." Harriet paused, taking a deep, shuddering breath. She turned her bright, fearsome eyes on Lonnie.

"Then one night on our way home from Marelli's, he pulled me into an alleyway. . ."

Lonnie sucked in a painful breath and began trembling. Aunt Millie's arm went round her shoulders and squeezed tight.

Harriet's voice grew hoarse. "When I came to my senses, he was gone. I stumbled my way home, bruised and bleeding, and—and *spoiled*." She spat the word out angrily, her voice rising. "When my mother saw me, she refused to let me into the house, saying I'd gotten what I deserved for refusing to obey her. She turned me out, and I had nowhere to go." Silent tears rolled down her cheeks.

Harriet continued, her voice dripping with sarcasm. "And my dear, beloved brother, Phillip, who'd just returned from Seminary College, was the newly appointed minister of the church. I thought if anyone would help me, he would; being the good Christian man he was.

"I begged him to go hunt that evil man down, to defend me in some way because our parents refused to do so. But he was so self-righteous and so concerned for his own precious reputation before his new little flock that he refused to find the man or do anything for me. He wouldn't even give me a roof over my head. So I went to stay with a friend, working to earn a living until I could leave this God-forsaken town behind me, because by then word had spread that my beau was gone and had stolen hundreds of dollars worth of things from almost everyone we knew. I was utterly ruined."

Lonnie stared at her mother. It was no wonder she was so bitter all these years, but she still didn't understand why her mother's anger was directed at her all the time. What had she done?

Her mother rounded on her, taking a few steps towards her. "And then, horror of horrors, I found out I was pregnant. With *you*." The word was growled. "I hid it for as long as I could, but when I was discovered, my friend's parents insisted I leave. This entire town turned its back on me—when I was helpless and faultless."

Lonnie gasped, trying to catch her breath. Was this really happening? Was all of this true?

"But then Martin Hamilton stepped in and offered to marry me. He was a boy I knew in high school who'd always been sweet on me. I don't know how he found out about my situation, but I agreed, because where else did I have to turn?"

Harriet went back to pacing. "I never loved him; my heart was still broken by the betrayal. But I was stuck with him in this town, forever facing the people who'd turned their backs on me. And then you were born, screaming and red-faced. Martin loved you as if you were his own, and I despised him for it. You received more care and love than I ever did from anyone."

She glared hard into Lonnie's face. "And then your eyes—those big blue eyes were always following me. It was as if that man, whom I'd loved and trusted, was always watching, mocking me."

Fresh tears stung and fell down Lonnie's cheeks, the full realization of her mother's bitterness sweeping through her. "I was a baby, Mother. How could you hate me so much? Why couldn't you have ever seen me as *your* child?"

"Don't you see? You were a *bastard*. You were the product of my foolishness and stupidity. Every day you reminded me of my mistake, but I raised you for Martin's sake. He doted on you so much, it disgusted me."

Lonnie clenched her fists. "So you eventually chased Father away? You pushed away the only person who'd truly shown he loved and cared for you—because of one mistake?" She scoffed, fiercely wiping away the tears. "You were so miserable and selfish he couldn't stand to be with you any longer, is that it? How could you do that?"

"Because I hate you!" her mother shouted. "And I hate myself. I hate Martin, and I hate every other miserable person in this town."

Lonnie clenched her teeth against her words. "But I love you, Mother. I always have. Why can't you see that there are still people here who care for you? Tunie and Marty, Uncle Phillip and Aunt Millie. Why can't you see that?"

Her mother clamped her mouth shut and turned away. Lonnie marched over to her and for the first time she could remember, she wrapped her arms around her mother. She was cold, her shoulders were limp with weariness, and Lonnie mourned for the woman her mother had become.

"I love you, Mother," Lonnie whispered. When Harriet didn't respond to her embrace, Lonnie stepped back, determined to make her mother listen. "However much you regret what happened to you, Mother, there's something you have to know—I'm not a mistake. Do you hear me? I am not a mistake!"

Harriet's face reddened. "You can think that all you want," she rasped, "but it doesn't change what you are and what you've done, the same mistake you've made. But this time I won't let him get away with it." Her eyes bulged as her face warped into something ugly. "I'm going to kill him. I'm going to kill that dirty bastard! How dare he lay a finger on you?" And then she was gone in a whirl of fresh fury. Her aunt's noisy sniffles were the only sound left.

Lonnie sank into the nearest chair, her mother's words a jumble in her mind. Martin Hamilton wasn't her father? How could this be? It was as if someone had taken her heart and scooped out the most precious parts, leaving it hollow and bleeding. She wrung her hands tightly together, trying to understand. Who was she? What was she? She was the daughter of a faceless beast. One that was capable of haunting her nightmares, of lurking in her darkest shadows. And she had nowhere to run.

Chapter Thirty-Four

HIS WORLD HAD cracked open, and he'd fallen through a bottomless chasm. He was still falling, still reeling from what Lonnie had told him. Sprawled out on the couch in the living room, he turned to address the photograph of Thomas.

"What do I do?" he whispered. "It's best if I leave everything now, isn't it? There's no point in staying. Not after this." Thomas was no help. He grinned down at him as if he knew a secret and had no intention of sharing.

Alex turned away, his eyes burning. He'd been so sure about leaving—it was the best decision for them both. Even now, it seemed he had more reason than ever to turn his back on this place. What was keeping him here? He held up the money, still crushed in his fist. He wanted to burn it. What good did it do him now? It would've been better never to know what had happened to it. Of all the people to have the cursed money—why did it have to be Lonnie?

Alex stood. He left by way of the back door and out the garage, down the back lane, and away into the country. He breathed deeply, allowing the earthy smells of melting snow and rotting leaves to clear the fog in his brain.

Without realizing he'd been heading there, he found himself outside Xiao Lin's house. What made him come here? He went up to the door and knocked. No one answered. He was walking back out to the dirt road when a voice called out to him from the garden in the back.

"Oh, good. You've come at the perfect time."

He followed the voice to the generously sized garden that peeked out with the first signs of new growth. The early thaw had forced many buds out of hiding. Upon reaching Xiao Lin, he bowed. "*Anyeonghasaeo*," he murmured, feeling strangely humbled all of a sudden.

She reached out to him. "Come, Yeong Su. I have some jobs for you. First you work, then you eat. Oh, my back is aching so." Quick as a wink, she had him raking, moving piles of compost, and scrubbing pots in preparation for housing seedlings. Alex was worn out by the time she brought him inside and sat him down in front of some steaming, comforting food.

Alex clutched at his chopsticks as if they were a sort of lifeline, shoveling as much food in as he could to avoid talking, to avoid thinking. The more he ate, the more his eyes stung until finally, tears filled them and spilled over. Even then he continued to eat until he thought he'd burst.

Xiao Lin, who'd watched him the entire time, lightly touched his arm with her soft, worn hand. "What is it, Yeong Su? Why are you so troubled?"

It was as if by her touch, she'd opened the floodgates. Alex poured out everything that had happened from the first time he arrived in town to Lonnie's last parting words that afternoon. When he finished, he was as hollow and empty as an old well.

He sagged against the wall by the low kitchen table and shut his eyes. If only he could stay right here and turn into a rock Xiao Lin could plant in her garden, maybe he could deal with that kind of a fate. But right now, he couldn't face his life as it was. To think about living without Lonnie, and how she'd deceived him—the two conflicting emotions threatened to tear him apart.

"Appalone came to me many weeks ago and told me about the money," Xiao Lin announced without ceremony.

His eyes flicked up to her in sudden suspense.

The old woman nodded her head. "You must understand how she agonized over it and how much she wanted to tell you. She knew she should, and I encouraged her to do so. But knowing and doing are two different mountains to climb."

"She lied to me," Alex said in a small voice.

"Yes. We all lie sometimes, whether it's to others or even to ourselves. Seldom do we understand how one prick of a lie can grow to be a vicious thorn."

"I love her, but I don't see how I can ever trust her again. She's not even the same person to me anymore."

"You do know her, Yeong Su. She was wrong in not telling you, it's true, but she did finally reveal the truth. So now, the question is whether you'll forgive her. Trust is fragile, but it can be built again if sorrow and the desire to mend are there. And I think they are, don't you?"

Alex wanted to pout. "She didn't even say she was sorry."

Xiao Lin cocked an eyebrow. "Did you give her the chance?"

"No," he mumbled. "We were too busy yelling at each other."

Xiao Lin chuckled and struggled to her feet. "Well, young man, it seems you have some more work to do, and it's best not to leave it too long."

Alex got to his feet. "More gardening?"

The old woman's eyes twinkled. "I think you have your own tidying up to do, don't you?"

***

Alex took his time walking home. He shoved his hands deep into his pockets, kicked clumps of ice-sheathed snow, and tried to think about forgiving Lonnie. But no matter how hard he tried, he didn't feel like forgiving her. Not yet anyway. It was still so raw, the pain that came from feeling betrayed. It wasn't an unfamiliar feeling. Feeling betrayed by his country, though, was far different from feeling betrayed by the woman he loved.

He appreciated that she had a hard time telling him the truth. He tried to put himself in her place, and in a way, he was flattered she'd wanted him to stay so badly, but he was still left with that hurt, empty feeling.

It was heading toward dusk when he approached Mike's house. Alex's footsteps slowed when the sounds of shouting and commotion at the front of the house reached his ears. Cautiously, he poked his head around the corner. A sizable, angry crowd was gathered at Mike's front door. Mike stood on his front step with a stony expression.

"Just bring him out, Hardy, and we'll leave you be. We don't want to cause you trouble."

"I don't see why I need to cooperate with an unruly mob, John Pickering," Mike growled.

"Come now, Mike, we aren't being unreasonable here. Alex Moon is guilty of getting Mrs. Hamilton's daughter, not to mention my secretary," here John cleared his throat, "in the family way. We're here to make him answer for his crime. We don't tolerate his kind here."

Alex nearly fell over in shock. Lonnie in the family way? What was he talking about?

Mike grunted. "I don't see Mrs. Hamilton here. What does she have to say? Is there any evidence of his guilt?"

A woman pushed her way to the front. "I'm right here, Mike. I don't know what kind of 'evidence' you expect me to provide for something like that, but he did hit her. I saw the mark on her face. She was despondent and heartbroken when I found her. What other evidence do we need?" She sounded spitting mad. Alex swallowed with difficulty. He'd hate to face her just now.

Mike crossed his arms. "Are you sure the mark on her face wasn't from your own actions, Harriet?"

"Stop changing the subject, Mike, and just get the mangy Jap out here," Harriet shouted. "Or else, we'll come in and drag him out ourselves."

"No," Mike stated. "Now, get off my property." He turned and went into the house, slamming the door behind him.

Alex leaned against the side of the house away from the crowd, a strange mix of fear and amazement stealing over him. How in the world had this happened? He'd talked to Lonnie not three hours ago and now there was an angry crowd on his doorstep demanding he pay for a crime he hadn't committed. How had her mother come to such a conclusion? Surely, Lonnie hadn't been angry enough with him to blame him for something preposterous like that, especially when Teddy was to blame for her wounded face. Today was the first time he'd seen Lonnie so angry. There was no telling what she'd do, but he sensed no matter how mad, she'd never accuse him of something he wasn't. A coward, maybe. Hitting her and taking advantage of her like that? No.

After Mike shut the door, the crowd grumbled hotly. Banging echoed out into the street. "Hardy, bring him out! Don't make us take him by force."

Mike didn't answer, and Alex grew nervous. What were they going to do? It's not like Mike could cooperate, even if he wanted to. Would they really barge in and ransack the house looking for him? Alex shook himself. Why was he still standing here, hiding like he was guilty? A simple testimony from himself and from Lonnie would surely clear up this misunderstanding. Lonnie said she trusted the people in this town. Perhaps he needed to trust in them too. Like Mike had already told him after the fire. He couldn't let a handful of people's hatred destroy his life. He had to face this. Become strong by it.

He peered around the corner. Even if they were borderline violent? Were they even worth trusting?

Without stopping to analyze his quavering doubts, he stepped from around the house. He strode up to the porch, reaching into his pocket for his key. At that point, he was spotted by Harriet.

"You." Her voice cut the air like a jagged knife. She stomped up to him and jabbed a finger in his face. "I've been searching for you, you bastard."

Alex's calm demeanor belied how his lungs squeezed with trepidation. "Did you have to bring half the neighborhood to talk?

You're welcome to come inside, and we can clear things up over a cup of coffee."

She scoffed and the mass of faces shouted their own indignation. "Don't be an idiot. Of course I won't. Why should I trust myself with you, especially considering what you've done? We're going to make you pay for what you did to my daughter."

He felt the door open a crack behind him. Mike was listening in. "I don't know where you heard I've done something to her, but I only saw her a few hours ago. She was upset, but it wasn't because I'd touched her or done anything to her. It was because we argued. I love your daughter, Mrs. Hamilton. I would never dream of hurting her."

The crowd roared in anger as one. "So he did see her." "He's as good as admitting it." "He's guilty!"

"You lie," Harriet hissed. "Trash like you has no right to love my daughter. How dare you." She stepped even closer and the crowd pressed in with her. She grabbed the front of his shirt, shaking him, the whites of her eyes showing in her vengeance. He stumbled back into the door, finally knowing exactly why Lonnie was so terrified of her mother.

"You've ruined her!" Harriet screamed. "You've ruined my daughter, and now she'll bear your horrible, yellow baby." A sob escaped her. "She'd be better off dead. Better dead than to face that humiliation." She pounded on his chest, tears falling down her worn face, but Alex didn't fight back. He was paralyzed by the cutting wound of her words.

Mike opened the door and calmly tried to separate her from Alex's shirt. "That's enough, Harriet."

"No!" John yelled. "It isn't. Look at him, he's not even denying her accusations. It's about time we took him to task—to teach him he can't just waltz into our town, take advantage of our daughters, and get away with it. And he's a Jap on top of it. Who knows what kinds of secrets he's been spying out and sending to the enemy? This needs to stop here and now."

Everyone cried out in agreement and pushed in. Rough hands grabbed at Alex, pulling his arms, his hair, his legs. It was as if a hundred-armed creature was lifting him, pulling him in to maim and swallow. He landed on the ground and a few got kicks in his side. Mike roared in protest, trying to fight his way in. Alex hissed from the jabbing pain, curling into a ball and covering his head. The kicks and blows continued to fall, raining down like a nightmare of burning hail.

Chapter Thirty-Five

LONNIE LAID HER head in her hands, trying to think calmly and rationally about everything her mother had told her. Besides her father, she could barely wrap her head around her mother's accusations. It was as if upon seeing her, her mother had already formed her hated assumptions just from the brief talk with Aunt Millie in the street. Why would her mother think Alex had ruined her? It's true her cheek was ugly with the bruise, but Teddy was to blame for that. Oh, why hadn't she thought to say that? It would've corrected her mother's outrageous assumptions. But would she have listened? She never listened.

Aunt Millie had her own regrets, and she voiced them as she set the table for dinner. "Oh, I never should've said anything to that ridiculous sister of mine. Of all the nerve, barging in here and just spilling her guts to you like that. It wasn't the right time. But then she never thinks of anything but herself. She never even thought to ask me for help back then. Even though I was married and had a baby of my own, I would've taken her in. She seems to forget I'd offered. She was always too proud, thinking I was Mama's favorite. Stupid woman."

Just then there was a knock at the front door. Before either of them could get up to answer it, Uncle Phillip strode in looking harried.

"Phillip. Well, it's about time." Aunt Millie scowled.

"I've only just now been able to get away. There's been a rash of food poisoning in the town. Mrs. Simmons has apparently been packaging frozen food herself and passing it off as the real thing. It's been terrible."

Aunt Millie hurried out and returned with another cup of coffee. Handing it to her brother, she said testily, "You'd think *you* were the town doctor the way you're going on."

"It's not like my duties are imaginary, Mildred. I got here as quickly as I could."

"You just missed everything. Harriet was here spewing the past like a flood, and poor Lonnie had to take the brunt of it, hearing everything. There's no way I could've stopped her."

He came up to Lonnie and gripped her hands. "I'm so terribly sorry, my child. I never wanted you to go through that, but I suppose it had to come out in the end." He bowed his head. "And now you see what a cowardly, despicable man your uncle is. I couldn't even protect my own sister. I was self-righteous, and proud, and too afraid for my own reputation to risk saving hers. I've tried to make it up to her in the best way I could by watching over you."

"Thank you, Uncle Phillip. I've always appreciated everything you've done for me." She paused. "But right now I'm really worried."

"About your mother?"

"No, about Alex. Mother thinks he took advantage of me. I think she's gone to find him. I don't know what she'd going to do."

Aunt Millie paled as she faced her brother. "She's gone mad. I think she's still reliving that nightmare."

Right then, the phone rang, and Aunt Millie hurried from her seat to answer it. "Hello, Mrs. Godfrey. Oh. Yes, he's here." She held out the receiver, brows knit together. "It's for you, Phillip."

He took it from her. "Yes?" As he listened, he became grave, his face sagging with the weight of the words they couldn't hear. "I see. And the police have been called? Yes. I'll be right there." He hung up and took a seat on the couch, pulling Lonnie down next to him. He took her hand in his, and her pulse quickened in alarm. He addressed them both. "Lonnie's right about her mother. But I'm afraid it's gone far past just going to find Alex. Mrs. Godfrey just informed me a mob came looking for Alex claiming . . ." He swallowed. "Claiming that he'd gotten you in the family way, and they'd come to make him pay. Harriet was at the front of it."

Lonnie nearly choked on the cry that wrenched from her body, her hands flying to her mouth. She stared at her uncle in horror. Aunt Millie fanned her face with her hand. "Good heavens," she breathed.

Uncle Phillip continued sadly. "Mr. Hardy called the police, but . . . I don't think Alex is in such a good state."

Lonnie sprang from her chair. "I have to go to him." Uncle Phillip got up and pulled her to him in a hug. "He's going to be fine, Lonnie. The Sheriff is on his way. Things will be taken care of. Now, I need to go. I'll do my best to help him. I want you to stay here and wait for my phone call. Do you understand?"

Lonnie grabbed his arm as he turned to go. "Please, Uncle Phillip. I have to go with you. I have to see Alex."

"Millie, please see after Lonnie. She's looking terribly pale." He gently extricated his arm and left.

The moment the Ford's motor roared to life, Lonnie turned to her aunt. "I have no intention of staying here. I'm going to him."

Aunt Millie wrung her hands in despair. "What about dinner? It'll be ruined if we leave it." But then her face hardened, and she grabbed Lonnie's hand. "The devil take it. Let's go."

***

Alex didn't know how much time passed, but in his haze, the wail of a police siren cut through the roar of the surrounding crowd. Then came police whistles and shouts. Eventually, Alex felt himself being pulled to his feet.

"Stand up. Come on, son," a familiar voice said in his ear. Alex craned his neck to see the wavering image of Sheriff Wilcox come into view.

"Sheriff?" Alex took a step, but his knees buckled, and the sheriff caught him.

"Steady. Come with me." Another set of strong arms assisted the sheriff, and Alex's head swung to see Walter, who wore a determined expression. Alex was too numb to register surprise.

"Hold on, Sheriff," John Pickering spoke up. "We still have some things to sort out with this man. As a town, we need to decide what's to be done with him."

"John, I'd say you aren't in a position to decide anything in regards to Alex Moon." His voice was calm, but there was a stern edge to it that got everyone's attention.

"Maybe not me, but you can't deny the mother of the young woman this man has wronged."

"And who would that be?"

"It's me, Howard." Lonnie's mother stepped forward then.

Alex drooped in the Sheriff's grasp, and Walter readjusted his grip to take all the weight, leaving the sheriff to deal with things. "You're saying he's done something to Lonnie?"

"I am."

The sheriff's eyes travelled from face to face, and Alex wondered through his fog what was about to happen.

"I don't begrudge you folks the chance to talk out your grievances, but there's to be no mob violence in my town, you understand me?" He shouted the last words and slowly, reluctant nods and murmurs of agreement came. "Come on, son. Let's get you to see Doctor McDonnell." Sheriff Knox moved to lead the way to his police car, but Alex resisted.

"No." His voice emerged from his parched throat in a croak. "No, I want to stay. I want to hear what they have to say."

Mike stepped forward as Sheriff Knox hesitated. "It's all right, Sheriff. He can sit up on my porch while you keep an eye on everything."

Alex found himself supported not only by Walter, but by Mike Hardy as well. In the glow of the setting sun, he thought he saw the glimmer of moisture in the man's eyes, but he turned his head before Alex could be sure. Mike and Walter gently set Alex down in the rarely used porch swing, and that's when he noticed the crowd. It had gotten larger. Since the sheriff's arrival, the gossip network must have been busy. The street was full of what looked like half the town.

Alex's accusers didn't waste any time.

***

By the time Lonnie and Aunt Millie got to Mike Hardy's house, the violence had stopped, and it seemed an impromptu meeting was underway. The street was thronged with people, and it didn't seem to matter that the sun was going down. The street lamps were beginning to turn on. People had lanterns and flashlights and were bundled against the cold.

Lonnie gaped at the tall figure of her boss, Mr. Pickering, speaking at the front of the crowd. It was clear he'd organized the gathering from the authoritative way in which he spoke. Something in the pit of her stomach soured.

"We've tolerated him walking freely about, buying from our stores, eating at our restaurants, conversing with our neighbors. But he's sullied the name of a good, Christian young woman, and it's the last straw. It's been shown he's guilty. He should be sitting in jail, but even that isn't good enough. I say we run him out of town and see his back for good."

A great hum of chatter arose from the crowd at his words. Lonnie craned her neck, trying to find where Alex might be, and finally spotted Mike with a protective hand on Alex's shoulder, a stony-faced Walter standing guard nearby. Alex sat on the porch swing looking weak and bloody. Her heart leapt into her throat.

Without thinking, she pushed her way to the front. She was rewarded with sympathetic smiles and scowls of contempt. But she only had eyes for Alex.

Mr. Pickering pounded his fist into his hand. "So how many are with me? Who says we should run this man out?"

Cries of 'Aye' arose, but they died away as Lonnie stumbled out in front of the gathered crowd. Alex started at seeing her and struggled to stand. She could see in his face he wanted to go to her, but Mr. Hardy held him back.

Mr. Pickering spotted her then. He quickly glanced over at Harriet, uncertainty clouding his resolve. Harriet glared at her, but Lonnie refused to acknowledge her mother's hatred any longer. There was no way Harriet Hamilton was going to have the last say about Alex. She turned to face the crowd.

Someone shouted from the back, "Let her speak." Others took up the demand until, reluctantly, John Pickering conceded and stepped away. On the outside, Lonnie exuded calm and confidence. Inside, she was a quivering bowl of gelatin.

She stood before the sea of expectant faces. Panic reared its ugly head, and the details of the crowd washed together like a watercolor drawing left out in the rain. She shut her eyes briefly to muster all the scraps of courage she had. All she had to do was to think of Alex's current condition. Defiance and determination surged through her veins.

"My name is Lonnie Hamilton. I'm the young woman who's the subject of the recent rumor that Alex Moon has somehow taken advantage of me. I'm here to tell you that rumor is absolutely not true."

Heads tipped toward one another and murmurs washed over the crowd. They silenced again as she continued to speak. "Alex Moon and I became friends soon after he arrived and was stranded in this town last year. He's only ever treated me with the utmost respect. He's kind and thoughtful, and I dare say many of you who've met and talked with him can say the same."

Lonnie was met with silence and more than a few stony glares. She really wasn't sure what else to say. She searched the crowd for those who might agree with her, even familiar faces. It was hard to pick them out from among so many.

Mr. Pickering spoke from his position at the front. "I find all this very hard to believe, Miss Hamilton. Personally, I think you're only trying to salvage your reputation. As a pretty-faced young woman, you're easily charmed. All the young women are, especially since young men are so scarce. I just find it disgusting that you're going around town, openly flirting with the enemy our brothers and sons are off fighting."

Lonnie's quivering bowl of gelatin returned to her stomach at the angry shouts of affirmation to the man's statements. She swallowed. It was going to be harder to convince everyone than she expected. Out of the corner of her eye, Sheriff Wilcox's form prowled the edge of the crowd along with a few of his officers. His presence was reassuring, though the shouting was slow to abate.

To her surprise, a familiar red head emerged from the edge of the crowd and came to the front. Rose came to stand beside Lonnie, and she squeezed her friend's hand in relief.

Rose turned to face everyone. "I can testify that what Lonnie says is true. I'll admit I was wary of Alex Moon at first. I worried what his association with my friend would do to her. And, so I watched carefully, observing Mr. Moon's actions. I never once saw him treat her with disrespect, ever giving the indication he'd hurt her in some way." She took a quick glance over at her and Lonnie smiled her encouragement.

"And I can attest to Mr. Moon's kindness," Rose continued. "He found a letter that my beau, Thomas Hardy, had written before he joined up and—and was killed. He sought Mr. Hardy's permission to give me the letter. If it wasn't for him, I never would've had those last words of Tommy's." Rose's voice broke at the end.

The crowd seemed to digest her words, but Mr. Pickering spoke again. "A very nice sentiment, but once again you prove my point—you young women are easily charmed by a young man with a nice smile, however inappropriate it may be to like someone like *that*."

Mike Hardy spoke from the porch. He leaned forward and eyed Mr. Pickering "So, John, do you think young and handsome Alex Moon, with his dazzling smile and sparkling personality, has charmed *me*?"

Laughter broke out, and Lonnie tried unsuccessfully to hide a small smile.

Mike grew serious. "This young man is extraordinary—a hard worker, and the most brilliant mechanic I've seen in years. Many of you have him to thank for your cars still running, that your tires, as bald as they may be, still hold air. I've seen him repair kids' bicycles and old wagons, sharpen widows' lawn mowers and even mow their grass, all out of the goodness of his heart. I took him into my home because I saw things in him that I admired—honesty, respect, and determination.

"You may wonder why I took someone like him into my home in the first place when my boys were killed by those Japs in the Pacific. War is an ugly thing, but I don't need to tell you all that. I can tell you this, folks: this young man is no enemy to you. I think he's done a lot of good in this town. I dare any of you to say different."

One by one, more people came forward and told of one thing or other they'd noticed about Alex, and how he'd served them. Lonnie's heart warmed as she saw the trust she'd placed in her town be rewarded. There were so many little things Alex had done that she'd never seen herself.

Uncle Phillip came forward to stand by her as well. He offered her an understanding nod, then turned and spoke. "I've always been reluctant to take sides in instances such as these, but I feel strongly that I must add my voice to those who've spoken. I will only say I can vouch for Alex Moon's good, Christian character. As a regular attendee of my church, I've only ever seen him treat those around him with respect and honor, even in the face of cruelty and unkindness. I think our whole town would be better off focusing our energies on fighting the real enemy."

One woman raised her voice, wringing her hands. "Miss Hamilton, I think we all understand Mr. Moon as a person better, and maybe he has done a lot of good in this town, but—" Her voice broke and it took her a moment to gather herself. "But to be perfectly honest, every time I see him walking down the street I just think how angry I am that some Jap is roaming free in our town while my Billy is off fighting the war against his kind and Hitler and the rest. I just can't abide that. I think a lot of us feel that way. To be fair, it's nothing personal against his character, I see that now, but I don't want him here anymore. I don't need that reminder."

Shouts of agreement arose and the crowd became rowdy again.

Lonnie swallowed, her heart racing. This was the moment she'd been waiting for. The chance to redeem herself for her mistake and to finally set her town straight as far as Alex was concerned.

Before she could speak, Mr. Pickering stepped forward. "Miss Hamilton, it's clear to me that the apple doesn't fall far from the tree." His comment stirred the mass of people behind him. Heads nodded, whispers were exchanged behind hands, expressions darkened.

Uncle Phillip shouted in protest. "That is out of line, John Pickering. You've no business dredging up past events in a situation so unrelated—"

"Unrelated?" Mr. Pickering's voice rose, and a few more people shouted in support of his disagreement. "Isn't it obvious, Reverend? Like mother like daughter. I wouldn't be surprised if Mr. Moon was to disappear, and the rest of us would be the ones to suffer like last time." Rage erupted from the crowd, and Sheriff Wilcox and his officers moved in.

Lonnie grabbed hold of the porch post in alarm at seeing their livid exchange. Watching the crowd was like viewing a violent film unfold before her eyes where she was the only one in the audience. Did the entire town know what had happened all those years ago?

Off to her right, her mother cursed loudly, and then pushed her way through the crowd to make her escape. Lonnie pitied her. She was reliving her humiliation all over again.

"Pipe down. All of you," Sheriff Wilcox roared, his hands raised as if he were keeping the Red Seas of animosity apart. A hush descended until only the shuffling of feet and a few sniffles from cold noses could be heard. "I don't want to see another outbreak like that or we're going to declare this meeting over and clear the street. Understood?" No one contradicted him, so he gave Lonnie a nod. "Miss Hamilton, you may resume."

Lonnie found the woman who'd addressed her and smiled with sympathy. "Ma'am, I understand how you feel, but I want to make this clear—Alex is not Japanese. He's Korean. And while they look similar, their countries and cultures are very different. Korea is under the dictatorship of Japan, just as Poland and France are under Hitler's dictatorship, and they long for independence. For Koreans, this war means the chance of freedom for their people! They despise the Japanese as much as any of us—if not more so because of the horrible things they've been experiencing much further back than the bombing of Pearl

Harbor. Alex's own brother is fighting with American forces against the Japanese. His whole family is passionate about America winning this war."

Lonnie paused to take a deep breath. Somewhere someone coughed, but they continued to let her speak. "I understand all of your frustrations and heartache, but every action you've taken against Alex for the sake of satisfying your hatred of the Japanese has been spitting in his face and on the sacrifice of his family and his people. I don't expect the world to change overnight, but . . . I believe our town has the capacity to accept this man for who he truly is—a good and worthy American who deserves respect as a human being and fellow citizen of this great country."

She relaxed. Finally, she'd said everything she wanted to say. Lonnie searched the faces of the people and found Tunie grinning proudly.

Mr. Pickering spoke one last time. He seemed determined to make his case. "That all may be very well and good, Miss Hamilton, but you still haven't answered how your face came to look like that. If Mr. Moon didn't do that to you, then who did?"

Lonnie's vision jerked from face to face as the murmurs of dissidence erupted at this question. She didn't want to expose Teddy, but she didn't want them thinking Alex had anything to do with it. She needn't have worried. Mr. Stanton cleared his throat. Only then did Lonnie see Teddy standing beside him, pale and drawn as his father spoke.

"I'm ashamed to say my own son is responsible for Miss Hamilton's injury. From speaking with Sheriff Wilcox, he informed me there were witnesses saying Mr. Moon defended Miss Hamilton after my son struck her. I'm deeply ashamed of his actions, and I apologize to you, Lonnie, on Teddy's behalf." Teddy stared at the ground, his face a stone mask as the street burst into a frenzy of whispers. Eyes turned to stare, heads shook in disbelief, and not a few people displayed disgust.

Lonnie's heart broke in sorrow for Teddy. They had over a decade of friendship behind them. It hurt that he'd thrown all of that away in one heated moment.

John Pickering came to the front once again. He held up a hand as if signaling peace. "I apologize for my accusations, Miss Hamilton. Perhaps it's best we leave the past in the past, eh?" He smiled, though the sincerity didn't reach his eyes. Lonnie nodded with reluctance.

He cleared his throat and spoke again, this time addressing the crowd. "I think we all owe Miss Hamilton an apology. A young woman's reputation is an important thing to protect, and if I've done anything to harm it, then I sincerely apologize. There seems to be enough testimony vouching for Mr. Moon and his innocence. Are there any that would say against him?"

No one stirred. No one spoke. Lonnie suspected Mr. Pickering's generosity was merely for show.

Mr. Pickering nodded. "I think I've changed my mind myself. We should give this young man a chance to stay. Mr. Hardy, you're right—Alex Moon fixed my brother's truck when no part was available, and it's still going strong. He's still able to feed his family as a result." He took a deep breath. "So I guess we can adjourn this meeting and leave the poor young man in peace."

People began drifting away, the air filling with the hum of conversation. Lonnie suddenly felt the need to sit down. It was all over. She was filled with a strange mix of emotions—disbelief and triumph. Had she succeeded? Had she really just spoken up for herself and Alex? And everyone had listened? A grin slipped onto her face of its own accord. Her heart soared.

Without waiting another moment, she stumbled up the steps and rushed across the porch to Alex's side. With Mr. Hardy's help, he managed to stand on unstable legs until Lonnie caught him in her arms.

"Oh, Alex," she gasped. "You're all right. Aren't you? Mrs. Godfrey called and told us what was going on. Uncle Phillip didn't want me to come. I didn't care if we'd fought, there's no way I was staying behind when I knew you'd been hurt. I'm so sorry. I'm sorry about everything."

He was having difficulty breathing. Nevertheless, he continued to hold her, his smile gentle. It wasn't until he wiped the tears away that she realized she was crying.

"I know. Wild horses couldn't keep you away. Am I right?" He blinked slowly and swayed a little. Lonnie tightened her hold on him. He gazed down at her, his expression full of love and wonder. "Thank you for what you did. You've got some nerve, Lonnie." He laughed lightly, but a moan escaped from the effort. "I've lost track of how many times you've stood up for me." He swayed again. "What . . . what would I do without you?"

Before she could respond, Alex's eyes slid shut and he stumbled forward. Lonnie cried out as Mike leapt to help catch him. "We need to get him inside."

Uncle Phillip ran up the steps to assist. Lonnie followed them into the house where they laid Alex on his bed.

"I've been told Dr. McDonnell is on his way," Uncle Phillip said. "He's been busy tonight helping Dr. Warner with the rash of food poisoning. He should be here soon."

"Good," Mr. Hardy grunted. "Alex will be in good hands until then."

"Come away, my dear." Uncle Phillip took her arm.

"No," she stated firmly. "I'm not going anywhere." She challenged him with a stubborn glare, and Mr. Hardy chuckled.

"It was her hands I meant, Reverend. Come on. I'll get us some coffee while we wait."

Chapter Thirty-Six

ALEX DRIFTED UP from the wavering clutches of slumber. He took a few moments to become fully awake and then turned his head to take in the sight of Lonnie dozing in a chair close beside his bed. He reached a bandaged hand over and grasped her hand resting on the covers. Instantly she awoke.

"How are you feeling?"

He struggled to sit up and she jumped to her feet to help him get adjusted. "Lonnie, it's been three days. You don't have to sleep by my bedside while I take a nap. Please, go home. You need to rest. Mike's here and can take care of me too."

"No. I want to be here."

A grin slid onto his face at her expression toward his request. Was she actually pouting? "That may have worked on your father when you were six, but . . ."

Lonnie flinched and nervously brushed away a stray hair. "That's something I've been meaning to tell you about, but I was afraid to with how you've been feeling."

"About pouting when you were six?" He teased.

"No. My father."

Her serious tone made him instantly sober. "What do you mean?"

Slowly, reluctantly, Lonnie spilled out the story of her mother's confession regarding her true father and the ensuing consequences. Alex could only stare in disbelief.

When she'd finished, he swung his legs out of bed and gingerly scooted forward, reaching out for her. She leaned into his embrace. As soon as his arms were around her, protecting her from everything outside their circle, she cried heavy, aching sobs.

When she'd quieted down, she wiped her face. "I'm sorry. I've been in such shock about the whole thing; I haven't even thought to cry. It's just so hard to comprehend. I'm not the person I thought I was."

"I'm sorry. I should've been there to comfort you."

"You are right now." She sighed deeply. "Oh, Alex. I feel as if a bomb's been dropped on my house, and my world's just exploded. I lived my whole life clinging to my father's love for me, because there was none offered from Mother. And to find out he's not even my father. My real father is someone who . . ." Her voice caught.

Alex cut in. "Martin Hamilton *is* your real father, Lonnie. He raised and cared for you. Bonds like that don't always have to be forged by blood." As he spoke, his mind turned to Mike. He'd been as much of a father to him as his own.

"But who am I?" she whispered. "I don't even know what he looks like or where he is now. How can I ever look at myself in the mirror the same way again, knowing I'm the daughter of such a heartless, dishonest man?"

Alex leaned back, brows furrowed. "You are Appalone Hamilton, the most extraordinary woman I know. You aren't defined by your parents. You're your own person and always have been. It's incredible what you've become despite everything that could've dragged you down. Nothing, not even what you've learned from your mother, is going to stop you. You can do anything."

She stared at him, her blue eyes wide with amazement. He laughed when she didn't say anything. "What is this? Have I made you speechless?"

Lonnie offered a tiny smile and ducked her head. "Well, that's nothing new."

***

The next day, a knock sounded on the door while Alex sat listening to the latest news report on the radio. He slowly got up to answer it since Mike was busy working in the shop. The door swung open, and there stood the sunny-faced Lonnie.

"Hi," she said.

His entire mood lifted at the sight of her. Listening to war updates had put him in a sour mood. They were a sharp reminder of the duty to his father he'd shunned. "I thought you'd be at work."

She shrugged. "I lost my job."

"What?" He frowned. "Why?"

"Mr. Pickering sounded conciliatory in front of the crowd, but he made it very clear to me he disapproves of anything between us. He feels my association with 'people like you' is unseemly and reflects badly on his business." She laughed. "But it doesn't matter. I came by to see if you'd like to go out for a picnic. It might even be warm enough to sit out by the river."

The story about her job was unsettling. He tried to brush off her boss's words. "My morning's all yours. A picnic sounds great. Being an invalid doesn't suit me at all, and I'm dying to get out. Let me get my hat and coat."

They stepped out into the beautiful day together. Lonnie had a small basket slung on her arm. She took his hand with her free one, happiness etched all over her face. "We'll go slowly. I don't want to tire you out."

They walked in pleasant silence for a few blocks before she spoke again. "I had a letter from my father. He says he looks forward to meeting you." Her eyes twinkled.

"So you wrote your dad about me, eh?"

"Does that bother you?"

"I suppose it depends on what you wrote." He eyed her warily, but ended up laughing.

"Nothing but the truth, which were all good things." She stuck her chin in the air.

"I've written my mother about you." He took delight in her gasp of surprise.

"Oh, really?"

"She wants to meet you too. She's curious what kind of young woman took my head out of my books. I was a pretty serious student before I came out here."

Lonnie sighed. "I suppose we'll have to wait until after the war for all these meetings, whenever that will be." She turned to him. "Did you study mechanics?"

"I was studying engineering. I really miss it."

"Well, I'm sure you'll be able to go back to school some day."

"I'd like to. I try to study in my spare time so I don't fall too far behind."

They enjoyed a leisurely lunch, sitting on the bench overlooking the water. Alex liked how the river curved around their little bluff as if it protected them from everything beyond, though he knew it couldn't hold back the tide of the war forever. He wished it was more lasting, that the feeling of protection wouldn't leave him just by walking away from the view. He couldn't stop thinking about his draft card. They'd changed the age requirement for the draft from twenty to eighteen back in December. At any moment, the military could lay claim to him, forcing him to leave Lonnie behind, perhaps for good. But what could he do? The uncertainty only left him feeling sick.

Alex insisted on walking Lonnie back home despite her protests about his health. The house was quiet except for some music drifting out from Aunt Millie's bedroom.

He hesitated as Lonnie tried to pull him inside the house. "I should probably go home."

"It's all right," she assured him. "I hinted to Aunt Millie you might want to walk me back. She was gracious in saying she'd give us the living room to talk."

Alex conceded and followed her inside. She turned on a lamp, and they removed their coats. That sick, nervous feeling returned, and on an impulse, he went over to the Victrola to flip through the records in the nearby box. He wasn't avoiding her exactly, but she seemed to catch on that something was wrong. She came to his side, studying him.

He selected a record, put it on, and set down the needle. Alex turned to Lonnie and held out his hand. "Dance with me?"

She blushed prettily and took his hand. With relief, he held her in his arms, and they danced slowly to the music of "The Very Thought of You." Alex breathed in the scent of her hair and closed his eyes. As Al Bowlly's voice washed over them, Alex sang along.

When the song ended, they stopped dancing, and Lonnie turned her face up to his, eyes bright. "I didn't know you had such a beautiful voice."

"That's just one of my many hidden talents. I can't show them all off at once, now can I?" He winked at her, grinning.

"I want to learn about all of them, and I hope it takes a lifetime." Her gaze was passionate, and he traced her bottom lip with his thumb.

"It just might take that long." Cupping her face in his hands, he kissed her.

***

A week later, Alex was feeling more like himself. His broken rib was healing, and overall he was on the mend. He was grateful Mike gave him an additional week off work, in fact he insisted upon it. Alex definitely needed the time to recuperate. Rolling over in bed during the middle of the night was still agony, and it took more effort than he liked to admit getting dressed. He gave himself extra time to get ready. He wanted to look his best for the plans he had that morning, but his body wasn't cooperating very well.

His fingers fumbled with his buttons. When he went to groom his hair, he dropped his comb and could only stare at it, wondering if he should bother the misery of picking it up. In the end, he gave up and went to find some breakfast.

Mike was already having his breakfast. When he saw Alex, he burst out laughing. "Had a bit of trouble this morning?"

Alex frowned. "What? Okay, so my hair probably looks ridiculous, but I dropped my comb. Do you know how hard it is to pick up a dropped comb with a broken rib?"

Mike grunted. "There's nothing wrong with asking for some help." He got up, retrieved the comb and came back, handing it to Alex. "That explains the hair, but what about the buttons?" He sipped his coffee, trying unsuccessfully to hide a smile.

Alex's chin dropped, and he sighed. There were missed-matched buttons on more than one hole. He sat gingerly to fix them. "I'm nervous."

"Oh?"

"Yeah." Alex swallowed, not wanting to talk about what was on his mind, for fear he'd lose his nerve.

"Well . . . good luck with that." Mike winked and folded up his paper. "I'm off to the shop. Don't get yourself into any trouble."

"I won't." His reply was only half-hearted though. He might very well get himself into trouble.

After a simple breakfast, he walked to the church and knocked on Reverend Hicks's office door.

"Come in," the man called. His face lit up at seeing him walk in. "Alex, what brings you here? Have a seat."

Alex acquiesced, but his jaws instantly clenched together. He shifted uncomfortably in his chair.

"How are you feeling? Recovery going well?"

"As well as can be expected, I guess." Alex's eyes wandered the familiar office full of papers, books, and a few art prints of Christ.

Reverend Hicks leaned forward in his seat. "You're here to talk about Lonnie, aren't you?"

"What?" His eyes shot back over to the reverend, and his stomach rocked. "How did you know that?"

"Come now, Alex," Reverend Hicks chuckled. "You're not the first man to cross my threshold to talk about marriage."

Alex gulped. "Well, you're right, sir. I do want to marry Lonnie . . ." And just like that he lost steam. Everything he'd fixed in his mind to say was gone in a puff of smoke. His mouth gaped open for a second. "I—I had a speech all prepared . . ."

Reverend Hicks laughed again. "It's all right, Alex. Save the speech for my niece." His expression grew serious. "Even after everything you've been through, I would be remiss if I didn't tell you honestly about my reservations about you marrying her. I hope you see you both have a rough road ahead of you. Do you understand that?"

Alex nodded. "I do understand. Lonnie and I both do. We'll work through everything together, and I swear to you I'll protect her with my life."

"I know you will. And so I'll give you permission to marry her, but it's mainly because of this." He held up an envelope. "This is a letter addressed to me from Lonnie's father, Martin Hamilton. Apparently, she wrote to him about you, explaining quite a bit of your relationship."

Alex's face reddened wondering how her father had responded.

"Do you know what he said?"

Alex shook his head.

"He said he trusted his daughter's judgment, and while you aren't what he'd imagined as his son-in-law, if I could vouch for you, then he'd accept our decision. He looks forward to meeting you."

Alex stared at the man, amazed. Now, he understood where Lonnie's kind, unassuming nature came from. Something else occurred to him. "But, Lonnie would've had to write that some time ago."

Reverend Hicks smiled. "Yes, it would seem she's had her eye on you for a while now."

Alex's heart skipped a beat. "Just like that—I can ask her?"

The man nodded. "Just like that. And my best wishes and blessings go with you, young man, though I expect to see you two in here for some ecclesiastical counseling before the big day."

He came around his desk, reaching out his hand. Alex shook it, grinning like an idiot.

After a moment, the reverend raised questioning brows, his mouth hitched up with humor. "What are you still here for?"

Alex laughed and bid him farewell, hurrying out into the sunshine.

***

The dishes clinked together in the wash water as Lonnie ran a dishrag over them. Since being fired from her job by a disapproving and unsympathetic Mr. Pickering, she was grateful for this extra time she had to think and to plan. Alex's words bolstered her—she could do anything! The question was what. Should she muddle along in town, helping her aunt and uncle, still watching over her siblings? Should she get another job, perhaps in a factory in a bigger city like Indianapolis?

She sighed, rinsing the cups and bowls. What she really wanted was for Alex to speak up, to ask her to marry him. But would he? They'd never openly talked about marriage. It was obvious he wanted to be with her, but after the recent events, would he be too intimidated to take that kind of a leap? In the background, the telephone rang and Aunt Millie answered, but Lonnie hardly acknowledged it. Her thoughts kept churning forward.

What if Alex wasn't ready to make that kind of a commitment with her? Should she join up and help in the war effort in a greater way? She loved him, but what was next for them if he didn't ask for her hand? She wasn't content to leave things as they were. She'd determined to marry that man, and by golly, she would!

Lonnie threw down the dishrag and wiped her hands dry, frowning. Well, if he wouldn't ask her, she'd ask him. It was unconventional, to be sure, but it wasn't completely unheard of. How did one go about proposing marriage to a man? Down on one knee? With a bouquet of roses? She giggled.

In the end, she told herself to calm down. "Be patient, Lonnie," she said aloud. "You can wait."

"Wait for what?" Aunt Millie said, walking into the kitchen.

Lonnie blushed. "Oh, nothing."

"You did the dishes. How darling of you." Her aunt's face shone, her smile bigger than usual.

"It's no problem." Lonnie paused as her aunt went about fixing herself a cup of tea. "Aunt Millie, do you think I should ask Alex to marry me?"

Her aunt nearly choked on her first sip. "Whatever for?"

"Well . . . I just don't know if he'll ask me. I think he might be afraid to what with—oh, you know. Everything."

Aunt Millie set down her teacup. "That boy is besotted with you, Lonnie. Why wouldn't he ask you? And it's not like he's had a lot of time to get around to it either, you know."

"I know." Lonnie frowned. "I suppose I'm being impatient, but I feel anxious. It's as if we're at a crossroads, and either we set out on the same path together, or we don't."

Her aunt reached forward and hugged her. "Oh, my dear. You don't need to feel so anxious."

"Why not?"

"I wasn't supposed to tell, but I will anyway. That was Phillip who just called. Alex already spoke with him today. And Phillip gave you both his blessing." She pulled back to wink at Lonnie. "There might have been a little help from your father as well."

Lonnie's surprise and excitement grew like a balloon until it burst inside of her. She leapt to hug her aunt, jumping up and down. "Really? Oh, really?"

Aunt Millie laughed. "You're acting as if you've bet on a winning racehorse."

"I have! I have, Aunt Millie." She clapped her hands to her flushed cheeks. "Maybe you shouldn't have told me. I won't be able to concentrate on anything today."

"Not even if you were to help me do some cleaning before our family dinner party tonight?"

Lonnie laughed. "I suppose I might be able to help with that, though don't count on the quality of my work."

Lonnie and her aunt tied their hair up in scarves and changed into slacks and old button-up blouses. Then Aunt Millie put some music on the Victrola, and together they got to work taking down curtains, vacuuming, and scrubbing. Aunt Millie and Lonnie hummed and sang along to the music.

As she worked, Lonnie wondered what it would feel like to someday take care of her own home. She liked how her aunt tackled chores—with fun music and a happy heart. There was no walking on eggshells or worrying if her efforts were good enough. She knew through helping Uncle Phillip in his church duties that work could be a joy. She wanted her own home to be that way.

As they moved on to cleaning the bedrooms, Lonnie began to wonder about the reality of being married to Alex. She paused in vacuuming her room to remember that time at Christmas when she'd held Alex's coat in her hands and breathed in his scent. How familiar that smell seemed now, but the image of hanging up his coat after a long day at work, of ironing his pants and shirts, and cooking his meals filled her with a shy little thrill. To know Alex in all those intimate details of life . . .

Lonnie continued vacuuming busily, trying to move onto something a bit safer. Right then, Aunt Millie popped her head around the doorframe. "Done in here yet?"

Lonnie stopped. "I think so."

Aunt Millie sauntered in, a suspicious smile on her face. "Why is your face so red? It's not from working too hard is it? Or is it because you're thinking of a certain *someone*?" She wiggled her eyebrows, and Lonnie flushed.

"Aunt Millie!"

The woman laughed, and gasped happily as the strains of "For Me and My Gal" came on in the living room. She grabbed Lonnie's hands, swinging her arms and teasing her with the lyrics.

Lonnie burst out with laughter and blushed an even deeper shade of red. "That's hardly fair."

Her aunt pinched Lonnie's cheeks. "You delightful girl. You realize I'll never have the chance to tease like this. At least not until David comes home and finds some girl."

"That's true," Lonnie conceded. "Very well. I suppose I'll allow you your fun at my expense."

Aunt Millie crooked her arm around Lonnie's as she pulled the vacuum out into the hall. "So tell me," she said with a wink. "Is he a very romantic dancer?"

Lonnie gasped. "You peeked?"

Her aunt sauntered away with the vacuum, dancing with it clumsily into the next bedroom. "I'll never tell."

There was a knock at the front door, and Lonnie shook her head in disbelief as she went to answer it. She was surprised to see Alex there looking just as surprised.

"Alex, I'm so happy to see you." Then she remembered how she was dressed and laughed. "We were doing some cleaning . . ." Her words died away. There was something troubling in his eyes.

She held open the door. "I'm sorry, please come in. I hope you don't mind the state of the house." She rushed to pick the couch cushions off the floor and straighten the coffee table, turning off the music on the way.

"Please, don't worry about it. Lonnie."

She froze at the sound of her name and turned slowly to meet his gaze. Only the sound of Aunt Millie vacuuming filled the space between them now. The little bubble of happiness in her deflated. Something was wrong.

"Lonnie," Alex said. "We need to talk."

"Okay. Would it be all right if I changed?"

He nodded and sank onto the couch without removing his coat. Alex clenched his hands together, and the muscle in his jaw twitched.

She hurried to her room and changed into a fresh dress, wondering what could possibly be the matter. Could he have heard bad news from his family? Had his brother been killed? Had something else happened to him in town?

Dark thoughts swirled around her head as she touched up her hair and spritzed on a whiff of perfume. She looked at herself in the mirror and took a deep breath. Whatever it was, she was going to be there for him. Whatever it was, they'd face it together.

Steeled with determination, she joined him back in the living room. Seeing her, he got to his feet. His expression hadn't improved. In fact, he looked worse; his face had grown ashen. She went up to him.

"What is it, Alex? Please tell me. Do you want to sit here? Do you want to go for a walk or sit out on the patio?"

He grabbed her hands and clung to them. "*Sagwa.*"

Her heart seized. "What?" Was he apologizing to her? Or was it just her nickname?

"There's so much I want to say. So much . . . so much I don't know—" He stopped and gulped. "You know I love you, don't you?"

Lonnie tried to remain calm. "Of course." The wait was agony. Why didn't he just say it?

He began again. "You losing your job wasn't something I was expecting. I spoke with your uncle, and I was just reminded that a relationship between us—"

Lonnie felt the color drain out of her, right down to her toes, bleeding onto the floor. He was breaking things off. He was leaving her.

He riveted his eyes on hers. His beautiful, dark amber eyes. "Things will be hard. We can't pretend they won't be. You'll be subjected to the same treatment and hatred I've gone through, if not worse. You'll be cursed at, spit on, shunned. Our—our children will forever be like me, trapped between two worlds and dual identities. And besides that, there's the war. For heaven's sake, I could be drafted any day. Or what if—what if I decide to join up?" He squeezed her hands, his breathing growing rapid. "I don't know if I can face the idea of leaving you, of you losing me. Just thinking of our road ahead, I don't know how I can in good conscience . . ." He turned away with a growl of frustration. "I don't know what to do."

Lonnie was motionless at his words, at what he was trying to say. Then she reached out to him and made him face her. "I love you,

Alexander Moon. It's true we've already been through so much, and no doubt, we'll have more to face in the future. I've also been considering joining up to help more with the war effort. But you know what? The wonderful, exquisite thing is that we'll be able to face it together, even when we're apart. Whatever comes. Whatever it is. We'll have each other. I wouldn't have it any other way. So, please. Let me join you on your path. Let me be a part of your life."

His expression evolved from awe to hope and finally to relief. He grabbed her hands. "Oh, Lonnie. I was so afraid to ask you. I was elated your uncle gave me permission, but then all of those other doubts came crashing down. I didn't know if I was right in even asking."

She smiled to encourage him, aching and needing to hear the words at last.

As he kissed her fingers, his face completely lit up with his joy. "Lonnie, my darling, sweet Lonnie. Will you? Will you do me the incredible honor of becoming my wife?" He was so earnest in his declaration that her heart overflowed. She gazed at him, drinking the image in, storing it away, forever locked in her memory.

She grinned, and flinging her arms around his neck, she kissed him.

Alex pulled back after a moment. "Does this mean you feel the same way?" He teased.

Lonnie laughed in return. "Yes," she cried. "Yes, of course!"

And then Alex kissed her in a way that even Aunt Millie would have blushed to see.

THE END

Korean Word Definitions

abeonim — father (formal)

anyeonghaseao — hello

Chuseok — Korean Thanksgiving

eomma — mother (informal)

halmeoni — grandmother

hangul — Korean script

joesonghamnida — I apologize

joka — nephew

kimchi — traditional fermented cabbage

kimchi sok — red pepper paste mixture for coating the cabbage leaves for kimchi

maejakgwa — a traditional Korean cookie

meet banchan — side dishes prepared in advance

sagwa — apple or sorry

sarang hae — I love you

samchon — uncle (on father's side)

Seollal — Korean Lunar New Year

seonsaengnim — teacher

songpyeon — traditional stuffed rice cake

sookmo — aunt (by marriage on father's side)

tteokguk — traditional rice cake soup served for Korean New Year (Seollal)

Historical Notes

Near the spreading shade of a large tree in a cemetery in Anderson, Indiana stands the headstone of my great aunt—Elaine Hazelrigg Chan. Carved dragons colored in fading chalk grace the top; black Chinese lettering marches beneath her English name. Backing her headstone is a matching stone with the names of her four children, their death date all the same, victims of a house fire. What's even more sad, is that Elaine's own death date precedes her children's by mere months. Nearby are Elaine's in-laws and a few dozen paces away rests her Chinese husband, Shaungee "Harry" Chan.

I grew up knowing about the misfortune of my great aunt and her children, a tragedy indeed for my Great Uncle Harry to live through, losing his entire family in less than six months. But I never knew much more beyond the cause of their deaths.

When I began writing this book, I knew I wanted to write about the plight of the Korean American experience during World War II and wanted to include a love story. As I wrote, I was drawn once again to my great aunt and uncle's story. They married in the late 1930s and were together through the war until she died in 1947. It was such a tumultuous time for them to marry, that I wondered at their decision. Surely, there must have been some amount of prejudice and challenge to marrying outside their individual cultures. Harry was born in China and immigrated with his parents to Indiana as a young man, where he helped his father run a Chinese restaurant in Anderson. Elaine was a Christian girl of English descent from the Midwest attending school at Anderson College. She worked as a waitress at Harry's restaurant.

I was fascinated by Aunt Elaine's choice and asked my great uncle, her brother, about her decision. He told me that the book *The Vintage of Yon Yee* by Louise Jordan Miln, which I have my main character Lonnie read, was a major influence in her decision to marry Harry Chan. I couldn't help but smile over the idea that a book could have such an impact.

So while this story is not based on Harry and Elaine's lives, they did serve as a muse and motivation to explore this fascinating aspect of our country's history—a long history of immigrants and their posterity making their way in a complicated, imperfect world.

As for the plight of Korean Americans and other Asian minorities during World War II, it's an aspect that, outside the tragic Japanese interment camps, is sadly under told. It was my hope to bring their story into greater light. Research was very difficult to come by, but through a few books, some wartime magazines, and Lili M. Kim's doctoral thesis, I was able to piece together the Korean American wartime experience.

At the outbreak of World War II, Korea was under the rule of Japan, and early on in the war, the U.S. government questioned the loyalty to the wartime cause of Koreans living in the U.S. Koreans were fiercely opposed to the Japanese and fought hard to be recognized as American allies and to free Korea from Japanese power.

The fascinating dilemma the Korean community faced was that of the second-generation, the Korean American youth. They had no memory of the homeland, and many of them grew up alongside Japanese Americans, holding no hostilities toward them. They didn't fully grasp the urgency in fighting for the Korean cause and identified themselves as Americans. Unfortunately, Americans in general had difficulty distinguishing between the different Asian ethnicities, or in their eyes, between an enemy or not. Due in part to fear and suspicion, many Asian Americans suffered from discrimination and violence. Alex's story draws on their experiences and frustrations.

Just before publication, I discovered an article in the March-April 2013 issue of "America in WWII" magazine discussing the additional wartime internment of Germans and Italians. In my story, Alex wonders why Germans haven't been put into camps. I didn't have sufficient time before publication to do more research into the public knowledge of these other government-interned groups, so I left Alex's statement as it was. I felt it was important to mention it here though.

River Bluff, Indiana, is a fictional town, but I did draw inspiration from three specific Hoosier towns: Anderson, Bloomington, and Madison. Madison, in particular, was featured in a government wartime film and was a valuable resource for my research.

The Indiana wartime experience differed, depending on where you lived. If a town was located close to important military forts or key factories, the town experienced more air raid blackout drills. Some rural towns, like Madison in southern Indiana, only experienced a few blackout drills late in the war. For the sake of my book, which takes place early in the war, the southern town of River Bluff has yet to experience blackouts, and they still keep the street lamps burning.

Many factories during the war were retrofitted to produce wartime goods, thus making many everyday items scarce for Americans when before they were plentiful and easily obtained. At the turn of the century, Indiana was home to many glass factories due to the temporarily plentiful natural gas resources in the state. The Ball glass factory, famous for producing canning jars, is one example. To honor the tradition of glass making in Indiana, I wanted there to be a glass factory in my story, which is what the fictional Stanton family runs as their family business.

Food rationing in America began in mid-1942 with just sugar, followed by coffee in November, and everything else in March of '43—canned goods, meats, fats, and processed foods. Rubber imports had been cut off in '42.

I make mention of Mrs. Simmons's packaging her own frozen foods and passing it off as the real thing. In my research on the frozen food industry, I found mentions of such occurrences—where grocers who were trying to cut corners would stock their rented Birdseye freezer cases with their own frozen foods. This act was a breach of contract, and they were penalized and the frozen case removed from the store. The major difference in the foods themselves was the process of freezing. Birdseye used a quick-freezing method utilizing specialized equipment. The common grocer had no such equipment available and had to rely on traditional freezing, so the food froze at a slower rate and the quality differed greatly.

Women's magazines offered many helps to women during the war. They published ration-friendly recipes, tips on "making do," and even advice for quick wartime weddings. In the story, Lonnie makes use of wartime recipes, as well as a favorite resource of mine—Westinghouse's Health-for-Victory Meal Planning Guides. All of the recipes she makes are ones that I've made myself. They can be found at my history blog: http://history-preserved.blogspot.com.

V-Mail is another fascinating aspect I wanted to include in my story. The millions of paper letters mailed back and forth between families and soldiers weighed a lot and were bulky to transport. An ingenious method borrowed from the British was introduced to Americans in mid-1942. The method was to photograph letters written on a special V-, or Victory, Mail form. The photographs were stored on a microfilm reel, which could hold hundreds of letters. These reels were then transported back and forth for a fraction of the weight and space as traditional paper. Once at their destination, the letters were then photocopied to a readable size. The script was still pretty small, so special magnifying lenses were made for reading them. Many times, V-mail letters arrived faster than usual, though letters from soldiers were still subject to the ever present wartime censor.

Lastly, I was always fond of my third great grandmother's unique name, Appalone Hamilton. We don't know how she pronounced her given name, but we've always said it like "appa-lone" with the "o" long and the "e" silent. My character Lonnie and her actions bear no resemblance to my grandmother of the same name who died long before I could know her.

When it comes to my Great Aunt Elaine, I'm still unraveling the mystery of her life. I've found newspaper articles about my Great Uncle Harry, as well as notice about the death of herself and her children. Pictures are elusive and any further records of their lives are even harder to come by. But I will always be inspired by Harry and Elaine's courage to be together during such a difficult time of struggle and change in the history of the United States.

Selected Bibliography

Choy, Bong Youn. *Koreans in America.* Burnham Inc. Publishers, 1979.

Furnas, J. C. *How America Lives.* Ladies Home Journal, 1941.

Kim, Hyung-Chan, ed. and Patterson, Wayne, ed. *The Koreans in America, 1882-1974: A Chronology and Fact Book (Ethnic Chronology Series, No. 16).* Oceana Publications, 1974.

Kim, Lili M. *The Pursuit of Imperfect Justice: The Predicament of Koreans and Korean Americans on the Homefront During World War II.* Thesis (Ph. D.)--University of Rochester. Dept. of History, 2001.

Schenning, Craig S. (2012) *The Collector's Encyclopedia of Indiana Glass; Volume 1 — Early Pressed Glass Era Patterns (1898-1926),* Unpublished manuscript, Old Line Publishing, Hampstead, MD.

Takakai, Ronald. *Double Victory: A Multicultural History of America in World War II.* Boston: Little, Brown and Company, 2000.

The National World War II Museum.
http://www.nationalww2museum.org/ (accessed November 19, 2015).

Acknowledgments

First of all, my deepest gratitude goes to the Lord for His inspiration, for His strength, and for blessing me with perseverance in writing this story which was so important for me to tell. He helped me to accomplish what felt like a very daunting task.

It's difficult to express how grateful I am to my best friend, Mairi McCloud, for her enthusiastic support and tireless reading of my drafts, new, sometimes disjointed scenes, and multiple rewrites. Her constant encouragement and excitement for my story was just what I needed to keep going, even when writing certain scenes was difficult to face.

I also want to thank my mother, Constance Yerden, for spending many hours with me on the phone, listening to my ideas, brainstorming, and working out kinks.

I'm extremely appreciative to my mini army of beta readers: Mairi McCloud, Constance Yerden, Lisa Rector, Lisa Swinton, Jane Pearce, Megan Hirschi, and Laurie Lewis. Their feedback really helped to make this book shine. I'm also indebted to Kim Kuhn and Michelle Muller for their feedback on the Korean aspects of my book. Without their help, this book would've been riddled with inaccuracies. *Gamsahamnida!*

I want to extend a huge thank you to my wonderful writer's group: Lisa Rector, Lisa Swinton, Laurie Lewis, Beth Bentley, and Misty Pulsipher. They gave me such invaluable feedback on my manuscript and endured and answered numerous questions about publishing my first book. They're all wonderful, talented writers that I'm very blessed to know. Thanks especially to Lisa Rector for showing me the formatting ropes and for being my proof reader. A very special thank you goes to Melissa Lemon who went over my second proof in one day!

I'm very thankful to Loris Simcik, whom I had many a delightful conversation about everything World War II and who was such an inspiration and motivation for my research. I especially appreciate the loan of so many of her original wartime women's magazines, which I was able to use in research for my book.

I am so grateful to my editor, Sabine Berlin, and the other wonderful ladies at Eschler Editing. I learned so much from them, and I appreciate all of Sabine's hard work in helping polish my book. It meant a lot to share this project with someone who could understand all the subtle Korean drama references I snuck in to honor Korean culture, past and present. Fighting!

I'm very appreciative of my talented cover artist, Cindy Canizales. She did wonders with the photo for the cover and was very patient with all my last minute changes. Thanks also goes to my talented friends—make-up artist, Christina Cook, and photographer, Keslie Houser, for making my author photos turn out far better than I could've imagined. My gratitude also goes to my college roommate and longtime friend and librarian, Christine Baker, for all her wonderful help and research.

I want to extend a special thank you to Craig Schenning for the use of his Indiana glass factory research, as it's not an easy topic to research in Maryland! Also, a big thanks goes to Lili M. Kim for her wonderful doctoral thesis. Without it, this book would've been very difficult to research.

While I didn't end up needing the information for my book, I'm very grateful to Rebecca Koford and Judy G. Russell, genealogists extraordinaire. I now feel very well-versed in the often confusing draft age changes of WWII, as well as 1940s marriage laws.

Words cannot adequately express the gratitude in my heart for all those American men and women who sacrificed so much and served so faithfully at home and abroad during World War II in defense of freedom. I've loved becoming more familiar with their lives and the time in which they lived. I especially enjoyed getting to know more about Fred Ohr, a pilot who became the only Korean American Fighter Ace in WWII.

And lastly, but certainly not least, this book wouldn't have happened at all without the tireless love and support from my incredible husband, Erik. Thanks, honey, for your "guy" feedback and serving as my sounding board for my musings, triumphs, and frustrations. I can't leave out our two wonderful children. Being able to slip away to the library a couple times a week to write and to work at home on my "homework" really helped me focus and get this done. They displayed such great patience and understanding. Thank you, my sweetie-pies!

About the Author

Sarah Creviston Lee started first grade wanting to be a writer and has been writing ever since. Then at the age of thirteen, she fell in love with history and the World War II era while working as a volunteer at the Monroe County Historical Society Museum in Bloomington, Indiana. Since then she's volunteered and worked for various museums including the President Benjamin Harrison Home, Conner Prairie, and the Utah State University Museum of Anthropology where she worked for three years as Collections Photographer.

Many research papers later, including retaking her capstone course twice, on purpose, she went on to earn her bachelor's degree in History with a certificate in Museum Studies from Utah State University in 2009. Her favorite topics of study are the World War I & II American and British home fronts, wartime food rationing, and the Industrial Revolution.

Sarah is a proud Hoosier, born and raised. She currently lives in Maryland with her wonderful husband, two adorable children, and flock of clever chickens.

You can visit her blog, "History: Preserved," where she writes about all things History and museums found at:
http://history-preserved.blogspot.com

Made in the USA
Columbia, SC
07 November 2017